Longbarrow

Mark Morris

PIATKUS

Copyright © 1997 by Mark Morris

First published in Great Britain in 1997 by
Judy Piatkus (Publishers) Ltd of
5 Windmill Street, London W1

This edition published 1999

The moral right of the author has been asserted

A catalogue record for this book is available from the British Library

ISBN 0 7499 3053 5

Set in Times by RefineCatch Limited, Bungay, Suffolk

Printed and bound in Great Britain by
Mackays of Chatham PLC, Chatham, Kent

This one's for my daughter, Polly Rose.
I love you, peach.

Acknowledgements

I know I say it every time, but it continues to be relevant, so first and foremost, a massive thank you to Nel for her incredible love and support this past year.

Thanks also to the Kent contingent, Hilary and Ali, for technical input; Suzanne for information on trees (safe, me?); Pete for his unflagging efforts with Americans; Nige for medical stuff and Karen for school stuff.

Thanks just for being there to Mum, Trevor and Margaret, Jo and Michael, the Chisellers, Kev, Chris (who *is* a chiseller, so that's two thank yous in one), Shareena, Justina and Richard, assorted friends, and probably some other very obvious and important people whom I've forgotten about.

Finally, another massive thank you to my children, David and Polly, for . . . well, just for being perfect.

Part One
Susan and David

Chapter One

'Bergkamp!' shouted Ian Lubensky, drawing back his foot for the shot. Simo 'the Cat' Dyer, crouched between two piles of sports bags that served as goalposts, readied himself to spring to the left or the right, unconcerned about the damage that the concrete playground could inflict upon his knees and elbows. Simo was the only kid that David had ever seen dive full-length on gravel to tip a ball round the post, and come up grinning with sheer joy at having made the save, despite the blood oozing through the holes in his torn jeans. Sometimes he dipped his fingers in his own blood and drew symbols on his forehead – a cross or a third eye.

'All the great goalies were a bit el loco,' he would say, tapping the side of his bristly head. 'That's how I know I'll make it as a professional. I'm not scared of putting my face where the boots are.'

On this occasion, however, Simo didn't need to make the save. Chris Sinclair nipped in on Lubo's blind side and prodded the ball away from him. Chris looked a bit like a rat, with his sleek black hair and sharp features, but he was a good player; he played for the local district under-thirteen team, which was made up of the best players from around two dozen schools in southwest London.

As he streaked away with the ball, Lubo, caught off-balance, swung his foot at empty air and landed on his arse. Simo whooped and rotated his fist in the air. 'Oh yes!' he bellowed. 'Beauty! Beauty!'

David Wisher – Wish to his friends – didn't hear Lubo's response (though he suspected it might take the form of a suggested sexual liaison between Simo and his mother), because he was scampering down the field – or rather, across the playground – hoping to get on the end of one of Chris's pin-point crosses. Like Chris, David was small for his age, though there the similarities ended. David possessed neither Chris's pace and skill, nor his sinewy strength and balance. He was okay, though. He tried hard despite his asthma, and knew the other lads respected that. 'You're okay for a cripple,' Simo would say, punching his arm both softly enough for the blow to be companionable and hard enough to prompt a retaliation that usually degenerated into a scuffle. Sometimes, when his asthma was particularly bad, David had to sit out games altogether. He'd be stuck in a classroom with all the other geeks, reading or doing his homework. Not that he really thought that guys like Marvin Butler, who had cerebral palsy, or Ahmed Akram, who had been born blind, were geeks, of course. Ahmed in particular was a really funny guy. Sometimes he would offer to referee their lunchtime games just so that the lads could shout, 'What are you, ref – fucking blind or something?' Ahmed loved that; he'd bend double over his white stick, cackling uncontrollably. Once he'd been hit in the face with the ball so hard it had knocked him off his feet. As his classmates crowded round, Ahmed had sat up, groggily shaken his head, and had then cried out, 'I can see!'

It was summer term: 3rd July 1995. Only two and a bit weeks to the holidays. It had been warm and dry for most of the past month, and already optimists were talking about the most glorious summer for twenty years whilst pessimists muttered about global warming and skin cancer.

David was looking forward to the summer. He and Mum were planning on spending a couple of weeks at the coast, and then he'd stay with Granddad and Grandma and all the animals for a while in Kent while she went back to work. As much as anything he was looking forward to putting Year 7 behind him. He wouldn't exactly relish coming back in September, but at least when he did he'd no longer be a member of the youngest year in the school. There'd be a whole new batch of eleven- and twelve-year-olds to act as prey for the older kids. Not that he himself had been too badly victimised. The worst that had happened was that he and his friend, Steve Foreman, had had their shoelaces tied together by a bunch of Year 10s, who had then pushed them down the street until they fell over. Some of the other kids in his year had fared far worse, like the two lads who had been burned with cigarettes for refusing to try Ecstasy, or the girl who had been made to eat dog shit by a gang of older girls after being stripped from the waist down and tied to a lamp post. And there were other kids who had been pushed off their bikes which had then been stolen, or who had been beaten up and their trainers nicked. Drug dealing, extortion, violence, cruelty – it was all part of the everyday life of a typical secondary school in southwest London.

'Chris!' David yelled now, raising his arm. 'Cross it, cross it!'

He sprinted into the danger area, screwing up his eyes against the glare from the sun, which was coming from behind Chris as he ran with the ball, reducing his head to a shimmery blur.

'*Chris!*' David shouted again, waving his arm wildly.

And that was when the sun was blotted out by a huge wall that David ran into full-tilt.

Something massive and heavy, something that felt like a tree-branch or an anvil or a slab of concrete, slammed into David's stomach, smashing the air out of him so instantly and totally that he could do no more than utter a strangled little 'ug' of surprise. He rebounded off the wall, feeling like a brain in a body he had no control over. The world whipped past in a smear of light and dark as he crumpled to the ground. Insects made up of tiny points of light were buzzing angrily in front of his face.

He couldn't breathe.

He tried, but it was as though the shock of the collision had flicked a switch inside him that had locked all his inner workings. His mouth opened and closed as if he was actually trying to chew chunks of air like it was meat, but as the seconds passed and still nothing happened he felt the familiar bright blossoming of panic inside him.

When he had an asthma attack, and was labouring vainly for breath, it was easy to panic, but that only made things worse, and so to some extent he had learned to control it. This was different, though. This was like being in a vacuum. He felt his nerve endings starting to go cold, his senses starting to shift out of phase, the familiar feeling of a weight on his lungs as the dark, buzzing walls closed in on all sides. He began to flail as the panic filled his head and shifted over into terror, swamping his senses. Dimly he was aware of a growing darkness full of bobbing shapes, which felt like the approach of an airless unconsciousness, but which an isolated part of his mind realised was merely his classmates crowding round him. Distorted, echoing voices reached him as though from the far end of a narrow tunnel.

'What did you smack him for, Paddy, you fat tart?'

'It wasn't my fault, he just ran into me.'

'Do you think he's all right?'

'He's going blue.'

'His eyes are going all funny.'

'Get his inhaler.'

'Where is it?'

'It'll be in his bag. The Liverpool one. I think he put it down over there.'

Running footsteps. A girl's voice:

'What's the matter with him?'

'What's it to you?'

'Shall I get Mr MacDonald? He's just over there.'

'Yeah, I think you'd better.'

'Sir! Sir!'

Slipping into blackness.

There was a moment of absolute terror, a moment when whatever remained of David's conscious mind – which, in fact, felt like the intrinsic nugget at the centre of his being – knew it was going to die and screamed and scrambled frantically in an effort to escape the tar-black surface of the water at the bottom of the well he was sliding towards. But there was nothing to hold on to, and a moment later the black water closed over his head.

And that was it.

Dead.

The end.

No more struggling. No more anything.

Now that it was over, the terror and the panic ebbed away, and a vague sense of peace and acceptance flowed over him. It didn't occur to David for a moment that he might not really be dead. He genuinely felt that what he was experiencing now was more than sleep, more than unconsciousness. He felt as though he had passed through some portal, come out on the other side of something.

Without being aware of any great change in his state of

being, he suddenly found himself walking up a drive between a mass of mature oak trees, whose branches were so entwined with their neighbours', and whose foliage was so luxuriant, that they completely screened what he was walking towards. Nevertheless, David's surroundings seemed familiar to him, as if he had been here many times before. Somehow he *knew* that behind him the driveway started at a set of iron gates which opened on to a tree-lined road that led down between fields and clumps of woodland to a village. He knew also that the house at the end of this drive was large and spacious, a place made of grey sandstone with lots of windows and an impressive portico, ivy the colour of blood swarming over the left-hand side, as high as the eaves.

He looked down, and saw that he was following a golden, shining strip of light – or rather, something that seemed *more* than light, something that pulsed and glowed, but which at the same time gave the impression of being ethereal. A path of pure energy.

A ley-line, he thought, surprising himself, feeling simultaneously as though the phrase was new to him and yet at the same time oddly familiar.

The trees seemed to retreat, to step back like obedient courtiers, or open like a doorway, as the drive widened into a parking area. And suddenly there was the house, just as he had imagined (*remembered*) it.

He saw more ley-lines, saw them as though from above, as though he was hovering high in the sky, like a bird or an angel. Paths of energy – pure, effulgent, breathtaking – they traversed great tracts of land, running for miles like streams winding towards a common destination. They seemed to run right into the house, suffusing the stonework with a soft radiance, creating an aura, like a glowing cushion of mist, around the base of the house. Or perhaps they didn't end *at* the house, but instead pushed their way into its foundations, or deeper still, through the earth and the bedrock, pooling beneath the building like some vast underground lake.

With the instinctive, intense emotion of dreaming, David sensed that the energy was purity given form – it was the essence of beauty, happiness, generosity, perfection, gentleness, love.

Was this Heaven then? This house? Was this the final

destination for everything that was, or had ever been, good and positive in the world?

He was walking round to the back of the house now as if he had a purpose, crossing the ley-lines that converged upon it, feeling their goodness welling inside him, purifying his soul.

He came to a well that was little more than a hole in the ground, but it was a hole full of light, of energy that resembled the sun made liquid. David plunged in his hands, cupped them, feeling the energy tingle and sparkle against his flesh. The energy flowed into him, making him feel as though he was composed of it. It was a feeling so immaculate that it was beyond words, beyond emotions, beyond the human capacity to explain or understand. He brought the liquid to his lips, drank it, washed his face in it, gave himself up to it completely.

And now he was walking around *inside* the house, as if a chunk of time had been taken away from him, removed as if he had no need of it. The walls of the house were wood-panelled up to waist height, and then papered up to the high ceiling with a subtle yellow floral pattern. A stained-glass panel above the front door scattered coloured blocks of light across the polished floorboards of the hallway. There were two doors to the right of the front door, a grandfather clock resting against the wall between them, and then beyond the doors was a wide staircase, carpeted in a rich burgundy, ornate wooden banisters curving to an upper landing, inset with more doors, which disappeared into shadow.

To the left of the front door were four doors marching along a corridor which led presumably to the back of the house. It was along this corridor that David now found himself walking, his feet tapping on the wooden floor with the exaggerated clarity of footsteps on a movie soundtrack.

He had no idea why he was going this way – and then suddenly he did. It was as if one of his senses had suddenly started working again after a period of inertia. He was following a heartbeat – or rather, something that he interpreted as a heartbeat. Pulse or not, it seemed to be summoning him, and at that moment David felt he could more easily have cut off his own foot than ignore it.

At the back of the house was a huge kitchen with an Aga and a china sink you could take a bath in, the centre of the

8

room dominated by a battered wooden dining table that would comfortably seat a dozen people.

But it wasn't from in here that the heartbeat was coming. It was from beyond a door tucked away beside a Welsh dresser in the far corner of the room. A door that could only lead into a cellar or storage area beneath the house.

Without hesitating, David approached the door, reached out and grasped the handle. The heartbeat was so loud now it was almost painful. It was like the engine that drove his *own* heartbeat; his blood ebbed and flowed in sync with it, contracting and expanding juicily in his head. It occurred to him that if he opened the door, the pulse (*the calling*) might overwhelm him, every cell in his body acting like a tiny sponge, absorbing the summons as he had earlier absorbed the energy from the well.

However, the thought did not frighten him, or even concern him. He felt incapable of fear here, felt as though this was a place where negative emotions had never been able to gain a foothold, as though hate and fear and anger and misery were germs that couldn't withstand the climate.

Slowly he twisted the handle and tugged the door open.

The heartbeat stopped.

It was replaced by a silence so profound it was as if the universe and everything in it had paused to catch its breath.

Then the moment passed, and the planets resumed their orbits, the seas recommenced their tides, and every living creature that swam and crawled and walked upon the earth slipped back into the endless cycle of life and death.

And in this place where Heaven met Earth and where death met dreams, David stood at the top of a flight of cellar steps, his face caressed by the cool darkness below. He began to descend, his breathing shallow, his steps light but sure. The darkness enfolded him, erasing the steps at his heels, blotting out the doorway above.

He was in another place now, another domain, and yet despite the darkness he still did not feel afraid. He reached the bottom of the steps, alighting on a floor that produced a bright *spat* of sound beneath his feet like smooth, polished stone. He took three steps forward and then stopped. Wherever his destination was, he had reached it.

Patiently he waited, the darkness gelling around him. And suddenly, behind him, there came a rustling, slithering sound, as of something large and heavy propelling itself through dry leaves.

David waited, unafraid. The slithering approached his back, moved to the right of him, and then was passing in front of him, seemingly no more than a couple of feet away, though he could see nothing. Then the sound moved to his left and back behind him again, as if whatever was making it was circling him, appraising him, or perhaps (and again this thought came with no attendant fear) entwining itself loosely around him.

The rustling was behind him again now, and then to the right of him once more. And then something nudged his foot. A light touch, although somehow giving the impression of considerable bulk and strength.

David squatted down, reaching out his hand in the darkness to touch whatever had touched him. His fingers made contact with something cool and dry and silky-smooth, something that seemed to have the shape and girth of an adult thigh, though when it moved beneath his touch, sliding and rustling, it seemed to go on forever, an endless length of silken, tensile muscle.

Rustling and slithering. Coiling around him. Slowly David rose to his feet. He sensed movement in the darkness beside his head, and turned to face it.

Something hissed right into his ear.

Someone spoke his name and he woke up.

Chapter Two

As usual, the tube was hot as a sauna and smelt like an armpit convention. Susan Wisher breathed shallowly through her mouth, a little nauseated at the thought of the tainted air, thick with microbes, that was sliding down her throat and circulating in her lungs.

It was little better in the streets, car fumes greying the air, encasing everyone with an extra epidermis of grime. She hated London in the summer, the pollution covering the city like a sweaty blanket ripening in the heat, tourists doubling the population, choking the tubes and the buses with backpacks as big as themselves.

David's asthma was always worse in the summer. Heading down to the coast when the schools broke up, or even out to Kent to see her parents, always felt like being released from prison. It was only then, when she got out into the country, that she'd realise she hadn't walked without hunching or taken a deep breath for months. She'd look at David and see how pinched and pale he was, and she'd curse Gerry for springing the trap on her, even whilst knowing that the trap was old and rusty now and that the only reason she hadn't escaped from it long ago was because she was afraid of what might lie beyond its confines.

Gerry was – had been – her husband. September would mark the seventh anniversary of his death. The realisation that so much time had passed since that anguished, empty, bewildering period in 1988, that David had now lived over half his life without his father, still had the capacity to shock Susan. Although the grief and the guilt and the anger had long ago become manageable (not so much eradicated, but incorporated into her, put away in the attic of her thoughts like a trunk of old toys she was unable to get rid of), there still emerged now and then a bubble of resentment, a tendency to blame Gerry for her situation when things weren't going well.

It was Gerry, after all, who had brought the family to London in 1985, when David was two and a half. Susan and he had met at Canterbury University in 1978 and had remained in the city after graduating, marrying in some haste in June 1982, after Susan discovered she was pregnant. By the time David was born in December, Gerry was well established with a firm of stockbrokers in the city and Susan was in her second year of training to become a nurse, a vocation which she put on hold when her son was born, finally qualifying in 1984. Then Gerry had got his job with Peabody and Golding, a firm of high-flying stockbrokers in the capital, and although he could easily have commuted from Canterbury each day, the three of them had moved to London, buying a three-bedroomed house overlooking Wimbledon Common.

To be fair to Gerry, at the time Susan had not objected too strongly to the move. She had been twenty-five then, and although she had always been a country girl, the progression from Canterbury to London had seemed a natural one, the big city holding a mystique and an excitement that the more genteel environs of Kent simply couldn't match. If she had any reservations at all, they were to do with the thought of her little boy growing up in a big, bad, dangerous city, but those reservations evaporated the instant she saw Wimbledon's leafy streets that were certainly no busier than the street where they had lived in Canterbury, and the great expanse of green that was the Common on their doorstep.

Looking back, Susan supposed that they had been happy years. It was odd, but in many ways she felt detached from them now, unable to recall her day-to-day thoughts and emotions over the ten-year period that she and Gerry had been together. She supposed she must have loved him too – certainly she couldn't remember ever being unhappy or disillusioned with her marriage – but whenever she thought of him now, it was not with warmth or affection, but with resentment for what he had done, and that saddened her.

Gerry had been a taciturn, introverted man, reluctant (unable even) to show his true feelings, embarrassed by emotional outbursts. Even when they had made love, they had done so silently, with the lights off, she making a conscious effort to stifle her moans and gasps of pleasure. Now, when she looked back, she couldn't recall how they had ever got together and although she remembered days out with him, they were like silent movies in her head; she couldn't for the life of her recollect what they had used to talk about.

Neither could she picture him laughing; his face, as she remembered it, seemed incapable of such liveliness. Yet there must have been occasions when he had laughed, mustn't there? Whenever she brought his face to mind now, it was either the stern, tight-lipped, bespectacled image that stared out from the pine frame on her dressing table, or it was the sallow, sunken mask he had worn in his coffin, where, deprived of his spectacles, he had looked achingly vulnerable.

His death had been typical of him – controlled, secretive, single-minded. The first inkling Susan had that anything was wrong was when Gerry failed to return home from work at his usual time one Thursday evening. Even then she had thought little of it, had thought he was working late or had been held up in traffic, or had even (though it was the unlikeliest option) been persuaded to join some of his colleagues for an after-work drink. It was only around ten o'clock that she became worried, and almost midnight before she had called the police.

His body had been found the next morning, slumped in his car in a lay-by off a dirt-track near Canterbury, where they had used to live. He had fed a hose from the exhaust pipe back into the car, and had taken a full bottle of sleeping pills for good measure, washing them down with three-quarters of a litre of Evian water. Apparently he had been sitting reading *The Times* when he had slipped into unconsciousness. The newspaper had been found crumpled in his lap.

He had left no suicide note, a fact which accounted for much of Susan's initial bout of anguished guilt and bewilderment. During those first few weeks she had asked herself over and over why he had done it. Was she to blame? Should she have shown him more love, more support, more understanding? Should she have spotted the tell-tale signs of stress or depression? Had he been crying out in his own way for months without her hearing him? Oh, how could she have failed him so utterly?

13

Finally, after an arduous police investigation, a likely reason for Gerry's suicide had come to light. Although he had played the stock market, both for himself and his clients, with considerable acumen for a number of years, it transpired that in the few months leading up to his death he had hit a streak of bad luck. He had made a series of disastrous decisions that had resulted in his running up a number of quite considerable personal debts. By the time of his death, the family's finances were in dire straits, a fact of which Susan was completely unaware. Gerry had always insisted on being responsible for the household money, had always seen it as his domain, and as such had never once discussed financial matters with his wife.

Looking back, Susan couldn't believe how naive and ignorant she had been, how completely Gerry had dominated certain areas of both their lives. She had been blindly content with her little personal account, with the fact that the bills and the mortgage were always paid, that there was always food on the table, and that they always went on nice holidays. She had been vaguely aware that somewhere, somehow, Gerry had been 'making their money work for them', though exactly what that had involved had been a mystery to her. He could have been trafficking heroin or selling arms to Iran for all she knew.

The police came to the conclusion that Gerry had killed himself for one of two reasons. Either he had done it purely to avoid losing face with his friends and family, or he had done it to stabilise the financial situation for his wife and child, knowing that with his death the mortgage would be paid off and his life insurance would not only wipe out his debts but provide his family with a nice little nest egg. In other words, his suicide had been either a selfish gesture or a noble sacrifice. At the time, Susan, confused and distraught and still blaming herself, had been incapable of making up her mind which theory to accept. Now, though, she thought that there was some truth in both arguments. Gerry had been a proud man but also a protector. He hated failure, was in fact critical of anything but one hundred per cent effort, which had sometimes made him hard to live with (especially for little David, who had craved his daddy's praise but rarely got it). And yet at the same time he had been fiercely devoted to his wife and child, determined to shield them from harm come what may, even to the extent of dying his lonely death far enough away from home to be certain that they wouldn't be the ones to find him.

Nevertheless, for a long time the dominant emotion in Susan's heart had been not sadness but bitterness. How dare Gerry be so presumptuous as to place their financial security above their emotional well-being! How dare he do something so drastic, so final, without discussing it with her! She saw his suicide as an insult to her intelligence, an act of betrayal and cowardice, manifesting complete disregard for the needs of herself and her son. For a long time she hated her husband more than she grieved for him; the anger burned in her belly like an ulcer. He had left her with an almighty mess to clear up.

How could you explain to a five-year-old boy that his daddy had gone and that he was never coming back? How could you respond to questions like: '*Why* isn't Daddy coming back, Mummy? Doesn't he love us any more?'? Susan could still picture David's little face as she had tried to explain it all to him. He had looked bemused and vaguely disappointed rather than grief-stricken; at times he had become frustrated with her, as if by sticking to her story she was insisting on flogging some joke that had long ago ceased to be funny. But he had never cried, unless he had done it privately, and that still worried her. She couldn't help thinking that there must be some knot of unreleased emotion somewhere deep inside him, something that had grown gnarled and calcified with time. She was terrified that he might end up like his father – introverted, emotionally stunted. But were such things genetic or merely learned? Had Gerry, by killing himself, ultimately *contributed* to his son's emotional growth or damaged it?

These were questions that Susan would never know the answer to. Certainly David *seemed* like a normal boy, particularly when he was with his friends, when he would be as rowdy and cheeky as the rest of them. At home he would be quieter and more creative. He would read and draw, make things out of cardboard or clay or Lego. He was more open than Gerry had ever been, and more affectionate; he was not averse to giving Susan an involuntary kiss or hug when there was no one else around, and telling her that he loved her. He was sensitive to her feelings, sometimes eerily empathic. In fact, there were times when he actually seemed *tele*pathic, able to read her emotions as if she had them written on her forehead, to tell

15

when she was feeling down or worried, no matter how cheerful she pretended to be. Susan supposed circumstances and necessity meant that she and David had a closer relationship than most mothers and sons, but she tried hard not to stifle or mollycoddle him. The future did frighten her, though, the thought that in another six or seven years, David would probably be going away to university or wanting to branch out and find a place of his own. She honestly didn't know whether she'd be able to stand being all alone in her big house, or alone anywhere, come to that. Gerry's death had made her strong and resourceful in many ways, but there were still some things that could arouse a kind of dull panic inside her when she thought about them too deeply, and this was one of them.

She looked up as the tube began to whine as it slowed, and the black walls of the tunnel were replaced by the crowded platform and sloping, ivory-bright walls of Green Park station. She stood up, 'Excuse me'ing her way through a group of German teenagers with brightly coloured T-shirts and shorts, then stood shoulder to shoulder with a plump black woman who was holding a string bag stuffed with shopping and dabbing at her sweaty face with a handkerchief.

When the train stopped and the doors opened, Susan hopped off before the crowd on the platform could press forward. Her handbag clutched tightly against her side, she fought her way through a fug of sweat and stale perfume to the escalators, then stood weary-legged as the metal stairs carried her upwards, gazing at posters for Kickers boots, West End shows, new books by million-selling authors. Everyone in the endless procession of people clanking up the stairs to her left looked harried and hostile. Susan had to resist the urge to grab the sleeve of a beautiful but sour-faced young woman in a pink suit and to proclaim, 'Oh, for God's sake, cheer up!' She glanced at her watch and saw that it was almost five past one. Hopefully Beth had been her usual punctual self and had arrived at Alfred's early enough to grab them a table.

This was Susan's half-day from her job as doctors' receptionist at a small surgery in Putney, and was the only time in the week when she really treated herself. After finishing work at 12:30, she would travel into town to have lunch with her friend, Beth, then spend the afternoon wandering around the shops, occasionally buying herself a little something to wear before ending up at a deli-cum-coffee shop she knew near Covent Garden. Here she would sit at a table by the window, nibbling carrot cake and sipping the best coffee she had ever tasted, contentedly watching the world go by. She would buy herself and David something special for dinner from the counter (their spinach and ricotta tortelloni with arrabbiata sauce was one of David's favourites) and then make her way home on the tube, usually arriving to find her son doing his homework or sprawled on the sofa, watching TV.

The brightness hit her as soon as she stepped out on to the pavement, making her screw up her eyes. Alfred's, where she and Beth ate most Mondays, was a small and unpretentious pizzeria just off Berkeley Street, a couple of minutes' walk from the tube station. When Susan arrived, she thought two things: one, that Beth was uncharacteristically late, and two, that they'd never get a table. She was pressing her lips together with disappointment when she saw a slender, bangled arm rise like a periscope from behind the bald pate of a middle-aged businessman with grease on his chin who was leaning forward as if to impart confidences to a sceptical-looking woman sitting opposite him.

The hand on the end of the arm waggled strawberry-red fingernails at her, and the next moment Beth was standing up, her mass of blonde curls and generous, red-lipped mouth attracting admiring glances – both blatant and covert – from at least ninety per cent of the men in the room.

'Yoo-hoo, chuck, over here!' she called in her broad Manchester accent. Susan grinned and waved and made her way across to where her friend was sitting.

Beth was commissioning editor for a women's magazine. Susan had first met her at a yoga class almost nine years ago. Oddly, the two had been little more than casual acquaintances until Gerry's suicide, which was when Beth had really come into her own. Hearing about Gerry's death through a mutual friend at the class, she had turned up on Susan's doorstep one day, armed with a bottle of wine. 'You can tell me to piss off if you like,' she had said, 'but I heard about what happened and I thought I'd come round to see if I could help.' Then, as an afterthought, she had thrust the wine towards Susan. 'Oh, and I brought this. I was going to bring flowers, but I thought you'd have enough of those.'

Beth had been invaluable all the way through that long, dark period. She had adapted herself to be whatever Susan required at any particular time: a sounding board, an advisor, a comforter, a pick-me-up. The two had become fast friends, added to which David adored her. He had known her most of his life, but even now his eyes would light up whenever she came to the house. Until the recent advent of his still-burgeoning sexual awareness, he would hug Beth as uninhibitedly as he still hugged Susan. It was only in the last year or so that he had stopped doing that, at around the same time as he had stopped declaring, 'When I grow up, Beth, I'm going to marry you.' Beth seemed to understand, though, and she never teased him about it. She might put herself across as a brash, simple Northern lass, but she was one of the most sensitive and astute people that Susan had ever met.

Beth remained standing long enough to give Susan a hug, then the two of them sat down.

'Started without me, I see,' Susan said in mock admonishment, nodding at a plate of half-eaten garlic bread and a glass of white wine.

'Sorry, love, I couldn't wait, I were starving,' said Beth, then tossed her blonde curls and grinned her generous grin. 'The fella I were with last night didn't have anything in – typical bachelor. Well, no, I tell a lie. He had three bottles of Michelob, a well-squeezed tube of tomato puree, and half a tin of Alphabetti Spaghetti with furry mould growing on the top.'

'You haven't got *another* man?' exclaimed Susan in shocked delight. 'What happened to Alex?'

'Oh, Alex couldn't keep up,' said Beth cheerfully. 'You know me, chuck, I like to be out enjoying meself. Alex was more your slippers and pipe sort.'

'So who's this new one, then?' said Susan.

'Oh, I wouldn't say he was a new one as such. He were just some fella I met in a club. Ray, I think his name was. I don't know if I'll see him again. It were just lust at first sight, if you know what I mean.'

'You're terrible,' said Susan affectionately.

'I know. I'm a right slag, aren't I?'

'Course not. There's nothing wrong with having a good time. But you ought to be careful. I worry about you.'

'Don't worry,' said Beth, tapping the handbag that was slung over the back of her chair, 'I always carry my little rubber friends around with me.'

'I didn't mean that. I meant there's some scary people around nowadays.'

'I'm a big girl. I can look after meself,' said Beth airily. Then she grinned. 'Dear old Sue. You're like the big sister I never had.'

'Patronising cow,' said Susan. 'And less of the old, if you don't mind.'

Beth laughed uproariously, showing her white, capped teeth. She was just under six feet tall and always looked as though she was dressed for a party, wearing well-cut, often tight-fitting clothes that showed off her fantastic figure. Her skin was flawless and permanently tanned, her eyes cornflower blue, her mouth, which was never without its carefully applied coating of bright red lipstick, mobile and expressive. In some ways her mouth actually looked too big for her face, and yet at the same time managed to be her best, most alluring feature.

Much as she loved Beth, Susan could never help feeling stumpy and dowdy in her company. Even though she knew that she wasn't, the feeling was hard to dispel. She was six inches shorter than her friend, with dark brown hair cut in a bob. She had a delicate, fine-boned face and a trim figure. More than once she had been told she looked like a slightly older Winona Ryder, which she took as a great compliment. She dressed simply, but (she liked to think) flatteringly. Today she was wearing a sleeveless cotton dress in yellow and grey that came to just above her knees, and black sandals. Her legs were good enough to remain uncovered, besides which she hated tights and avoided them whenever possible; horrible, hot, suffocating things.

They spent the next five minutes poring over the menu and ordering the food. Susan went for tuna steak in black peppercorn sauce with a tomato and basil salad, and Beth opted for a pepperoni and mushroom pizza with a Niçoise salad. Beth ordered the wine, flirting with the waiter, who boasted a chiselled jaw and eyebrows so thick and black they looked like chunks of coal.

'So,' Beth said when the waiter had swaggered away, 'how are things?'

19

'Oh . . . okay,' said Susan.

'You don't sound too sure.'

'No, I'm fine. It's just this heat. I hate London in the summer.'

'Pining for the fjords again, are you?'

Susan smiled. 'Something like that.'

'How's Davey's asthma?'

'Not brilliant. All the pollution stays at ground level when the weather's like this.'

'Well, why don't you do what you've been threatening to do for the last five years, girl, and move out of London for good?'

'Oh, trying to get rid of me, are you?' said Susan in mock indignation.

Beth smiled. 'Chance'd be a fine thing. Nah, chuck, I'd be down to visit you every weekend, armed with me galoshes.'

'There aren't any night clubs in the countryside, you know,' said Susan.

'Who needs bloody night clubs with all those lovely farm labourers about?' said Beth, waggling her eyebrows. Then she suddenly became serious. 'No, but what's stopping you, chuck? You're all right for money, you've got no real ties, and it'd be great for Davey. All that fresh air.'

'You *are* trying to get rid of me, aren't you?' said Susan. She wrinkled her nose. 'I don't know. I've got my job and Davey's just finished his first year at secondary school. I wouldn't want to disrupt him.'

Beth rolled her eyes. 'Excuses,' she said. 'First of all, you don't really need the job and you don't really enjoy it; you only do it to fill in some time. And secondly, Davey'll settle in just as easily in a new school. I mean, it's not as if he's in the middle of his O-levels or whatever it is that kids take these days.'

'I know, but . . . well, we might not be able to sell the house,' said Susan defensively.

'Excuses, excuses, excuses. The only way you'll find out is to put it on the market.'

'And where would I find the time to go house-hunting?'

'Quit your job. You'll have all the time you need then. Besides, I thought you said your mam and dad had offered to look around for you?'

Susan pulled a face. 'I wouldn't want to live near Mum and Dad. I mean, don't get me wrong, I love them both dearly, but whenever I'm with them for any length of time they start trying to run my life. My mum has little digs about the way I bring Davey up. Nothing nasty, just subtle little things. She'll say something like, "When you were a little girl we never let *you* do that, but I suppose things are different nowadays." And then if I have a go at her, she'll look all wounded and say she was only trying to give me a bit of advice.

'And then they'll start going on about the fact that I'm "on my own", and that they know how tough it is for me, bringing up a child "on my own", and they'll ask me whether I've met "anyone nice" recently, and my mum'll say, "Oh, so and so's son is about your age, and he's never married, and he's *ever so nice*", and then before you know it they'll have signed me up with Dateline and enrolled me in the bloody Singles Club or whatever it is.'

The waiter came back with the wine and uncorked it with a flourish. 'Would madam like to taste?' he asked Beth, trying for suave, but only managing to make it as far as lascivious.

On this occasion, Beth barely glanced at him. 'No, no, love, just bung it in the glass. We'll drink it whatever it tastes like.'

He did so, then retired, looking bewildered and hurt. Beth finished off the glass of house white she had ordered, then took a gulp of the bottled stuff.

'Yeah, well,' she said, picking up the conversation, 'you know what my thoughts are on that subject. You're wasting yourself, girl. All that lovely man-flesh to choose from and you're waiting for Mr Right.'

'I'm not waiting for Mr anybody,' said Susan.

'So what's holding you back? Get in there!'

Susan grimaced. 'You may find this hard to believe, Beth, but I'm not really all that interested.'

Beth looked stunned, as though she had witnessed all that she held most dear being ground casually underfoot. 'You're right,' she said, 'I don't believe it.'

The food arrived, and they were silent for a few minutes as they applied condiments and sampled what they had ordered.

'It's just . . . I'm not like you,' Susan said after chewing and swallowing a mouthful of tuna. 'Call me boring if you like, but I've never been interested in sex just as a physical thing. For me, sex is like . . . this is going to sound corny, but I suppose it's like an expression of my love. I'd have to love – or at least really like – someone before I'd consider going to bed with them.'

Beth was silent for a few moments as she digested this. She put a forkful of pizza into her mouth and chewed thoughtfully. Finally she said, 'Do you mind if I ask you a personal question?'

Susan shrugged. 'Why should I? You usually do.'

'Have you slept with anyone since Gerry?'

Susan paused before answering. Then she said, 'No, not really.'

'What do you mean, not really?' said Beth. 'Either you have or you haven't.'

'Well, there was that one guy. You remember? Richard. I met him in the park with Davey. We couldn't get Davey's stunt kite to fly and he helped us.'

'Oh yeah, I'd forgotten about him. God, how long ago was that? Two years?'

'About that, yes.'

'So you slept with him, did you?'

'No, I didn't. I nearly did, but I couldn't go through with it. I mean –' she leaned forward, whispering, '– we got undressed and got into bed and everything, but as soon as he put his hands on me I froze.'

'So how did he take that?' asked Beth.

'Oh, he was okay about it once I'd explained the situation, but things cooled off between us after that.' She shrugged and looked down at her plate. 'And that's the full extent of my sexual exploits over the past seven years. Hardly Sunday tabloid stuff, is it?'

'He just wasn't the right fella for you, that's all,' said Beth. 'Sooner or later you'll meet someone and it'll be like – pow! There'll be no stopping you.'

Susan shrugged. 'It better be sooner rather than later. I'm thirty-five now. I'm no spring chicken any more.'

'Nonsense, girl. A woman's just reaching her sexual peak at your age. Tell you what, you come out with me one night. I know lots o' fellas I could introduce you to.'

Susan chewed a piece of tuna and shook her head. 'That's really kind of you, Beth, but I'm really *not* all that bothered. I'm happy enough as I am.'

At that moment there came a faint trilling from underneath the table.

'What the bloody hell's that?' said Beth. 'Have you got a budgie in your handbag?'

Susan looked both embarrassed and alarmed. 'It's my mobile.' She put down her knife and fork and picked up her handbag. 'Only Davey and his school have got this number. I hope nothing's wrong.' She rummaged in her handbag for the phone, then put it to her ear, feeling a fluttering in her stomach. 'Hello?'

'Mrs Wisher?'

'Yes, who's this?'

'This is Mr Egerton, Mrs Wisher. David's headmaster.'

The fluttering turned into a crampy feeling. Susan was aware of Beth watching her with concern, but tried to keep her voice level. 'Hello, Mr Egerton. What can I do for you?'

It seemed to take a long time for him to reply, and when he did his tone was apologetic.

'Mrs Wisher, I'm afraid there's been an accident.'

Chapter Three

The first thing David saw when his eyes flickered open was an angel's face surrounded by a halo of shifting white. It was a beautiful, serene face, like a painting in a church, but as it leaned towards him it seemed to acquire lines of worry, imperfections; the light seemed to fade around it, to become hard and stark. He saw the lips in the face move, heard a sound that his sluggish brain absorbed but failed to comprehend. All he knew was that he was filled with a sense of warmth, of love, for this imperfect, worried face.

Opening his mouth felt as though someone was tearing a strip of paper in half somewhere below his nose. His throat felt like an old machine, fused with rust, that was being forced back into service after decades of inactivity.

'Mum?'

The word emerged as a creak of sound, nothing more. Yet David saw his mother's face suddenly blossom with relief and joy. It was the most wonderful thing he had ever seen.

'Hello, Davey,' she said, her voice clear but distant, as if she was speaking to him underwater. 'How are you feeling?'

It was a difficult question. Just at that moment he wasn't feeling anything, except confused. He tried to swallow, but couldn't find any saliva to do it with.

'What happened?' he croaked.

'You're in hospital. You had an accident. I'll tell you all about it in a minute.' She spoke this last sentence quickly as if he had started to interrupt her, then she asked him again, 'How are you feeling?'

David applied himself to the question. He tried sending messages from his brain down to where his arms and legs ought to be. Little by little he became aware of his body, weight and pain settling into the familiar shape of it that he now realised was laid on its back in a hard-mattressed bed.

'My chest hurts,' he said, ' . . . like it's bruised . . . and my throat's so dry.'

He saw his mum leaning forward, reaching out beyond his field of vision. He heard the splash of liquid, and then she was leaning back, holding a glass of water. 'Can you sit up a little bit?'

He tried, but when he put weight on his arms his chest flared with pain. It felt as if his breastbone had been sawn in half and then welded back together. The pain was so bad he couldn't speak, but he managed to give a small shake of the head.

'Here, I'll give you a hand,' his mum said, and put the glass down. She slid her arms around him in exactly the right places to lessen both his weight and his pain and helped him sit up a little bit. 'You never lose the knack,' she said in reference to her nursing days, then picked up the glass again and held it to his lips. 'Here you go, sip this. Don't gulp it, though, or it'll make you sick.'

The water was like a magic potion, seeking out the sore, dry places in his throat. David remembered the well in the dream, the way the water or the light or whatever it had been had refreshed and purified his entire being.

He looked around. He was in bed in a small cubicle surrounded by white curtains on runners. For the first time he became aware of the clamour beyond the curtains – the buzz of conversation, the odd burst of laughter, the occasional clank of unidentifiable metal objects banging together.

'Am I in hospital?' he asked.

'Yes.'

'Did I have an asthma attack?'

'Eventually.' She stroked the back of his hand. 'How much do you remember?'

'I had an amazing dream,' he said immediately. 'There was this house . . .'

'How much do you remember *before* the dream?' she interrupted gently.

He frowned, thinking hard. The dream was still uppermost in his mind, still so vivid that it seemed as if *it* was the reality, and what had gone before was no more than dim fragments of a half-remembered dream.

'I was . . . playing football,' he said. 'I was running along, and then . . . I think I must have crashed into something. Everything went black.'

'You swallowed your tongue,' she told him. 'Luckily one of your teachers realised what had happened and he managed to save you.'

David looked at his mum, the implication of what she had said slowly dawning on him. Awe-struck, he said, 'You mean I could have *died*?'

'You could have done, or been brain-damaged if your teacher hadn't acted quickly enough.' She spoke matter-of-factly, but all at once her face crumpled and she pressed a fist against her mouth.

As tears filled his mother's eyes, David realised how much of an ordeal this had been for her, how much she must have been struggling to hold herself together. He understood in an instant that she had wanted to present a calm face to him when he woke up so as not to frighten him. Now relief had snapped the tension and all her bottled-up emotions were coming out.

He reached out and stroked her arm. 'Don't cry, Mum,' he said in his croaky voice. 'I'm okay.'

'I know,' she said tearfully. 'I'm sorry.' She rummaged in her handbag for a handkerchief with which to dry her eyes and blow her nose.

'I'm sorry I worried you,' he said.

She blew her nose loudly and wetly. 'And so you should be.' She sniffed and stood up. 'Are you too old for a cuddle?'

He shook his head, and she hugged him to her, tightly but taking care not to squeeze his aching chest. She kissed his forehead through his fringe. 'Don't ever do that to me again,' she said.

'I'll try not to.'

She held him a little longer and then let go, settling back in her chair. She looked earnestly into his face as if committing every little detail of it to memory.

'I don't know what I'd do if I lost you as well,' she said.

For a moment the spectre of Gerry seemed to hang over both of them, then David shrugged and said, 'Well, you're not going to, so you don't have to think about it.'

Tentatively, wary of upsetting her again, he asked her what had happened after he had been saved from swallowing his tongue.

'Your lungs kept going into spasm,' she said, 'and your heartbeat was all over the place. The doctors seemed to think that what had happened had triggered some kind of severe asthmatic reaction.'

She looked as though she was going to add something to that, but had then decided not to. David wondered whether she was going to say that she thought the doctors didn't really know why his lungs had gone into spasm, that they were only speculating it had something to do with his asthma. But wouldn't saying that be tempting fate, suggesting that because they didn't really know why it had happened the first time, there was nothing to prevent it happening again?

'In the end they put you on a respirator to help you breathe and eventually things settled down. They monitored you for a bit in intensive care and then they transferred you here.'

Again she was making it sound simplistic, matter-of-fact, but David knew how terrible it must have been for her.

'How long have I been asleep?' he asked.

She looked at her watch. 'It's nearly four now, so it must be about three hours since you got knocked out.'

Three hours. Weird to think of everything that had happened to him in that time, and he completely unaware of it. School would be over for the day now. His friends would be on their way home, or home already.

'Where's my inhaler?' he asked.

'Why?' she said, alarmed. 'Are you feeling breathless again?'

'No, I'm fine. I want to know where it was, that's all. Just in case I need it.'

'It's here,' she said, picking it up from the bedside table and holding it in front of him as though he might not recognise it otherwise. 'But if you feel breathless, you're to ask for a nebuliser.'

He nodded. 'Okay. When can I come home?'

'Tomorrow. They want to keep you in overnight for observation.'

He sighed, but made no protest. 'I must have looked a complete geek, falling down in the playground. It's bad enough when I get my asthma, everyone crowding around me. I know they're only trying to help, but I wish they'd just leave me alone. I'm all right when I've got my inhaler.' He scowled and then said with feeling, 'I really *hate* asthma.'

'I hate it too,' she said, 'for your sake, I mean.' She paused and then asked, 'How would you feel about living in the country, Davey?'

He blinked at her, and saw that she looked almost as surprised as he must have done, as if she hadn't known what she was going to say until she said it.

He didn't reply for a moment, and then, warily, he said, 'You mean move out of London? Sell the house?'

'Well . . . yes.'

'But what about school? And my friends?'

'We'd find you a new school. You'd make new friends.'

'But what about your job?'

'I'd quit it. I don't really need it. When your dad died, he left us quite well off.'

David stared at the white drapes at the end of the bed and thought about his mum's proposal. He had to admit, his first reaction was to oppose the idea. He liked the life that he and Mum had together. What was the point of changing it, starting all over again? Okay, so London wasn't perfect, but it was familiar. Moving out to the country would be like . . . like stepping into the unknown.

'What brought this on?' he asked.

'Nothing brought it on. Well, if you must know, I was discussing it with Beth over lunch. But it's something I've been thinking about for a long time.'

'Why? Aren't you happy in London?'

'It's not a case of being happy. Well, not entirely. I *am* happy with you. But no, I don't like London, not any more. It's too crowded, too dirty, too noisy.'

He remained silent, sullen or perhaps just thoughtful, staring at the plastic hospital bracelet on his wrist. After twenty or thirty seconds she said, 'What about you? Are *you* happy in London?'

He shrugged. 'Yeah, I s'pose so.'

'But don't you think you'd be happier somewhere else? Somewhere with fresh air where you might never have to use your inhaler ever again?'

He pursed his lips. 'I dunno.'

28

'Well, why don't you have a think about it? There's no rush. We'll talk when you're better.'

'Where would we go?' he said, almost defiantly.

'Well . . . I don't know. I haven't thought that far ahead. Your gran and granddad have said that they'd help us find somewhere nice in Kent if we ever wanted to live out that way.'

He looked at her shrewdly. 'You wouldn't like that, though, would you, Mum?'

Startled, she said, 'What makes you say that?'

He shrugged his shoulders. 'I just thought that maybe you'd find it a bit much, being so close to them all the time. I mean, I love them and everything, but they're always trying to tell you what to do, aren't they?'

The expression on his mum's face graduated to astonishment. 'You're incredible, you know that?' she said.

He grinned and said airily, 'Of course.' Then he became serious again. 'So where *would* we go?'

She looked now as if she wished she had never started this conversation. 'Oh, I don't know. I haven't thought that far ahead. We'll talk about it some other time, Davey, all right?'

'Okay,' he said. 'Can I tell you about my dream then? It was really weird.'

She smiled indulgently. 'Go on then.'

'Well, I was walking towards this house . . .'

Chapter Four

By the end of July, London was baking in a heat wave. Temperatures soared into the nineties daily, and never dropped below the mid-seventies even in the dead of night. It was enervating, inescapable heat. Much of the time it was too hot even to sit out in. Weather reports were full of dire warnings about the dangers of sunburn and the high levels of pollution in the capital which the dense heat was keeping at ground level. On Saturday 29th July, almost four weeks after his accident in the school playground and two weeks into the summer holidays, David was at home playing Monopoly with Beth. He was wearing shorts and a Flintstones T-shirt, drinking ice-cold Coke and sitting in the coolest room in the house, yet even so sweat oozed constantly from his pores.

Mind you, just looking at Beth was enough to make him feel hot these days. Especially when she wore the kinds of things that she was wearing today – a black low-cut T-shirt that was so tight it looked as though she had simply spray-painted her upper body, and white shorts that showed off her long, smooth, tanned legs. David was finding it hard to concentrate on the game. He couldn't keep from glancing at the outlines of Beth's nipples when he thought she wasn't looking, feeling sick with embarrassment and guilt and a yearning but panicky desire. In bed at night his penis would become iron hard as he fantasised about Beth seducing him, peeling off her clothes as she panted how irresistible she found him, how she couldn't hold herself back any longer. In the fantasy he was cool and commanding, though he knew only too well that if anything like that ever happened in real life he'd be utterly terrified.

Beth was the top hat and he was the battleship. Despite the distraction of her, he was winning. He had three of the best sets – the yellows, the greens and the navy blues. He'd just bought hotels for Oxford Street, Park Lane and Piccadilly. It was only a matter of time now before she went bankrupt.

'I'm all out of cash. Perhaps I could offer you something else,' he imagined her saying while pulling down the strap of her T-shirt. He swallowed and closed his eyes briefly, feeling breathless. If the way he felt about Beth brought on an asthma attack, would she guess? Since the incident four weeks ago he hadn't had a bad attack, though since the heat wave had really kicked in his chest had felt almost constantly tight. He used his inhaler perhaps two or three times a day, the Ventolin providing almost instant but temporary relief. Never mind; next Saturday he and Mum were going to Cromer for a couple of weeks, after which he would spend the time before school started again with his gran and granddad in Kent.

Since their conversation in the hospital, he and Mum had talked about the prospect of moving out of London on only a couple of brief occasions. The latest conversation had taken place in McDonald's on Oxford Street last Saturday, where the two of them had adjourned for lunch after a morning spent traipsing round the shops in the heat.

Putting ketchup on his Big Mac and fries, David had said, 'They don't have McDonald's out in the country, do they, Mum? Or Virgin Megastores,' he had added, glancing at the plastic bag she had put on the table which contained a CD for her (*Tuesday Night Music Club* by Sheryl Crow) and a video for him (*Batman Returns*, reduced to £4.99).

She had looked up from her Diet Coke (she had decided not to eat here, but to buy a sandwich from 'her' deli in Covent Garden later on), and said, 'Are those things really that important to you?'

'Well . . . no,' he said, wrinkling his nose, 'I suppose not. But . . . well, what would I *do* if we lived out in the country?'

'You could do anything you like,' she replied. 'There'd be fields and woods to run about in. We could have a big garden, grow our own vegetables. Just think, Davey, there'd be no traffic, no pollution, no lunatics roaming the streets. You'd be able to breathe clean, fresh air. You might even be able to throw away your inhaler.'

'Yes, but who would I play with?' he wanted to know, speaking around a mouthful of bun and meat.

'I expect you'd make new friends.'

'How would I? No one else lives in the country.'

She frowned, showing a flash of irritation. 'Of course they do. I'm not proposing living in the middle of the Sahara Desert in a tent. You'd still be going to school every day. Are you just being awkward for the sake of it?'

'No,' he said cautiously, though in truth he knew that that was exactly what he *was* being.

Mum sighed, and then said more calmly, 'You're not really such a city boy are you, Davey?'

'No,' he said.

'I mean, you enjoy it when you go to grandma and granddad's, don't you?'

'Yeah.'

'Well, then.'

And that was where they had left it. Since that conversation exactly a week ago, nothing more had been said on the subject. Mind you, he and Mum had had something else to occupy them this past week, which was the reason why Mum was out now and why Beth had come over to keep him company. Last Monday Mum had received a letter from a firm of solicitors called Robinson McGann. The letter had requested that she be present at the reading of the last will and testament of Mrs Mollie Boscombe at the firm's London office on Saturday 29th July at two p.m.

At first Mum had thought the letter had been wrongly addressed to her; she didn't *know* anyone called Mollie Boscombe, and, as far as she could remember, she never had. After a couple of days spent racking her brains, however, it had finally occurred to her who Mollie Boscombe was. She was Dad's granddad's sister, which made her Dad's great aunt or something. Mum had explained to David that she had met the woman only once before, and that had been when Mrs Boscombe had travelled down to London with Dad's mum for Dad's funeral seven years earlier. Not that Mum had been able to remember much about her, beyond the fact that she was old and fat. David knew that Mum had never got on with Dad's mum – his other grandma – which was why David never saw her. All David knew about her was that she lived in Yorkshire and that she 'disapproved' of Mum. When he had asked Mum why, she had said with a smile that David could see concealed a great deal of bitterness, 'Oh, she didn't think I was good enough for her precious son, but then in her eyes I don't think anyone would have been. She's a spiteful, possessive woman, Davey. She's nothing like your other grandma. Do you know, all the time that I was with your dad, she never came to visit us. She never even sent us a Christmas card. In fact, apart from the funeral, I only ever saw her three times – once at our wedding, where she spent the whole day glaring at me, once at someone else's wedding, and the third time when we went up to see her in Yorkshire just after you'd been born.

'I'll never forget the way she looked at me at the funeral. You'd have thought I was your dad's murderer, not his widow. She wouldn't talk to me. I tried once, but she didn't want to know, so I left it.'

She had looked sad and defiant and a little upset. Then, in a voice that seemed to contain all of these emotions and more – thoughtfulness, a kind of wonder, a little shame – she had said, 'Do you know, I'm not even sure whether she's still alive.'

'What time is it now, Beth?' David asked, doing his best to fight his instincts and to look directly into her face without first glancing at her chest.

Beth, who seemed oblivious of the effect that she was having on him, said, 'It's about ten minutes later than the last time you asked me.' Then she rolled her eyes and looked at the slim gold watch on her wrist. 'Quarter to four.'

'Do you think Mum'll be home soon?'

'I've no idea, chuck. I don't know how long these things take. There's probably a lot of rigmarole to go through, papers to sign and whatnot. I don't think it's just a case of, "Hello, Mrs Wisher, you've inherited fifty million quid. Here it is. See ya."'

David sighed. 'I wonder how much we *have* inherited.'

'Enough to get bloody air conditioning, hopefully. Oh, pardon my French. I'm parched. D'you fancy another Coke?'

David nodded, his mouth going dry and his heart fluttering excitedly as Beth leaned forward to push herself to her feet, presenting him with a generous glimpse of her cleavage. He watched her long brown limbs as she strolled across the living-room carpet to the door. A trickle of sweat meandered down his spine.

He heard the front door open while she was in the kitchen, and jumped up, his foot catching a heap of Monopoly money, which avalanched across London, destroying most of his hotels. He emerged from the living room into the hallway just as Beth came out of the kitchen, clutching two cans of Coke that were filmed with condensation.

Mum was pushing the front door shut. She looked tired and hot, and, David thought, a little shell-shocked. She was clutching a clear plastic envelope with some papers in it.

'Well?' Beth said. 'Don't keep us in suspense. Are you a millionaire or what?'

Mum looked up as though she hadn't realised they were there, and her lips tweaked into a smile. 'Oh, hi,' she said. 'God, it's so hot. The tube was like an oven. One woman nearly passed out.'

'*Mum*,' David said as though she was teasing them, 'tell us.'

'All right, give me a chance. I need a drink first.'

'Coke?' said Beth, holding up a can.

'I'd prefer tea.'

The three of them trooped back into the cluttered kitchen, on whose walls were framed prints of farm animals and drawings that David had done at school. A cork board was covered with leaflets and cards advertising night school classes, taxi cab firms, takeaways, plumbers. Beth passed David his Coke, then put the kettle on and grabbed a mug from the overhead cupboard. Susan pulled out a chair from under the little dining table opposite the magnet-bedecked fridge and dropped into it as though her tendons had been cut. David sat down opposite her.

'Come on then, spill the beans. How much did she leave you?' said Beth, leaning against the counter and crossing her arms.

'Money-wise, nothing,' said Susan, and then, noting their disappointed expressions, added pointedly, 'But.'

She let the word hang teasingly in the air until Beth raised her eyebrows. 'But?'

'But David and I are the sole beneficiaries of Great Aunt Mollie's will, and as such she has bequeathed to us her house and all its contents.'

It took a moment for this to sink in, and then David said disbelievingly, 'A house?'

'You're kidding,' said Beth.

34

'I'm not. I've got all the details here.' She held up the plastic folder.

'Bloody hell,' said Beth. 'Well, come on, girl, tell us more. Where is this house? How much is it worth?'

'It's in a little village in the Yorkshire Dales called Longbarrow. I don't know exactly how much it's worth, but it's a big place. It's set in its own grounds and everything.'

'Jesus,' said Beth, 'you lucky sods. I wish I had a rich old aunt who'd leave *me* something.' She turned to pick up the kettle, which had switched itself off, and poured boiling water on to the teabag in the mug. 'What will you do? Sell it?'

'I don't know,' said Susan. 'We'll go and have a look at it in a couple of days, shall we, Davey? It could be just what we've been waiting for.'

'But Yorkshire's *miles* away, Mum,' David protested.

'It's not that far. A few hours in the car. Anyway, there's no harm in looking, is there?'

David shrugged.

'Have you got any details about this house of yours, then?' Beth asked.

Susan picked the plastic folder up off the table and leafed through it. She drew out two sheets of paper stapled together. 'There's a photo and all the details.'

Beth took the sheets from her. 'Oh, it looks lovely.' She began to run down the details. '*Five* bedrooms. What will you do with five bedrooms? A library . . . a dining room . . . and what's a bloody reception room when it's at home?' Finally she shook her mass of blonde curls. 'Well, you've really landed on your feet this time, chuck.' She held out the sheets to David. 'Here you go, love. Have a look at what you've inherited.'

David took the sheets reluctantly, as though by doing so he was committing himself to the place. He glanced at the half-page photograph preceding the details and then froze, snatching his hand back and letting go of the sheets so that they seesawed to the floor.

Surprised by his shocked reaction, Susan said, 'David, what's the matter?'

When he looked at her, his eyes were wide, and for a moment he seemed not to recognise her.

Then, in a small, tremulous voice, he said, 'That's the house from my dream.'

Chapter Five

'Come Up and See Me (Make Me Smile)' by Steve Harley and Cockney Rebel came on the car radio, and Susan began to sing along, bopping in her seat as she drove.

God, this brought back memories. She must have been about fifteen when it came out. It made her think of school discos, of sitting giggling with her friends, while the boys with their long hair, wide-collared shirts and enormous flares eyed them up.

She'd started going out with Stuart Cooper, her first real boyfriend, at one such disco. They'd smooched to Barry White, and afterwards he'd walked her home, holding her hand all the way. Stuart had been the first boy she'd allowed to get his hand inside her bra. It had happened in the back of Mark Hunslet's dad's car, which had been parked in the garage at the time.

Mark Hunslet had been going out with her friend, Suzanne Fielding. On this particular evening, Mark and Suzanne had occupied the front seats, whilst she and Stuart had had the back. It had been dark, she remembered, probably sometime around October or November. From the front seat had come the squishing of lips, the soft squeak of leather, the occasional groan or urgent but unintelligible whisper. She and Stuart had settled down for their own snogging session, and for a while that was all they had done, entwined together on the back seat, their lips (and occasionally their teeth) grinding together. Stuart had stroked her breasts over the top of her clothes before, but had never tried to touch her actual skin. On this occasion, however, he did. She didn't even notice him pulling her shirt out of the waistband of her jeans, but as soon as she felt his warm hand on her stomach she froze. As his hand crept up towards her bra, she remembered feeling both terrified and exhilarated, wanting to tear herself away and urge him on in equal measure. If Mark and Suzanne had not been in the car she might have asked him to stop, but she hadn't wanted to make a fuss in front of her friends. She had been at an age when it had been important to appear mature, worldly. Afterwards she had felt ashamed, but it hadn't stopped her wanting Stuart to touch her again. Now, whenever she thought of sex, it was accompanied by an abstract association of dark, smoky, autumnal evenings, and the faint smell and creak of leather car seats.

She glanced at David, slumped in the passenger seat next to her, mouth partly open as he slept. Sleeping, he looked so perfect, so innocent. Even now, whenever she checked on him at night, she had to fight an urge to wrap her arms around him and cover his smooth, pale cheeks with kisses.

The breeze drifting in through the half-open window ruffled his hair like a loving touch. It was Monday, the last day of July. Another hot one, though at least driving up the M1 at eighty miles an hour meant that the heat couldn't enfold you like a heavy suit of armour.

The drive had been fun. Despite David's reservations about the house, both of them had been in high spirits. Susan had felt almost as if she was going on holiday, though she supposed it was just getting out of London that had made her feel that way. They hadn't been too happy at work about her taking the whole day off, but they could get stuffed as far as she was concerned. As Beth had said, she didn't really need the job, and at least if they sacked her it would save her the bother of resigning.

It was twenty to two now. She and David had left London in her red Citroën that hardly ever got used at nine o'clock that morning. The first hour of the journey had been spent disentangling themselves from the barbed wire of London's rush hour, but since then they had been making steady progress, and now Susan guessed that they were no more than an hour from their destination.

They had played car games (Who Am I? and A to Z), eaten most of a bag of Fox's Glacier Fruits, sung along to the car radio (as she was doing now), and stopped at a Little Chef for lunch.

David had become subdued just before falling asleep around half an hour ago, but Susan wasn't sure whether it was because he was tired or whether he was becoming more anxious the closer they got to their destination. Certainly he had remained adamant that the house they'd inherited was the one in his dream. What Susan tended to think, however, was that he had mentally superimposed the image of their new house on to his dream-memory, convincing himself that the house in Longbarrow and the house in his dream were one and the same. She was hoping that actually seeing the house would convince him of his error. If not, she would have to remind him that the dream-house as he had described it to her was a good place, and that therefore there was nothing to be afraid of.

The song she was bopping along to finished just as she passed Junction 31 on the M1. The next junction would be where she changed motorways, from the M1 to the M18. She indicated and shifted over into the slow lane, easing down to sixty-five. Beside her, David stirred, groaning and moving his head from side to side. There was a mottled red impression of the seat belt on his cheek.

He remained sleeping, however, until they had left the M18 and were heading north on the A1, which was being converted into a motorway. He came awake grumpily, forehead crumpling like newspaper as he opened his eyes and looked around.

'Where are we?' he growled as if she had managed to get them lost.

'We're on the A1.'

'Where's that? In Yorkshire?'

'The bit that we're on is.'

He scowled at the hedges lining the road as if he didn't trust them. 'How long before we get there?'

'Half an hour or so. Do you think you can cope with a bit of navigating?'

He picked up the road atlas and the envelope on which she'd jotted their route and compared one to the other. For the next half an hour he directed her along a series of increasingly minor roads until eventually they were heading along the B6451, parallel with the vast expanse of pale green on the map that was the Yorkshire Dales National Park.

Scrutinising the atlas, David said, 'There's a place here called Bedlam.'

'You'd be mad to go there,' said Susan.

'And one called Blubberhouses.'

'Made from whales, no doubt.'

David grinned. His trepidation, if that was what had caused him to become subdued earlier, seemed to have dissipated, at least for the time being. 'What about Kettlesing Bottom?' he said as though testing her.

'I had that once. Very painful.'

Soon they had even left the B6451 behind, and were meandering along a series of narrow country lanes that high hedges and trees were doing their best to convert to sun-pierced tunnels. Occasionally there would be a break in the trees, giving them breathtaking glimpses of the ground sloping to the valley floor below, where fields were divided by dry-stone walls that from this distance looked like the thick black strokes of a marker pen, before rising again to low hills encrusted with foliage and clumps of woodland and white flecks that were sheep.

The breeze coming in through the car window was stronger now and free of car fumes, though the sun was still fierce enough to imbue the greens in the landscape with such vibrancy that it prickled the backs of their eyes. The sky seemed vast, incredibly blue; somehow in London it was never given the chance to stretch out like this.

'Isn't it beautiful?' Susan breathed.

David nodded, albeit reluctantly. 'Yeah.'

The narrow road continued to twist and turn for the next ten minutes, Susan shifting the gears from second to third and back to second, and occasionally even into first when the road became so steep that it seemed in danger of curling back on itself.

'Are you sure this is the right way?' she asked.

David consulted the atlas. 'It must be. There isn't any other way.'

Five more minutes elapsed, and then the road started to broaden out a little, to curve subtly downhill.

'Look, there's a sign,' said David. 'Longbarrow one and a half.'

Susan began to hum the *Twilight Zone* theme tune. 'You

are about to cross the boundary between light and dark, science and superstition,' she announced in a cod American accent.

They came to a signpost for a hump-backed bridge, though had barely registered it before they were on the bridge itself, a sturdy stone construction only wide enough for one car, which arched across a stream that had been reduced to little more than a trickle by the lack of rain over the past few weeks.

A metal sign on their left read LONGBARROW, and immediately they were driving between rows of pretty, tightly packed stone cottages with well-kept front gardens.

The narrow road curved uphill and then down. They passed some larger, though no less pretty, houses, a rustic-looking pub called The Druid's Arms, the occasional shop or business. Longbarrow appeared to be set in a dip in the land, the houses like little stone blocks clustered in the centre of a natural basin.

'Where's our house, Mum?' David asked, looking around as if he expected it to leap out at them.

'I think we must be coming into the village from the south,' Susan said. 'Our house is on the other side somewhere. What does it say on the instructions?'

David consulted the envelope. 'Follow the main road into the village until you see a garage on your left and a church on your right. Straight ahead you'll see a war memorial and some shops. Ask at the travel agent's for the key.'

'Sounds simple enough,' said Susan. She grinned suddenly at him. 'This is lovely, isn't it?'

David had to admit that it was. Longbarrow seemed a peaceful, picturesque place, unspoiled by tourism. The buildings were generally of either sandstone or red brick with slate roofs, and seemed, almost without exception, old and quaint and lovingly maintained. There were children playing out on bikes, people walking their dogs or tending their gardens or washing their cars or simply passing the time of day with their neighbours. David had half-expected the locals to stare silently after them as they passed, marking them instantly as outsiders, but the residents of Longbarrow seemed like ordinary people doing ordinary things and the red Citroën barely merited a second glance.

Abruptly the road widened, branching into four. The

turning immediately to the right appeared to lead between more housing, as did the one to the left. The second right turning cut up by the side of a churchyard before following the curve of the churchyard wall and bending out of sight. The church itself, set atop a hummock so that it seemed to watch over the houses below, was small and picture-postcard beautiful, constructed of weathered stone and surrounded by shrubs and flower beds.

Most of the land which comprised the churchyard appeared to drop away behind the church, set on different levels, presumably to keep the graves upright. Yews grew in abundance around the perimeter of the church grounds and in the churchyard itself, giving the place a tranquil, cosily enclosed feel.

David pointed out the church and then the garage.

'And there's the war memorial,' said Susan, pointing ahead. She looked right and left and then drove straight across.

The road encircled the war memorial, which took the form of a large stone cross carved with the names of the local dead of two World Wars. To the left was a row of shops, and to the right a stone wall inset with a lych-gate which was the main entrance to the churchyard. The path from the lych-gate rose up a slight gradient to the church's entrance porch. Susan took the left-hand fork around the memorial, pulling almost immediately into the forecourt of the garage, which was actually someone's house with a petrol pump outside.

'Can I go and look at the graves while you get some petrol, Mum?' David asked.

Susan's first instinct was to tell him not to be morbid, but then she nodded. 'Yes, if you like.'

As he crossed the road, stopping at the war memorial to look both ways before heading for the lych-gate, Susan tried not to be troubled by her son's behaviour, tried to tell herself that being interested in graveyards was perfectly natural for a twelve-year-old boy. Back home David would happily spend hours poking around in Highgate cemetery; he seemed to find it a fascinating occupation working out exactly how long people he had never met or even heard of before had lived. Perhaps she was being too sensitive, but sometimes she thought that this preoccupation with death might be something to do with his father, a subtle but persistent attempt to come to terms with what had happened. Occasionally David would lapse into periods of broodiness which she never allowed him to work through himself but always tried to get to the bottom of, because they frightened her; they reminded her too much of how Gerry had often been.

She tried to comfort herself with the thought that David was probably just looking for Aunt Mollie's grave, or was perhaps curious to discover whether any of their other relatives were buried here. She bought her petrol, parked the car in one of the designated spaces outside the post office, and then went off in search of her son.

Though it was still hot here, the heat was not stifling or fume-clogged like it was in London. Indeed, the air smelled dizzyingly fresh – of grass and flowers, wood and earth. When she passed through the lych-gate into the churchyard, what little sound there was from the road outside seemed suddenly blocked out. She paused a moment, listening. All she could hear was the whisper of the breeze through the dry grass and the spiky foliage of the yew trees, the occasional buzz of a bee busily collecting nectar. It was so peaceful; she sighed a deep sigh of contentment. She strolled up the flagstoned path towards the church, veering to the left when she reached the entrance porch, following it around to the back.

The trees were more prolific here, trapping the sun in their branches, throwing dapples of light on to the little flights of stone steps that divided one level of ground from the next. The different levels and the graves they contained did not look planned, but higgledy-piggledy, formed by accident rather than design, by the simple necessity of accommodating more and more graves. For the moment Susan could not see David, but she felt loath to call out his name and shatter the silence which seemed to have accumulated over long years. She pushed between two trees which were bent towards each other like old women deeply engaged in conversation, down yet another short flight of stone steps which were overgrown with weeds and worn by the passage of many feet over many years, and suddenly found herself in a relatively open area, on the crest of a gently sloping bank.

And here was David, standing on grass parched brown with

the sun, his face uptilted as he stared at something on the back wall of the church. It was obvious that he hadn't yet registered her presence. Susan felt a little jolt of unease watching him there, so small and still, his face pale, lips pressed into a terse line, as if he was mesmerised or shocked into immobility by whatever he was looking at.

This time she had no qualms about calling out. It suddenly seemed more important to rouse David from his reverie than it did to maintain the tranquillity of the churchyard. The instant she waved and called his name, he turned his head towards her and smiled. It seemed such an easy transformation that Susan wondered whether she had been making too much of his stance of a few moments before. She walked down towards him, and when she got close enough to make herself heard without having to raise her voice, she asked, 'Are you all right?'

He seemed surprised by the question. 'Yes, I'm fine. Why?'

Susan didn't answer, but instead countered his query with one of her own. 'What were you looking at?'

David pointed. 'That thing there.'

She had reached him now. She turned and squinted up at the back of the church, using her hand to shield her eyes from the sun.

Carved on the church tower, quite high up, above the stained-glass windows, was an enormous eye. It was extremely weathered, but still striking and instantly recognisable.

'What is it, Mum?' David asked.

'That is the Eye of God,' said a voice behind them.

Both of them turned to see a man trudging up the slope. He was in his early fifties, straight-backed and distinguished-looking, debonair rather than handsome, with wavy grey hair and a wide mouth that looked used to smiling. The dog collar he wore immediately identified him as the local vicar. He looked, thought Susan, rather like one of those British gentlemen actors from a bygone age – David Niven or James Mason.

He was sweating as he joined them, and produced a checked handkerchief from his pocket which he used to dab at his forehead.

'I'm sorry if I startled you,' he said.

Susan smiled. 'It's all right, you didn't.'

'Then I'm sorry for eavesdropping on your conversation.

43

Actually I wasn't really eavesdropping. I was just walking up from the vicarage.'

He gestured towards a copse of trees beyond the wall at the bottom of the slope. Above the trees Susan saw a couple of red brick chimney stacks and a television aerial on which a line of sparrows perched.

David turned back to the carving on the church tower. 'What's it looking at?' he asked.

The vicar gave Susan a secretive smile, almost as if he was complimenting her on her son's inquisitiveness. 'It's a witch-craft eye. It dates from the sixteenth century. It's supposed to protect the church from witches.'

'Were there witches here?' David asked eagerly.

'Oh, some say there still are,' said the vicar, apparently in all seriousness.

David's eyes were wide. 'Wow, really?'

Brusquely Susan said, 'There aren't such things as witches, Davey. Not real ones.'

The vicar looked at her. 'Oh, I wouldn't be so sure of that,' he said good-humouredly. 'Longbarrow is quite a magical place, you know.'

'How do you mean, "magical"?' asked David.

'Oh, the place is steeped in folklore, legends of witches and wizards and ghosts and holy wells and goodness only knows what else. Quite a few of the locals claim to have psychic abilities of one sort or another, passed down from generation to generation.'

'Isn't it a bit incompatible?' said Susan. 'You being a vicar and believing in magic?'

The vicar smiled. 'Oh no, I don't think so. If black magic is said to be the Devil's work, then white magic has to be the work of the Lord, doesn't it?'

'I suppose you could look at it like that,' said Susan dubiously. 'But I'd always thought God was supposed to be a bit more than a . . . a galactic magician.'

The vicar laughed. 'Indeed He is.' He glanced at his watch. 'Look, I'm sorry to be rude, but I really ought to be going. I have a rather pressing appointment. Are you just visiting the village?'

'No,' said Susan. 'That is . . . well, we had a relative who lived here. Mollie Boscombe. We've inherited her house.'

'Really?' said the vicar, sounding genuinely pleased. 'Yes, I knew Mrs Boscombe. She was rather reclusive, but a very nice lady. Will you be moving in to the house, then?'

'Well, we don't know yet. We only found out on Saturday that we'd inherited it. And to be honest, we didn't know Mrs Boscombe. She was a relative on my husband's side, my . . . er . . . late husband, that is. So all this has really come like a bolt from the blue.'

The vicar listened, nodding. 'Well, it's a beautiful house. I'm sure you won't be disappointed.' To David he added, 'Actually your house is reputed to be the focal point for all the magic in Longbarrow, apparently built where a number of ley-lines converge.'

The vicar's words set off a mental echo in David's head. Ley-lines. He thought of the glowing paths of energy in his dream.

Susan laughed as though to make light of his words. 'I knew there'd be some catch. Subsidence due to ley-lines.'

The vicar laughed too. 'Oh, I wouldn't worry. The energy from ley-lines is generally regarded as beneficial; it's not a destructive or an evil force. In fact, many churches are said to be built on ley-lines, though this one isn't. It seems we rather lost out to your aunt's house there.'

'Is our house haunted?' asked David.

The vicar looked at Susan, who was frowning slightly. 'Oh, I don't know about that,' he said. He glanced at his watch again. 'I'm very sorry, but I really must be going. Perhaps we'll meet again. My name's Steven Farrar, by the way.'

Susan introduced herself and David, and she and the vicar shook hands. His grip was warm and damp with sweat, but firm.

'Very nice to meet you,' he said. 'Well, cheerio for now. I hope you like the house.' He began to move away, hurrying towards the stone steps at the bottom of which Susan had first seen David staring up at the church. Just before he disappeared from sight, Farrar turned back and called, 'Ask someone to tell you the legend of the Seven Sleepers. Ask Mr Toot, the grocer. Goodbye.'

He waved and then stepped between the two overhanging yews.

'Mr Toot, the grocer,' said Susan incredulously. 'It sounds like a name from . . . from a game.'

'Or a fairy tale,' said David. He looked up again at the eye carved on the back of the church. 'Do you believe in magic, Mum?'

'No, I don't,' Susan said firmly, and began to walk in the direction the vicar had taken. 'Come on, Davey. I think it's time we went and had a look at our inheritance.'

Chapter Six

David felt a nervous energy in the pit of his stomach, almost a tingling, like an electric current, as they drove north out of the village. *Ley-line energy*, he thought, and glanced up at the road ahead, half-expecting to see a trail of golden light illuminating their way. But of course there was nothing except dusty, pitted Tarmac, crumbling at the verges where weeds flourished. Like the road into the village, the road out was narrow and winding, the flanking trees and bushes providing them with welcome shade from the sun's heat.

Mr Charles, the estate agent, who had had a set of keys waiting for them, together with directions to the house, had kept referring to the place as Longbarrow House, which made it sound important. He had fussed and fawned over them as though they were cherished customers, though maybe, David thought, he treated everyone that way. He had told them that Aunt Mollie's house was 'on top of the hill', about a mile outside the village, and as he had said this he had gestured vaguely upwards as though referring to some castle in the clouds.

The short drive up to the house had been undertaken mostly in silence, and David wondered whether his mum too could feel the odd and growing tension in the air, the sense not of foreboding but of expectancy. It was strong enough now to have become a physical sensation, but David had been aware of a subtle heightening of his perceptions the instant he had stepped out of the car in the village, as if the air was loaded with positive ions, or as if his body was soaking up a faint but discernible charge of energy (*magic*) from the concrete beneath his feet.

Now, as they got closer to the house, the tingling in his

stomach intensified, suffusing his entire body. His fingertips felt as though they were twitching with invisible sparks, his hair felt stiff and prickly, and his mouth was filling with a slick, metallic taste. His senses, too, seemed to be ballooning beyond their capabilities, filling his head with strange thoughts. It was almost as though the world that he saw outside the car was nothing but an elaborate cover for something far more significant.

Like a snake moving beneath a blanket, he thought suddenly. You can't see the snake, but you can see the blanket rippling and you know that the snake is under there.

Suddenly, almost without realising he was speaking, David said, 'In a minute the trees'll stop and there'll be a big cornfield on the left and a wall on the right. That's where our house is.'

Susan looked at him. 'Is that what the estate agent said?'

'No,' said David. 'I just know.'

Ten seconds later, Susan rounded an uphill curve, immediately squinting and squeezing down gently on the brake as they were ambushed by sunlight. The reason for the sudden brightness was that the trees which had craned towards the road, blotting out much of the sun, had all at once petered out, or more likely been cut back to make way for farmland. As David had predicted, there was a cornfield on their left, enclosed by a dry-stone wall that looked in need of repair. The corn seemed imbued with a golden glow, as though it had been sown from seeds of the sun. The ears bobbed gently in unison as a breeze stirred them. In a week or so the crop would be ripe for harvesting.

Susan slowed the car to a crawl as a high stone wall topped with broken glass appeared on their right. She gave her son a strange look. '*How* did you know about this?'

David looked back at her wide-eyed. 'I don't know. I just did, that's all.'

She sighed and gripped the steering wheel hard as though bracing herself for something. 'Was it part of your dream?'

David thought about it. He hadn't actually *seen* this in his dream, but hadn't he somehow known about it? Couldn't he picture it in his mind the way anyone could picture a familiar route?

He shook his head as if to clear it. Although the tingling in

48

his stomach was still there, the intensity he had felt a moment before, the way the energy had expanded and filled his entire body, was gone, released like the zap of a lightning flash when he had voiced his foreknowledge.

'No, not really,' he repeated lamely. 'I just knew.'

Susan pressed her lips together and said nothing. She drove on a little further, parallel with the high wall, until they came to a set of iron gates set into stout stone pillars.

She indicated out of habit, even though they had not seen any other cars since leaving the village, and pulled in in front of the gates. David noticed that on each of the pillars was a stone carving, in the form of a spiral or vortex. At first he thought that the carvings were stylised eyes, like on the church tower, which would have given the gates the look of a huge face with a cavernous mouth full of bared metal teeth. Then he noticed that each of the spirals culminated in reptilian heads with forked tongues, and he realised that the carvings were in fact coiled snakes.

His mum made no comment on the carvings as she got out of the car and inserted one of the keys that Mr Charles had given her into the lock of the huge padlock that hung from the gates. The padlock sprang open and his mum unwound the heavy-duty chain encased in its plastic sheath. David opened the passenger door, intending to help her pull the gates open, but they swung apart easily despite their size and apparent weight. Beyond, he could see a gravel drive scattered with acorns from the oak trees that flanked it. The house itself was not visible.

They drove through the gates, the wheels of the car crunching on gravel.

'Aren't you going to close the gates?' David said as his mum eased up to second gear.

She glanced at him, her lips pressed together, and he thought she wasn't going to reply until she said a little curtly, 'Why should I? It's our house.'

He was silent for a moment, and then he said, 'Are you mad at me because of my dream?'

She glanced at him again, and immediately her face softened. 'No, of course not. I'm just a bit . . . unsettled, that's all.'

David looked around. 'I don't think there's anything to be scared of, Mum. I think this is a good place.'

'I'm sure it is,' said Susan, 'but that doesn't stop this whole situation from being spooky.'

The gravel drive meandered on for another quarter of a mile before – just as in David's dream – the trees seemed to step back, giving the impression that they had parted like the gates into another world. Immediately the driveway widened out into a parking area bordered by flowerbeds in front of the house.

It was exactly as David remembered it – a big, square, stone-built building with lots of windows and an entrance porch, red ivy crawling up the left-hand side, high enough to tickle the eaves. One detail that did surprise him, however – a detail that had either been absent from his dream or that he simply hadn't noticed – was the carving in the stonework above the stained glass panel over the big front door. It was the same as that on the gateposts, a coiled snake.

'Wow!' Susan said. 'This is amazing. It's even bigger than I imagined it would be.' She brought the car to a halt and asked David almost reluctantly, '*Is* it the place you dreamed about?'

He nodded, looking apologetic. 'Yes, definitely.'

She looked up at the house again, silent for a moment, and then she said, 'Well, maybe your dream was a good omen. I mean, it's not as if you had a nightmare about the house, is it?'

David thought of how the dream had ended – with the great serpent coiling around him in the blackness. The image itself was nightmarish, but the dream had not had the flavour of a nightmare. He shook his head.

They got out of the car. The house seemed to glow in the sunlight. The reflection of the sky on the windows gave the impression that screens of white tissue paper had been laid across every pane of glass, offering the vaguest suggestion of darker shapes inside.

David pointed up at the carving above the door. 'Why are there snakes everywhere, Mum?'

Instinctively Susan's gaze followed the direction of his pointing finger before she looked quickly away. 'I don't know,' she said, and the tone of her voice was obvious: I don't know and I don't *want* to know.

She unlocked the heavy oak door and they went inside. The instant David crossed the threshold, a wave of energy similar to that which had heralded his prediction in the car ten minutes earlier sluiced through him. The difference this time, however, was that the charge of energy was accompanied by an incredible sense of well-being, a sense that he was being joyously welcomed, though whether it was by the house itself or by some force inside the house, he couldn't say.

He looked at his mum and saw a beatific, almost soppy smile on her face.

'You feel it too, don't you, Mum?' he said.

She looked at him, dewy-eyed. 'What?'

'The . . . the *feeling*.' He didn't know how to describe it. 'The *good* feeling. I felt it as soon as I walked in.'

The blissful smile remained on her face a moment longer, and then she blinked and shook her head as if to stimulate thoughts that had turned slow and syrupy.

'I don't know about that,' she said. 'I was just thinking how incredible this was, how lucky we were. I don't think it had properly sunk in until a few minutes ago when I actually saw the place . . . This is *ours*, Davey. This house belongs to us.'

He nodded. They were standing in the entrance hall of his dream. The walls wood-panelled to waist height, the polished floorboards of the hallway, the wide staircase carpeted in burgundy with ornately carved banisters, the position of the doors, the grandfather clock . . . it was all just as he remembered it.

They walked forward cautiously, perhaps even a little reverently, as if uncertain what to do, where to start. Their tapping footsteps echoed up to the high ceiling. Susan crossed to the first door on the right, opened it and peered inside.

'This must be the reception room.'

David joined her. Various mismatched items of old but comfy-looking furniture were clustered around an inglenook fireplace. The carpet was richly patterned but threadbare. Light poured in through the three long sash windows, out of which David could see his mum's red Citroën parked on the gravel, and the beginnings of the driveway before it curled out of sight between the myriad, somehow guardian-like oak trees.

'Smells a bit musty,' he said.

'The house has been closed up for three weeks. It just needs a good airing, that's all.'

They exited the room, Susan pulling the door shut behind them. David stopped to examine the grandfather clock which stood against the wall between the door of the reception room and the next one along.

It was perhaps eight feet tall, its woodwork edged with intricate carvings of vines and leaves and flowers. A fan-like section had been cut from the beautifully painted dial, behind which had been inset a smaller dial, this one painted with images which seemed to depict the different times of day, or perhaps the changing seasons. At any given time, only a quarter of this smaller dial was visible. David supposed that it rotated weekly or monthly when the clock was going. At the moment the image revealed was of a smiling, fat-faced moon hanging in a stormy sky.

'Look at this, Mum,' David said, and pointed up at the smaller dial. 'I wonder what the other pictures are.'

'Maybe we can get it going and find out,' she said. 'It might just need winding. It's a lovely piece of work, isn't it?'

The room beyond the reception room was a dining room containing a huge oak table and eight chairs. The walls were painted brick-red and hung with paintings depicting rural scenes. There was an open fire in this room too, a chandelier suspended above the table like a vast diamond, and a bay window which gave a view of the land at the side of the house – an area of lawn, flowerbeds, more trees.

'All oak trees,' Susan noted curiously.

'I wonder what it means,' said David.

She gave him a sharp look. 'Why should it mean anything?'

He shrugged, unable to answer. It was the snake under the blanket syndrome again. He felt certain there was a significance underlying everything, if only he could see it.

Leisurely they examined the rest of the ground-floor rooms. As well as a downstairs toilet, there was a library whose floor-to-ceiling bookshelves contained everything from a seventeenth-century Bible to a collection of well-thumbed Catherine Cookson paperbacks; a study dominated by a vast oak desk with an inlaid surface of worn green leather, its walls decorated with dead insects in glass cases and framed maps of the British Empire; and a sitting room large enough to accommodate comfortably two three-piece suites which were upholstered in damask woven with a fruit and flower pattern.

'Wow! Look at the fireplace, Mum,' David said, entering this room.

'I bet they've roasted a few pigs here in their time,' Susan said.

The fireplace was cavernous, its cluttered mantelpiece on a level with Susan's forehead. Beside it, on the hearth, was a basket of logs that looked as though it would need four men to lift it. Even the companion set looked as though it had been made for a giant; the tongs and poker resembled ancient, creaking torture implements.

Looking around, Susan said, 'My God, you could hold the Antiques Roadshow in here.'

Every bit of wall space was taken up with a cabinet or a dresser or a sideboard, the majority of which looked very old. There was a great amount of china and glassware on display, and Susan wondered how much it would all fetch before silently reproving herself for her mercenary thoughts.

'Is all this ours as well?' David asked.

Susan nodded.

'But there won't be any room for our stuff.'

Susan raised her eyebrows and teasingly said, 'Oh, so you've decided we're going to live here, after all, have you?'

David reddened. 'I meant *if* we do.'

The only unexplored downstairs room now was the kitchen at the back of the house, but David knew what to expect from his dream. Already he was becoming used to living his dream, and the positive vibes or good magic or whatever it was that the house continued to exude made him feel fairly relaxed about it. He considered describing to his mum exactly what the room would be like before she opened the door, but decided that she would find that neither amusing nor clever.

The kitchen held no surprises for him. There was the rough-hewn table, the Aga, the massive sink, the Welsh dresser – and of course the door in the corner of the room leading down to the cellar. As his mum looked around, making complimentary noises, David listened with his newly attuned senses, half-expecting to hear – or at least to sense – the pulse or summons that had drawn him down to the cellar in his dream.

However, he heard nothing. The house was steeped in a silence that nevertheless seemed somehow companionable. Susan leaned on the sink to look out of the window above it. Beyond a fence enclosing a small, well-kept garden, complete with shed, was an overgrown paddock, and beyond *that* was a wilderness, weeds and long grass replacing the usual flower-beds and well-clipped lawn. She turned back round to face him, her back now against the sink. Nodding at the door in the corner of the room, she said boldly, almost as if challenging him, 'According to your dream, that should go down to the cellar, shouldn't it?'

'Yes,' said David, and almost added, *where the snake was*, but the words wouldn't quite come. It was silly really, this game his mum was playing with him. David knew she wouldn't want him to mention the snake in his dream, even though she was probably thinking about it herself. It was as though by not talking about it she could make herself believe that the snake in his dream had nothing to do with the ones carved on the gateposts and on the house.

David, however, *knew* there was a connection, although for the time being he didn't know what that connection was. He fell into step behind his mum as she marched across the room to the cellar door.

'Come on then, let's have a look,' she said determinedly.

She opened the door and the two of them peered in. Apart from half a dozen stone steps descending into blackness there was nothing to see. There was a light switch on the wall to Susan's left, but when she pressed it nothing happened. For a moment the two of them stood there as if uncertain how to proceed, and then David said, 'I could look through some of these drawers for a torch?'

The minor setback, however, appeared to have drained Susan's resolve. 'Maybe we'll leave it for another day,' she said. 'We've still got upstairs to look at.'

She closed the cellar door and the two of them left the room and went back along the corridor. They ascended the staircase, David in the lead. The upper landing seemed gloomy after the relative brightness of the ground-floor rooms, largely because the three doors facing them before the landing curved around a corner out of sight were closed. Together they checked out the rooms. There was a bathroom which smelled vaguely of stagnant drains, with pink fluffy rugs on the floor and dead flies on the windowsill, a carpetless bedroom that was stacked so full of dusty old furniture that David sneezed eight times in a row and had to use his inhaler because he became so wheezy, and a square room with nailed-shut windows that had evidently once been a nursery judging by the recurring pattern of dolls and teddy bears and wooden trains and marching tin soldiers on the wallpaper.

This room, too, was dusty, and with each step that David took into it he felt his chest tightening and the itch intensifying at the back of his throat. He persevered, however, because he wanted to check out the stack of interesting-looking stuff beneath the window. In a cardboard box bearing the legend *Winalot* he found curls of rail-track and the tin carriages of a toy train; a cross-eyed doll with a face dirty as a coalminer's; loose wooden building blocks painted in chipped primary colours; a wooden bagatelle game; a stack of children's books; board games and jigsaws with jumbled pieces; and some Matchbox cars in various states of disrepair.

He poked among what was evidently the debris of several long-ago childhoods like a prospector searching for a nugget of gold in a panful of dirt. The whole lot was covered in a thick grey crust, and in the end he was forced to retreat, sucking on his inhaler.

'Anything decent?' Susan asked.

'Maybe. I'll have to have a proper look some other time.'

They rounded the corner to be faced with three more doors. It was even gloomier up this end of the corridor, and just for a second David imagined he heard a light set of footsteps underlying his own. He stopped, and so did the footsteps – if they had ever been there at all. At the end of the corridor was a further set of stairs. Narrow and winding, they led presumably to one or several attic rooms.

All three doors in this part of the corridor opened into bedrooms, two of which were thick with dust and sparsely furnished. The third, by contrast, was clearly where Aunt Mollie had slept. It had sunny yellow walls with paintings of geese and ducks and sheep hanging on them. There was a brightly coloured quilt on the large, lumpy bed, a dressing table cluttered with an old lady's things – brown plastic prescription tubes of tablets, a roll of surgical bandage, some corn plasters, various creams and ointments – and a wicker chair painted white, on which was a stack of neatly folded cardigans and thick, tweedy-looking skirts.

'My God,' Susan said. She marched across to the dressing table and snatched up a framed photograph.

When David asked what it was, she silently handed it to him. It was a black-and-white family snapshot, slightly out of focus. There was a big, moustached father in a wide-lapelled suit, a stern-looking mother with her arms folded, and a boy of about ten, squinting through a long fringe, wearing shorts and a school blazer.

'Who's this?' David asked.

'Don't you know?'

She sounded surprised, even a little disappointed. He looked again. The boy looked a bit like him. 'It's Dad, isn't it?' he said.

'Yes, your dad and your grandparents. I never met your granddad. He died of a heart attack when your dad was fourteen.'

David looked at the photograph once more, then handed it back. Photos always made him feel a bit sad, because even when the people in them looked happy you knew that one day they would all be dead and gone.

It was the first time he had felt sad since entering the house, but once they were out of Aunt Mollie's room the feeling passed.

'Can we have a look up there?' he asked, pointing to the twisty flight of stairs at the end of the corridor.

'Of course. Ever upward,' said Susan.

David took the lead. At the top of the stairs was a tiny landing, little more than a four-foot square platform, with a door to either side and a high ceiling that rose in a point and was inset with a small skylight.

David opened the left-hand door. The room beyond was dingy and hot and full of cobwebs which stretched like grey netting from the stacked furniture and piles of boxes and propped rolls of carpet to the sloping ceiling. There was so much stuff in here that there was barely any floor space. It would have taken a week to sort through everything – and probably another week to have cleaned the room afterwards.

David squeezed into the room between a sludge-brown settee and a wooden crate which appeared to be full of rolls of curtain material. The layer of dust on the bare floorboards was so thick that it muffled his footsteps. The shafts of sunlight forcing their way through the grime on the skylight window teemed with dust motes, and immediately David felt his bronchi contracting again, probably due as much to the psychological effect of actually *seeing* all that dust as to any physical reaction. He took his inhaler from his pocket and had two more long blasts, knowing that if he had much more Ventolin he would start to get the jitters.

'Are you okay?' Susan asked.

He didn't answer immediately, but stood, breathing deeply, imagining the dust motes as a swarm of tiny, virulent insects invading his body, only to be instantly neutralised by the bug-killing cloud of Ventolin in his lungs.

After a few moments his breathing eased and he nodded. Often the Ventolin made him feel light-headed, but today his senses were so attuned that he probably wouldn't have noticed much difference.

'You wait here by the door,' Susan said. 'I just want to have a quick poke through some of this stuff.'

She squeezed past him into the room. The grainy light slanting in through the window formed a fuzzy white nimbus above her dark hair. 'I can't believe how old some of this furniture is,' she said, looking around. She reached out for a roll of carpet that was propped against the wall above a chaise longue that she wanted to look at more closely. She shoved at the carpet gingerly, trying to shunt it along the floor, out of the way, without making it topple over. David was about to ask her if she needed a hand when he became aware of a curious pattering sound. He looked down and saw hundreds of fat yellow maggots spilling out of the carpet and across the floor.

'*Oh, gross!*' he yelled, jumping back instinctively, though the fan-shaped area of blindly wriggling life was a good four feet away from him.

'Oh my God,' Susan said, turning pale. Her hands jumped back from the carpet as if the fabric itself had begun to squirm. Mouth stretched open in a grimace of disgust, teeth gritted, she took an exaggerated step over the teeming mass, joining David at the door.

She shuddered with her whole body. 'Urgh! Horrible things,' she said.

'Insects must have been laying eggs in the carpet,' David said, peering around. 'They probably laid thousands of them all over the place. We could have opened the door and stepped right into the middle of a massive swarm of flies, like in that film—'

'Don't,' Susan said, looking queasy. She turned away. 'Shut the door. I can't stand looking at those things any longer.'

David obliged, then indicated the other door. 'Do you still want to look in here?'

'I'm not sure it's a good idea now. What if they've hatched out in there?'

It was a sobering thought, but although he'd been content to leave the cellar for another day (he had, in a sense, already been down there, after all) David felt loath to leave even a small section of this part of the house unexplored.

He put his ear to the wood. 'I can't hear any buzzing.' Before she could say a definite no, he added, 'Don't worry, Mum, I'll protect you', and shoved the door open.

No flies flew at them, no insects scuttled away into crevices. There *was* a big spider in the corner of the room, crouched balefully in its web, but that was far enough away not to be a problem.

This room was bigger than the one across the landing – or perhaps it was simply its emptiness that made it appear so. It was certainly lighter; the two velux windows set into the dramatically sloping ceiling were evidently recent additions. The walls and ceiling had been painted with a white undercoat, and there was not so much dust in evidence here. It was as though Aunt Mollie had decided to give the house a thorough overhaul, working from the top downwards, just before she died.

David crossed to the furthest velux window and shoved at the bar that sealed it shut. It swung open with a faint *shluk* sound. Standing on his tiptoes, he stuck his head out.

The view from here was spectacular, and made him realise how high up they were. He could see the boundary of their estate at the back, the high wall topped with broken glass stretching all the way round what the estate agent's details had informed them were fifty-odd acres of land. The wilder land beyond the paddock, still heavily populated with the ubiquitous oak trees, contained patches of undergrowth so dense in places it practically merged with the woodland that took over where their boundary ended. Away to the right was the village of Longbarrow itself. From here the impression he had gained earlier of the buildings being clustered at the centre of a natural basin was borne out. Longbarrow House, by contrast, seemed high enough up the valley to be almost nudging the clouds.

Susan joined him, the breeze up here ruffling her fringe. 'Wow, just smell that fresh air,' she said.

'I didn't realise we were so high up.'

'The house on the hill,' she murmured, and grinned at him. 'Isn't this fantastic? You could almost believe there are only the two of us in the world.'

David thought of London, where you were never alone. Even in bed at night there was always the sound of traffic somewhere close by. His earlier reservations about moving out to the country, his fears that he would have nothing to do, now seemed petty and unfounded. He felt wonderful here, at peace with himself and the world. The forces that moved in this house were benign ones. He wanted to stay here for ever. It was the thought of having to drive back to London tonight that depressed him now.

He lowered his heels to the floor so that his head was back inside the room, and looked around once more. 'Can I have this as my bedroom, Mum?' he said.

Susan turned away from the view and draped an arm across his shoulders, seemingly fully recovered from her encounter with the maggots. 'Who says we're going to live here?'

'Aren't we?' he said, unable to hide his disappointment.

She smiled enigmatically. 'Come on, let's go and have a look at our grounds.'

They went downstairs and out through the kitchen door into the little back garden that David guessed had been Aunt Mollie's personal domain. Someone had evidently been tending it since her death because the plants were healthy despite the drought and there were few weeds. Butterflies fluttered from flower to flower, erratic in flight, becoming creatures of beauty and grace when they stopped to rest. Bees like fat little workers in striped uniforms collected nectar, whilst at ground level ants marched in file along the cracks in the flagstones.

Beyond the shed at the end of the garden was a gate which led into the paddock. Susan unlatched it and the two of them wandered through, their feet now swishing through the long dry grass.

All at once a dark flicker of movement caught David's eye a

few feet to his left, and he paused, a little startled, half-expecting to see a large insect or a fieldmouse beating a hasty retreat. What he did see, in fact, was a grass snake, no more than a foot long. It made a quick, lithe S-shape and was gone.

'Did you see that?' David breathed, but Susan had wandered ahead and was squinting up at the sky as though looking for something. It was obvious she hadn't heard him. He took a couple of steps towards her, opening his mouth to speak, but before he could say anything a voice called out, 'Hey, stop!'

Susan spun round as though she'd been shot, arms jerking up as her shoulders hunched instinctively. David, too, felt shock jolt through him, and turned a split-second after his mum.

He saw a man standing on the path at the side of the house, beside the thigh-high fence that bordered Aunt Mollie's little flower garden. The man was about his mum's age, and had muscles and a tan that looked as though they came not from a gymnasium and a sunbed but from working outside. He was stripped to the waist, wearing a pair of ratty jeans so ingrained with grease and dirt that it looked as though no amount of washing would ever get the stains out. The sun had bleached the man's unkempt, mousy hair blond in patches. He began to walk towards them, and as he got closer David noticed two things: one, that the man looked a bit like a younger version of the film star, Harrison Ford, and two, that he had a small but upraised scar in the shape of a question mark curling from just below his lower lip to the dimple on his chin.

David glanced at his mum, and saw that she had unconsciously adopted a defensive stance, shoulders still hunched, back straight and stiff, face set.

'What's the problem?' she called, sounding aggressive without, David suspected, even realising it.

'Don't move,' the man said, half-raising a hand. He came to a stop perhaps six feet away from them.

'This is my house and my land. My great-aunt left it to me in her will. We're not trespassing.'

The man smiled then, and it transformed his face. It was a slow, almost goofy smile. David, who had the instinctive caution of any kid who had been brought up in the big city, surprised himself by deciding on the spur of the moment that he liked this man.

'It's not that,' the man said. 'You were heading straight for the well. You might have fallen down it and broken your neck.'

The well. Of course. David should have remembered that it was around here somewhere.

Susan was looking around suspiciously. 'What well? I don't see one.'

David remembered the energy that had filled the well, and filled him too when he drank it. No, not just filled him, but *transformed* him, as though allowing him a glimpse of what he could become.

The man was pointing over Susan's shoulder. 'It's just over there. Do you want me to show you?'

Still she looked hesitant, her lips pressed tightly together.

'I'd like to see it,' said David.

The man glanced at him, his smile returning, then he looked again at Susan. 'I'll show you if you want me to,' he said. 'It's up to you. I just didn't want you to fall down it, that's all.'

Susan licked her lips and shifted position slightly. Now she didn't look quite so tense. 'I don't mean to be rude,' she said, 'but we don't even know who you are or why you're here.'

'My name's Jack Bradley. I live in the village, got my own business – Jack of All Trades. I've been working for Mrs Boscombe ever since I started up: gardening, plumbing, decorating, building, electrics. I'll turn my hand to anything.'

'You're not a jack of all trades, master of none, are you?' Susan asked teasingly.

For the first time Jack frowned. 'I've been working in this village for fifteen years, and no one's ever complained about a single job I've done.'

Susan smiled. 'Sorry, I couldn't resist it.'

Jack Bradley's frown persisted for a moment longer, and then the smile resurfaced. 'Aye, well, you're not the first one to make that joke. The lads in the pub are always saying it to try to rile me. Doesn't work, though. Water off a duck's back.'

'*I* nearly riled you,' said Susan.

Jack laughed. 'Nah, you didn't. Sun got in my eyes for a minute, that's all.'

Susan's smile was genuine rather than teasing now. 'So who's employing you to work on the place now that Aunt Mollie's gone? The local estate agent?'

Jack Bradley flushed, and actually looked a little sheepish.

'Well . . . no,' he admitted. 'To tell you the truth, I'm just doing it off my own bat. Like I say, I've worked for Mrs Boscombe for fifteen years, and she's always been really good to me, and . . . well, to be honest, I love this house and I couldn't bear to see it fall to rack and ruin. So every time I've had a spare minute I've been popping up here just to keep things ticking over – doing a bit of gardening, bit of maintenance, that sort of thing.'

Susan's smile was widening all the time. 'You mean you've been doing this out of the goodness of your heart?'

Jack was almost squirming with embarrassment. 'Well . . . yeah, I suppose you could put it like that. But don't tell anyone, will you?'

'Why not?'

'If the lads in the pub found out, I'd never hear the end of it. They'd think I'd gone soft.'

This time Susan laughed out loud. 'It's all right, Jack,' she said, 'your secret's safe with us.'

His consternation turned to a grin of relief. His face was so expressive that it gave him an air of great openness. He seemed to David like the kind of man who would find it hard to mask his emotions or tell lies.

'Thanks,' he said. 'Now, do you want me to show you this well or not?'

Susan said yes, and Jack led them through the long grass, stopping after about twenty yards and dropping on to one knee. At first David could see nothing, and thought that Jack had perhaps stopped to tie his shoelace or pick something up. Then the handyman reached out and began to yank weeds and clumps of long grass out of the ground, tossing them aside. The muscles in his forearms stood out like thick cables. After a few moments he sat back, wiping a sheen of sweat from his forehead with the heel of his hand.

'There you go,' he said.

He had revealed a round black hole, lined with stone blocks that descended into the earth. There was no lip on the hole, and when David craned forward to peer down into it all he saw was blackness.

'I've been meaning to board it up for a while, but I haven't got round to it. Bloody dangerous thing. As quick as you clear all the weeds from around it, they just grow again.'

'How deep is it?' asked David.

Jack shrugged. 'I don't know. Very deep. Some people say if you fall in there you'll never stop falling.'

David looked around in the long grass and picked up a chunk of rock. 'Can I drop this in it?' he asked.

Jack glanced at Susan as though for her approval, then said, 'I don't see what harm it can do.'

David dropped the rock. The three of them waited for almost a minute, but they never heard it hit bottom.

'It must go right into the centre of the earth,' David breathed.

'Or maybe all the way down into Hell,' said Susan, wiggling her eyebrows to show she was joking.

Jack, however, seemed to take her comment semi-seriously. 'Oh, it's not an evil place. In fact, Mrs Boscombe told me that it was once a holy well. It was supposedly given as a gift to the villagers by a mage called Decumen. Its water was supposed to be able to cure any ailment.'

'What's a mage?' asked David.

'A magic man.'

'Like a wizard, you mean?'

'Aye, if you like.'

'Has there ever been water in the well?' Susan asked.

'Not to my knowledge.'

'It was full of water in my dream,' David said, a comment which earned him a warning glance from Susan.

'What dream's this then?' Jack asked.

'I had a dream about the house and the well before I even knew anything about them.'

Jack nodded as if he didn't find this at all unusual. 'You're another one of them then, are you?'

'Another one of what?' said Susan.

'Whatchamacallums ... psychics. The village is full of them.'

David looked at Jack, wide-eyed, then turned to Susan, grinning delightedly. 'Is that what I am, Mum? A psychic?'

'Of course not,' said Susan, and frowned at Jack, who looked suitably apologetic.

'Have you heard of the legend of the Seven Sleepers, Jack?' asked David.

'Oh yeah. Everyone around here knows that.'

63

'The vicar said we should ask someone called Mr Toot about it.'

'He's the best person to ask, all right. He's quite a character is Mr Toot.'

David's eyes were shining. 'Can we go and see him, Mum?'

Susan looked doubtful. 'Oh, I don't know, Davey. We really ought to be thinking about getting back.'

'Oh, *please*? It wouldn't take long, would it, Jack?'

Jack shrugged his broad shoulders and looked cautiously at Susan. 'His shop's just down in the village opposite the church.' He seemed to take her silence as a sign that she was willing to be persuaded, and added, 'He's an amazing man. You'd love him if you met him. Everyone does.'

Susan sighed. 'All right. I suppose it won't do any harm to say hello.'

David cheered. 'Can we go now?'

Susan turned and took another look at the house, as if afraid that if she didn't keep an eye on it, it would disappear. 'I don't see why not,' she said. She hesitated, and then added casually, 'Why don't you come with us, Jack? You could introduce us.'

Jack looked surprised, though flattered, by the invitation. 'Oh . . . er . . . all right. I mean, yes, I'd like that.'

She smiled briskly. 'Right then, let's go.'

As they began to move away, Jack said, 'There's only one snag about introducing you.'

'What's that?'

'You haven't told me your names.'

Susan smiled again and shook her head, then indicated her son. 'This is David,' she said, 'and I'm Susan.'

'Pleased to meet you, Susan,' said Jack.

Chapter Seven

There were two parking spaces side by side, right in front of Mr Toot's grocery store, and as Susan pulled into the left-hand one she couldn't help reflecting that it was almost as if the spaces had been reserved for them. Oddly, she didn't find that thought as fanciful as perhaps she might. Despite her earlier scepticism, Longbarrow did seem to possess a kind of magic, a sense of . . . of predestination, of things falling neatly into place.

However, this wasn't to say that she was entirely happy with the notion that she and David were somehow meant to be here. Since Gerry's death she had developed an instinctive opposition to change, a need to have control over her environment. She hated London, but at least she *knew* it, and understood her place in it. Longbarrow, on the other hand, she loved, but it frightened her a little. It was not the place itself that was frightening, it was her own feelings she didn't quite trust. It was the old trap thing again. If you were in prison you might hate the place, might yearn for your freedom, but if you were in there long enough to become institutionalised, then freedom when it came might be a two-headed beast – exhilarating, yes, but disorientating too, perhaps even terrifying.

Before today, David's resistance to her suggestion that they should leave London and move out to the countryside had acted as a kind of safety valve, an excuse not to put her plans into action. Now, though, in the space of half a day, everything had turned around. Now he was talking as if the move was imminent and she was the one with the ifs and buts. But what reservations could she really have about moving out here? The village was beautiful, the house incredible, the people she had met friendly. Okay, so there were a few practical things, such as David's schooling, to consider, but his school in London was not exactly a centre for educational excellence, was it? They could have a good life here, a *great* life, they could be truly happy. She glanced across as Jack's blue van pulled into the space beside her, and smiled at him. He smiled back.

Jack was nice. After her initial caution, she had decided that he was a genuine, warm-hearted person. True, she knew next to nothing about him, and would not have come to such an instant conclusion in London, but things were different here. Here she felt she had room to breathe, felt more in tune with her emotions, at least where other people were concerned. She was, however, a little daunted about the prospect of meeting Mr Toot. From the way Jack had talked about him, he sounded like someone very special.

She looked across at Davey, who had unbuckled his seat belt and was opening the car door. He looked healthier already, his eyes sparkling, cheeks glowing with colour. Susan felt a sudden surge of well-being, almost as strong as that which she had felt when she had entered Longbarrow House. As if he sensed the emotion like a blast of heat, David paused and turned to her.

'Are you all right, Mum?' he asked.

'Fine,' she said and got out of the car. She looked up at the sign for 'Mr Toot's', the words painted in rather flamboyant golden script on an olive-green background. Below the wooden sign was a convex window made up of small leaded panes, behind which were displayed fresh hams hanging from hooks, delicious-looking loaves dusted with flour, and all manner of tins, jars and packets, some of which were of recognisable brands, others more unusual and exotic.

Jack got out of his van and locked the door. He was wearing a baggy grey T-shirt now with a small Guinness motif on the breast. He led them across the pavement and opened the shop door, which caused an old-fashioned bell to ring, then stood aside to allow them to enter. Susan did so first, trying to adjust her eyes to the sudden gloom.

The interior of the shop was like a grotto, fitted out in cherry-coloured wood, with a couple of thick but raddled supporting beams holding up the low ceiling. From hooks screwed into the crossbeams hung strings of garlic, wind chimes, wicker baskets and other paraphernalia. The shelves were stuffed to capacity with tins and packets and bottles of foodstuffs, together with copious supplies of virtually every other household item that Susan could think of. Plastic buckets, cans of paint, bundles of firewood, bags of weedkiller and God knew what else were stacked up on the floor, turning the aisles into obstacle courses. At the end of the room was a counter, around which a kind of stanchion had been erected, from which hung a variety of magazines and newspapers. Behind the counter were rows of big jars containing sweets, spices, different types of tea and coffee, even nuts and bolts and screws.

Susan had come to the conclusion that there was no one here when a sing-song voice that seemed momentarily to come from nowhere and everywhere called out, 'Mrs Wisher! And David! How lovely of you to come and visit me!'

Next moment a little bespectacled man with a perfectly smooth bald head was hurrying forward, hands outstretched, reminding Susan of the words of the narrator in an old children's TV programme: 'As if by magic, the shopkeeper appeared.'

Before Susan could react, the little man had clasped both of her hands in his and was squeezing them, and then turned to David, who had entered the shop behind her, and gave him the same treatment.

Ordinarily Susan might have recoiled from such a greeting by a complete stranger, but she sensed such warmth and sincerity radiating from Mr Toot that she was instantly enchanted. She stood there, grinning, her fingers tingling slightly where he had touched her, as he released David and shook Jack's hand with a delighted cry of, 'Jack Bradley! How lovely to see you too! Well, this is a surprise! Come in, come in!'

They followed him into the shop as he bustled towards the counter, Susan aware that neither she nor David nor even Jack had so much as uttered a word since they had entered. Although Mr Toot had said their visit was a surprise, she had the strange feeling that it wasn't at all, that in fact he had been expecting them.

She opened her mouth to speak and was surprised to find that her lips felt dry and sticky, and that she had to make a real effort to pull them apart. Similarly, her tongue felt awkward and unfamiliar, too big for her mouth. However, she managed to make herself say, 'Er . . . excuse me, Mr Toot?'

He stopped abruptly and spun round, light glancing on his spectacles and his smooth forehead. 'Yes, my dear?'

'How do you know our names?'

He smiled, and Susan suddenly got the peculiar impression that his head was perfectly round as well as perfectly smooth, like a large pink snooker ball. His smile, however, made her feel warm inside, even secure.

'I keep my eyes and ears open,' he said. 'Now then, David, my guess would be that you're particularly partial to Poor Bens.'

David looked bewildered. 'Poor Ben's what?'

'They're sweets,' Jack muttered. 'Liquorice things.'

'Oh,' said David, 'right. Er . . . yes, I love liquorice.'

'Thought so,' said Mr Toot. 'All boys your age love liquorice.' He scurried behind the counter, reaching up to the shelves behind it and taking down a jar full of coin-shaped liquorice pieces. He unscrewed the lid, produced a paper bag from somewhere, and then filled it with Poor Bens until it was bulging. He screwed the lid on the jar, put it back on the shelf, and presented the bag to David. 'Here you are.'

'Oh . . . er, thanks,' said David, taking the bag. 'But I haven't got any money.'

Mr Toot wafted a hand. 'Please accept these as a gift. A housewarming gift, perhaps.'

Susan wondered whether the whole village knew of her and David's arrival. Longbarrow House was evidently an important building in Longbarrow, after all; it was only natural for the villagers to be curious about the potential new owners. Or perhaps it was simply that Mr Toot was a busybody – in the nicest possible sense, of course – who knew all about them because he happened to own a shop three doors along from the estate agent's.

David popped a Poor Ben into his mouth and offered the bag around. Chewing, he said, 'Mr Toot, we saw the vicar earlier. He said you'd tell us about the Seven Sleepers.'

'Did he indeed?' said Mr Toot, and Susan almost said, 'You mean you didn't know?', but managed to stop herself. 'Then I shall.' He crossed to the shop door, locked it and turned the

'Open' sign round to 'Closed'. Beaming at them he said, 'We'll go into my cubbyhole and make ourselves comfortable, shall we? I'll put the kettle on.'

The cubbyhole turned out to be a small storeroom behind the main shop. It was piled high with boxes, leaving only around eight square feet of floor space. Beside a door which led presumably into a back yard was a sink beneath a net-curtained window through which could be seen the hazy impression of an angled brick wall and a patch of sky, and beside this was a counter covered with tea-making things, including four mugs waiting in a row as if he *had* been expecting them. Stacked against the door, like a flimsy barrier against intruders, were a number of plastic chairs with black metal legs. As Jack dealt with these, unlinking one from another and handing them to David, Mr Toot made tea, humming tunelessly as he did so.

'Here we are,' the little man said a couple of minutes later, coming across with a tray. He set the tray on the floor and handed the mugs out. 'No sugar for you, Susan, two for you, David, and another two for you, Jack.'

'How did —' Susan began.

'Biscuit?' said Mr Toot, thrusting a packet of Ginger Nuts at her.

'No. Thanks.' The first word was spoken irritably, the second resignedly. She sighed and sipped her tea, deciding to let it go. She had already been here long enough to know that Mr Toot wouldn't give her a straight answer to her question anyway.

Mr Toot settled in his seat, a cup of tea in his hand, and abruptly said, 'Centuries ago there was a mage called Decumen. He was a very wise and wonderful man, and many junior mages came from far and wide to hear his words and to learn from him.

'One day a group of seven came to him and asked him if he would teach them all that he knew, so that they could spread his words and his good deeds throughout the land. The names of the seven were Redcap, Uther, Vinegar Tom, Gerennius, Shuck, Pyewackett and Cullen.

'Decumen agreed, and for many months he taught the seven, until their combined power was almost as great as his. What Decumen did not know, however, was that each of the seven was touched by darkness, and that their intention was not to spread good words and good deeds but evil and pestilence and destruction.

'They waged war on Decumen, intending to cast him down into the pit from which they had come. The conflict was long and furious, but after a final terrible battle, Decumen defeated the seven. He didn't kill them, though – some say because he was merciful, others that the war with the seven had weakened him, drained his power. Instead he trapped them in another dimension and cast a spell that made them fall into a deep, deep sleep. And there they have stayed ever since, their powers dormant.

'As for Decumen, some say that he went away and was never seen again, others that he died of his injuries and is buried deep in the earth in a golden coffin.'

'And Longbarrow was where all this supposedly took place?' said Susan.

Mr Toot nodded. 'Longbarrow was the site of the final battle.'

'And your house,' added Jack, 'is where Decumen is supposed to be buried. Isn't that right, Mr Toot?'

Mr Toot smiled his radiant smile. 'There are many legends and rumours in Longbarrow and the surrounding areas associated with the battle of the mages. Many people say that the final battle was so terrible that the land became saturated with magic, which was absorbed into the blood-lines of the people who lived here and has been passed down from generation to generation.'

'That's why there are so many psychics in the village,' said Jack. 'Like Mrs Dyer and old Jonas – they reckon his powers drove him barmy. He lives on his own in a shack in the woods up by the river now.'

'Generation after generation,' repeated Susan. 'You mean none of these families have ever moved away?'

'Some have,' said Mr Toot.

'Aye, and there's a lot more that have either stayed here or come back,' said Jack. 'Longbarrow has this effect on you. Once you've lived here for a bit you don't want to leave. Nowhere else seems . . . right.'

'Maybe it's the magic,' suggested David.

'Maybe.'

'Or maybe it's just because it's a nice place,' said Susan.

'What about ghosts?' asked David, his eyes shining. 'Is Longbarrow haunted?'

Jack glanced at Mr Toot, who smiled and said nothing. Taking this as his cue to continue, and clearly warming to his subject, Jack said, 'People have seen weird things up by the river, about half a mile beyond your house.'

'What kinds of weird things?' asked Susan.

'Little men. Too small to be human. Some folk reckon they're trolls, though there's some that say they come out of the water.'

'Is that it?' said David. He sounded disappointed.

'Well, there's Black Shuck. Some reckon that Decumen changed one of the sleepers into a big black dog with glowing red eyes whose restless spirit roams the country lanes at night. They say if you see him it means someone's going to die.'

Susan shuddered. 'This is giving me the creeps. I don't think I want to know any more. It might put me off ever coming back.'

She saw a look of dismay cross Jack's face, and wondered whether that was because she didn't want to hear his stories or because she had said she might not come back.

'What about snakes?' asked David.

'Snakes?' repeated Jack.

'Yes. On the gateposts of our house and on the wall over the door there are carvings of snakes all curled up, and in my dream there was a snake as well. I just wondered whether they meant anything.'

'Well . . . I don't know,' said Jack. He looked at Mr Toot.

'The serpent is a symbol of occult knowledge,' Mr Toot said. His eyes, deep and green as the sea, seemed to fill the lenses of his spectacles. 'But the coiled serpent is representative of a vortex and therefore may be a source of destruction.'

'Oh,' said David in a small voice and popped another Poor Ben into his mouth.

Unexpectedly Mr Toot said, 'Your asthma can be cured if you want it to be.'

For a moment Susan and David were so taken aback by the abrupt change of subject that neither of them said anything. Then Susan stammered, 'W-what do you mean?'

'Just what I say,' said Mr Toot. There was no impatience in his tone and only gentleness in his eyes.

'But . . . but how?'

'Follow me and I'll show you.'

He jumped up and marched out of the storeroom and into the shop before anyone could react. Susan looked in bewilderment at Jack, who shrugged in apology as if the little shopkeeper was an eccentric relative whose actions he felt responsible for.

'I think we should follow him,' David said, and hurried after Mr Toot.

Susan shook her head as if she'd dozed off and missed some vital part of the proceedings, then stood up and wandered out after her son, Jack bringing up the rear.

Mr Toot was unlocking the door. 'You'll have to drive, I'm afraid, Susan. I don't, and Jack's van is only a two-seater. We'd be rattling about in the back like pebbles in a tin.'

'Drive where?' Susan asked, following him outside.

'To where we're going.'

She sighed. 'And where might that be?'

'To a place I know. Come along.'

Outside in the sunshine Mr Toot seemed almost to gleam, as if the brightness of the day was inordinately attracted to him, as if shadows recoiled before they could touch his skin. He scuttled round to the passenger door and stood there, smiling expectantly. Susan couldn't help but smile back. Despite his evasiveness, it was impossible to dislike Mr Toot, or even to feel any sense of exasperation towards him. She unlocked the car and they all got in.

'Where to?' she asked, winding down the window and opening the sun roof.

'Back towards your new house,' Mr Toot said.

'We're going back to the house?'

He smiled as if at some secret joke, and looking up at the sky murmured, 'Sometimes it's better to show than to tell. Isn't that right, David?'

David, who was sitting next to Jack in the back, chewing another Poor Ben, looked uncertain. 'Er . . . I suppose so.'

Mr Toot settled back in his seat, crossed his pudgy pink hands over his stomach and closed his eyes. 'Wake me up when we get there.'

72

Susan raised her eyebrows, then started the car and backed out of the parking space. She headed back in the direction from which they'd just come, wondering even as she did so why she was doing this, why she didn't stop the car right now and demand some straight answers. No one spoke as she drove out of the village, leaving the houses behind as the road narrowed and the trees on either side closed in. Dapples of sunlight that the trees couldn't block flickered on the car and on their faces like confetti. Mr Toot began to snore quietly.

They were halfway to the house when the little man suddenly opened his eyes and sat bolt upright, making Susan jump. Pointing straight ahead he said mildly, 'Pull into this lay-by on the right, would you please, Susan.'

Susan did so without question, pulling off the road on to a patch of dirt and gravel, and bringing the car to a halt beside a rusted crash barrier. Beyond, the ground sloped away into what appeared to be a particularly dense patch of woodland.

'Splendid,' Mr Toot said, unbuckling his seat belt and hopping out of the car. 'Come along, come along.'

He clambered over the crash barrier with astonishing ease and began to stride downhill into the woods through ankle-deep grass and clumps of wild flowers.

The others had no choice but to hurry after him, Susan having to run to catch up with David and Jack after locking the car. Mr Toot was thirty or forty yards ahead by this time, appearing only to stroll and yet moving at an incredible rate. His bald head bobbed between the trees like a pink balloon; his feet negotiated the uneven terrain with unerring, almost balletic, grace. Within a few minutes, Susan's breath was rasping in her throat and her head was itchy with sweat. By the time Mr Toot stopped, twenty minutes later, she was exhausted.

As she slumped to the ground, she realised that they had stopped in a large clearing, like a natural amphitheatre. Glancing at David and Jack, Susan saw that the walk had taken its toll on them as well.

Despite his muscles and his washboard stomach, Jack's grey T-shirt had big dark stains under the armpits and down the centre of his back, and sweat was dripping off the end of his nose as he bent forward, splashing on the grass between his feet.

73

David, still sitting on the grass, had his left hand pressed against the centre of his chest, and was breathing hard and fast in what Susan recognised was the prelude to an asthma attack. For the first time since meeting Mr Toot she felt angry, and glared at the little man, who was standing on the far side of the clearing, staring up at the sky as if looking for something. She was not entirely surprised to see that he appeared unaffected by his rapid progress through the wood. There was no hint of sweat on his smooth pink brow; he was not even breathing hard.

'What's . . . the point . . . of this?' she said between gasps. 'Look . . . what you've . . . done to . . . Davey.'

Mr Toot barely glanced her way before placing a finger to his lips. 'Shhh.'

Susan sprang to her feet. 'I will not shush,' she blurted, her breathlessness momentarily forgotten. 'You drag us out here on a wild goose chase . . . ' She broke off, placing a hand to her throat, blinking as white sparks danced in front of her eyes.

Mr Toot ambled across and gave her a reassuring pat on the shoulder. 'Don't upset yourself, my dear. All I ask is for a little trust and a little quiet, and if you can give me that, then I promise that in a few moments everything will be fine.'

Susan looked into his depthless green eyes and felt all the anger and indignation flowing out of her. Suddenly she felt tired, though calm. She found herself nodding.

'Splendid,' he murmured, treating her to one of his dazzling smiles. 'Now, why don't you sit down and have a nice rest. You look as though you could do with one.'

'Yes, I . . . I will,' Susan said. She sat down, wondering if she had been hypnotised, but finding that she didn't much care. Mr Toot strolled across to David, who was still struggling for breath, and squatted down beside him. He leaned forward and murmured something to her son that Susan couldn't quite catch. She saw David nod his head briefly and reluctantly let his hand drop away from his chest. Then Mr Toot placed his own right hand on David's chest and looked up once again at the sky.

Suddenly he opened his mouth wide and made the most incredible sound Susan had ever heard. It was high-pitched and crystal-clear, a pure, unwavering note. And yet it was more than that – it was awesome, unearthly; it seemed impossible

74

that such a sound could come from a human throat. Susan felt the hairs prickle on the back of her neck. She had the feeling that she was privy to something very rare and very special here.

And then Mr Toot closed his mouth, and the sound cut off as abruptly as if a needle had been raised on a record. What Susan realised now was that all the other woodland sounds she had barely noticed before – the birdsong, the drone of insects, the rustling of small animals in the undergrowth – had ceased as if in deference to the sound Mr Toot had made. Surrounding them now in their little clearing was a silence and a stillness so total that Susan felt as if she was part of some profoundly mystical, almost religious experience. It was as though, for a moment, Mr Toot's song or cry (Susan struggled to find an appropriate word for the sound) had caused all the disparate, opposing forces of the universe to shift into alignment, creating a moment of such perfection it was breathtaking.

Susan felt an almost epiphanous sense of peace descending over her. Though she wanted to weep with the sheer joy of it, she dared not blink or even breathe for fear of breaking the spell. She might have stayed there for ever, motionless as the trees and the air around her, if Mr Toot himself had not spoken. The little man stood up, looked around and then said to David, 'You can throw your inhaler away now.'

David, and then Jack, began to stir, like waking courtiers after the prince had broken the spell by kissing Sleeping Beauty. Jack looked bewildered, but David began to smile. He took his inhaler from his jeans pocket and without hesitation turned and hurled it into the trees. Susan felt the briefest pang of dismay, and then the feeling was swallowed by the peace that was still flowing through her. She grinned at David and said dreamily, 'How do you feel?'

He grinned back. 'Better than I've ever felt before. My asthma's . . . gone. Left me for ever. I just know it.'

Susan turned to Mr Toot. She felt as if she were floating on air. 'What did you do?' she breathed.

'A favour, that's all,' said Mr Toot. 'Everything will be fine now.' He squinted up at the sky again. 'We'd better be getting back. As it is, you good people won't be reaching home much before midnight.'

He turned and tramped off through the woods. Like awe-struck disciples, the others drifted after him.

No one said anything until Susan was pulling up in front of Mr Toot's shop once again. All four of them got out, and Mr Toot squeezed Susan's hands as he had done when he had greeted her an hour or so earlier.

'It's been such fun,' he said with boyish enthusiasm. 'I'll see you again soon. Goodbye.'

'Goodbye,' said Susan. 'And . . . and thanks for everything.'

'Thank *you* for coming to visit me,' he said. 'Goodbye, David. Goodbye, Jack.' He waved, then turned and walked away.

The moment he had stepped inside his shop and closed the door, Susan felt herself drifting back down to earth.

'What . . . what happened back there?' she asked.

David shrugged. 'He cured my asthma.'

'He's always been able to do that,' said Jack. 'Cure people.'

'Yes, but . . . but what *happened*? I mean, that noise he made . . .'

She looked helplessly at Jack and David, but they simply looked back at her, unable to provide her with answers. Finally Jack said, 'He's always done stuff that people don't really understand. But it's always in a good cause and it always seems to work. We just let him get on with it.'

Susan looked at the gold and green sign above the leaded window. The building was quaint, but relatively unassuming. Who would have thought that such magic and mystery could be contained in there? She felt oddly as if she had spent the whole afternoon missing the point.

'Has Mr Toot always lived in Longbarrow?' she asked.

Jack shrugged with his face, pushing out his bottom lip. 'Far as I know. He's owned that shop ever since I was a kid.'

'I wonder how old he is,' Susan said thoughtfully. 'It's difficult to tell.'

'I don't think anyone knows,' said Jack. 'He's always looked the same, never changes. And he's never married or even been out with a woman. Not that he's . . . What I mean is, I don't think he's bothered.'

'Toot,' murmured Susan, still looking at the sign. 'Such an odd name. Like something out of Enid Blyton. I wonder where it comes from.'

'A toot is a magical place,' said Jack, 'or a haunted one. It's a place where elves and fairies are supposed to live.'

Susan looked at him as if he was joking, but his face remained earnest. After a moment she said, 'This really is an extraordinary place.'

Jack smiled. 'Aye, it is. So what do you reckon? Are you going to come and live here?'

Susan looked at Jack and then at her son. 'What do you think, Davey?'

David's eyes lit up. 'Can we?'

Susan felt the shackles of the last seven years loosening around her 'Well, it *is* our house,' she said.

Part Two

The Barrow (1)

Chapter Eight

Because of the unusually lengthy heat wave that had gripped the country this summer, it wasn't yet chilly when Jake Sissons' alarm went off at 4:30 each morning, but it was certainly darker than it had been two or three weeks ago. It was almost like waking up underwater these days, his room filled with a pearly blue half-light. Odd to think that for the first time in eleven summers he wouldn't be going back to school when August clicked over into September in two weeks' time. He had left full-time education a month ago with four GCSEs and no real idea what he wanted to do for the rest of his life. He supposed he ought to be busting a gut looking for work rather than just biding his time, helping his dad on the farm, but to be honest it was impossible to make long-term plans or even to think straight just at the moment. The question that occupied all his waking thoughts was: What were he and Lucy going to do about the baby?

Only Jake (and Lucy herself, of course) knew that she was pregnant. They were both sixteen and had been going out together, secretly, for four months. Lucy was the eldest of John and Julia Benson's three daughters. Mr and Mrs Benson owned the post office in Longbarrow and were both a bit snotty, especially Mr Benson, who used to be the manager of some big retail firm in Bradford. They disapproved of Jake and his family, which was why Jake and Lucy had had to see each other secretly. This was frustrating for Jake as he knew it was Gary, his fourteen-year-old brother, they actually disapproved of.

Gary was uncontrollable, always causing trouble, and it was his antics that had tarred Jake, and even his mam and dad, with the same brush. The trouble was, people round here seemed to think that when a kid went off the rails it was the parents' fault, but Jake had never had any problems with his mam and dad, and they had always treated Gary the same as they treated him. As far as Jake was concerned, his brother had simply been born with bad genes, though God knew where he had got them from. He had never wanted for anything, never been mistreated, and yet he was a lazy, sneaky, lying little thief, and a bully too. Last year he had been suspended from school for beating up younger kids and nicking their dinner money. He was happy enough eating the food that Mam cooked and sleeping between the sheets that she washed, but he would never lift a finger around the farm unless Dad made him.

Jake pushed his duvet aside and got out of bed. He yawned and stretched, scratched his blond head vigorously, then crossed the room and pulled on his smelly work-clothes. He really loved Lucy – she was clever and funny and sensible – but the thought of the two of them having a baby to look after terrified him. What would they do for money? Where would they live? Could they really cope with being tied down so early in their lives? Before she had discovered she was pregnant three weeks ago, Lucy had been talking about starting her A-levels next month, then going on to university. She'd left school with ten GCSEs, six of them grade As, and had ambitions to become a research scientist, trying to find cures for cancer and AIDS and stuff like that. It was a future that Jake, in all honesty, hadn't been able to see himself being part of, but at the time it hadn't seemed to matter too much. He had just been happy that he and Lucy were going out *now*, that she liked him enough to defy her father's wishes, and that, despite their differences, they got on so well. He hadn't wanted to think about the future, about where they might be in five or ten years' time.

But now the baby had changed all that, because even if he and Lucy split up tomorrow he would still be the father of that child for the rest of his life. That was if they decided to have the child, of course, which was something else they had to think about. Over the last few weeks, he and Lucy had talked and talked over all the possibilities – abortion, adoption, marriage, money, the future – without really getting anywhere.

Jake felt like a hamster on a wheel, going round and round and round. What they really needed was somebody to stand back, look at their problem and give them advice on what to do. But who could they ask? He had suggested Mr Toot, who was always helping people, but Lucy had been reluctant. What did he know about such things? she had said. He'd never been married or had children. Of course, the obvious people to ask were their parents, but so far both he and Lucy had been putting off telling them. Jake thought that once his mam and dad got over the shock and stopped yelling at him, they would be all too willing to help however they could, but Lucy's parents were a different matter altogether. Knowing Mr Benson, he would insist on his daughter having an immediate abortion and would then whisk her off to some remote college somewhere so that Jake and Lucy never saw each other again.

'He'd probably make me go to the police and tell them that you'd raped me as well,' Lucy had said to him earlier that week. 'He'd never be able to live with the shame of having a daughter who'd gone to bed with a Sissons because she actually wanted to. I'd be the black sheep of the family, a scarlet woman.'

They had both laughed at that, but only because it was preferable to crying. Lucy had cried a lot at first; when she'd had her pregnancy confirmed with one of those little kits she'd had to go all the way to Ripon to buy because she hadn't dared buy it in the village, she'd been crying so hard she hadn't been able to tell Jake about the baby, and he had got really scared, thinking she had some terminal disease or something. When he had finally got the truth out of her, he had been relieved at first and then had got scared all over again. The thing was, this wasn't something that you could put into perspective once a bit of time had passed, or that would go away of its own accord. On the contrary, with each day that passed Jake's anxieties grew. He felt that if he didn't discuss it with someone other than Lucy soon he would explode.

For the past four mornings he had considered mentioning it to his dad during the twenty minutes that they had alone together at the beginning of the day. The routine was this: Jake would get up and get dressed, and would then wake up Gary who would tell him to fuck off. Gary would then spend a while coming to, which usually involved him stomping about bad-temperedly, glaring at whoever got in his way and muttering obscenities under his breath. Rather than chivvying him along, which did more harm than good, Jake and his dad had got into the habit of going downstairs and having a cup of tea together until Gary deigned to join them. When Gary appeared he would respond to their good mornings with surly grunts, and then all three of them would go out together to milk the cows. For the next two hours, before they broke off for one of Mam's cooked breakfasts, Jake and his dad would work their arses off whilst Gary slouched around, did as little as possible, and generally looked as if he'd rather be anywhere other than where he was.

Although Gary's attitude was a pain, one positive outcome of it was that it had brought Jake and his father closer together. When Jake had been younger, Dad had simply been a big, loveable, but slightly intimidating man. Now Jake regarded him as more of a friend, particularly first thing in the morning when he felt the two of them were united against the common enemy of Gary's bad temper. Those twenty-minute cups of tea in the stillness of the big kitchen were warm, companionable times; sometimes, listening to Gary thudding about upstairs as if he was punching the walls and wishing it was them, Dad would look at Jake and smile and shake his head, as if Jake was not his son, but someone on an equal footing, someone who understood exactly what he was thinking and sympathised with it.

A number of times over the past few mornings, Jake had been on the verge of telling Dad about Lucy and the baby, had had the words backed up in his throat, eager to emerge, but had never quite managed to give them voice. It wasn't so much his dad's anger that he was scared of, it was more his disappointment. Although he wanted his dad's help and advice, he also wanted him to think well of him, to be proud of him; he didn't want him to know how stupid and careless he'd been. And yet sooner or later Jake knew he would have to come clean. It wasn't something that could be put off for ever.

This morning, he thought determinedly as he approached the door to his brother's room, I'll tell him this morning. He opened Gary's door, stepped in – and immediately recoiled. God, the stench! The place stank of puke, which was underpinned by the high, sharp odour of regurgitated whisky. Jake put a hand over the bottom half of his face and breathed through his mouth. His brother was a dark, motionless hump on the bed, completely covered by the duvet.

With the curtains closed and the carpet patterned in green, brown and yellow, it was difficult to pinpoint the source of the awful smell. Jake reached out and switched the light on. Immediately colours and objects jumped into stark, bright clarity. Now he could see the spatters of vomit on the carpet, leading to the bed, and the smears and stains on the duvet too. He curled his lips in disgust and crossed the room gingerly, avoiding the foul-smelling pools on the carpet. Jake knew that his brother drank when he was with his mates, and he suspected that sometimes he also took drugs, but he had never come home in this state before.

He took hold of a corner of the duvet, examining it first to make sure he wasn't putting his hand in anything nasty, and cautiously peeled it back. Gary was curled up on the mattress, fully dressed (including his muddy steel-toe-capped boots) and fast asleep, though he screwed up his face as the light hit it. The inside of the duvet, the sheet on which he was lying, his clothes and his spotty chin were stained orange-brown with puke. Worst of all it was matted in his hair, which stuck out in gluey spikes clotted with bits of undigested food.

'Gary,' Jake hissed. He prodded his brother in the shoulder. 'Gaz, come on, wake up.'

Gary groaned and rolled over, covering his clothes in even more puke. 'Ugoff,' he slurred.

'No, Gaz, come on, it's twenty to five. You've got to clean yourself up before Dad sees you and does his nut.'

Gary scowled and opened his eyes the merest fraction. 'Fucking leave me alone, you cunt,' he muttered, the words thick and barely audible.

Jake hesitated, caught in two minds. If he persisted in trying to rouse his brother, there was the possibility that Gary could turn really nasty, lashing out like a wounded animal, but if he left him to it then sooner or later Dad would want to know why Gary wasn't up, and once he found out he would go totally ballistic, which wouldn't be pleasant for anyone.

'Come *on*, Gaz,' Jake coaxed, progressing from prodding his brother's shoulder to actually shaking it. 'I'm saving your life here. You're covered in puke.'

'So what?' growled Gary, still half-asleep or half-cut, and made an attempt to shrug off his brother's hand.

'So Dad'll know you've been drinking,' Jake said, trying to make each word as urgent and clear as possible in the hope that the message would permeate his brother's alcohol-sodden brain.

'Fuck Dad 'n' fuck you. Jus' let me fucking die,' Gary said. He closed his eyes and rolled over again, burying his head in his arms.

'I'll make you some coffee,' Jake said.

'Don't want no fucking coffee. Jus' want you to fuck off.'

Jake sighed. 'All right,' he said finally, 'but don't say I didn't warn you.'

He negotiated his way past the noxious pools and out of the room. Downstairs his dad, dressed in a pair of blue overalls unbuttoned to the waist over a white T-shirt which was stretched tight across his beer belly, was brewing up.

'All right, lad,' he said. 'Fair morning again.'

'Yeah,' said Jake, looking miserably out of the kitchen window at the brightening sky.

'Our Gary coming, is he?' Bill Sissons said.

'Er . . . I'm not sure,' said Jake, sitting down.

His dad looked at him, eyes narrowing in the big square block of his head. Jake had to make a conscious effort not to squirm in his chair or avert his gaze.

'Not sure? What do you mean? You did wake him up, didn't you?'

'Er . . . yeah, but . . . I don't think he's well. I think he's got some sort of bug. He's been sick in the night.'

'He told you that, did he?'

'No, he . . . I mean yeah.'

'You don't sound right sure.'

'No, I meant . . . you can tell he's ill. He looks awful. We can manage the milking between us, though, can't we, Dad? We'd probably even be quicker, just us two.'

His dad smiled at that. 'We probably would an' all,' he said, 'but that's not the point, is it? That lad's got to learn some responsibility. I'll take him a cup o' tea and see for meself whether I think he's fit to work.'

'I'll take it, Dad. You have a sit down,' Jake said quickly.

Bill Sissons gave his son a shrewd look. 'You're hiding summat from me, aren't you, Jake?'

'No,' Jake said, but he couldn't help blushing.

Bill Sissons frowned. 'What's that little bugger really been up to?'

'Nothing, Dad. He is ill, honest.'

'I'll see for meself, shall I?'

Before Jake could react, his dad had put down the tea things, crossed the room and was out of the door. 'Shit,' Jake muttered under his breath. He pushed back his chair and went after his dad. He had almost caught up with him at the door to Gary's room, but not quickly enough to say or do anything to prevent his dad shoving open the door and marching inside. There was a second of silence and then Bill Sissons bellowed, 'What the bloody 'ell's been going on 'ere?'

Jake followed his dad into the room, switching on the light. 'Dad, watch—' he said, but too late; Bill Sissons' size elevens slid straight through the biggest pile of puke on the carpet. Jake saw his dad's neck and cheeks turn brick-red as he stared in disbelief at the mess on his boots, the mess on the floor, the mess in which his youngest son was lying. Gary, meanwhile, oblivious to his father's presence, was moaning, 'Turn that fucking light off, you wanker.'

'You filthy little bugger!' Bill Sissons bellowed and stomped across to the bed. His rage overwhelming his distaste at touching someone else's vomit, he reached down towards his son's throat, grabbed a handful of his puke-spattered T-shirt and hauled him upright. Gary gagged and spluttered and flailed his arms. 'Let go of me, you big cunt,' he croaked.

Bill Sissons shook his son until his teeth rattled. 'Shut your filthy mouth,' he roared.

Jake had never seen his dad so angry. He quailed as the big man turned towards him, thinking that he too was going to get a bollocking for trying to protect his brother. However, his dad simply growled, 'Jake, go into the bathroom and turn the shower on. Make sure it's as cold as it can be.'

Jake nodded and hurried out of the room, trying to close his ears to the sounds of his dad dragging his brother out of bed and across the stinking carpet, and his brother's weak but venomous protests. In the bathroom he turned the shower on, twisting the temperature dial down to as cold as it would go as his dad had requested, and as the water began to batter against

the plastic tub like a tropical downpour, he decided that today
would not be a good day to tell his dad about Lucy, after all.

Chapter Nine

'Oh, Audrey, my love,' muttered Joyce Morrow, 'I miss you so much.'

Gently, as if placing a blanket over a sleeping child, she laid the lilies she had bought on her ex-lover's grave, beside the headstone. It was exactly a year since Audrey had succumbed to the lymphatic cancer that had plagued her for the last eighteen months of her life, and even now the house the two of them had shared for the past quarter-century seemed too big, too quiet, without her hustle and bustle to fill it. Until the cancer had been diagnosed, Audrey had seemed indomitable, as if she would march into her nineties or beyond. She had seemed the sort of woman who would choose her time to die, the sort who – when she put her mind to it – could very probably have put the fear of God into God himself.

Remembering her, Joyce smiled. Audrey had always been the confrontational one of the partnership, the one who drank pints and smoked cigars in the Druid's Arms (she did neither at home) because she believed that living the stereotype was sometimes the only way of defying the wagging tongues, of showing she had nothing to be ashamed of. She wore her pink triangle with pride too, and sometimes when Joyce got upset because of a remark a pupil had made, or a parent, or even one of her staff, Audrey would be the one to say, 'Dang what other people think, Joyce. *We* know we're happy, *we* know we love each other, and as long as we're together then nothing else matters, does it?'

'No,' Joyce whispered now, the sun warm on her head and back, 'nothing else matters.' She stared at her partner's silent grey headstone and thought how lonely she had been these last twelve months. She was no longer living her life, she was merely existing, drifting from one pointless day to the next. She sometimes thought that if it hadn't been for their boxer dog, Bella, she might simply have given up, stopped like some old clock which had ticked for too many years and now no longer cared what time it was.

Indeed, it was almost as if time was suspended, for although she had been alone for a year now, she still found herself wondering how she would fight the fight without Audrey beside her, who she would turn to for a hug at the end of the day.

Audrey had been sixty-two when she had died, six years older than Joyce, who was now fifty-seven. Three years ago, at Audrey's riotous sixtieth birthday party, Joyce had said, 'My God, Audrey, we're starting to get *old*.' Audrey had pooh-poohed the idea, little knowing that six months later she would find a lump in her armpit that she would be surprised she hadn't noticed before. It was ironic, but now that Audrey had gone the years ahead no longer seemed precious and few to Joyce, but endless and desolate. My God, she thought, I might live for another twenty years yet, or even thirty! What would she do with all that time? Thirty years ago she hadn't even *met* Audrey. In three years she would be retiring from Longbarrow Comprehensive where she had been headmistress for almost a decade and a half, and *then* how would she fill her days? She imagined herself turning out like Jonas Miller, shuffling through the village in filthy clothes, mumbling to herself, a crazy old dyke whom nobody loved.

'I know what you'd say,' she murmured, placing a graceful, long-fingered hand on the headstone, which in this heat was warm as human skin. 'Chin up, girl. Pull yourself together. Dang everyone else, you just look after yourself.'

She sighed, looking up. A yew tree was nodding gently as if agreeing with her; bees busied themselves in the wild flowers that grew in the long grass between the graves. 'But you weren't so tough, were you, Audrey, old girl? You pretended to be, but you were a big softy really. Gentle as a lamb.'

Tears filled Joyce's eyes, turning the day to a bright blur, and then spilled down her cheeks. She remembered how angry in public but upset in private Audrey had been during that unpleasant time when Mrs Darracott and her WI cronies had tried to get Joyce sacked. Her relationship with Audrey was a disgrace, they had said, a shocking example to set the children. The Narrows, as Audrey had named them, had made so much noise that all the normally anonymous strait-laced brigade had crawled out of the woodwork to support them. At first Audrey had been defiant ('Dang the lot of them, dried-up old harridans. Just because they haven't got decent lives of their own, they try to mess things up for those that have'), but as the battle had become a war of attrition, and things had actually begun to look so bad that Joyce had considered resigning just to get them off her back, Audrey's tough exterior had gradually disintegrated. In the end it had got to the stage where Joyce would be the one comforting Audrey, where Audrey would weep in Joyce's arms, wailing, 'Why don't they just leave us alone? We haven't done anything to hurt them.'

The whole unpleasant episode had finally been brought to an end by Mr Toot, the grocer, who had turned up on their doorstep one evening and had told them over a cup of tea that things had gone quite far enough and that he aimed to have a quiet word with Mrs Darracott the very next day.

And that had been that. Neither Joyce nor Audrey had ever found out what Mr Toot had said, but from that moment the victimisation and the campaign to get Joyce sacked had stopped.

Her fingers were wet. It was this that tugged Joyce from her reverie. She had been gazing unseeingly at the nodding yew tree as her memories unfolded, oblivious to the constantly changing jigsaw pieces of sunlight between its subtly shifting leaves, but now she drew her attention back to the headstone.

Gasping, she snatched her hand away and stumbled backwards. The fingers that had been resting on the headstone were wet because black fluid was leaking from the grey granite. Even as Joyce watched, a dark pinprick appeared just above the chiselled-out A in Audrey's name, swelled to become a bubble tipped by a shimmer of light, and then burst sound-lessly, running into the clean lines of the A, emboldening her ex-lover's name.

Heart thumping, Joyce regarded the phenomenon with wide eyes, and wondered what could be causing it. Had the intense heat perhaps stimulated the release of some excess moisture in the rock? It sounded unlikely, ludicrous even, but what were the alternatives? That she was hallucinating? That she was actually witnessing some paranormal (or at least inexplicable) event? The dark fluid was still oozing from the stone even now, trickles running together to form rivulets, some of which were filling in the indented letters in the inscription.

Her heart began to beat even faster. Was it a coincidence that this had happened on the anniversary of Audrey's death? Perhaps her partner was trying to send her a message from the other side? She looked at her fingers which had been resting on the stone, and drew in a breath so sharply that it was like swallowing something solid.

Whereas the fluid oozing from the stone looked black against the granite, on her skin it was a deep and vivid red. She sniffed it, registering a faint coppery odour. That settled it: it was undoubtedly blood. Same colour, same smell, same texture and stickiness. She wondered fleetingly whether it was her own blood, but then dismissed the notion. No, this had come from the stone. Impossible as it seemed, Audrey's headstone was actually weeping blood.

Joyce took two more steps back. Her heart was still thumping madly inside her chest, but there was a little part of her that felt almost uplifted by what she was seeing. If it *was* a message from Audrey then it was a wonderful thing, but what could it possibly mean, and why communicate in such a macabre fashion? She considered saying something, perhaps asking Audrey what she was trying to tell her, but the words jammed in her dry throat. Perhaps her best course of action would be to consult Reverend Farrar, see what he had to say on the subject.

Audrey's grave was behind the church, quite low down the slope; Joyce had had to negotiate several sets of worn stone steps to reach it. It was a nice spot, secluded and peaceful, closer actually to the vicarage beyond the stone wall and the copse of trees at the bottom of the hill than to the church itself.

Joyce stumbled down the hill in a daze, through the creaking metal gate in the wall at the bottom, and then along the shaded, dappled pathway through the trees to the narrow, quaint house that was the vicarage. She rang the bell and waited, her blood-smeared hand held a little away from her body, fingers outstretched.

It was Reverend Farrar himself who answered. He looked surprised to see her, but greeted her warmly. Joyce had always thought Steven Farrar a kind man. He had never quite known how to take the relationship between her and Audrey, had always seemed a little awkward in the presence of the two women, but at least he had *tried* to accommodate their sexuality; as far as Joyce was aware he had never been judgemental or condemnatory.

'What can I do for you, Miss Morrow?' he asked now, and then, stepping back and wafting a hand towards the interior of the house, 'Would you like to come in?'

'Er . . . no, I won't, if you don't mind, Reverend,' Joyce said, surprised at how calm she was being. 'I . . . er . . . well, I wanted to ask your advice about something.'

Again Farrar looked surprised, though he masked it quickly. 'Ask away,' he said.

'Well, actually . . . I'm sorry to be an awful nuisance, but I think it would be easier if I showed you. I know it's early, but . . . well, I wouldn't ask if it wasn't important.'

'No, no, that's no problem. Excuse me for asking, Miss Morrow, but . . . are you all right? You look a bit . . .'

'Pale?'

'No, not pale, but . . . as though you've had a fright.'

Joyce laughed, and was alarmed at how high and splintery it sounded. 'Do I?' she said. 'Well, I suppose I have. Audrey died a year ago today, you know. I went to her grave to lay some flowers.'

The vicar's face fell. 'Oh dear. The grave hadn't been vandalised, had it?'

'Oh no, nothing like that. No, it started . . . well . . . bleeding before my eyes.'

The vicar became very still, his face immobile, as if her words had stunned him. 'Bleeding?' he said.

She held up her hand, showing him her fingers. 'Weeping blood. Just . . . just came oozing out of the stone. I saw it.'

Suddenly she began to tremble. Her outstretched hand groped for the doorframe to steady herself, but was intercepted by Farrar, who held her upright until the feeling had passed.

'Oh dear, I think all this has affected me more than I realised,' she said weakly.

'Look, come inside, have a cup of tea,' he invited.

'No, no, I must show you.'

'Are you sure you're up to it?'

'Quite sure.'

Gently but insistently she pushed herself away from him, standing unaided. She still felt a little dizzy, but was determined not to make the Reverend think of her as weak and fanciful. Not that he was giving any indication that that was what he *was* thinking, but Joyce didn't even want to give him the chance.

She led him back along the dappled, tree-lined path, through the gate and up the slope to Audrey's grave. As they rounded one of the many yew trees that shielded the grave from sight until they were almost upon it, she braced herself to witness the phenomenon again, but was actually a little disappointed when the gravestone came into view.

Although the black fluid was still very much in evidence, the bleeding itself had stopped. Furthermore, the fluid was now congealing beneath the hot mid-morning sun and looked nothing like the blood on Joyce's fingers. Indeed, it now looked as though the grave *had* been vandalised, as though it had been copiously spattered with ink or tar. Joyce glanced at Reverend Farrar, who wore the expression not of a man witnessing an inexplicable event, but of a man appalled by the desecration of a hallowed site.

'I *saw* it bleeding,' Joyce said as though he had questioned it. 'It started when I was here. This . . . this liquid just came seeping out of the stone.'

'I'm sure it did,' the Reverend murmured.

'It *did*,' she insisted, and then her shoulders slumped. 'You don't believe me, do you?'

'On the contrary,' he said, as though eager to reassure her, and then for a moment he appeared uncertain. Suddenly he seemed to come to a decision. 'Would you allow me to show you something?'

'What?' she asked.

He gave a grim smile. 'Like you, I'd rather show than tell. It's something up in the church. If you'll follow me?'

He led the way along the higgledy-piggledy overgrown paths and up the little flights of stone steps to the church. The witchcraft eye carved on the church tower stared out over the landscape, ever watchful. By the time they reached the plateau where the church sat like a tiny but proud castle, they were both panting and the Reverend's face was damp and red with exertion.

'This heat,' he said, and then was unable to say any more.

'When I was a little girl, my mother always used to tell me that the sunshine was the glow of God's teeth when he smiled and the rain was his tears when he cried.'

'Then we must have a very happy God looking over us at the moment,' the Reverend said.

They walked around the flagstoned path to the front of the chuch and in through the entrance porch. The vestibule, normally cool, was today stifling.

The heavy oak double-doors leading into the church proper were closed but not locked. Reverend Farrar turned the black metal ring that lifted the latch and pushed the left-hand door open.

St Luke's, though a small church, was light and airy. The windows were long and wide, and whoever had commissioned the stained-glass inserts (which were not original features but post-war additions) had favoured pale rather than heavy colours – pinks, sky blues, soft yellows. Furthermore, the interior walls were of light rather than dark stone, the pews and pulpit of blonde wood. The most impressive feature was an enormous rose window behind the altar, through which sun poured in a broad and brilliant beam of colour. It was warm in here, but not stifling like it was in the vestibule, and perhaps not even as hot as it was in the direct sunlight.

'Notice anything different in here?' Farrar asked.

Joyce looked around. 'No, I don't think so.'

The Reverend pointed down at the aisle between the pews. 'Look again.'

'Oh yes, the rug. What's that doing there?'

Farrar walked down the aisle, halting at the edge of the long, faded rug that covered the middle third of it. Joyce attended church infrequently (the last time had been three weeks ago), but she was certain she had never seen the rug before. Although she hadn't noticed it immediately, now that the vicar had pointed it out to her it did seem incongruous.

She watched as Farrar bent and lifted the rug clear of the aisle, draping it over the nearest pew. On the brown tiles beneath was a large black stain, as if someone had dropped a bottle of ink.

Joyce came closer 'What is it?' she asked.

Farrar's voice was oddly matter-of-fact. 'Blood.' When she looked at him, startled, he said, 'When it was wet I got some on my handkerchief and sent it off to be analysed. It's human blood. Type "O".'

Joyce stared down at the stain again and then turned her attention back to Farrar. 'But it's black,' she said, thinking of Audrey's headstone even as she spoke the words.

'It looks black on the floor, but on my handkerchief and my hands it was bright red.'

The vicar seemed almost resigned to the impossibility of the phenomenon. 'But . . . where did it come from?' Joyce asked.

He sighed. 'It just appeared. Last Tuesday morning. I locked the church up on Monday night, came in on Tuesday morning, and . . . there it was, just sitting there, glistening.'

'It was wet?' said Joyce.

'Oh yes. At first I thought a pipe had burst and it had come up through the floor, or perhaps dripped through the ceiling. I started cleaning it up, and that was when I was shocked to discover that the stuff actually came up not black but red. Anyway, the mess mopped up easily enough, but I was unsettled by the incident to put it mildly. I rang up a scientist friend of mine and asked him to analyse it for me.' He shrugged unhappily. 'You know the rest.'

Joyce stared down at the stain again. She didn't know what to think. 'And it came back after you'd cleaned it up?' she said.

'Yes. On Wednesday morning it was here again, exactly the same place, and I cleaned it up again. But then when it was here again on Thursday morning I decided to leave it. Eventually it dried and I put the rug over it.' He looked a little desperate. 'I didn't know what else to do.'

Joyce felt as though insects were crawling under her skin, congregating in her belly. 'Human blood,' she said in disbelief. 'What can it mean?'

The Reverend grimaced. 'It is said that a mysterious bloodstain on a church floor can be a symbol of impending disaster.'

When she looked at him, his already flushed face turned an even deeper shade of red and he laughed unconvincingly. 'I know,' he said. 'Ridiculous, isn't it?'

Chapter Ten

Every morning Mike French thought: What if Ted's found out? Recently his days had been spent in a heady, exhausting state of lust and terror, which he knew would only end when he went off to university in six weeks' time. He couldn't bring himself to end it before then. Mary Sheridan was like an exquisite drug to him; once sampled, she was unrefusable. Despite his fear of her psychopathic husband, Mike couldn't stop himself going back for more.

Perhaps it would have been easier if he hadn't been the Sheridans' temporary postman. His dad's friend, Chaz Recchia, had got him the job to tide him over the long twelve weeks between finishing his A-levels and starting uni. If his grades were good enough (and he'd find out in a week's time) Mike wanted to go to Liverpool to read Political History. It was his dad who'd got him interested in politics. He worked on the buses and was high up on the local TWU. Like many small and exclusive village communities, Longbarrow was a Conservative stronghold, the mainly moneyed residents terrified that if Labour got in they would encourage developers to rip out great chunks of Green Belt land and throw up housing estates for the poor. Nevertheless, come election time the French household would display their allegiance with pride, a tiny red boat on a deep blue sea.

Mike was proud too, but sometimes he felt uncomfortable, like a City fan who had wandered into the United end by mistake. As he tramped the streets now, his sack growing lighter with each delivery, but his guts growing heavier with dread and anticipation as he drew closer to the Sheridans' house, he wondered what Ted Sheridan's political affiliations were.

Probably voted Conservative, if only because the local constituency had nothing more extreme to offer. He imagined him with his mates in the pub on a Friday night, spouting about how all of society's ills were down to the Niggers and the Pakis before getting into a drunken fight, smashing up a chip shop and Sieg Heiling all the way home. He probably wore that big black beard to hide the swastikas tattooed on his cheeks. One thing was certain, if Mike's covert enquiries since starting his affair with Mary Sheridan were anything to go by: it was a very stupid man indeed who made Ted Sheridan his enemy.

His dad had told him that Sheridan used to ride with a biker gang who had terrorised the village back in the seventies. Most of the members of that gang were dead or gone now. Indeed, there were only two of them still in the village – Sheridan and Jack Bradley. But whereas Bradley had put his wild youth behind him, Sheridan had simply found other outlets for his viciousness. Mike knew for a fact that he treated his wife and son, Jason (who at seventeen was the same age as Mike), like shit. In fact, it was Sheridan's violence that had brought Mike and Mary together.

Four weeks ago he had had a package for the Sheridans which had been too big to fit through the letter box. He had rung the doorbell and Mary Sheridan had answered, looking dazed, blood trickling out of one ear. Mike had been shocked. 'Are you all right?' he asked. When she gazed at him as if she didn't understand the question, he moved from one foot to the other, wishing he was somewhere else because he wasn't sure he would know how to handle whatever kind of situation this was. Raising his voice a little he said, 'Have you had an accident?'

She burst into tears then and slid down the grubby wall to the floor.

'Oh God,' Mike said, looking up and down the street in the frantic but vain hope that there would be someone about to help him. 'Oh bloody hell, please don't cry. Look, I'll . . . I'll see if next door are in.'

He was about to move away when Mary Sheridan blurted, 'No!'

Mike hovered, looking at her indecisively. 'Well . . . why not? I just—'

'I don't want that nosey cow knowing my business.'

Mike looked down at her for a few seconds more. He had never felt so helpless. 'Is there . . . is there anyone else in the house who could help you, then?' he asked.

The trickle of blood from her ear, dizzyingly red, had bisected her jawline and reached her chin by now. 'It's that bastard that did this.'

'Who?'

'My fucking husband. He's a fucking animal.'

Mike looked along the dingy hallway behind her, half-expecting to see some twenty-ton bruiser with sledgehammer fists – someone very like Ted Sheridan, in fact – come thundering towards him.

'Is your husband in?' he asked nervously.

'No, he isn't. He's gone to work. Fucking bastard.'

'Well, can I call the doctor or . . . or anything?'

'No, I don't want anyone else to know about this.' She looked at him sharply. 'You won't tell anyone, will you?'

'Not if you don't want me to,' he said.

She sighed. 'Thanks, love. Look, give us a hand up, will you? All I need is a cup of tea and a good sit down. You wouldn't make us one, would you?'

'Well . . . I've got the rest of my round to do,' he said lamely.

'It won't take a minute, love. Please? I'd be ever so grateful.'

Unable to refuse, Mike had gone into the house, put down his postal sack and helped the woman to her feet. She had leaned on him heavily, pressing her body against his. Despite the circumstances, it had not escaped Mike's attention that Mary Sheridan was an attractive woman. She was in her mid-thirties and wearing a white towelling dressing gown that only reached to halfway down her thighs. Her face was fine-boned, her mousey-blonde hair pulled back in a ponytail that swished between her shoulder blades. She had a good body, a little on the heavy side, but shapely, sensuous. Her large breasts pushed against the white towelling material of the dressing gown, and against his arm when she leaned on him. Her legs, though blotched with the odd bruise, were long, the muscles well defined.

Mike had escorted her through a grubby, messy sitting room with videos piled up beneath the TV, and old, tired furniture, into a kitchen that smelled of fried food. Dirty crockery and breakfast debris were piled up on every surface.

'Sorry the place is such a mess,' she said, crossing to the sink to clean the blood off her face with water and kitchen roll before sitting at a table cluttered with empty milk bottles, old newspapers, crumbs, screwed up food wrappers, a full ashtray and some small oily bits of machinery that might have come from a bicycle.

'It's your house,' Mike said, and looked around. 'Er . . . where's the kettle?'

That was when she had burst into tears again. Mike looked at her helplessly for a moment, willing her to stop. However, instead of stopping she raised her arms like a child which had fallen and wanted its mummy, and said, 'Hold me.'

He felt trapped. Unable to think of an excuse not to, he crossed the room and put his arms awkwardly around her shoulders. Still sitting, she wrapped her arms around his waist, her cheek pressed against his stomach as she sobbed. When her tears finally subsided, which seemed to Mike to take a very long time, she said, 'What's your name, love?'

'Mike.'

'You wouldn't hit a woman, would you, Mike?'

'No,' Mike muttered, horrified to discover that he was getting an erection because her breasts were squashed against his groin.

He was relieved when she pulled away and looked up at him. 'Have you got a girlfriend, Mike?'

'Not . . . not at the moment,' he said.

'I wish I was your girlfriend. I bet you treat your girlfriends well, don't you?'

He shrugged. 'I don't know. I try to.'

'I bet you do. Do you want to see how that bastard treats me?'

Before he could answer, she pulled the dressing gown off her left shoulder, revealing not only that and her bruised collarbone, but three-quarters of her left breast.

Mike felt his throat tightening. He was scared and uncomfortable, wishing he was somewhere else, but his erection was iron-hard. He didn't dare look down at the front of his trousers for fear of seeing what felt like a broom handle pointing with embarrassing candour at the object of his desire.

100

'I . . . I think I'd better go now,' he stammered.

'Please don't,' she said, standing up, the dressing gown slipping a little lower. 'I still feel a bit shaky. We haven't had that cup of tea yet.'

'I've got to finish my round.'

'I think you'd rather stay, though, wouldn't you?'

'What?' he all but squeaked.

She walked towards him, and then, shockingly, reached out and took hold of his erection through his trousers. 'My husband doesn't make love to me,' she said. 'He just fucks me.' She released his erection only to wrap her arms around him. 'Don't go,' she pleaded.

That had been the first time, the first taste of the drug, the first unbelievable high. Before Mary Sheridan, Mike's sexual encounters had been uncertain, fumbling affairs. Mary, though, had taken him to places he thought only existed in the pages of magazines like *Escort* and *Penthouse*, which he and his friends used to buy from the Barratt twins at school for 50p. Now, when he was with his friends and they talked about their sexual conquests, he knew that ninety per cent of the time they were lying. He longed to confide in someone about his affair, his habit, but he couldn't afford to take the risk. It would only take one tongue to wag for the secret to become local gossip, and Longbarrow was a small enough place for that gossip eventually to become loud enough to reach the ears of Ted Sheridan. Likewise, although he and Mary had tried to be careful, it only needed one suspicious neighbour or a slip from Mary herself to let the cat out of the bag. Which was why, as he turned into the Sheridans' street each morning, Mike's guts began to ferment, his saliva to thicken to tacky paste beneath his tongue and in the roof of his mouth.

One of these mornings he was certain Ted Sheridan would be there waiting for him, armed with a baseball bat or worse. It had got to the stage where Mike would jump every time he heard a motorbike engine, though he wasn't sure whether Sheridan even owned a motorbike any more. Last week Mike and two of his friends had been drinking in the White Hart when Sheridan had walked in. Mike had actually felt the blood draining from his face, the beer he had drunk turning to poison which his stomach wanted to expel. Will Trent, whom Mike had known since he was five, had asked him if he was all right, giving Mike the excuse to mumble something about food poisoning and slip out through the side entrance. He had run all the way home in a blind panic, his lungs hurting, his breath jagged and coppery, like slivers of rusty tin in his throat. A couple of times he had been certain he could hear running footsteps behind him, but he had reached home safely with no sign of a pursuer. Next morning, naked with Mary, he had recounted the incident. She had assured him that Ted didn't know about their relationship and never would.

Mike's heart quickened as he turned into Hawthorn Close where the Sheridans lived. It was a hot day, the latest in a seemingly endless succession, but Mike would have been sweating even if it had been the most bitter of winter mornings. For a split-second the dazzling sun and his imagination conjured a bulky black shape which was turning its head towards him at the gate of number 16. Then the shape was gone, and he released the breath that was jammed in his chest, and started his Hawthorn Close deliveries, trying to look as innocuous as possible.

On the pavement outside number 16 he had to make a conscious effort not to sneak a quick glance up and down the street before pushing open the gate and strolling up the path. Only his eyes moved as he glanced at the right-hand upstairs window. One curtain was open, the other closed, which meant that Mary was in the house alone. Without hesitating or looking behind him, Mike walked up to the front door, opened it and stepped inside. He closed it quickly behind him, dropping the catch so no one could gain entry without a key.

Only now did he allow himself to breathe more easily, though his mounting excitement was still interlaced with an edginess which he knew he would never completely shake off. His mind was full of what ifs. What if Ted injured himself at work and had to come home? What if he'd forgotten something? What if Jason should turn up, even though Mary had told him her wayward son couldn't get out of the house quickly enough in the morning and only came back for the occasional meal and to sleep? What if this was a trap and Ted and Jason were waiting for him upstairs?

That was the worst one, the thought of Ted Sheridan lying in wait, Mary close by, too terrified to shout a warning, perhaps even gagged and bound so that she couldn't.

'Mary,' Mike called softly. 'Mary, where are you?'

No reply at first, and then he heard her voice. 'Up here.'

He started to ascend the stairs, still carrying his postal sack because that was another what if: What if Ted came home and found the sack in the hall? At the top of the staircase he called again, 'Where are you? In the bedroom?'

'Yes.'

He crossed the landing, which creaked intolerably, passing doors which were all closed except the one which led into the bathroom. The house smelled not precisely bad but certainly not fresh. When he passed the bathroom door he was lovingly embraced by the heavy, fetid odour of bad bowels.

Holding his breath, trying not to think of Ted Sheridan stinking the house out with his morning dump before stomping off to work, Mike gingerly pushed the half-open bedroom door all the way back. Mary was on her back on the bed, spreadeagled like a laboratory rat. She was wearing a black bra and a pair of black pants. The pants were so flimsy that her pubic hair curled out at the sides. She was motionless as if she was unconscious or dead, and a bright, juicy, terrifying thought suddenly sprang into Mike's mind: *Bait! He's using her as bait!*

Not just his erection but his whole body wilted with terror, the energy to fight or even run draining out of him. Mike looked around wildly, wondering from which direction the first blow would come.

Then Mary lifted her head from the pillow, looked at him and said, 'Well, don't just stand there, lover boy. Come and get it.'

Chapter Eleven

Millicent Birkin lowered the binoculars, her hands trembling with excitement. That settled it. That young postman and Mary Sheridan were definitely up to something, and it didn't take Albert Einstein to work out what that might be. Dirty old trollop. The boy was young enough to be her son. She had first noticed him going into the house on Friday morning and coming out looking flushed half an hour later. Saturday, of course, Ted had been home, and Millicent didn't think it was only her imagination that the boy had looked decidedly nervous as he had approached the house, and had all but scuttled up the path as if he had a yapping dog at his heels after delivering the Sheridans' mail. Yesterday, of course, had been Sunday; Millicent, frustrated and impatient, had spent the entire day willing Monday morning to come around. Now it had, and she had been amply rewarded. Just wait until she told the girls about this.

Wheezing and wincing, she hauled herself up from the chair by the window in which she'd been conducting her vigil, and made her way slowly and painfully over to the telephone by the bed. Millicent was fifty years old and had never married. She had only ever had one boyfriend, in fact, and that almost thirty years ago. She suffered from spondylitis and chronic obesity, the former a direct cause of the latter. She had always been a large woman, but in the last five years, since the spondylitis had become bad enough to reduce her mobility, she had ballooned from fifteen stones to almost twenty-two.

The greatest period in her life had been seven or eight years ago when she had been Anne Darracott's right-hand woman during the campaign to get that dreadful, disgusting pervert,

Joyce Morrow, removed from her all-too-influential position as headmistress of Longbarrow Comprehensive. It had been a heady, exhilarating time; Millicent had spent weeks feeling giddy with importance. In the end, mysteriously, the whole campaign had fallen apart virtually overnight; Millicent had never quite found out why. What had upset her most about their failure had not been that Joyce Morrow had got to keep her job, but that her own prestige had taken something of a nose dive.

Well now, here was a chance to claw back a little of that prestige. Gossip was always welcomed by the girls, the juicier the better. For a few days at least her name would be lauded; the prospect made her vast stomach quiver with excitement. She lowered her huge bulk gingerly down on to the bed and reached for the telephone.

Chapter Twelve

'Lucy, what *are* you doing in there?'

Julia Benson began to hammer on the bathroom door, as if she honestly believed her eldest daughter might not have heard her. If she had been able to see Lucy at that moment she would have received a shock. Lucy was slumped in front of the toilet, hands clutching the peach-coloured plastic seat, puking her guts out. She was almost eight weeks pregnant and her morning sickness was getting worse with each passing day. She didn't know how much longer she would be able to keep her secret from her parents. She swept her long chestnut hair away from her face and made a gargantuan attempt to control her roiling stomach.

'Just on the loo, Mum. Won't be a minute,' she called, hoping her voice wouldn't betray the effort it took simply to speak.

'Well, hurry up. Other people have to use that bathroom as well as you. Your father wants a shower before he opens up.'

'Yeah, okay,' Lucy said, and then her stomach lurched again and she lunged for the toilet bowl. She stuck her head as far down it as she could, praying her mother wouldn't hear her retching.

Eventually her stomach settled a little and she sat back on her heels. She felt weak and tired and emotional and alone. Just a few weeks ago she'd had it all mapped out, her mind full of plans and ideas for the future, but now everything seemed such a mess. She wondered whether Jake had told his parents yet. Maybe they were all sitting round their big kitchen table at this moment, discussing the situation. The thought frightened her, but it also gave her a degree of comfort. She liked Jake's mum and dad. They were always so straightforward, and

106

despite the fact that her father had made his disapproval of Jake plain, there was always a warm welcome for her when Jake took her back to his house.

God, if Dad ever found out she'd been seeing Jake he'd go spare. She dreaded to think what he would do if he found out about the baby. She was still clinging to the hope that maybe they could sort things out without her parents having to be told. Of course, the only way they *could* do that was for Lucy to have an abortion on the quiet.

The problem was, she found that thought just as horrifying as going through with the pregnancy. Jake had tried to convince her that it was only a blob, that it didn't have feelings, but Lucy couldn't help thinking that once she had been a blob too, that the little thing inside her was a potential human being and that if left alone it would grow into a proper baby and then a child. It would smile and call her 'Mummy' and hold her hand when they crossed the road. In some ways it would be nice to be a young mum, because when her son or daughter was entering his or her teenage years, she would still only be thirty, young enough to understand their problems, to be treated more as a friend than a parent.

She knew if she had an abortion she would feel like a murderer. She would feel as if she had killed her child just because she was too selfish to look after it. Of course, she knew that it wasn't as simple as that, that there were many other factors to consider – Jake for one. Were she and he going to spend the rest of their lives together just for the sake of the child? Were they going to give up everything? And how were they going to manage? They had no jobs, no home of their own, no money.

She pushed herself unsteadily to her feet and crossed to the sink to wash her hands and face. She looked in the mirror above the sink and was shocked by how pale she was. If Mum saw her like that she'd know immediately that something was wrong. She flannelled her face vigorously with water as hot as she could stand. There, she looked better now, enough to convince her parents she was just tired, at least. She wondered whether the baby would have her brown, almond-shaped eyes, snub nose and wide mouth, or whether it would be more like Jake, who with his straw-blond hair and fine features looked more like an Aussie beach bum than a Yorkshire farmer's son.

Did she love Jake? She thought so, but was it a love that

would last for ever? It was certainly a love strong enough to persuade her to lose her virginity to him. It had happened at Roger Jaffrey's party to celebrate the end of school. Maybe if they hadn't both been tipsy on Diamond White they wouldn't have let their lust get the better of them, would have waited until Jake had managed to pluck up the courage to buy some condoms at the little chemist's on Bellwood Road.

It was so unfair. One little mistake and their lives had been turned upside-down. If there was a God, then he had a very nasty sense of humour. Her stomach rolled again, and she breathed deeply, trying to quell it. When it had settled as much as it was going to, she flushed the toilet, then crossed to the bolted door, bracing herself for the ordeal of breakfast.

Chapter Thirteen

'I saw the lights again last night,' Chris Farrar said.

'Oh yeah?' said Colin Dyer carefully.

'Yeah. Same place as before. They started at our gate and floated up through the graveyard. I watched them through my dad's binoculars until they disappeared behind a load of trees and stuff.'

Chris squinted at his friend through his spectacles. He was a small, thin boy with bony wrists and knees, but he had sharp, intelligent features, and when he spoke he did so quickly, as though eager to impart what was on his mind.

Colin Dyer was the complete opposite. He was big for his twelve years, and though not exactly fat was heavy-looking, measured – even slothful – in his movements. He had a round face, hooded eyes, and ears so large he looked as though he was in danger of taking off in a high wind. Some of the kids at school called him Dumbo, but Colin, who despite his size was a gentle soul, never reacted beyond shrugging his shoulders as if the insult was a regrettable but inevitable fact of life.

Standing astride his bike, he looked beyond Chris, through the lych-gate of St Luke's to the graveyard, as if just talking about the lights might summon them. As usual his face gave nothing away beyond a certain thoughtfulness which too many people mistook for stupidity.

'Did you ask your gran about them?' Chris asked.

Colin's gran, though somewhat fearsome, was generally regarded by Chris and Colin and the two other self-named 'Barrow Boys', Brian Pockett and James Couzens, as the fount of all knowledge, because of her ability to 'see things' and to make strange but often uncannily accurate predictions.

Colin nodded his head slowly.

'And what did she say?'

Colin turned his attention to the church tower, though his expression became even blanker than usual. As if preoccupied he said, 'She says they were probably fireflies.'

'Col,' Chris said, sharply enough to make his friend look him in the eye, 'what did she really say?'

Colin sighed and pretended to fiddle with the brake cables on his bike. 'You know what she's like,' he said. 'She says some daft things. She's ninety next year, and my dad reckons—'

'Col!' snapped Chris in exasperation.

Colin stopped talking. He sighed again. A wasp cruised past, humming menacingly; heat shimmered around the war memorial as if it was really a disguised spaceship, pulsating with alien energy.

Reluctantly Colin said, 'She thinks they might be Jack o' Lanterns.'

Chris's perpetual squint was more a nervous affliction than anything, and now his eyes opened wide in awe. 'Really?' he said. 'That sounds pretty cool.' Though he was standing still, his body gave the impression of being forever active, his head and hands making little darting movements as if he was constantly ingesting and processing data from the world around him. Now those movements became more pronounced, his hands fluttering like moths. 'So what *are* Jack o' Lanterns?' he said. 'What do they do?'

'They're green lights. People often see them in graveyards at night.'

'Well, I *know* that, don't I? But what *are* they? What do they *mean*?' He shuddered in delicious anticipation. 'Are they the restless souls of the dead, condemned to roam the earth for all eternity?'

'Not really,' said Colin pedantically. 'But my gran says the reason you always see them in graveyards is because they float up to the church door and disappear.'

'Why do they do that?'

'I don't know. But she says that if you can get to the church door before they do, you'll see the face of someone who's going to die soon in the lights.'

'Wow!' exclaimed Chris, his eyes glittering now, his hands

110

tapping his leg, rubbing his chin, scratching his head, as if they were independent of him. '*Ultra*-cool!'

Colin shrugged, looking uncomfortable. 'It's just what my gran says.'

'Yeah, well, I'm going to see if it's true,' Chris announced. 'Next time the Jack o' Lanterns come, I'm going to bomb up to the church door before they get there.'

'Your mum and dad'll never let you out at that time of night,' said Colin.

'I'm not going to tell them, am I, brain-dead? I'm going to pretend to go to bed and then I'll sneak out. It'll be brilliant.'

Colin said nothing. Though he had lived in the same house as his gran all his life and was used to her predictive abilities, he was not comfortable with things that he didn't fully understand. He knew his gran regarded her ability more as a curse than a blessing, particularly that of being able to foresee a person's death, which disturbed her so much that these days she remained virtually housebound by choice, shunning large crowds. He had asked her once how she knew when someone was going to die, and she had told him that she saw something white fluttering above their heads, something that looked like a dove trapped in a net, but which moved so quickly that she could never quite focus upon it. Though Colin accepted most things without too much fuss, that particular image had worried him so much that for weeks afterwards he had kept glancing above his own head, had even lain awake at night, scared of hearing the flutter of phantom wings in the dark.

Despite his unease at his friend's recent preoccupation, Colin had to admit that it had been a good summer. Admittedly there were two weeks of it left yet before school started again, but although it still felt hot enough to fry eggs on the pavement, he couldn't shake the feeling that it was now winding down, that autumn was just around the corner. Maybe it was something to do with the fact that they had already packed so much into the long, hot days, or that two of their four-strong group were spending the last two weeks of freedom on holiday with their families, Brian in Scotland and James in Florida. On the way over on his bike, Colin had not been able to help thinking about the time they had spent together almost

111

wistfully, almost as if it was the last summer they would ever share. He looked back fondly at the games of football and cricket and tennis, the snooker tournament on Brian's half-size table in his garage, the fishing trips, the water-fights, the den they had built in the woods where they had played cards and ogled at pictures of naked women, and almost coughed their guts out trying the cigarettes that James had filched from his mum's bag. They had ridden their bikes for miles, had camped out in James's back garden (where they had even had a camp fire on which James's dad had helped them cook sausages which they had eaten in sandwiches beneath the stars), and had gone ghost-hunting at dusk up at the big house before the new people had moved in. It had been Chris who had proposed that particular expedition, of course. The four of them had left their bikes concealed behind the hedge across the road and then had climbed over the high double gates, scaring each other witless imagining dark shapes flitting between the oak trees that had flanked them as they had crept towards the house.

However, although they had not *really* seen anything, Chris had not been deterred. A week or so later he had announced importantly, 'My dad's met the people who are going to move in to the big house. There's a lad about our age. When we see him we can ask *him* about the ghost.'

'Yeah,' James had said. 'Maybe we could even let him join the Barrow Boys. Then we could stay over. Maybe he'd let us sleep in the haunted room.'

'*Is* there a haunted room?' Colin had asked.

James had looked at him exasperatedly. 'Course there is. Bound to be, isn't there?'

The new people had moved in a few days ago, though so far none of the Barrow Boys had seen them. Chris had wanted to go up there to say hello, but the rest of them had decided that that wasn't a good idea because they would have had to climb over the gate again to get to the house, which probably wouldn't have gone down too well.

Now, though, Chris had a new obsession – the so-called Jack o' Lanterns, which he had first seen last Wednesday, then again on Friday, and then for the third time last night. If what his gran had said was true, Colin hoped that the third time would also be the last. He had no doubt that if Chris saw the mysterious green lights again, he would be as good as his word and would attempt to reach the church door before they did.

' . . . for the lights,' Chris said.

Colin looked at him, his mind drifting back to the present. 'What?'

Chris tutted, shook his head, flapped his fingers. 'What are you, deaf or something? I said, why don't you ask your mum and dad if you can stay over, then we can both look for the lights?'

Colin shook his head slowly. 'No, I don't think so.'

'Why not?'

'I just don't want to, that's all.'

'You're scared!' Chris exclaimed, head darting forward, eyes squeezing into slits.

Most twelve-year-olds would have denied the accusation at once, but Colin considered it carefully. At last he shook his head. 'I just don't see what's so good about knowing who's going to die.'

Chris tutted, though offered no further argument. He made a chopping motion in front of his face as if he was being pestered by midges, and said, 'What shall we do today?'

Colin shrugged his big shoulders. 'Don't know.'

'We could get some Cokes and sweets and stuff from Mr Toot's and take them to the den.'

'Yeah, okay.'

The boys wheeled their bikes across the road to the grocer's, the bell ting-a-linging as they entered. They both loved Mr Toot's shop; everyone did. Mr Toot was his usual beaming self, asking after their families as he took down sweet jars and totted up what they owed him. He rounded the figure down as he always did, even popping a couple of extra sweets into their bags. Colin didn't know whether it was Mr Toot's soothing, mesmeric voice or the shadowy warm stillness of the shop, or the comforting combination of smells – coffee, apples, pastry, fresh newspapers – but he always stepped out of Mr Toot's feeling calm and content, sometimes almost soporific.

Today was no exception, though what he saw when he set foot on the pavement outside the shop caused the bubble of tranquillity that was surrounding him to burst. Gary Sissons was standing astride his bike. Colin suspected that if he had remained in the shop for ten seconds longer, he would have come out to find an empty patch of pavement where his bike had stood.

'Er . . . hi, Gary,' he said. 'What're you doing?'

He was aware that he ought really to be angry, indignant, but that wasn't the way to handle Gary Sissons. Besides, it wasn't really his style.

Gary looked at him, not in the least embarrassed at being caught in the act. Indeed, his upper lip curled in disdain. 'Scuba-diving, what's it fucking look like?'

Despite being two years younger, Colin was as tall as Gary, and certainly wider, but what made Gary frightening was that he had dead eyes. Shark's eyes. He looked as though nothing fazed him, as though he'd fight anybody anywhere any time. He looked too as though once he started on you he'd never stop, as though he'd tear you apart without feeling anything at all.

'It's just that . . . well, that's my bike,' said Colin mildly.

'So?'

'Um . . . well . . . could I have it back, please?'

Colin was aware that Chris had come out of the shop now and was standing silently behind him. However, he didn't expect his friend to help him, and he wouldn't blame him later for not doing so.

Gary's face was deadpan, though his shark's eyes remained fixed on Colin. 'I'm borrowing it for a bit.'

Colin didn't know what to say. Gary's answers seemed to be designed to get Colin to say something that would give Gary an excuse to turn nasty. Not that the older boy *needed* an excuse.

'But . . . er . . . I need it,' Colin said at last.

'No, you don't.'

Another pause as Colin considered how to respond. Finally, carefully: 'Chris and I were going on a bike ride.'

'You'll have to think of something else to do then, won't you?' Gary said, making the words sound like a challenge.

Colin sighed, glancing up at the sky, perhaps in the hope of divine inspiration. Resignedly he said, 'How long would you want to borrow it for?'

'As long as it takes.'

'How long would that be?'

'I don't fucking know, do I? Fucking stupid questions. Do you want to make something of this, cunt?'

114

'Perhaps you ought to ask more questions yourself, Gareth. An enquiring mind is a healthy mind, so they say.'

Colin half-turned. Behind a cowering Chris stood Mr Toot. He had somehow managed to slip out of his shop without making the bell ring. He was smiling as if exchanging pleasantries with friends, apparently oblivious to the tension in the air.

Gary turned his shark's eyes on the little grocer. 'What?' he said dangerously.

Mr Toot strolled forward until he was standing at Colin's shoulder. Still beaming he said, 'How are you feeling now, Gareth, incidentally? Better, I hope.' To Colin he said, 'Poor Gareth overindulged last night and was terribly ill this morning. Made an awful mess, I understand. Tell me, Gareth, did you manage to get the stains out of your carpet?'

Gary's face was an exquisite blend of fury, confusion and embarrassment. 'Who fucking told you about that?' he said. 'I bet it was my fucking brother, wasn't it?'

Mr Toot ignored the question. Instead he said pleasantly, 'It's very kind of you to keep the seat of Colin's bike warm for him, though hardly neccessary on a day like today.'

'Why don't you just fuck off, you little bald bastard?' Gary said.

Though a model of equanimity, Colin felt a chill pass through him. No one *ever* talked to Mr Toot like that. He glanced at the little shopkeeper, but his expression had not faltered. Mr Toot did, however, move right up close to Gary, who was still standing astride Colin's bike, his hands gripping the handlebars as if the bike itself was a weapon he intended to use.

And then, to Colin's astonishment – and Gary's too, judging by the expression on his face – Mr Toot reached out and placed his chubby pink hands over Gary's grubby, nail-bitten ones.

For a few seconds the world seemed to pause. The birds and the insects fell silent; all background noise ceased; even the drifting white clouds overhead appeared to cruise to a halt.

Colin felt as though his heart was slowing, slowing. He looked at the two motionless figures in front of him, and a question his general science teacher, Mr Bellis, had posed to the class earlier in the year popped into his mind: What happens when an unstoppable force meets an immovable object?

Gary was the first to break the spell. 'Let go of me, you fucking woofter.' Colin thought it was surely his imagination that made the beginning of Gary's sentence seem slurred as though his voice was a recording initially played at too slow a speed. Indeed, his tension must have stifled his senses, for suddenly the world was normal again – a car over-revving three or four streets away, a dog that sounded equally distant yapping then falling silent. He glanced up at the sky. A cloud the shape of a wolf's head was inching towards some unknown destination, its jaws yawning wide.

Mr Toot's smile remained on his face without ever seeming fixed. 'You're quite at liberty to remove your hands if you wish, Gareth,' he said genially.

Gary, however, seemed either unable or unwilling to slide his hands from beneath Mr Toot's – even though Colin would have sworn that Mr Toot was applying no pressure whatsoever. An expression flickered in his shark's eyes that looked astoundingly like distress, but which was so brief that Colin couldn't even be sure that he had seen it at all. Then Gary said something that sounded like, 'I don't ... ' before his voice dropped so low that Colin couldn't hear it.

Mr Toot leaned forward like a confidant, the sun gleaming on his pink scalp. Colin wasn't quite sure what happened next. When he went over it in his head later, the incident seemed odd, almost dream-like. What *seemed* to happen was that Mr Toot whispered something to Gary, which made the fourteen-year-old rear back, a startled expression on his face. He snatched his hands from beneath Mr Toot's with no apparent difficulty and swung his left leg over the bike so quickly that he lost his balance, all but sprawling on the pavement. He staggered to his feet and slouched away without so much as a threat or a backward glance. Mr Toot turned and, still beaming, wheeled Colin's bike over to him.

'Wonderful things, bicycles,' he said. 'Good for the spirit and the circulation. If we all had them the world would be a far better place.'

Colin was still watching Gary Sissons' rapidly departing back. He couldn't help thinking the boy resembled an animal bettered in a tussle with one of its fellows. What could Mr Toot possibly have said that had made him react like that? Colin couldn't think of any threat or insult that wouldn't have prompted Gary to come back snarling and spoiling for a scrap.

He turned his attention to Mr Toot, a little bemused. 'Er . . . yes,' he said, 'thanks.' Part of him wanted to ask Mr Toot what he had whispered to the bully, but a bigger part assured him it was wiser not to know, to leave well alone.

'My pleasure,' Mr Toot said and ambled over to his shop. At the doorway he paused and said, 'You two boys enjoy the summer while you still can.'

Then he was gone.

Colin turned and looked at Chris, who was still standing in exactly the same position as before, mouth agape. For a few moments neither boy said anything, Colin because he rarely spoke without a certain amount of reflection, Chris because he seemed too overawed by what he had witnessed.

Then, as his curiosity came to the fore, Chris twitched and jerked back into life. His mouth closed with a snap, his eyes narrowed into their customary squint, and he spread his hands wide as if in the blind hope of catching answers he had momentarily lost in the sun.

'What happened?' he blurted, sounding almost accusatory.

Colin looked at him a moment longer and then shrugged. 'I don't know.'

He started to wheel his bike away from Mr Toot's shop. Chris scampered over to get his bike, which was propped up against the shop's convex window, and ran to catch him up.

'What did he say to Sissons?' he wanted to know, almost squawking in his excitement.

'I don't know,' Colin said. 'I didn't hear him.'

'But you were closer than me,' said Chris in frustration.

'I know, but I still didn't hear him.'

'Well, why didn't you ask him?' Chris said.

Colin came to a sudden halt and looked at Chris levelly. 'Why didn't you?'

Chris's reddening face went through all kinds of contortions. 'Well, I . . . I mean, it was just . . . I . . .' Finally his eyes opened wide as an excuse occurred to him. 'It was *your* bike.'

'So?'

'So don't you want to know how Mr Toot got it back for you?'

'No,' Colin said, and it was only partly a lie.

'Well, *I* do,' said Chris. His eyes narrowed again. 'I think I might ask him later.'

117

'Might you?' said Colin, knowing full well that he wouldn't.

'Yeah . . . What do you *think* he said?'

'I've no idea.'

'Do you think he threatened to rip Sissons' heart out or something? Or maybe he hypnotised him. Yeah, I bet that's it. Because whenever *I* talk to Mr Toot, I feel all sort of . . . woozy.'

'There's that kid,' said Colin.

Chris looked up, surprised. 'What?'

'That kid. The new one who's moved into the big house.'

'Where?'

'There, by the chemist's. Carrying a skateboard.'

'Oh yeah, I see him. Come on.'

The two boys jumped on their bikes and pedalled furiously up the street, towards the corner into Bellwood Road where the chemist's was with its red neon PRESCRIPTIONS sign in the window. The new kid was no taller than Chris, though maybe not quite as skinny. He was carrying a snazzy-looking skateboard under his arm and wearing an even snazzier-looking pair of trainers, together with a black *X-Files* T-shirt which hung out over a pair of old Levi's with frayed turn-ups.

He passed the chemist's and stopped to look in the window of the tiny video shop next door. He seemed quite taken with the poster for Stallone's *Cliffhanger*.

'Hey!' Chris shouted. 'Hey, you!'

He screeched to a halt in the gutter, his back wheel skidding impressively, as the kid turned round. Colin, more conventionally, slowed to a stop, putting his foot out to the kerb to steady himself.

Strands of the kid's fringe reached down like dark fingers towards his left eye. He looked wary. 'Me?' he said.

Chris nodded. 'Yeah. You've just moved into the big house, haven't you?'

'Yeah,' the kid said, still cautious.

'Is it haunted?' Chris asked.

The kid seemed unfazed by the question. He looked from Chris to Colin and then shrugged. 'I don't know. We've only been there a few days.'

'We reckon it's haunted, don't we, Col?' Chris said.

'You do.' Turning to the kid, Colin said, 'We saw you from

118

up the road, so we thought we'd come and say hi. I'm Colin and this is Chris.'

'I'm David,' said the kid, less wary now.

Colin produced the rather crumpled paper bag of sweets he had bought in Mr Toot's and held them out. 'Fancy a sherbet bon-bon?'

Chapter Fourteen

Monday lunchtime, and thanks to the continuing hot weather the Druid's Arms was once again doing a roaring trade. It was a pub that lovingly cultivated its image as a traditional country inn, with its low ceilings, dark beams and profusion of horse brasses. However, the illusion was undermined somewhat by the large restaurant extension which had been built on to the back of the building, one wall of which was all windows, offering a magnificent view of the fields and woodland that formed the upward sweep of the valley.

The food in the Druid's Arms was renowned throughout the area (as evidenced by the framed newspaper reviews rubbing shoulders with the Yorkshire landscapes, hunting prints and anatomically scrupulous flower studies on the walls), but on weekdays it was mostly a labouring crowd who came in, interested more in a few pints and a cheese roll than in lamb *en croute* with a nice bottle of Cabernet Sauvignon.

There were the farm workers, the car mechanics, the lads from the tannery (to whom the oily, pungent aroma of sheeps' hides seemed perpetually to cling) and the lads from the sheet metal works, as well as the occasional suit and of course the locals, like old George, who would next miss an opening time on the day he was measured for his coffin.

This day was much like any other, the raucous chatter and ching of the cash registers reaching a peak at around one p.m. At two the landlord, Trevor Paine, who had come up from Peterborough eleven years ago, and though treated well enough by the locals was still regarded as something of an outsider, peered through the blue gauze of cigarette smoke whose stink would force him to shower and change his clothes before the evening shift, and allowed himself a sigh of relief.

He was delighted with the business his pub was doing, but he was always glad when the lunchtime rush hour started to draw to a close and the lads began drifting back to work. His corns had been playing him up something rotten these past few weeks, and what with the heat and the smoke, and the crush of sweaty bodies all requiring liquid refreshment, there were times when working behind the bar became almost unbearable.

'Afternoon, gents,' he called as a group of tanners upped and left in unison. They grunted and waved, trooping to the door and stepping out into a brightness so intense their features seemed momentarily to be erased by white light.

Before the door could swing closed behind them, forcing the sunlight back outside, it was shoved open again and three people entered the bar. They were wearing filthy blue overalls and steel-toe-capped boots, and though Trevor's smile remained on his face he groaned inwardly. He thought, with it being past two, he had escaped having to endure the company of Ted Sheridan and his cronies. Yet here they were, Sheridan in the lead, his big beard clamped around his fat face, his piggy eyes staring out from beneath eyebrows like tangles of thick black wire.

Although Sheridan had never done anything serious enough to get him barred from the Druid's Arms, Trevor regarded him as twenty stones of unadulterated viciousness. He was surly and monosyllabic, and he addressed everyone as though he had some grudge against them. Trevor never failed to feel uncomfortable beneath the man's stony gaze.

Ted clumped to the bar, his two friends swaggering in his wake like courtiers basking in the reflected glory of their leader. Trevor's two senior barmaids, Janice and Andrea, were working with him today, and though they were used to fending off drunken proposals from middle-aged men and dealing with crude comments from young lads emboldened by inebriation, even they hated serving Ted Sheridan, and avoided it whenever possible. Today, Trevor was aware of Janice scurrying off on a phantom errand to the kitchen, and of Andrea sliding along the L-shaped bar to ask old George if he wanted a top-up even though his glass was still over half-full.

Forcing his grin to widen, he placed his hands on the bar. 'Now then, gents, what can I get you?' he said.

Sheridan's deadpan expression didn't change, but the look he gave Trevor made the landlord feel as though he had said something unutterably puerile.

'Three pints o' bitter,' the big man said at last, his voice gruff and flat.

Trevor lifted down three glasses and began to fill them, the creamy-brown liquid dribbling out of the tap excruciatingly slowly. He felt a trickle of sweat run down his face. 'Another hot one,' he ventured.

Sheridan not only ignored the comment, but actually turned his back to look around the bar, the end of his greasy ponytail brushing the tip of the triangle of sweat that had soaked through his clothes to darken his overalls. It was left to one of his cronies to answer, a seedy-looking man called Ed Perdew, who had thinning sandy hair and a badly clipped moustache.

'Aye. S'fuckin' boilin' at work. I could fill a pint glass wi' the sweat in me boots.'

Trevor laughed and placed the three pints on the drainage tray. Sheridan dropped a screwed-up five-pound note on the damp beer mat beside the tray, then scooped up his glass and plodded towards the snug where the pool table was, leaving Perdew to collect his change.

For the next fifteen minutes nothing much happened. More people left than entered. The smoke dissipated a little, coiling in the sunlight that jabbed in through the windows and turned dark wood to glowing gold with its Midas touch. Ed Perdew scuttled back to the bar to order three more pints, as if servility was the price he paid for the dubious honour of being part of Ted Sheridan's inner sanctum.

Trevor wasn't sure exactly how the trouble started. He was telling Janice how he must be on about sixty a day if it was true what they said about passive smoking when he heard raised voices coming from the snug. He and Janice both turned their heads to look in that direction, as did the two dozen or so other people still in the pub.

What he saw made his heart sink. Ted Sheridan was looming over a lad of about twenty with short dyed-blond hair and a large silver loop in his left ear, who Trevor knew worked as a car mechanic at Matty Hanson's garage on Church Street by the war memorial. The lad was holding a pool cue, though his posture suggested defence rather than aggression. He was wearing a white T-shirt smeared with oil and dirt, and even though he looked as though he worked out regularly, he still appeared puny next to the bear-like bulk of Ted Sheridan.

'Sorry, mate. It was an accident. Look, I'll buy you another,' the boy said.

'Fuck that!' Sheridan boomed.

'What about his clothes?' said the other man who had entered with Sheridan, a craggy-faced individual with a DA so plastered with oil it looked moulded from shiny black plastic.

'They're only overalls. They'll dry,' the boy said, his voice a mixture of exasperation and desperation.

Ed Perdew, who was still sitting and watching proceedings as if they were an interesting piece of theatre, took a gulp from his pint. The instant he put the glass down, Sheridan snatched it up and hurled its contents all over the boy.

'What did you do that for?' the boy spluttered, beer dripping from his hair and face and arms, plastering his white T-shirt to his body, forming a puddle around his feet.

'It'll dry,' Sheridan said sarcastically.

'But what I did was a fucking accident, you stupid fat twat!'

'Who you calling a twat?' Sheridan roared.

At which point, Trevor lifted the bar flap and hurried through to the snug. 'What seems to be the trouble, gents?' he asked, trying to keep his voice calm and reasonable.

'Look what this stupid cunt did to me,' the boy said, his cheeks red, his voice shrill with an anger fierce enough to overcome his natural caution.

'Fuckin' warned you,' Sheridan grunted, and waded forward, swinging his massive arms.

The boy retaliated by taking a swipe at Sheridan with the pool cue, but the big man smashed it aside. As the cue clattered against the wall, the boy retreated, as did his friend who had been standing silently by the bottom right-hand pocket throughout the encounter. The two of them ran around to the other side of the table, using it as a buffer between themselves and the man-mountain that was pursuing them.

'Ted, stop this before someone gets hurt!' Trevor shouted.

'It's got nowt to do wi' you,' Sheridan barked.

'It's my pub!'

'It's got nowt to do wi' you,' Sheridan repeated stubbornly, 'so fuck off!'

Suddenly he grabbed hold of the table, lifted it up and heaved it at the boys. They leaped out of the way as the table smashed on to its side, pool balls spilling out of the pockets and rolling all over the floor.

Before the boys could regain their balance and composure, Sheridan grabbed an empty beer glass from the table where they had been sitting and hurled it at the blond-haired boy. He ducked just in time, but the glass shattered against the wall above his head, showering him with sharp, glittering splinters.

'Stop this, Ted!' Trevor shouted again, and ran forward with no real idea of how he was going to restrain the human juggernaut rampaging through his pub. He saw Sheridan reaching for another empty beer glass and lunged for him, both hands outstretched. 'Ted, stop—' he shouted, but got no further.

He never knew whether Sheridan acted instinctively or with deliberation, but as his hands closed on Sheridan's tree trunk of an arm, the big man snatched up the beer glass, swung round and smashed it into Trevor's face. Trevor's head snapped back with such force that it felt as though the vertebrae in his neck had torn apart; accompanying this was an incredible explosion of light and sound.

It wasn't until he was lying on the floor, the cupped hands around his face slippery with blood, that he really became aware of the pain. His cheek suddenly felt white-hot, but far worse were his eyes, which felt as though they had become embedded with dozens of razor-sharp hooks that ground together, tearing and pulling, whenever he blinked.

He began to scream then, his own deep-throated sounds like a weird echo of the high-pitched screams of Janice or Andrea that seemed to be reverberating down a long tunnel towards him. He wasn't screaming only because of the pain, though that was reason enough, but also because the explosion of light had dwindled and died, leaving only a thick, agonising darkness behind.

His eyes were open – he *knew* they were open – but try as he might he couldn't see a thing. Terror surging within him, he crawled about on the floor, hands and knees crunching on broken glass.

'I'm blind!' he screamed, tasting blood and glass splinters in his mouth. 'I'm blind! I'm blind!'

He felt hands on him, trying to pull him to his feet. Someone shouted, 'Get Des Brewer down here. And call a fucking ambulance!'

Chapter Fifteen

Her family and many of her friends thought they were mad for
rushing into it, but Susan didn't care. She loved the house and
so did Davey, despite the maggots and the dust and the isolation. It was odd but she felt safe here, even though it became
so black at night you couldn't even see the closest of the surrounding oak trees when clouds smudged out the moon. When
she and Davey had returned to the house to live, only seventeen days after having first viewed it, it had felt like coming
home.

To facilitate the move, they had had to cancel their holiday
in Cromer, and Davey had had to forego his two weeks in Kent
with her parents (which hadn't gone down too well, even when
Susan explained that she wanted to get installed and settled
before the new school year started), but all the hassle had been
worth it in the end. The last two hectic weeks in London had
been spent completing the paperwork, putting their house on
the market, arranging to have their furniture placed in storage,
and packing their lives into crates, cardboard boxes and
suitcases.

They had finally moved in on Thursday, 17th August, four
days ago. Since then they had been making the place their own
– cleaning and decorating, and sorting through the contents of
the house and deciding what to keep and what to throw away.

On Friday, Susan had given Jack Bradley a ring to ask if he
knew of anywhere local where she could hire a skip to be
delivered on Monday morning. He had offered to arrange it
for her, adding tentatively that if she needed a hand sorting
stuff out, he was willing to come over for the day.

Susan's first instinct had been to refuse his offer – she liked to make it clear to would-be Sir Galahads that she and David were quite capable of managing by themselves, thank you – but after only a few seconds' hesitation she had relented, deciding that by asserting her independence she would only be cutting off her nose to spite her face.

Jack was upstairs now, sorting through the junk in the attic room next to the one that David had appropriated as his bedroom. David had spent virtually all of yesterday decorating his new room with paint he had chosen himself from the hardware store in the village. Now, as the walls dried, he was taking the morning off, a break which Susan thought was well earned. He had set off on his skateboard at 9:30 that morning, telling her he was going to go down to the village to explore and would be back later.

Susan had spent the morning throwing rubbish into the skip that had arrived just before Jack at 8:30 that morning, cleaning the Aga (a thankless task which she had decided she could put off no longer), and making phone calls – to the solicitor and the estate agent, to an auctioneer (whose number the estate agent had given her) who had promised to come round on Wednesday morning to view the items she had decided to part with, to the headmistress of the local secondary school which David would be attending in a couple of weeks' time (she had been out, but Susan had left a message on her answerphone), and to a local clock repairer called Arnold Thrasher, whom Jack had recommended. Mr Thrasher had promised to pop over later to take a look at the grandfather clock which Jack had told Susan had been silent for at least five years and maybe more. He had had a tinker with it once, but had been unable to get it going. 'Probably wants stripping down and cleaning,' he had said. 'I'd do it for you, but I might bust it for good. It's a bit of a specialised job.'

Now Susan had decided it was lunchtime. She made a stack of ham sandwiches and a pot of tea, which she put on a tray with two mugs and a plate of Digestives, and carried the whole lot upstairs.

From the landing below, she heard Jack banging about in the room that she and David had dubbed the Maggot Room. It was odd, but despite hardly knowing him she felt completely at ease with the fact that there were just the two of them in the house. She didn't know whether this new relaxed attitude was down to herself or to Jack or perhaps even to the tranquil effect of her surroundings.

'Lunchtime,' she shouted, standing at the bottom of the winding staircase and looking up.

'Oh, right,' he called back, sounding surprised, and then, perhaps realising his response had shown a certain lack of gratitude, 'Smashing. Thanks a lot. I'll come down, shall I?'

Susan looked around. All the rooms on this level were still thick with dust and grime apart from Aunt Mollie's, which Susan didn't particularly fancy eating her lunch in.

'No, it's okay, I'll come up,' she said, and did so, taking care not to trip on the narrow staircase.

Jack was standing in the open doorway to the Maggot Room, waiting for her. His clothes, his hair, even his skin looked dusty. He reached out to take the tray.

'How's it going?' she asked him.

'Not too bad. There's not a lot of room to work in, but I've managed to sort through most of it. That there's rubbish,' he said, indicating with his head, 'and that's all the stuff I thought you might want to keep.'

'Any more maggots?' she asked, grimacing.

'A few. Plenty of other creepy-crawlies as well. I've dealt with them, though.'

Susan smiled. 'You must think I'm a complete wimp.'

He grinned his slow grin. 'I'll tell you a secret: I'm terrified of earwigs. When I was a lad I put my dad's slippers on, and there was an earwig in one of them which grabbed me with its pincers and wouldn't let go.' He shuddered. 'I've hated them ever since.'

Susan grinned with him, then nodded at the closed door to the other attic room. 'I thought we could eat our sandwiches in here.'

'Fine,' he said. Susan opened the door and led the way inside.

The smell of fresh paint hit her like a wave of well-being, and she hunched her shoulders, unable to suppress a shudder of happiness. The room was warm and bright, sun blazing through the open velux windows, but Jack, noting her reaction, said with concern, 'Are you cold? Shall I close the windows?'

Susan couldn't keep the grin off her face. 'No, I'm not cold,

I'm just happy. It's just . . . walking into this room summed it all up for me. It's so bright and sunny, like the future will be. And the smell of paint –' she lifted her face, breathing it in, '– it's like . . . like the smell of a fresh start, a new life. Does that make any sense to you?'

He nodded solemnly. 'Oh yes. I sometimes feel a bit like that myself here, when I'm working in the garden or whatever. You feel so happy that you just sort of . . . tingle all over, don't you?'

She smiled at him and walked across to the wall and placed a hand on it. 'The wall's dry enough to lean on. We'll have to sit on the floor to eat our lunch.'

Jack placed the tray on the floor and they sat down, their backs to the wall. As Jack reached for a sandwich, Susan poured the tea.

'What do you think of the decorating?' she asked.

'Very good. Did you do it?'

'No, David did it all himself. He's never been able to do anything like this before because of his asthma . . . you know, with the fumes and everything.'

Jack was silent for a moment as he munched a mouthful of ham sandwich. He swallowed and said, 'So his asthma's better now, is it?'

'Yes. It's amazing. Since Mr Toot took us into the woods that day his asthma has just vanished. He's been helping me clean the rooms downstairs, with dust flying everywhere, and it hasn't affected him at all.' She sat back from pouring the tea and took a sandwich herself. 'Have you any idea what happened, Jack? What Mr Toot did?'

Jack shook his head. 'No. I've seen him do one or two things in my time, but don't ask me to explain any of them.'

'What else have you seen him do?'

'Well, there was this girl once, Liz something her name was, and she had the worst acne I've ever seen. I was in the shop one day when she came in in a terrible state, asking if he could help her. He sat her down and then he put his hand on her head and whispered something – I couldn't hear what. Then he told her to go for a walk and come back in an hour. Well, an hour later she came back and there wasn't a mark on her face. Her skin was as clear as . . . well, as yours or mine.'

'You're kidding,' Susan said.

'I'm not. And there was another time. This old boy came into the shop, crippled with arthritis. He didn't come in for treatment, he just came in for some milk or something. He could hardly walk, poor bugger. He had a stick in each hand and he just sort of shuffled along. Anyway, Mr Toot asked me if I'd mind the shop for half an hour and then he took the old boy out the back. I tried to hear what was going on, but I couldn't hear a thing. And then suddenly, after about fifteen minutes, I heard this sort of crack-crack and I thought Mr Toot had broken the poor bloke's legs or something. I went to find out what was happening, but the door was locked, and as I still couldn't hear anything, even when I put my ear up to it, I went back to mind the shop. Ten minutes later the door opened and out came the old boy grinning from ear to ear, walking perfectly normal – no sticks, nothing. I asked Mr Toot what he'd done, but he just smiled. One thing I've learned about him – if he doesn't answer you the first time, there's no point asking again.'

'But this is incredible,' Susan said. 'He must be some sort of miracle worker.'

Jack nodded sagely. 'I reckon that's about right. But you don't have to take my word for it, do you? You saw for yourself how he cured David.'

'Yes, but I thought . . .' She frowned, as if uncertain whether to continue. Then she said, 'I'm not saying that what we witnessed wasn't amazing, but it did cross my mind that Mr Toot had put the idea that he was cured into David's head and that David did the rest.'

'A psychosomatic suggestion?' said Jack.

'Yes,' said Susan, unable to hide her surprise.

Jack grinned. 'You didn't think I'd know long words like that, did you?'

Susan felt herself blushing, and stammered, 'No, it wasn't that . . . It was just . . . well, I mean . . .'

'It's okay,' said Jack, rescuing her from her discomfort, 'no offence taken.' He shrugged. 'I live on my own, so I read a lot.'

Susan put a hand to her burning face. She wanted to ask him why he lived on his own, why he wasn't married, but instead she said, 'Have the press ever got wind of what Mr Toot can do? I mean, a story like that would be massive.'

Jack shrugged again. 'People round here just accept what he

130

does. I don't think Mr Toot'd want a lot of newspaper people poking round.'

'No, I suppose not,' Susan said. She took a sip of her tea.

Awkwardly Jack said, 'You wouldn't tell them what I've told you, would you? Newspaper people, I mean? It's just that . . . Mr Toot's been good to me. He stood by me years ago, back when I probably didn't deserve it. I wouldn't want him to think I've let him down.'

Susan felt a little hurt that Jack could think she would do such a thing, but then she supposed he barely knew her. 'Of course I won't tell anyone,' she said. 'This is my home now too, remember. I've got no desire to turn the place into a media circus.'

Jack nodded, and for a few moments they munched sandwiches in silence, the atmosphere just a little soured.

Then Susan said, 'What did you mean when you said that Mr Toot stood by you when you didn't deserve it?'

When he looked uncomfortable she said, 'It's all right, you don't have to answer that if you don't want to.'

He shook his head. 'No, it's all right. It was a long time ago now. The thing is, I was a bit of a bad lad when I was about sixteen, seventeen. I fell in with the wrong crowd. We all rode around on motorbikes and caused a lot of trouble – stealing, fighting, smashing things up, taking drugs. I knew what we were doing was wrong, and even back then I was ashamed by some of it, but I suppose I was easily led – not that that's much of an excuse.'

'And it was Mr Toot who got you back on the straight and narrow, was it?'

'Not really. I had to do that myself. What happened was that the leader of our gang, a bloke called Richard Heap, got blasted out of his head one night and smashed his bike into a tree. We'd all done it loads of times – got drunk and then gone tearing off along the country lanes like nutters. But when Dicky got killed I sort of grew up overnight. I realised what a stupid, pointless life Dicky had had, and how I was heading the same way if I didn't do something about it. I realised that there were people in the village who must have been glad that Dicky had been killed, who must have thought he deserved it, and I didn't want them to think that about me.

'So I stopped seeing the rest of the lads, told them I'd had

131

enough, but it was hard for a while. The gang thought I was a wimp, and no one else in the village would give me the time of day, and I couldn't really blame them, considering the amount of trouble I'd caused.'

'Except Mr Toot,' said Susan.

'Yes. He was the only one who trusted me, who believed that I really wanted to change. I remember I walked into his shop one day, and he just came up and shook my hand and said that he always knew I'd come good, or something like that. He even gave me some work to do in his shop, even though I knew he didn't really need me. I'd stack shelves for him, or move boxes around, or replace washers in taps, little things like that. It was thanks to him that I started doing odd jobs for one or two other people, including Mrs Boscombe. And then one thing led to another and I started up the business, and that's it really. I've been on the go ever since.'

'What about the other gang members?' Susan asked. 'Are they still around?'

'Only one of them – Ted Sheridan. He works in the big sheet metal works that you pass as you come into the village. He's still a bit of a troublemaker. We don't really talk to each other. I just keep out of his way. All the others have moved away, except for a bloke called Eddie Burke. He and his girlfriend got killed when they skidded into an articulated lorry on the M1 about ten years ago.'

'Do your parents still live in the village?'

'No, they're both dead now. They're buried in St Luke's churchyard.'

'Oh, I'm sorry,' said Susan.

'No, that's all right. My dad died nine years ago, and my mum the year after. They were quite old for parents. They were both in their forties when they had me, and I was their only child. About three months after my dad died of cancer, my mum got it too – I reckon it was all the stress. She went downhill pretty quickly. Ten months after burying my dad I was burying my mum. I still live in the house I was born in on Russell Crescent. It's about halfway between here and the church. In fact, you can probably see it from here.'

He stood up and went over to the window. 'Yes, you can. It's the . . . one, two, three . . . sixth one in that row over there.'

'Where?' said Susan, joining him.

They stood, their bodies almost but not quite touching, their heads close enough for her to feel his breath on her hair as he pointed his house out to her. She liked the proximity of him. She even leaned back slightly until she felt the light pressure of his chest against her shoulder blades.

Nevertheless it was she who brought their closeness to an end, ducking back into the room, afraid that if she lingered too long the mood of the moment would change from enjoyment to mutual awkwardness. She sat down and began to nibble at a biscuit. Jack turned from the window.

'What about you?' he asked. 'Are you going to tell me your life story?'

'Not much to tell. Normal, middle-class upbringing in Kent. Did well at school, didn't rebel. Went to university in Canterbury. Got married. Trained to be a nurse. Had child.' She left it there, shrugging as if the rest of it was of no consequence.

'What about your husband?' he asked. 'Did you two get divorced or . . .'

'He died,' she said flatly.

'Oh. Right.'

'He killed himself. Seven years ago. Mollie Boscombe was his relative, not mine. If he'd still been alive, this house would have passed to him.'

He looked as though he felt he ought to respond but couldn't decide exactly what to say. Before he *could* decide, they both heard a noise from downstairs that made them pause and look at each other.

'What was that?' asked Susan.

'I don't know.'

'It sounded like something heavy being dragged across a floor. My God, you don't think someone's stealing something, do you? The front door isn't locked.'

'It's probably just David come back,' Jack said, but he was already making for the door. Susan followed him downstairs, almost running. From the landing that looked down on to the hallway she could see that the front door was closed and that nothing seemed to have been disturbed.

Jack preceded her across the wooden-floored hallway and into the library, which was where the majority of their crates and boxes were stacked.

'Everything seems all right,' he said.

Susan stood by his shoulder and looked around the room. 'No, something's different. That box of books there, look, it's been dragged right across the room and tipped over.' She approached the upended box cautiously, even though it was obvious there was no one else in the library.

'Are you sure it wasn't like this before?' Jack said, looking down at the fan of books that had spilled out over the floor.

'Positive. Someone's definitely been here.'

'I'll go and have a look outside,' he said.

He hurried out of the library. Susan heard his footsteps on the wooden floor of the hallway and then the clunk as he opened the front door. She pulled the box upright and squatted down to gather up the books that had spilled out of it. Her first assumption had been that someone had tried to steal the books, but had found the box too heavy and had perhaps fled when it had fallen over, certain that the noise would alert whoever was in the house. However, it was only as she was neatly re-stacking the books in the box that she was struck by the gaping flaw in her theory. She realised that whoever had moved the box couldn't have been trying to steal it because he, or she, had dragged it not towards the door, but further into the room. She frowned, mystified, then stood up slowly and stared down at the box, as if believing that if she stood there long enough it would reveal its secrets to her.

The silence was broken by the sound of the front door opening and footsteps approaching across the hallway. She turned as Jack reappeared in the doorway, panting slightly.

'I've been all the way round the house, but I didn't see anyone,' he said. 'I'll check all the rooms for you, but . . .' He let the sentence trail off.

'But what?' Susan said.

He looked a little hesitant. 'I was just going to say, maybe there was no one here in the first place.'

'No one here?' Susan exclaimed. 'There must have been. Boxes don't move across rooms by themselves, do they?'

His expressive features were now trying but failing to hide his embarrassment. 'Well . . . odd things have been known to happen in this house from time to time,' he said. 'Things being moved about when there's no one in the room, things being put down in one place and turning up somewhere else.'

Half-amused, half-nervous, Susan said, 'What are you telling me, Jack? That my house is haunted?'

He grinned apologetically. 'Well, I haven't actually *seen* anything.'

'That's not reassuring,' Susan said.

'Sorry,' he replied sheepishly.

She sighed. 'Oh well, better a poltergeist than a burglar, I suppose. Come on, let's go and finish our lunch.'

Chapter Sixteen

Dr Marcus Kerr knew what his colleagues thought of him: dour, unsympathetic, out of touch, incompetent, but to be perfectly frank he couldn't give a damn. Who were they to judge him? He'd delivered babies who were now older than each of them; he was making life and death decisions when they were all still shitting in their nappies. Just because he didn't pander to the hypochondriacs and the malingerers they rated him a liability. They claimed their workload was twice, three times what his was, and that the reason was because people preferred to wait five days to see one of them rather than be added to his rapidly diminishing patient list. But of course what they were still too wet behind the ears to understand was that it was quality, not quantity, that counted. They might put in more hours than he did, but how much of that time was spent writing out prescriptions for placebos, catering to people who had nothing that a couple of days in bed wouldn't cure? Well, his so-called colleagues could say and think what they liked, but he certainly wasn't prepared to give lip service to attention-seekers. And if that meant that the number of blank appointments in his schedule was increasing almost daily, then so be it.

He got out of his car and walked up the path to the door of the house he had shared with his wife, Hilary, until her death early last year. Coming back at lunchtime always brought back memories of that day. On that occasion the door had been unlocked (now, of course, the only person who came in and out was him) and Kerr had entered the house, calling, 'Hilary! Hilary, dear, I'm home!'

He had found her failure to reply a little curious, but had

136

thought she must be out in the garden or talking on the telephone upstairs. He had walked into the kitchen, expecting to see her through the window that looked out on to the back garden, kneeling on her little foam-filled mat, wearing her headscarf and gloves, digging out weeds with a trowel. When there had been no sign of her, he had strode back through the house again, calling, 'Hilary! Hilary!' Surely the silly woman hadn't gone out and left the house unlocked? He had pushed open the partly open door of the lounge and stepped inside, and that was when he saw her.

She had been lying on the settee, her legs dangling over the side so that her toes touched the floor, her arms sticking out before her. Her face had been partly obscured by a cushion, but he had seen at once that her right eye was open and glazed, and he had known from that and from the colour of her skin and from the absolute stillness of her body that she was dead. For a few moments he had simply stood and stared at her, his mind numb, not knowing what to do despite all the years he had spent as a medical practitioner. He had noticed a tray on a little table in front of the settee on which stood a boiled egg in an egg cup, a plate of buttered toast and a cup of tea. Lunch, he had thought, which she had evidently made and never got the chance to eat.

Finally he had walked into the hall, picked up the telephone and dialled the number of Des Brewer, Longbarrow's community policeman. He had felt icily calm, but not quite there, as if there was a barrier between himself and the world. Even as he was dialling, an almost casually precise voice was reminding him that as a doctor he was of course familiar with sudden death, that after forty-three years in general practice he had learned to expect the unexpected. And yet somewhere beneath the strange, calm lassitude that was creeping over him like hypothermia, was a lost soul, full of child-like bewilderment, which wanted to know how Hilary could be dead when he had seen her only that morning, when they had spent two-thirds of their life together, when there were still things left unsaid and undone, when he loved her so much.

'Des Brewer,' a voice had said into his ear, and he had listened to himself talking calmly and precisely, and it had been as if he was listening to somebody else.

Afterwards, he had gone to sit with his wife while he waited for Des to arrive. He had held her lifeless hand, stroked her greying hair, and had even tried to close her eyes, though he knew perfectly well that in real life the eyes of corpses wouldn't stay shut until the undertaker glued the lids to the eyeballs.

Hilary had been sixty-four, a year older than him. The post-mortem revealed that she had died of a brain embolism. She had always been a robust woman, who cultivated friends as successfully as she cultivated plants and flowers in her beloved garden. Her sociability and energy had been the counterpoint to his brooding introspection. Kerr knew that people found him difficult, that they were often uncomfortable in his presence, but that was their problem, not his. It was odd, but when Hilary had been alive he had not felt dependent on her, had been quite happy in his own company, simply knowing that she was around, that she was available to him if he needed her. Now that she was gone, however, he missed her terribly. He felt lost and desperately alone, had spent the last eighteen awful months with the idea that life was barely worth living growing more solid in his head.

He had always enjoyed a snifter, a Scotch or two after work to wind down, but in the last year or so his drinking had been spiralling slowly out of control. Now he was getting through four bottles of Bell's a week, which, coupled with the Valium that he was taking with increasing regularity, had turned his life into something that resembled a waking dream. Not that he thought his physical and mental state interfered with his work. His thoughts might be a little muffled, his judgement not as acute as it once was, but he had been doing this job for almost half a century, and he honestly believed that there was nothing left to learn, that he could drift through each day with his eyes closed if needs be, issuing prescriptions and advice without any danger to his patients.

Indeed, he believed that in many ways the whisky and the Valium were actually making him a *better* doctor than he would otherwise have been at the present time. They took the edge off his pain, dulled the grief and the depression that would have clouded his judgement far more than a few drinks and a few pills. His 'colleagues' at the Longbarrow Medical Centre had hinted to him – *more* than hinted on occasion – that perhaps the time had come for him to start thinking about retiring, that he had *earned* it after so many years of good work serving his community.

Bullshit. They wanted him out, plain and simple. Doubtless they wanted to replace him with some other wide-eyed upstart fresh from medical school, someone who was like the rest of them – high on ideals and enthusiasm, but woefully low on know-how and common sense.

Well, he wouldn't go that easily. His job was all he had left now. He wouldn't have admitted it to anyone but himself, but the prospect of retirement terrified him. If the day ever came when he was forced to give up his post, they might as well take him round the back and put a bullet through his head. He knew what he'd do the minute the retirement party was over, once they'd given him the carriage clock and the golden hand-shake: he'd go straight home and consume all the booze and all the pills that he had in the house. He'd lie on his bed and close his eyes and wait for the nightmare that his life had become to be over.

As he entered the house now, its silence seemed to mock him. Pouring a drink and popping half a Valium had become second nature to him, and that was what he walked through to the kitchen and did now, washing the pill down with Bell's that he diluted with a splash of tap water. He gulped the watered-down drink as though it was Ribena, then poured himself another, this one neat. He used to suck peppermints to hide the smell of the whisky on his breath when he went back to the surgery in the afternoon, but now he didn't even bother doing that.

He stood at the kitchen sink, sipping his drink, and looked out at the back garden. It was in a sorry state, the grass – brown and withered now after weeks of endless sunshine – desperately in need of a water and a cut. The weeds were rampant, the flowers overblown through lack of pruning, the raspberries spoiling, having remained unpicked. If Hilary could see it, she would have a fit; she had always tended her garden so lovingly. He had tried to keep up with it for a while, but every moment he had spent out there had reminded him of his loss and made him feel wretched – not that he didn't feel wretched now, seeing all her hard work reverting to the chaos it had been when they had first moved in, so many years ago.

A floorboard creaked above his head and he glanced up at

the ceiling. The thought that jumped into his mind seemed natural, instinctive: *Hilary moving about in the bedroom.* Almost immediately he realised his foolishness. But if it wasn't Hilary (which of course it wasn't) then who was it?

An intruder, he thought, the thrill of fear permeating the muzzy web that tranquillisers and alcohol had woven around him. One creak might have been explained away as the timbers of the old house expanding in the midday heat, but the sounds were continuing, and moreover they seemed both furtive and purposeful. He couldn't think of them as anything other than footsteps crossing the room above his head, that being the bedroom he had shared with Hilary, containing the big double bed that these days seemed too often like the vast beach of an island on which he had become marooned.

He tilted his head back and threw the rest of his drink down his throat, then hurried through into the hallway. Already tension was making him gasp for breath, his heart and lungs struggling to do the work required. Ever since the heat wave had begun some six or seven weeks ago, he had sweated day and night, but now it was pouring off him – darkening his grey hair and running down his face, glueing his shirt to his back, making his balls itch.

A weapon. He needed a weapon. He stepped into the lounge, looking around so wildly that droplets of sweat flew from his hair, speckling the furniture. There by the fire, the companion set. He grabbed at the poker, his hand clumsy, setting the whole thing jangling. Blinking to clear his head, grinding his teeth together as if that could lessen the din of clanging metal, he lurched from the room, the poker slippery in his sweaty grip. The sounds from upstairs had stopped. Maybe the intruder had heard the result of his fumbled attempt to procure a weapon and was now lying in wait for him. Kerr was frightened, but there was actually a part of him that welcomed this, a part of him that believed he might well be heading towards something like destiny.

He began to climb the stairs, aware of how heavy and old his body was, of his breath like a small, struggling animal trapped in the cavity of his chest. He had to stop halfway up because his heart was beating too fast. He swopped the poker from his right hand to his left, then delved into his pocket and produced a brown and white handkerchief which he used to swab the sweat from his face. He listened, but could hear nothing from the landing above. Once his heart had steadied to something like an acceptable rate, he resumed his ascent.

At the top of the stairs he stopped to listen again, but all was silence. He began to creep towards the bedroom door which was very slightly ajar. He winced as a floorboard creaked beneath him, and almost stumbled as he sought to shift his weight to his other foot. Instinctively he put out his left hand to steady himself and the poker clutched in it clunked against the wall.

Oh, well done, Marcus, he told himself bitterly. For God's sake, man, you bloody well *deserve* to get your brains bashed out. Deciding that the cautious approach was pointless now, he moved the poker back to his right hand and hefted it, then marched up to the bedroom door and shoved it open. As the door swung away from him he braced himself, expecting some bulky, snarling figure wielding a knife or a baseball bat to fly at him.

Nothing happened, except that the door reached to the extent of its hinges and began swinging back towards him. Kerr put out a hand to stop it, then stepped quickly into the room. It was a square room, the dressing table against the wall to his right, the bed against the left one, stretching almost halfway into the room. The long window, made up of sixteen panes, looked down on the back garden, dominating the wall opposite.

There were two places to hide – under the bed or in the big wardrobe that stood further along the same wall as the door. For the moment, however, Kerr forgot all about the potential danger from an intruder, his body jolting with cold shock at what was on the bed.

There, laid out lovingly, as if someone had been about to put it on but didn't want it creased in the meantime, was Hilary's wedding dress.

Kerr's heart began to pump twice as fast as before, further pulses jumping to life in his stomach and throat and temples. His legs started to tremble as if about to collapse beneath the weight of his body. Seeing the dress his wife had married him in spread out before him like this was more distressing than anything else he could think of.

How long he stood and stared at the dress he wasn't sure.

141

The shaken, sick dismay inside him was cutting right through the fug that stuffed his senses and blunted his emotions. Who had laid the dress out like this? And for what purpose? To steal it? He couldn't conceive of an act more cruel. The sheer callousness of it overwhelmed him.

Eventually he sank to his knees and looked under the bed. If there *had* been somebody there he doubted whether he would have had much energy to fend them off. However, there was nothing but a few dustballs and an old paperback propped like a miniature tent.

He rose to his feet with difficulty, trudged to the wardrobe and opened it, not even bothering to raise the poker in defence. He was almost surprised to find the wardrobe full of nothing but clothes, for it was obvious that *someone* had been here. He certainly hadn't removed his wife's wedding dress from the tissue-lined box in which it had resided for God knew how many years and laid it out on the bed like a suit he intended to wear to a conference. Whoever had done it must be in another part of the house, or had found an escape route. He glanced up and saw the box the dress had been in was still there on top of the wardrobe, in its usual place. How many years might have passed before he even discovered the theft? Perhaps he might never have discovered it.

As he closed the wardrobe door, he glimpsed movement out of the corner of his eye, over near the dressing table. He swung round, his hand instinctively tightening on the poker. For a split-second, but so clearly that he felt it couldn't possibly be his imagination, he saw Hilary reflected in the dressing-table mirror.

She was wearing dark clothes, though the image was too brief to ascertain exactly what colour or style. Her reflection moved from the left to the right of the mirror as if she had been walking past the end of the bed. Although she was visible for no more than a second, the image of her fine, strong-jawed face, large eyes and dark eyebrows flared in his mind like a match dropped into a box of fireworks, sending rockets of recognition whizzing through his head. His awe and excitement were the sparks cascading from the tails of the rockets, fizzing and burning through the rest of his body.

Kerr shambled towards the mirror as if it was a doorway, half-believing that if he was quick enough he might just be able to catch hold of Hilary's sleeve, speak to her. He all but collapsed on top of the dressing table, peering greedily into the lozenge-shaped mirror. His own wild-eyed, crimson, greasy-skinned face goggled back at him; he looked as though he was being strangled or suffering a heart attack. 'Hilary,' he croaked, 'Hilary, where are you?' There was no reply, and no sign of the image he had seen just a few seconds before. Bereaved patients had often told him of glimpsing their loved ones again – walking up the path to the front door, standing at the top of the stairs, stepping out of a room via another door just as they stepped in. Kerr had always glibly put such sightings down to delusional wish-fulfillment, but this hadn't been like that, this had been *real*.

He turned frustratedly from the mirror. Perhaps the dress was a sign. Yes, that must be it! The dress was her way of telling him that she was okay and watching over him. He staggered over to the bed, reached out and placed a trembling hand on the dress she had worn on their wedding day over forty years ago. The lace was dry and oddly cold, like the skin of a reptile; it rustled beneath his touch.

Gently, so gently, he began to stroke it, and as he did so he whispered his wife's name over and over.

Chapter Seventeen

All the way home on the bus, Jason Sheridan expected a hand to come down on his shoulder. Not that he'd done anything wrong. People didn't understand, that was all; they didn't know that all he wanted to do was play games with the children, not hurt them like Dad had hurt him. He wanted to teach them, wanted them to enjoy the games as much as he would. He knew he was bigger and stronger than them, but he wouldn't make them do things that they didn't want to do, not like Dad had made *him* do things.

Sometimes, when Dad had come into his room at night and made him do those things, Jason had thought he was going to die. He had thought that Dad's hairy, smelly, heavy flesh was going to suffocate him, or that when Dad made him kneel on the floor and bend over, he was going to be split in half. Although he knew what it was that Dad was really sticking up him, it felt like a sword, cutting him up inside, making him bleed. He had tried not to cry and scream and beg because that had only made Dad angry, and when Dad was angry he hit him, and he could hit far harder than any of the boys at school.

If people saw the magazines that Jason had been all the way to Leeds to buy that morning they would say he was as bad as Dad, but he wasn't, no way. He wasn't a pervert or a paedophile, even though they were the sort of people he had to see to get the stuff he wanted. But all Jason *really* wanted was someone to love, someone to play games with, someone to protect. But he wanted someone pure, someone who wouldn't laugh at him and make nasty, clever remarks that he didn't understand. All the girls his age were like that: dirty, nasty slags, like Mum.

They'd ask him to do things he didn't want to do, and when he said no they'd call him names and be horrible to him and spread stories about him among their friends and treat him like he was shit.

Like Kim Ellis. She'd done that to him. She'd got him into really bad trouble because she'd made him so angry by telling everyone he hadn't been able to get it up that he hadn't been able to stop hitting and kicking her. That had been in the school playground, before he left last year. In the end some teachers and some other kids had jumped on him and held him down on the floor so that he couldn't move. Then Des Brewer had come in his dark blue uniform and taken him away, and afterwards Jason had been made to go and see a whatchamacallit, a psychiatrist, who had got him all confused by asking him too many questions. He had thought he was going to be locked up, which would have been even worse than being at home with Dad, even though when Dad had found out about Kim Ellis he had kicked Jason so many times in the head that Jason had blacked out. Not that Dad was punishing him for hurting Kim, he didn't give a toss about that. It was because, thanks to Jason, Des Brewer had found out about Dad selling pirate videos.

The psychiatrist had shown Jason pictures of Kim Ellis in hospital and had kept asking him why he had done it, but Jason didn't think he had hurt her *that* much. He hadn't been able to tell it was her from the photos – and maybe it wasn't, maybe they were trying to trick him. Were you trying to kill her, the psychiatrist kept asking, and Jason said no he wasn't, he just wanted to make her shut up. Was it neccessary to fracture her skull and break her jaw and damage her vertebrae and scar her so badly that she would need plastic surgery, the psychiatrist had asked in that calm voice of hers, staring at him all the time, and Jason had got scared and had said I didn't do that, you can't make me say I did that, I only hurt her a little bit.

Anyway. All that was a long time ago now. In the end he had had to do some work with some other boys, painting an old people's home, and that had been all right, the other boys had mostly laughed when he had told them about Kim Ellis, had said good on you, mate, that's the way to fucking treat them, keep them in their fucking place a good kicking will.

Now Jason spent his days signing on and trying to keep out of Mum and Dad's way. Sometimes he mucked around with Gary Sissons and that lot, sometimes he went into Leeds on the bus, sometimes he went fishing up by the river, and sometimes he just wandered about, not doing much but content enough just to be on his own and not to have to think about anything or to be told what to do by anyone.

And there was one other thing he did, of course, and that was talk to the children. He went where he knew they'd be, like the playground up by the community centre, but sometimes it was hard to talk to them there and he had to be careful because a lot of them were with their mums or dads, and he'd get funny looks and he'd have to leave before the grown-ups asked him what he was doing.

Other places he went were the fields behind some of the houses, where a lot of kids played, especially in the summer. There were loads of fields in and around Longbarrow, but there was one in particular, behind Roslyn Street, that he went to a lot. The reason for this was that Cassie Herron played there with her friends. Cassie had hair so blonde it was almost white, and big blue eyes, and she was so pretty, and her skin looked so smooth, and she smelt so nice, so clean and fresh. Whenever she saw Jason she would smile and wave, as if she was *so* glad to see him.

Cassie was six years old, and Jason was in love with her.

One day soon he hoped to be able to get Cassie to come into the woods with him, and he hoped that she would come on her own and not with her friends. He knew she liked him and he liked her, so there wouldn't be any harm in it, would there? A sort of thrill went through him when he thought of the games they would play together. He'd be so gentle, and she would like it, he knew she would. The thrill, which was like a warm, lovely shiver inside him, went down between his legs and made him so hard that he ached. He laid his magazines, which were wrapped in a Sainsbury's bag and Sellotaped all over so that they wouldn't slip out, over his lap, and leaned forward, pressing his thighs together around his stiff, hot cock, half-closing his eyes.

He could feel his face getting as red and as hot as his cock. He was glad there weren't many people on the bus, just a couple of old biddies and a fat bloke with a moustache and a shaved head who had been staring out of the window the whole time. Every time the bus jolted over a bump, Jason's balls were ground against the hard, smooth leather seat and he had to stop himself crying out in pleasure and pain.

No, he thought, I'm not going to do it here, even though he quite liked the idea of walking around with his mess drying inside his undies and no one knowing anything about it. But no, what he'd do was go into the woods with his magazines and do it there, taking his time and wishing that Cassie was with him.

Ten minutes later the bus pulled up by the war memorial and Jason got out, walking gingerly because his cock was still hard and hot in his pants. Carrying the magazines around, even though nobody could see what they were inside the plastic bag, made him nervous. Silently he practised what he'd say if the magazines were discovered: *I found them on the bus. I was going to give them to Mr Brewer*. It sounded good in his head, but would it sound good in real life? Anyway, what would really piss him off would be having to hand the mags over before he'd even had a chance to look at them, especially as they'd cost him all his dole money.

He started off up the street, walking quickly, anxious to get to the woods, when who should walk round the corner but Des Brewer! Jason stopped dead as a variety of possible courses of action raced through his mind. Should he turn and run in the other direction? Should he try and stuff the magazines up his T-shirt and hope Brewer wouldn't notice? Should he just hand them over and say excuse me, Mr Brewer, but I found these on the bus?

In the end he did none of these things. He just stood there as if he couldn't move and watched Brewer getting closer and closer.

'Afternoon, Jason, lad,' Brewer said, nodding to him.

Jason thought he said Afternoon back, but he wasn't sure because the blood was pounding in his ears.

'You all right, son?'

Jason nodded. He felt certain that Brewer was toying with him, that somehow he knew what the magazines were, even though he couldn't see through the plastic.

'Have you been out all day, son?'

Jason nodded again.

'Where have you been?'

'Nowhere,' Jason said quickly.

Brewer frowned. 'But you haven't been home?'

Jason shook his head.

'Right. Well, I think perhaps you'd better get off home, son. Your mum might have something to tell you.'

Jason narrowed his eyes. What game was Brewer playing now? Did he want to expose him in front of Mum and Dad, show them the magazines and tell them their son was a pervert?

'What – now?' he said.

Brewer nodded. 'It might be a good idea.'

Jason took a step back. 'So can I go then?'

Brewer looked perplexed. 'Course you can, son. Unless you've got something to tell me, that is.'

'Like what?' Jason said, trying not to panic.

Brewer looked half-amused, half-irritated. 'Look, son, I was only joking. Just get off home, will you?'

'Right,' Jason said, and turned and fled before Brewer could change his mind. As he ran, leaving the policeman behind him, he grinned, victorious and relieved. He wasn't sure how, but somehow he'd outwitted Brewer. If the policeman thought he could catch Jason out by arriving at his house before him he was very much mistaken. Jason *would* go home eventually, but not before he had hidden the evidence in the woods where Brewer would never find it.

Chapter Eighteen

Bloody barmy family, Des Brewer thought, watching the boy running up the street with that ungainly, stork-legged stride of his. The kid was as crazy as his dad in his own way, crazier perhaps, for his dad was simply a thug, a troublemaker – dangerous, certainly, but predictable.

The lad, though, he was something different. A loner, a social inadequate, not as volatile as his dad but capable nonetheless of quite shocking acts of violence. Brewer still couldn't look at him without thinking of what he had done to that young girl last year. People who'd witnessed the attack had said he'd been like a machine, using the girl's head like a football, punting her in the face even when it was obvious she was unconscious. The girl had spent the last year having reconstructive surgery. It had been a nightmare for her, agonising and traumatic. And what punishment had the boy been given? One hundred hours of community service. It was pathetic, and, for Brewer, bloody frustrating. The boy's defence had claimed he was 'mercilessly provoked' and the judge had believed him.

As for the mother, Brewer had been in the same year as her at school, and even then she had been the local bike, giving a ride to anyone that asked. Mind you, that didn't neccessarily make her a bad person, and Brewer couldn't help feeling sorry for her, even if she had made her own bed to lie in, so to speak. She had certainly been civil enough to him when he had gone round to tell her about the incident at the Druid's Arms that lunchtime, and about Ted being taken away for questioning by the boys from Ripon that Des had had to call in to help him sort out the trouble. The place had been in a right mess when he had got there, as had the landlord, Trevor Paine, whom Ted had glassed in the face. Fortunately, once he had been cleaned up, Trevor's injuries weren't as bad as they had first appeared. His cuts were mostly superficial, though he had got some glass in his eyes, which he had had to go to the medical centre to have removed. He had been given some eye drops and told by the doctor that although his eyes would be unbearably irritating for a few days, he was to avoid rubbing them.

Des was a reasonable, fair-minded man – sometimes *too* reasonable, according to friends and colleagues who worked in the bigger town and city nicks, and who often informed him frankly that his outdated softly-softly approach would cut no ice whatsoever in today's inner-city climate – but he really hoped the law would come down hard on Sheridan this time. He'd had warnings and fines and even minimal prison sentences in the past, but none of it had made the slightest difference to the way he behaved. What Sheridan needed, in Des's opinion, was a year or two inside. Even if that didn't change him, at least it would get him out of the way for a while.

Talking of happy families . . . Des glanced at his watch. It was almost 4:50. He'd told Alison he'd try to be back by five, but he had to admit to himself (with a certain amount of shame) he didn't relish the prospect of going home just yet. He loved Alison, but she had not been the easiest person to live with since the birth of their son, Zack, ten months ago. In fact, that was an understatement: she had been unbearable. Not that it was her fault, and he had *tried* to be understanding, but it was hard not to react when someone was screaming at you, undermining you, telling you you didn't care, didn't understand.

She had been to see Dr Strang a number of times, had consulted the local midwife and health visitor, but none of what they had offered seemed to help. Des's mum kept an eye on Alison and Zack as much as she could when Des was at work, but she had received the sharp edge of Alison's tongue on occasion, and so didn't go round as often as she and Des would have liked, for fear of being accused of interfering. Alison's own parents lived in Northumberland, and only got down to see them once in a blue moon. Every time they came, Alison made a real effort to be positive and cheerful and capable, giving them the warped impression that their daughter was a model mum.

Not that Des believed Alison would ever be capable of hurting Zack. If he thought that, he'd never leave the two of them alone together. However, he did know that she found Zack increasingly difficult to cope with, especially now that he had started to crawl. And whereas initially Des had tried to help as much as he could – playing with Zack, feeding him, bathing him, putting him to bed – he now kept out of the way as much as possible, honestly believing that his presence only exacerbated Alison's feelings of inadequacy, which all too often manifested themselves as rage and self-loathing.

If he left his wife alone, then eventually she'd work her way through this, had therefore become his recent philosophy. How sound that philosophy was he had no idea, but it was one born of desperation rather than logic, and at least it meant (as far as he could see) that the longer he stayed out of the house, the less opportunity Alison had to reduce it to a war zone. Thus justified, though still unable to fully assuage the guilt he felt, Des turned and headed in the direction of the White Hart. Didn't he deserve a pint or two after the day he had just had? Not to mention a drop of Dutch courage for what would inevitably be waiting for him when he got home?

Chapter Nineteen

Even during a summer as hot as this, Joan Dyer felt the cold in her bones these days. There was nothing in this world for her now; her friends were nearly all gone, her good times long past. And she was frightened. Not for herself, because since her dreams had stopped, as if used up over too many years, she spent every night practising for the death that she knew could no longer be far away. No, it was something else that frightened her. Something terrible and devastating. Something that she sensed even now was moving inexorably towards Longbarrow, casting its shadow before it like a vast black net.

In the past, her precognitions, visions, call them what you will, had been clear, specific, like visual and aural radio signals beamed directly into her head. Sometimes the visions had been upsetting, even frightening, but nothing in the past had prepared her for what had been happening recently. The signals she had been receiving were no longer specific but cacophonous, as though not one but a thousand radio and TV channels were being beamed into her mind at once. Afterwards she would be left shaking with terror, so profoundly affected by the ordeal that she would be unable to speak, barely even able to breathe. She was never able to define exactly what she had experienced, was merely left with the impression that something destructive and vile and sickeningly evil had wormed its way into her brain, allowing her a glimpse of itself. All she knew for sure was that whatever this thing was, it was getting closer and more powerful with each day that passed.

She had tried to warn Brian and Sheila, urging them to pack their bags and get out of Longbarrow before it was too late, but even she knew how she sounded – like a hysterical old woman who was rapidly losing her marbles. Brian, her son, who was as calm and steadfast as his father had been (as was the son he and Sheila had produced in turn), had listened intently, but in the end had done little more than humour her.

'We can't just up and leave, Mam,' he had said calmly. 'We've got our jobs and the house, and Colin starts back at school in a few weeks. I mean, where would we go?'

'*Where* you go doesn't matter,' she said. 'As long as you get away from here.'

'But, I mean, when's this . . . whatever it is going to happen?'

'I don't know. I don't know anything except that it *is* going to happen, and that when it does it'll affect everyone in this village.'

He looked at her, his face troubled. 'Yes, but . . . can't you describe what this feeling's like? I mean . . . when you've had these feelings in the past, Mam, you've always known straight away what they're all about.'

She shook her head and clasped her cold, stiff hands together. 'It's different this time. I've never felt anything like this before. The way it makes me feel, it's as if . . . as if I'm looking down a crack in the earth, straight into hell.'

He balked a little at that, and then tried to smile and make a joke of it. 'Nothing can be that bad.'

'It is, Brian, it is! Just listen to me, will you! Do what I say.'

He looked concerned then, though not, she suspected, so much by what she had said but by what he perceived to be the state of her mental health. She sighed, and though she had never been a physically demonstrative woman, she took his hand, surprising him.

'I'm not going senile just yet, you know, Brian,' she said wearily.

'I know that, Mam,' he replied, but looked embarrassed all the same.

Joan knew how she was regarded in the village, knew that anyone describing her would have the words 'battle-axe' and 'matriarch' never very far from their lips. *She's got a quick mind and a razor-sharp tongue*, they'd say, *and she rules that Dyer family with a rod of iron.*

Yes, well . . . that was then and this is now. The truth of the matter was, she was a frail old woman, frightened for her

153

family and for the village where she had lived all her life. She had spent nine decades on this earth and never had she sensed the presence of such evil. But how to put that into words without making it sound like the kind of doom-laden ranting that old Jonas usually came out with?

Gripping his hand even tighter, as if to prevent him pulling away, she said, 'You've always trusted my instincts before, haven't you, Brian? I've never let you down?'

'Course I have,' Brian said, looking unhappy.

'Well, trust them now. Take Colin and Sheila and leave this place. There are . . . there are *forces* gathering here. Something very bad is on its way. I *feel* it.'

He looked at her for a long time then, his face expressionless, but his blue eyes earnest, intent, thoughtful. For a few moments it seemed as if he was actually considering her words. Then, softly, placatingly, he said, 'That's as may be, Mam, but we can't just leave. This is our home. If something is coming, like you say, then we'll face it together.'

And that had been that. Despite his solid, serene nature, Brian could be stubborn when he wanted to be, a trait he had inherited from her. All she could do now was sit and wait and hope that she had been mistaken, that her age was making her confused, causing her to panic needlessly, though she knew in her heart of hearts that that was not the case.

And yet, on a day like today, which was merely the latest of a seemingly endless succession of identical days, she could almost convince herself that nothing *was* going to happen. The sun was shining, the birds were singing, the flowers were blooming, and the sky was of such a creamy rich blue that it made you want to taste it.

She was sitting in her accustomed place, in the squashy green armchair by the unlit fire, staring down at the white ash through the grate, which was the residue of the final fire of last winter, well over four months ago now. That ash would not be cleaned out until October or November, at least – if those months ever came around again, she couldn't help thinking. She was doing what she did a great deal of these days, which was nothing at all – or rather, simply waiting, marking time. She had books and magazines to read, a television to watch, a radio to listen to, but she rarely availed herself of these facilities, regarding them not so much as distractions these days, but irritations, as pointless as watching the fat black houseflies, which were everywhere this summer, bumping their bristly bodies against the windows. Even chanelling her thoughts seemed like too much of an effort, and so she merely allowed her mind to wander aimlessly, sometimes drifting into an almost trance-like state in which her whole being seemed to revert to a blank, white page, uncluttered by the cramped and messy scribblings of life. She often wished she could remain in this state for ever, had decided that if death was at all comparable to it, then she would welcome it eagerly when the time came. There was always something that dragged her back to the physical plane, however – the discomfort of old bones, fused into one position for too long, the ever-present dread which her visions had left behind, like silt that ground constantly in her gut.

Today, she was on the verge of slipping into this state of mind when she was jolted back by the slamming of a door. Her scrawny hands, the flesh so dry and wrinkled around the prominent metacarpals that it looked as though it could tear apart like wet paper, jerked in her lap. She was wearing a black, knitted shawl, which she tugged tighter around her shoulders in response to a chill breeze, whether real or imaginary, that sniffed her out like a dog looking for bones.

She looked up just as her grandson, Colin, plodded into the room.

'Hi, Gran,' he said, and then concern crept into his voice. 'Are you all right?'

She stared at him in horror. The vision was terrifying. His features, though visible, were like gossamer, so faint that they appeared transparent. Through them she could clearly see his skull, the teeth stretching round the jaw in a tombstone-grin, the eye sockets forming panda-rings around his indistinct eyes.

However, this wasn't the worst of her vision. What was truly terrifying was that he was beset by fluttering, ghost-like shapes, too fast-moving and formless to be recognisable as birds or moths, though nevertheless akin to both. They appeared to be hatching from his body, pushing their way out of his eye sockets and through the filmy substancelessness of his face. They spun round his head, jerky and white, like scratches on old film. Some even seemed to cling to him like bats, twitching minutely as if feeding, though even these seemed somehow to defy the eye.

He spoke again, her horror making his voice seem blurred, dragging. 'Gran, what's the matter?'

She had seen these images before, many times, though never in such profusion. She had seen them hovering above the heads of people for whom death was very close. They were harbingers of death, though whether they appeared in readiness to accompany the soul to a better place or as vultures circling to feed, she had no idea. Certainly, she had never seen them actually hatching from a person before, and she couldn't rid herself of the impression that her grandson was some kind of incubator or walking plague, growing spores of death and expelling them into the air.

Mercifully, the vision was brief, and after a few seconds began to fade. The fluttering white shapes dispersed like steam; the skull sank back beneath the skin as Colin's eyes brightened and his flesh acquired its customary healthy glow.

The experience had left her profoundly shaken, however. Her hands trembled in her lap and she had to clench her jaw to prevent her old, yellow teeth from chattering.

Colin looked cautious now, his eyes narrowing in concern. He was used to his gran acting strangely, though he had never seen her so terrified before.

'Gran,' he said again, 'what's wrong? What can you see?'

She tried to speak. Her voice, usually so imperious, albeit a little rusty these days, emerged faint and high-pitched and quivering.

'Where have you been, Colin? What have you been doing?' she demanded.

He looked puzzled. 'What do you mean?'

'Just tell me, Colin!' she said, her voice shrill, cracking.

Colin was like his father – thoughtful, imperturbable. His only reaction to her disturbing, semi-hysterical behaviour was to frown and purse his lips.

'Nothing,' he said, 'just mucking about. Me and Chris met that new kid who's moved into the big house, and we took him into the woods and showed him our den.'

'A new boy?' she said. 'What's his name?'

'David Wisher. Him and his mum have come up from London to live here. He talks a bit like they do in *EastEnders*, but he's all right. He's got a brilliant skateboard, and he says we can go into the big house to look for ghosts.'

Could this be it, the key to her recent disturbing episodes? She reached out towards Colin and he came forward and took her hands. She felt a faint buzz, like a minor electrical charge, from his flesh, but that was all.

'Colin, I want you to stay away from that boy and his house,' she said.

His frown returned. 'Why?'

'Because something . . . something *bad* is going to happen in Longbarrow, and I think that boy might have something to do with it.'

'But there's nothing wrong with him,' said Colin. 'He's all right.'

'That's as may be. But that house acts as a focal point for the energy in this village, and whoever lives there can't help but be touched by it. Do you understand me?'

For a moment he just looked at her, his lips pressed together. 'Does that mean I can't go looking for ghosts?' he said at last.

She shuddered. 'No. Promise me, Colin, that you won't go anywhere near that place. Promise me!'

His silence was longer this time. Finally he said, 'But David's my friend, Gran. Chris wants to go to the house and the others will too. I can't stop David from mucking around with us, can I?'

She gripped his hands tighter as if she was prepared to hold him there by force if needs be. 'I don't care what the others want. I only care about you. I know it's hard, Colin, but I wouldn't ask if it wasn't important. Now promise me, please.'

He said nothing.

Chapter Twenty

David felt great, better than he'd felt in ages, better perhaps than he'd *ever* felt. It was weird, but when he and Mum had left Longbarrow after the first and only time they'd been to look round the house before moving in, he had felt a real sense of loss, a yearning to come back as soon as possible. The next two and a bit weeks in London had dragged. He'd never enjoyed the summer holidays less, though at least he'd been able to enjoy the novelty of breathing with lungs that didn't feel like a couple of Hoover bags stuffed with dust. Mr Toot's cure, if it could be called that, had worked instantly, and appeared to be permanent. David had thought the pollution in London and then the dust in their new house might set his asthma off again, but he had been fine.

What he had also found surprising was that leaving London had not been a wrench at all. He'd rung round those friends that he was unlikely to see before he went, to tell them he was moving to Yorkshire, and had even promised to write to a select few, yet the pang of actually leaving them behind, knowing that most of them he'd probably lose touch with and never see again, had been swamped by the sheer excitement of returning to Longbarrow.

It was an excitement he couldn't altogether explain, a more extreme and positive emotion than the nervous anticipation he might ordinarily have expected to feel. It sounded silly, but it was as though Longbarrow was drawing him towards itself, as though his heart belonged there now and he wouldn't feel complete until he went back.

Although she didn't say so, David felt sure Mum felt that way too. She and Beth, who had come to see them off, had cried in each other's arms before he and Mum had set off in the car, waving furiously. However, as soon as they got off the M25 and started heading north, Mum had turned to him with a radiant grin. 'I'm so happy, Davey,' she had said. 'This is the best thing we've ever done.'

Nothing had happened in the first four days to sour what David couldn't help thinking of as their homecoming. They had been cleaning the house, and he had been decorating his room, and his mum had been on the phone, making arrangements for this and that. And even though he had done nothing but work, and had seen no one but Mum over the weekend, he had remained as deeply content as he could ever remember.

On Friday morning, he and Mum had ventured into the cellar, armed with strong flashlights. He had taken the lead, and although he hadn't actually been scared, he had been unable to get the image from his dream out of his mind.

The place had been something of a disappointment. More cell than cellar, it was small and square, stone-walled and concrete-floored. All it contained was a rickety wooden wine-rack, festooned with cobwebs, and a pile of cardboard boxes, soft with damp. From the low ceiling hung a bare light bulb, similarly hammocked in cobwebs, on a dust-furred length of flex.

Mum had unscrewed the old bulb, cobwebs trailing from her fingers, and screwed the new one in. She tried the switch, exclaiming, '*Voilà*!' as the place flooded with light. Despite the heat of the day it was cool in the cellar. 'They must have used it to store food before they had fridges,' Mum said. Looking around, it seemed as though the cellar hadn't been used for anything for a long time. They had trudged back upstairs, turning out the light as they went, and hadn't gone back since.

On Sunday, as a break from decorating his room, David had gone out for an hour to explore their grounds, strolling between oaks that dripped sunlight on him, but today had been the first time he had gone outside the high walls topped with broken glass that surrounded the house. He had crouched low on his skateboard as the road took him on a gentle down-hill curve into the village, and for half an hour he had simply wandered around the shops, enjoying the unhurried pace of life.

Ever since returning to Longbarrow, he had felt as sharp and clear-minded as he had the first time he had come here. It was as if he had been cleansed of all the impurities that had clogged his mind and body in London. Colours seemed more vibrant, objects more defined, smells more piquant, sounds crisper. When he woke in the morning, he felt fresh and instantly alert; when he went to bed at night, he fell into a deep and refreshing sleep the second he closed his eyes. Even the way he moved and breathed and spoke felt different here, somehow more . . . purposeful. He had been enjoying this new-found zest, his senses soaking up the sights and sounds and smells around him, when Chris and Colin had come skidding up behind him on their bikes.

David had jumped, but had not been exactly scared; if it had been London, he would have tensed instantly, expecting trouble, but here he had merely been wary, and more than a little curious. As it turned out, he, Chris and Colin had instantly hit it off. They had shown him their den in the woods, and told him all about the Barrow Boys, and by the time Colin announced that he ought to be getting home for his tea, the three of them were laughing and joking as if they had known each other for years.

'I go this way,' Chris said, leaping off his bike at the lych-gate that led into St Luke's churchyard and twitching a hand towards the church.

'Sleep in a coffin, do you? That makes sense,' said David, grinning.

Chris grinned too. 'Up yours, Cockney. No, my dad's the vicar here. We live in the house at the bottom.'

'Oh, I've met your dad,' said David.

'Yeah, I know, he told me. You were interested in the witch-craft eye.'

David nodded. 'So does that mean you're religious then, if your dad's the vicar? You believe in God and all that?'

Chris squinted and shrugged, looking a little embarrassed. 'I suppose so. But I'm not mad on it like my dad is. I'm not going to be a vicar like him when I grow up.'

'What are you going to be then?' asked David.

'A ghost-hunter. And a scientist. I watched this thing on the telly about scientists doing research on this age gene in the body. They reckon in about twenty or thirty years' time we'll be able to live until we're about a hundred and fifty, but I want to find a way to live for ever.'

'Yeah, but the earth'd get too crowded,' said David. 'Everybody'd be starving.'

'We'd all be going off in spaceships to colonise other planets by then,' said Chris airily, 'and there'd be massive space stations orbiting the earth like in *Babylon 5*. Anyway, see you tomorrow.'

He wheeled his bike through the gate and up the path towards the church. David, who was standing with one foot on his skateboard, raised a hand. 'Yeah, see you.'

Chris turned back, the sun glinting on his spectacles, and called gleefully, 'And don't forget – it's your initiation into the Barrow Boys tomorrow.'

David waved a hand nonchalantly. 'No problemo.'

'Ha, ha, we'll see, Cockney. We don't just let any old wuss into the Barrow Boys, you know.'

'How did you get in then?' David shouted.

Cackling loudly, Chris flipped him the finger, then wheeled his bike round the side of the church, disappearing from view. Smiling, David used his foot to turn his skateboard back to face the way he had come, not exactly relishing the uphill trudge home.

And recoiled with a cry as a living scarecrow loomed over him, arms outstretched.

The scarecrow was too close to retreat from. It stretched out a hand that seemed made of long twigs and clamped it around David's left forearm. As David struggled to get away, the scarecrow leaned closer, leering into his face. It had a mass of dark, wild hair and a bushy, tangled beard that was full of burrs and dried grass and clots of congealed food. Its teeth were brown, and its face and arms and hands so ingrained with dirt that its spindly frame seemed wrapped in wood rather than skin.

David tried not to breathe as the thing breathed on him. It stank like a combination of rancid cheese and rotting vegetables. Perversely it was wearing a pink Hawaiian shirt riotous with yellow and green palm trees, though its stained and shapeless trousers, by contrast, seemed fashioned from sackcloth. On its filthy feet were open-toed sandals, toenails jutting from the ends like splintered chips of yellow bone.

161

'The Behemoth above and the Leviathan below,' the scarecrow hissed at him. 'You know this, don't you, boy? You are the Leviathan.'

'Let *go* of me,' David said, trying to tug his arm from the scarecrow's vice-like grip. To gain more leverage on the pavement, he kicked his skateboard away. It clattered into the gutter.

'The bringer of the dark and the provider of the light. Two in one. The divided circle. You know this, boy, don't you?'

'Let go of me, you nutter,' David repeated, more desperately this time, and then, raising his voice, 'Help! Help! Someone help!'

The scarecrow seemed unmoved by his pleas. 'If you don't know about the beasts, then I need to tell you,' it said reasonably.

Still struggling, David said, 'Go and tell someone else.' He aimed a kick at the scarecrow's spindly legs.

The scarecrow sidestepped his flailing kick easily. Its sludgy eyes were red-rimmed, intense, whites showing all the way round the pupils. 'You are the Leviathan,' it repeated, almost gently this time.

'No, I'm not,' David said. He tried to prise up the scarecrow's claw fingers with his right hand.

'Jonas,' said a soft voice behind David.

Immediately the scarecrow looked up. At the same moment, David stopped struggling, twisting his head to look over his shoulder.

Mr Toot was standing there, having apparently appeared from nowhere. The sun was gleaming on his bald head. He was smiling serenely.

He strolled forward to stand beside David. 'Good afternoon, David,' he said. 'How are you settling in?'

Taken aback by the question, David could only stammer, 'Fine . . . er . . . fine, yes . . . thanks.'

'Splendid,' Mr Toot said. Then without warning he reached out and placed a hand on the scarecrow's forehead, like a mother gauging a child's temperature. He leaned forward until his mouth was close to where David guessed the scarecrow's ear would be, lost amid its surrounding forest of hair. 'Gently sings the serpent, Jonas,' Mr Toot murmured.

At once the scarecrow's eyes widened and a look of

understanding crossed his face. He released David immediately, leaving white fingerprints on his arm. 'Sorry,' he mumbled.

David was so bewildered that he could only reply, 'Er . . . that's okay.'

Without another word the scarecrow turned and loped away. David and Mr Toot watched him go. Mr Toot, David noted, had an expression of something like affection on his face.

'Who was that?' David asked when the scarecrow was out of earshot.

'That was Jonas. He lives by the river. He sees a great deal.'

'Is he mad?'

Mr Toot smiled indulgently. 'Merely overburdened.'

'He said some mad things to me. He said I was a leviathan. What does that mean?'

Mr Toot looked at him for a moment, and then he said, 'The circle is the most universal of all occult symbols, David. It represents perfection, eternity, the never-ending cycle of creation, decay and regeneration. The divided circle, however, represents the two halves of magical transformation. The top half, the Behemoth, is the state of exaltation and enlightenment. The bottom half, the Leviathan, is the state of hidden potential.'

'Oh,' David said, and wrinkled his nose. 'I still don't know what you mean.'

Mr Toot smiled again. 'Don't worry, David, you will. Given time.'

Part Three
Breaking Spells

Chapter Twenty-One

Although he was determined not to show it, David was nervous when he set off on his bike to meet Chris and Colin the following evening. This was to be the day of his initiation into the Barrow Boys, and all day, as he had been helping Mum carry things up and down stairs, he had been wondering what that would involve.

It was five past seven when he arrived on Church Street and came in sight of the war memorial jutting into the summer sky like a miniature version of the church tower beyond it. However, although the boys had arranged to meet at seven, only Chris was there waiting. He was sitting on the pavement a few feet from the lych-gate, his back to the church wall, tossing pebbles between his outstretched legs towards the storm-drain. Every time a pebble went between the thick bars of the grate, he punched the air and made a sound at the back of his throat like a crowd cheering.

David worked the pedals for a couple of turns and then freewheeled towards his new-found friend, whose head jerked towards him when David was no more than ten feet away, as if he had been caught unawares.

Adopting his customary squint, Chris said, 'About time. I was beginning to think you'd chickened out.'

'No chance,' said David, applying his brakes. 'Where's Colin?'

Chris pushed out his bottom lip as if to say 'Don't know'. 'I haven't seen him today. I expect he'll be here.'

'Hey, guess what happened to me after you'd gone yesterday?'

Chris shrugged. 'You were abducted by aliens? Michelle

Pfeiffer appeared and dragged you into the woods for sex?'

'No, I'm serious, Chris. This tramp with a big bushy beard grabbed me and started saying all this weird stuff.'

Chris's eyes widened. 'You don't mean Old Jonas, do you?'

'Yeah, Jonas. That's what Mr Toot called him.'

'Oh, wow,' said Chris, awe-struck, 'you were lucky to get away. Old Jonas is a total psycho. I've heard that he was once put in a loony bin for chopping up little kids and eating them. They had to give him electric shock treatment to fry his brains before they could let him out.'

'Nah, I don't believe that,' said David, though he didn't sound entirely sure. 'If he'd done something that bad they wouldn't have let him out at all.'

Chris shrugged as if he didn't care whether David believed him or not. 'You ask anyone. So how did you get away? Did you belt him one?'

'No, Mr Toot came,' said David, unwilling to elaborate further. He still wasn't quite sure exactly what Mr Toot had done to persuade Jonas to leave him alone.

Chris, however, was nodding as though he needed no other explanation. 'Yeah, Mr Toot is well cool. I told you how he helped us yesterday against Gary Sissons?'

David nodded. Sitting around in the den yesterday afternoon, his new friends had told him all that a twelve-year-old newcomer could possibly need to know about Longbarrow and its inhabitants. He now knew which kids were okay and which to avoid, what the school and its teachers were like, and where the best places to muck around were. Chris had done most of the talking, often embellishing the information with anecdotes and observations of such high drama that he made Longbarrow sound like a cross between Mega City One and Disneyland. Colin, however, had acted as the voice of temperance, undercutting his friend's wild exaggerations with muttered comments or knowing shakes of the head.

'Anyway, never mind Old Jonas,' said Chris. 'I've got something *really* brilliant to tell you.'

'What?'

'Wait till Colin gets here. I want you both to hear this. But I promise you, it's totally amazing.'

As if on cue, they both heard the squeak of brakes, and turned to see Colin on the other side of the road, emerging from Paddock Lane between one row of shops and the next. His bike teetered for a moment as he looked both ways, then he was pedalling across the road towards them, circling the war memorial, his face solemn.

'You're nearly ten minutes late,' Chris said, tapping his watch.

Colin shrugged. 'If it was up to my gran I wouldn't be here at all.'

'Why, what's happened?' said David. Colin's gran, together with a number of Longbarrow's other notable characters, was another topic on which Chris had waxed lyrical yesterday.

Colin looked at David, his face deadpan, gaze steady. 'She thinks you're bad news,' he said.

'Me, why?' David replied, taken aback.

Briefly Colin told them about the conversation he had had with his gran yesterday. David felt both alarmed and indignant to be condemned by someone he had never met, but Chris's eyes were glittering.

'Wow,' he breathed, 'there are so many weird things happening at the moment. Do you think it's true what she said, Col? Do you reckon something bad really *is* going to happen?'

'I don't know,' said Colin, tight-lipped.

'*I* think it is,' said Chris, not without a certain amount of glee. 'I think all these things that are happening are *portents*.'

He imbued this last word with dramatic reverence, his eyes widening behind his spectacles and his head thrusting forward.

As ever unimpressed by his friend's predilection for over-statement, Colin said, 'What things?'

Chris flapped his hands frustratedly. 'Loads of things. There's your gran, and there's the Jack o' Lanterns—'

'And don't forget Jonas,' interrupted David. 'He grabbed me yesterday,' he told Colin, 'and called me a leviathan.'

Colin frowned. 'What's one of them?'

'I'm not sure. Mr Toot tried to explain it to me, but it was all a bit complicated. I know it's something to do with magic, though.'

Chris was all but hopping from foot to foot in frustration, waving his hands as if to bat away David's words. 'Never mind Jonas. There's something else I haven't told you yet. Something *really* weird. I went to look for my dad this morning because some bloke rang and said he wanted him to ring him

169

back urgently. Anyway, I went into the church and guess what? Dad was looking under this rug in the aisle, and when he saw me he dropped the rug on the floor really quickly and looked sort of guilty, so I asked him what the matter was. Well, he wouldn't show me at first, but in the end he did. And you'll never guess what was under the rug.'

'Dust?' said Colin pragmatically.

'A trap door leading to a cellar full of dead bodies?' ventured David.

Chris was shaking his head, his face smug. 'Nope,' he said, and then pausing for dramatic effect: 'Blood.'

There was a silence, then Colin said, 'What do you mean, "blood"?'

Excitedly Chris told them about the mysterious bloodstain on the church floor that couldn't be removed. 'And that's not all. My dad also told me about this gravestone in the churchyard that actually started bleeding when somebody was looking at it the other day.' His forehead wrinkled in a frown. 'Only problem is, he wouldn't tell me which one it was. I think he only told me in the first place cos it's been getting to him a bit and he didn't have anyone else to talk to about it.'

'Well, couldn't we go and look for this gravestone?' said David. 'I mean, if it's got blood on it . . .'

'Dad cleaned it off,' said Chris glumly, 'and it hasn't come back like the blood on the church floor keeps doing.'

There was a silence as the boys digested this. Finally David said, 'What about the bloodstain on the church floor? Could we have a look at that?'

Chris shook his head. 'Dad's keeping the church locked at the moment, and he carries the key around with him.'

'Nothing like this ever happened to me in London,' said David. 'What do you think it all means?'

'I've told you,' said Chris impatiently, 'it's portents.'

David squinted up into the perfect summer sky. 'Well, when's all this stuff that your gran was going on about supposed to start happening?' he asked Colin.

Colin shrugged. 'I don't know.'

'So what are we supposed to do in the meantime?'

'Keep watch,' said Chris confidently.

'What for?'

'Weird things.'

170

'And then what do we do?' Colin muttered. He was still standing astride his bike, hands gripping the handlebars as though in readiness for a quick getaway.

Chris looked momentarily at a loss, and then he said, 'We'll decide that when the time comes.'

Colin looked nonplussed. As though to avoid any further awkward questions, Chris clapped his hands together and said, 'Anyway, Davey-boy, are you ready for your initiation?'

The subject of his initiation had been temporarily pushed to the back of David's mind. Now he tried not to look nervous once more. 'Of course. What do you want me to do?'

Chris grinned, narrowing his eyes and rubbing his hands together. 'I've got an idea,' he said. 'It's not hard, it just depends on whether you've got the bottle to do it.'

'Name it,' said David, trying to sound fearless.

Still grinning, Chris said, 'Have you heard of the legend of the Seven Sleepers?'

David nodded. 'Mr Toot told me about it.'

'I bet he didn't tell you how to wake the Sleepers up, though, did he?'

David glanced at Colin, who had a frown on his face. 'No.'

'Thought not,' said Chris. 'Well, *I* know what you have to do. And as your initiation into the Barrow Boys, I dare you to do it.'

Colin's frown deepened. 'I don't think that's a good idea, Chris,' he said, 'not after what my gran said.'

Chris scowled. 'I'm not asking you to do it, am I? I'm asking *him.*'

'That's not the point,' Colin said. 'I don't think any of us should do it.'

Chris rolled his eyes in disgust. 'Bloody hell, you're just a couple of wusses.'

'What do you mean?' said David indignantly. 'I'm not a wuss. I didn't say I wouldn't do it.'

'So you *will* do it?' said Chris. 'Or are you too scared?'

It was an old trick, but David rose to the bait immediately. 'Course I'm not scared. I'll do it, whatever it is. It's only a stupid story, after all.'

Chris smiled. 'That's what I like to hear.'

'So what do I have to do?' David asked, wondering what he had let himself in for.

171

'Well, the legend goes that if you run round the church seven times in an anti-clockwise direction you'll wake the Sleepers. And then when you've done that, if you go into the church porch and look through the keyhole of the door, you'll see the Devil walking up the aisle towards you.'

David glanced a little uneasily at the church through the lych-gate, though his overall feeling was one of relief. He had been expecting something far worse – having to strip naked and sacrifice a chicken on an ancient altar, something like that.

'Okay,' he said, 'sounds easy enough.'

'I really don't think this is a good idea,' murmured Colin.

'Lucky you're not the one who's doing it then, isn't it?' retorted Chris. 'Right, Dave, whenever you're ready.'

David leaned his bike against the wall and strolled through the lych-gate, adopting an air of nonchalance. Just like the first time he had stepped through this gate, three weeks ago, he was instantly aware of a subtle change in atmosphere. It was as though the church and the churchyard were encased in a vast, invisible bubble, which negated sound and diffused the light and kept the air still. He glanced back and saw Chris and Colin waiting at the gate, Chris urging him on, Colin looking pensive.

He waved, then jogged up to the church door, where he turned right, heading round the church in an anti-clockwise direction. His Nikes slapped the flagstones, which he only now realised were gravestones laid flat to form a path around the church. So many feet had passed over these stones throughout the years that they had been worn smooth as glass; even the epitaphs were unreadable. David wondered whether grave-stones had been taken from the churchyard to create the path, or whether dead people were actually buried here, beneath the ground beside the church walls. It was a little unsettling to think that he might be passing over dozens of dead bodies. He imagined all those grinning skulls staring up through centuries-long darkness. Of course, it was impossible to awaken something that had been sleeping or dead for hundreds of years. He knew this, so why did his heart feel as though it was bruising his ribs?

There were weeds poking between the gravestones, sorry-looking things with mustard-yellow faces, and tufts of grass like little spiky wigs. Round the back of the church there were unexpected steps and dips, beds of nettles that he had to brush past, holding his arms in the air to avoid getting stung. Bushes and upright gravestones pressed close to the path; at one point David had to duck beneath the outstretched branches of a yew tree, which was leaning over as though desperate to touch the church. When he arrived back at his starting point, he was panting, sweat prickling his forehead. However, he turned to grin and wave at Chris and Colin, who were standing in exactly the same position as when he'd last seen them.

He timed his second circuit. It took him one minute and twenty-three seconds. He reckoned if it wasn't for all the nettles round the back, he could have done it in a minute, tops.

He spent most of his third circuit trying to work out what seven times one minute twenty-three was. He kept losing count and having to start again, but just as he jogged around to the front of the church for the third time he had it: nine minutes forty-one. Nearly ten minutes at jogging speed was probably a mile or more, he thought, as he rounded the back of the church again, and suddenly he realised he'd done three and a half circuits. Halfway there.

Chris and Colin had gone when he arrived back at the front of the church for the fourth time. He slowed, looking around, but they were nowhere to be seen. He carried on going, but the fact that he couldn't see them disturbed him a little. Maybe they'd got bored and gone to do something else, or maybe the whole thing had been a joke to make him look stupid.

Or maybe they were hiding somewhere round the back of the church, planning to jump out on him.

It was this last possibility which seemed to him the most likely. He was therefore cautious as he rounded the back of the church for the fifth time. There were plenty of hiding places here – they could be crouched behind one of the taller grey gravestones or concealed within one of the thick bushes which encroached on the path. They might even be hiding round the edge of the wall – he imagined them with their backs pressed flat against the rough stone, trying to stifle their sniggers, Chris whispering excitedly, 'Here he comes, here he comes.'

He slowed to a walk, his eyes jumping to every nodding branch, every rippling blade of grass. He listened for the rustle of stealthy movement up ahead, but there was nothing; even

173

the insects and birds seemed momentarily silent. Nevertheless, it was a silence that David couldn't help feeling was gathering itself, drawing itself in only to erupt outwards at any moment. He cleared his throat.

'Chris? Colin?' There was no reply. He tried to make himself sound casual, bored even. 'I know you're there. You might as well come out.'

Still no response. David sighed and began to move slowly forward. He bent almost double to peer around every bush and tree before passing it, keeping a wary eye on the larger gravestones, scouring their bases for protruding feet or shadows. He was so wound up that when a cricket started to chirrup it made him jump. Finally he was approaching the corner of the church, and moved as far to the right of the path as he could, again searching for tell-tale shadows, listening for the scrape of cloth on stone, the shuffling of feet, quiet breathing.

He crept up to the corner of the church and then leaped around it, shouting, 'Hah!' There was no one there. Puzzled, his stomach still tight with tension, he jogged around to the front of the church again.

Chris and Colin were still nowhere to be seen. David shouted their names, but got no reply. Should he stop and look for them or carry on? Only two more circuits to go. Better carry on. Perhaps their disappearance was simply part of the initiation.

He felt cautious running round the back of the church again, though not as much as the last time. He found a stick which he used to thrash at the bushes as he passed them. At one point he glanced up, unable to expel the ridiculous notion that they might somehow be above him. However, he saw only the looming church tower, its vertical plane broken by the ridge that was the bottom curve of the witchcraft eye, gazing out across the countryside.

When he arrived back at the church door again, prior to his final circuit, Chris and Colin were once again standing at the gate. David felt a flood of relief; Chris cheered and gave him the thumbs up.

'Where have you been?' David shouted.

Chris held up what David first thought were two shockingly long green worms, one in each hand, or two halves of a grass

174

snake, before realising they were ice pops. Now he understood. They must have nipped across the road to Mr Toot's.

'How many more to go?' Chris shouted.

'This is my last one. See you in one minute twenty-three seconds.'

David turned and jogged towards the corner of the church, putting his friends out of sight.

Well, he'd done it unless he stopped now. Seven times round the church, anti-clockwise. Were the Sleepers, whoever they were, even now beginning to stir, the mystical chains that had bound them rusting and crumbling away? He half-expected something to happen – the sky to darken; a chill breeze to whisper through the graveyard; a faint subterranean sound, stone grating on stone, to reach his ears – but nothing did. He finished with a sprint, arriving back in front of the church door panting and sweating.

He gulped in air, then shouted, 'Done it!'

'You've got to look through the keyhole, remember,' Chris shouted back, gesticulating, his lips green as a lizard's. 'Look through the keyhole and see the Devil.'

David raised a hand in acknowledgement, then turned and entered the vestibule. It was dark after the brightness of the day and stifling as an oven. He paused a moment, blinking, then crossed to the heavy oak doors that led into the church. The keyhole was at waist height. As he stooped towards it, he felt unaccountably nervous.

He closed one eye and lowered his face to the wooden door that age had made hard and smooth as polished rock. His eye came level with the keyhole, and as it did an image floated into his mind: a man in a dark suit with a saturnine face, horns curling from his head, clacking down the aisle towards him on hooved feet. He looked through the keyhole, heart beating wildly, and for a moment saw nothing but blackness. Had his seven laps round the church caused it to be filled with darkness? he wondered. Was the devil going to come striding out of it, snarling and drooling? Then he realised that the hole gouged out of the wood was much larger than the more modern lock that was set into it, and he adjusted position accordingly, stooping a little lower – just as a hand came down on his shoulder.

He cried out, and instinctively jumped forward, trying to

175

pull away, succeeding only in slamming his face into the heavy oak door, which boomed under the impact. For a few seconds he was blinded by tears caused by his smarting nose. He staggered round to face whoever had grabbed him, rubbing frantically at his eyes, ducking his head as if he feared some kind of assault.

Like someone trying to speak to him above the crashing of a waterfall, he heard a voice whose actual words were lost in the torrent. Then he felt a hand – perhaps the same one that had grabbed his shoulder – taking hold of his arm. Thinking of Jonas seizing him yesterday, he flinched, shrugging the hand away. At the same instant his vision began to clear and the roaring in his ears to abate. He blinked at his assailant, saw a tall figure dressed in black and grey. The figure leaned towards him, and although its voice was muffled, the words were now intelligible: 'It's David, isn't it? Can you hear me?'

David nodded, still blinking. The man's features swam into focus. Immediately David recognised Steven Farrar, the vicar, Chris's dad. He looked concerned.

'Are you all right?' Reverend Farrar asked. 'I didn't mean to make you jump like that.'

David nodded again. His nose was still sore, but already the pain was fading. He examined it with his fingers, and was a little disappointed to find there was no blood. Blood from a facial wound was always impressive; without it, you were generally regarded as a bit of a wimp if you made a fuss.

Chris and Colin came hurrying up, wheeling the bikes which they laid on the path. 'Wow, Dad, what did you do? Punch David in the face?'

The Reverend looked ashamed, as if in a moment of uncontrolled anger he had done just that. David, however, said, 'No, he just tapped me on the shoulder and I jumped into the door. My fault really.'

Chris rolled his eyes as if to indicate that *he* would never have done anything so stupid. Reverend Farrar, however, still looked a little shamefaced.

'I didn't recognise you,' he said, 'otherwise I would never have grabbed you like that. It's just that recently there's been . . .' His voice trailed off, and then he said, 'I thought you might have been trying to break into the church.'

'He was just looking through the keyhole, Dad,' said Chris.

Reverend Farrar looked at his son, frowning. 'Whatever for?' Chris reddened and stammered, 'Well, I . . . he . . . I dared him to.'

The Reverend's frown deepened, and all at once David realised how tired and anxious Chris's dad looked.

'You dared him to?' The Reverend looked at each of them in turn. 'What are you lot up to?'

Thinking that Reverend Farrar would not take too kindly to being told that his son had started something that was supposed to result in the raising of the Devil in his own church, David said quickly, 'I was just trying to see if I could see the bloodstain, Mr Farrar, that's all.'

Immediately he knew he had made a mistake. The Reverend's frown became a scowl and he glared at his son, who looked anguished and guilty. Chris flapped his hands and said, 'Sorry, Dad, it just sort of . . . slipped out.'

Reverend Farrar's voice was like ice. 'I told you not to tell *anyone* about this, Chris. I thought I could trust you. It seems I was wrong.'

Chris looked utterly miserable. He stared down at his hands which were twining together. 'I know, Dad,' he mumbled, 'I'm really sorry.'

David gritted his teeth, wishing he'd kept his big mouth shut. He glanced at Colin, who was standing at Chris's shoulder, stoical as ever.

As the awkward silence stretched out, David desperately tried to think of something to say to relieve the situation, but to no avail. Finally, it was Reverend Farrar himself who sighed and said, 'Well, what's done is done, I suppose. But I don't want news of this spread around. I don't want my church becoming a curiosity. Do you all understand?'

The boys nodded and mumbled that they did. Then tentatively Chris said, 'Could I show David and Colin the bloodstain, Dad? I mean, now that they know about it, it doesn't matter if they see it, does it?'

'You're pushing your luck, Chris,' the Reverend warned, though there was no real anger in his voice this time. He shook his head in resignation and produced a set of keys from his pocket. 'All right, one quick look. Then I want you all out of here. This is a place where people come for solace. It's not a playground.'

177

Once again they mumbled their understanding. As the Reverend turned to unlock the church door, David looked at Chris and mouthed, 'Sorry'. Chris grinned and shrugged. He could be over-the-top and opinionated, but he didn't appear to bear grudges. Reverend Farrar turned the metal loop that was the door handle and led the way into the church.

David expected the place to be dark and gloomy, like most churches, but it was warm and bright. If the Devil had ever been here, he had gone now; there was not even the faintest whiff of brimstone. Reverend Farrar strolled up the aisle, stopping when he reached the rug that had been laid rather incongruously on the brown tiles and lifting it aside. The boys crowded round to look at the black stain that the rug had been concealing. David couldn't help feeling a little disappointed.

'It . . . it doesn't look like blood,' he said after a moment.

Reverend Farrar had been staring broodingly down at the stain, but now he looked up. 'No, it doesn't, does it?'

'It *is* though,' Chris asserted. 'Dad's had it analysed, haven't you, Dad?'

His father nodded a little grudgingly.

Colin, who had been silent for a while, said carefully, 'What do you think it means, Mr Farrar?'

The Reverend looked surprised and a little cautious. 'I don't think it neccessarily *means* anything, Colin. It's just . . . here, that's all.'

'You don't think it's a portent then?'

'A portent? For what?'

Colin's face was serious, his voice calm and steady. 'Approaching evil,' he said.

Chapter Twenty-Two

Since Gerry's death, Susan knew only too well how pragmatic, even cynical, she had become. She was certainly not prone to flights of fancy, and yet in the few days she had been in Longbarrow she had to admit that her whole attitude to life had changed. She felt relaxed, happy, even carefree, felt as though she had emerged a butterfly from the stifling pupa of her London existence. Time seemed not so much a restraint here, compartmentalised into schedules, routines, appointments, but an endless commodity like air or water, a luxury even, in which she could indulge herself.

These past five days she had hardly been out of the house, had spent her time cleaning, unpacking, decorating, sorting out, and yet despite this they had been five of the most contented and fulfilling days she could ever remember. Even the moving box of books, though a little alarming at the time, had not really fazed her.

Ghosts? she had thought. Magic? It all seemed so much part of the natural landscape here that there really seemed little point in worrying about it. Longbarrow was undoubtedly a special place, and their house seemed to Susan like the heart of it all.

They were wild and wonderful thoughts, she knew, crazy thoughts even (a fact which had been brought home to her when she had tried to explain how she felt to Beth earlier on the phone that evening, and had been met with a kind of bemused indulgence), and yet they seemed *right* somehow. Perhaps the way she had been thinking about Jack today, the way he had managed to sneak beneath her defences, was merely symptomatic of her new-found *joie de vivre*.

It was ludicrous. She had known the man hardly any time at all, had little in common with him that she could see, and yet today she hadn't been able to stop thinking about him. She kept bringing to mind his disarming, almost goofy grin, kept thinking fondly of how selfless and gentle he was, how guileless and honest.

More, she had thought of the way their bodies had pressed briefly together when they had been looking out of the window in Davey's room yesterday, and the recollection had given her a thrill of pleasure.

But this wasn't like her at all! She was usually so wary, so careful. She didn't throw herself at men like Beth did, and neither was she the giddy romantic type. She had always believed categorically that love at first sight was a nonsense, was even dubious of the idea of instant animal attraction, always maintaining that her interest could not be seized, but had to be prised from her, slowly and gently.

It must be this place, she thought, weaving its magic, but if so was that neccessarily a bad thing? Did the influence of her surroundings make her emotions less valid, or was it merely loosening the straitjacket of her inhibitions, which Beth would maintain was something she had needed for a long time?

Whatever, it was all new territory to Susan, but although she was confused, it was a happy confusion; her life seemed full of possibilities. She wondered what her next move should be, or should she leave that up to Jack? Perhaps, if he didn't get in touch first, she could invite him to dinner at the weekend, as a thank you for helping her out yesterday.

She was currently in the old nursery, which she had decided to have as her bedroom, stripping off wallpaper that was still sticky and grey with accumulated dust and grime despite being swabbed with hot water. She had spent the early part of the evening working on the windowsills – prising the nails out of the frames (presumably they had been nailed shut so that children couldn't open them), scraping off the flaking paint, sanding down the wood. The toys that had been in here had been sorted out by David. Some he had cleaned and kept, but most had been thrown in the skip, though a couple of things David didn't want had been held back to show to the auctioneer tomorrow. It had got dark some time ago, though as Susan's watch was downstairs in the kitchen – removed earlier when she was washing up – she had no idea what time it was.

Not that it mattered. Time was an irrelevance here. It was so easy to lose track of it in a way she had never been able to do in London. She went to bed when she was tired and got up when she wasn't. She would have eaten only when she was hungry too if it hadn't been for David wanting his meals at their designated times.

Davey was in bed, in his own room for the first time tonight. Susan envied him; he could look up through his velux windows at stars which were breathtakingly clear here, as though fresh-minted. She was glad he had made friends so easily. She hadn't met them yet, though one of them was the vicar's son, so he couldn't be too bad. Unless of course he was going through his rebellious stage and dabbling in Satanism to annoy his parents. The thought made her smile as wallpaper bubbled beneath the steam she was applying to it, allowing her to sweep it off in a great swathe with the metal spatula she was holding in her right hand.

She puffed out her cheeks and looked around. Almost three walls done. Should she press on and finish the job or leave it until tomorrow?

An image came to mind: her dad, handyman extraordinaire, smiling smugly and saying, 'Never put off until tomorrow what you can do today.'

Right, that settled it. She'd leave it. She put her tools down on the wallpaper-littered floor, then stretched and yawned.

Tidy up, mug of Horlicks, bed, she thought. Tonight would be her sixth night on the camp bed in the reception room, wedged between a lumpy settee and the inglenook fireplace. Not that she really minded; it was kind of cosy, actually. It reminded her of sleeping round at her friends' houses when she was a girl.

She spent the next ten minutes clearing up the mess she'd made, then moved out on to the landing. She was instantly aware of the ticking of the grandfather clock in the hall below. It had cost a hundred and forty pounds to get it repaired, but it had been worth it. Its ticking was sonorous but restful. It permeated the house, lulled her to sleep at night, not that she needed much lulling. Even as she washed her hands in the bathroom, it began to chime in its delicate, silvery voice. Susan counted the chimes, whispering, 'Eight, nine, ten, eleven,' as she dried her hands.

She plodded downstairs, noting when she reached the bottom that the smiling, fat-faced moon on the smaller dial of the clock had already begun to edge from the left to the right of the fan-shaped aperture in the main clock-face. She knew that Davey was excitedly wondering what image would follow the moon, and she had to admit to a little curiosity herself. She supposed it would be a few days yet before the image was revealed; the smaller dial appeared to revolve on a monthly cycle.

She walked through to the kitchen, her limbs now full of the good ache that came after a hard day's work. Putting on the kettle, she thought about making herself a sandwich to take to bed. She glanced out of the window that looked out on to Aunt Mollie's little garden and the paddock beyond, seeing nothing but her own and the room's reflection in the glass that darkness had turned into a black mirror. Last night she had heard an owl calling, had gone outside to see if she could see it swooping through the night. She hadn't seen the owl, but she had seen a few flickering, squealing shapes that were bats, and then had spent a while gazing up in awe at the stars until she became dizzy. She didn't think she had ever felt so . . . *whole*. That was the only word she could think of to describe it. She had hugged herself, sighed a deep sigh of contentment. Coming here was the best thing she had ever done.

Tonight, it seemed, the owls were hunting elsewhere. If it wasn't for the ticking of the clock and the gurgling hiss of water boiling in the kettle, the house would have seemed encased in silence. There was not even a whisper of wind outside; summer warmth hung heavy in the atmosphere, like a blanket beneath which the landscape drowsed. Susan felt drowsy too. She opened the cupboard above the Aga to lift down the Horlicks, then plucked a mug from the mug tree on the counter. The plastic lid of the Horlicks container lifted with a pop and she began to scoop spoonfuls into her mug. The kettle rattled as it gouted steam, then switched itself off with a click. As Susan poured boiling water into her mug, a sweet, malty smell billowing into her face, she heard a slithering sound from the corner of the room.

She tilted the kettle up to halt the flow of water and stood absolutely motionless, head cocked, listening. Since coming here her senses had seemed acute, as if they had been removed, finely tuned, then put back again. Her hearing was particularly sensitive: music was amazing; she was able to distinguish each individual instrument in a way she never could before, to appreciate the way they blended together to form a complete and harmonious sound. The slithering had been so faint that last week she might not even have heard it. Nevertheless, she knew she had not been mistaken. The sound had come from behind the cellar door.

She put the kettle carefully back down on the counter, as if anxious not to draw attention to herself, then nimbly crossed the short distance to the cellar door and placed her ear against it. All she could hear now was the susurration of her own blood. She stepped back from the door and stared at it, as though willing it to become transparent. As soon as she had heard the sound she had thought of David's snake-dream. Could that have been a premonition? Had a snake somehow found its way into the cellar? If so, it must be a big one. She doubted that even her newly attuned senses would have been able to pick up the movements of a grass snake. She looked down at the one-inch gap between the bottom of the door and the tiled floor. Could a biggish snake have got under there? She had heard that rats could get into tiny spaces by compressing their skulls, but could snakes do the same thing? And how big *was* the biggest snake in Britain anyway? She knew there were adders, but how big did they grow? And were they poisonous or not?

She nibbled absently at the skin around her fingernails, which the last few days' work had turned dry and flaky, and wondered what she should do. She could seal up the door, but what if the snake had found some other way in? Through the drains, for example? She couldn't remember seeing any sort of grille in the cellar, or any breach in the walls or floor where it could have entered, but she might have been mistaken – she hadn't, for instance, had a look underneath the pile of soggy cardboard boxes against the wall. She supposed she could don wellies and gloves and go down there to tackle it herself, but what if it escaped into the house, or even worse, bit her?

Jack, she thought, I'll call Jack, though even as she plodded into the hall, closing the kitchen door firmly behind her, she was wondering whether she really needed him or whether she was just using this as an excuse to get in touch. She dialled his number, hoping he wasn't the sort of person who went to bed when it got dark and rose with the dawn. As the phone began to ring she felt a skittish nervousness start up in her stomach that she told herself was utterly ridiculous. She was thirty-five, for God's sake, not fourteen! Nonetheless the nervousness increased each time the phone rang, which it must have done seven or eight times by now.

With a sinking heart, she decided that he must be either out or in bed, and was actually moving the phone away from her ear, when a breathless voice said, 'Hello?'

'Jack?' said Susan.

'Yes. Is that you, Susan?'

Despite herself, she felt a thrill of delight that he had recognised her voice from just one word. Did that mean she had been on his mind as much as he'd been on hers? 'Yes,' she said. 'I'm sorry to ring you so late. I didn't wake you up, did I?'

'No,' he said. 'I was watching a film. I thought the answerphone was on. That's why it took me a while to answer.'

'Oh,' she said, 'I'm sorry. Do you want to get back to it – the film, I mean?'

'No, that's all right, I've seen it before. What can I do for you?'

Already she was beginning to think that this was a mistake. Feeling foolish, she said, 'Well . . . I just wondered if I could ask your advice?'

'Ask away,' he said, and despite what he'd said a few seconds ago, Susan couldn't help wondering whether perhaps he *did* want to get back to his film. Was his voice a little brisker than usual? Was he sitting there with one eye on the screen, only half-listening to her? Or maybe the phone was in another room to the TV and he was wearing an expression of impatience and exasperation?

These images caused her to stammer and speak quickly, all the while hating herself for doing so.

'Well, it's just that . . . I . . . I think there might be a snake in my cellar, and I'm not sure what to do about it. Er . . . I wondered whether you might . . . um. . . have any suggestions?'

God, that sounded so feeble. He was going to see right through that. Already in her mind she could hear him asking coolly, 'That's not the *real* reason why you called me tonight, is it, Susan?'

Instead he said, 'I'll come over straight away.'

She was shocked, could only say, 'What?'

Now it was *his* voice that sounded unsure. 'Sorry, I meant . . . only if you wanted me to.'

Well, of *course* I want you to, she exclaimed silently, but heard herself saying, 'Oh no, you don't have to do that. I don't want to drag you out at this time of night. I'm probably just being silly.'

'It's no trouble,' he said. 'I can jump in the van and be there in five minutes.'

'The gate's locked,' she said. 'I'll have to drive down and meet you in the car.'

'No need.' He sounded a little embarrassed. 'I've got a key for the gate. Mrs Boscombe gave it to me. I meant to give it back to you yesterday, but I forgot.'

'Keep it.' There was a pause, and then Susan said, 'Are you *sure* you don't mind doing this, Jack?'

'Positive. See you in five minutes.'

'All right.' She wanted to add, I'll look forward to seeing you, but it didn't sound right. In the end she just said, 'Thanks a lot.'

As she waited she resisted checking in a mirror to see how she looked, concentrated instead on digging out her wellies and two pairs of gloves – yellow rubber washing-up gloves for her, gardening gloves that she hoped would fit him (they had always been too big for her). The grandfather clock was just edging towards twenty past the hour when she heard his van outside. She went to the door to meet him, returning the wave he gave her as he got out.

'Thanks so much for coming, Jack,' she gushed, leading him into the house. 'I'm sorry I sounded so pathetic on the phone.'

'You didn't,' he said. 'Do you know what sort of snake it is?'

Now she felt even more foolish. She shook her head. 'No, I haven't seen it, I've only heard it, moving around.'

'How do you know it's a snake?' he asked. His manner was as easy-going as ever, his voice not at all accusatory, and yet Susan felt herself flushing.

'Well, it . . . it sounded like one,' she said lamely.

'You're sure it wasn't just mice or something you heard?'

185

'No, I don't think so. Mice sort of . . . scamper, don't they? But this slithered. It sounded quite big too, like . . . like someone dragging a tyre across a stone floor.'

He fixed her with his blue eyes, nodding sagely.

'I suppose I should have checked, shouldn't I,' she said miserably, 'before dragging you out in the middle of the night?'

'No, you did right,' he said. 'Well, come on, let's have a look.'

They went into the kitchen. Susan said, 'I've got some gloves for us. I hope these fit you.' She picked up the gardening gloves from the table and handed them to him. 'I'm afraid I haven't got anything for you to put on your feet, though. I only take size fives.'

'These'll do,' Jack said, lifting his right foot to draw attention to his steel-toe-capped work boots. He looked around the kitchen. 'You haven't got anything I can whack the bugger with, have you?'

'Like what?'

He shrugged. 'Baseball bat. Something like that.'

'Tennis racket?' she suggested hopefully, then held up her hands. 'No, forget I said that. How about . . . um . . . a garden fork? Then if it goes for you, you can pin it to the floor.'

'That'll do,' he said, nodding, and she went out to the shed to fetch it. When she got back he took it from her and hefted it in his hands while she pulled on her wellies. Now they were ready.

Susan was quite happy to let Jack take the lead, though felt a coward for doing so. If Beth was here she'd have labelled Susan a 'fluffy', though Beth herself was not averse to batting her eyelashes when she wanted something done for her. Holding the garden fork in his right hand, all set to jerk up the pronged head and impale whatever might leap at them, Jack curled his other hand around the door handle and eased it down. Before he pulled the door open, the two of them stood and listened, looking into each other's eyes as if that might establish a telepathic link that would boost their hearing. If there *was* a snake in there, it was motionless now – perhaps sleeping, Susan thought, trying to banish the ridiculous image of a twenty-foot long python full of cold reptile cunning that would strike like a bullet the instant they opened the door. Jack gave her a quick reassuring smile, then eased the door open a couple of inches and peered through the gap. Shadows flocked from the darkness within the cellar, filling the creases around his eyes and mouth, ageing him.

'The light switch is on the wall to your left,' Susan said. 'I'm afraid you'll have to lean right in to turn it on.'

Jack nodded. 'Hang on a minute.' He slipped through the gap and a moment later a block of light sprang out of it. His shadow preceded him, folding itself up the wall. 'I can see right down to the bottom of the steps, but there's no sign of a snake. Do you want to come down with me or wait up here?'

'I'll come down,' Susan said. Jack nodded and disappeared back through the gap. She slipped through the gap too, almost walking straight into him.

'Pull the door shut behind you,' he said, then looked at her face. 'Sorry. Stating the obvious, aren't I?'

She smiled wryly to show that he was, but that she had taken no offence. She pulled the door closed behind her and they started down the stairs. Susan was all too aware of the loudness of her movements despite her efforts to remain quiet. She couldn't stop the fabric of her clothes rubbing against her skin, though, or quieten the grit that her feet pressed into the concrete steps, no matter how light her footfalls. She wondered which sense was dominant in snakes. Did they hunt by smell or sight or sound, or did they respond to vibrations like spiders did?

Halfway down the stairs, she realised that this was the first time since she had been in the house that she had felt anything like nervous. It might be argued that this was the first thing she had had to be nervous about, though under normal circumstances she might have expected the dark, unfamiliar landscape and their relative isolation to play on her imagination a little. But no, the house gave off such an aura of friendliness, of security, that she had never felt uncomfortable here until now. Not that this was the house's doing – this was a rogue element, an invader. She knew that the sound she had heard, though faint, had not been her imagination.

And yet she and Jack were almost at the bottom of the stairs now, and craning over his shoulder she was able to see every square inch of the cellar floor and walls and ceiling, and there was not a snake in sight. There was not even a rat or a mouse or an insect. Susan was baffled, a little embarrassed, even a tiny bit disappointed.

'I don't understand this,' she murmured. Jack had reached the bottom of the steps now and was standing on the dusty concrete floor, looking around.

'Maybe,' he said, then stopped as though unable to think of even an implausible explanation. Finally he said, 'Maybe there's a gap in the wall somewhere.'

'It could be hiding behind the cardboard boxes,' Susan said, though she knew that if it was it must be a very small snake, no more than a foot or so long and thin as a finger.

Nevertheless, she ascended a couple of steps despite her wellingtons as Jack scattered and shredded the pile of damp boxes with his fork, knowing that even if only a tiny snake shot out from behind there she'd jump.

However, nothing came out from behind the boxes, not even a centipede or a woodlouse. Next, the two of them examined the walls and the ceiling and the floor, but they were all solid – not a gap, or barely even a crack, in sight.

'I just don't understand this,' Susan said again. 'I definitely heard something. I didn't imagine it.'

Jack looked relaxed now, the fork dangling loosely from his hand. He shrugged. 'There's loads of underground streams and things around here,' he said. 'Maybe it was water you heard.'

She gave him a sceptical look. 'I know you're only trying to make me feel better, Jack. God, you must think I'm a total dip-head.'

'Course not. To be honest, I'm glad there wasn't a snake. I don't mind admitting, I was a bit nervous.'

Susan took one last look round, as though half-believing that somehow they might have missed the twenty-foot python of her imagination. 'Oh well, I suppose we might as well go back up.' Almost hopefully she added, 'You don't suppose it could have got behind us into the house without us noticing, do you?'

He smiled as if she had meant the comment as a joke (though in fact she had been half-serious), and began to plod up the steps behind her. A little cautiously he said, 'You remember I was telling you that sometimes odd things happen in this house? Things being moved around and stuff?'

188

She nodded.

'Well, sometimes people hear things as well. A couple of times I've been working in the house and I've thought I could hear voices or someone moving about, but when I've gone to look there's never been anyone there.'

'So what are you telling me?' said Susan. 'That I heard a ghost-snake?'

He pulled a face and shrugged. 'I know it sounds daft.'

They reached the top of the cellar steps. Susan opened the door as Jack turned off the light. Pulling off her rubber gloves and dumping them on the kitchen table, she said, 'Look, let's forget about it. I feel stupid enough already. Can I offer you some supper or something, Jack, as compensation for dragging you out in the middle of the night?'

He didn't answer immediately, and Susan felt sure he was going to refuse. Then he said, 'Yes, all right. That'd be nice.'

She tried to moderate the grin that wanted to stretch her lips wide. 'It won't be much, just some cheese and bread.'

He rested the garden fork against the wall beside the back door and tugged off the gloves which, although he'd managed to pull them on, had been a tight fit. 'Are you trying to put me off now?'

'No, of course not.'

He grinned to show he was joking. 'You don't have to keep apologising about everything, you know, Susan.'

'I'm not!' she protested, then said uncertainly, 'Am I? I'm sorry.'

'There you go again.'

She grinned along with him and said, 'Oh, just go and do something manly – build a fire or something.'

'Isn't it a bit warm for a fire?'

She flapped her hands, shooing him. 'Do it anyway. It'll be . . .' She nearly said 'romantic', but managed to snatch the word back from the brink. Besides, she wasn't the romantic type, was she? '. . . nice,' she said finally.

'All right, if that's what you want,' he said, shrugging, and plodded from the room.

For the next ten minutes she busied herself throwing together what she hoped was a reasonably impressive supper: some Ciabatta bread together with two blocks of cheese – Stilton and Wensleydale – that she had bought from the small but well-stocked deli in the village when she'd popped out that afternoon, some pickle, a bowl of salad, and a bottle of Australian red that she wished she'd been able to let breathe for longer (feeling reckless, she opened another one and left it on the counter). She washed a bunch of fat red grapes, worried that adding them might make the whole thing look a bit Roman-orgyish, then thought, *Oh, what the hell?* and arranged them aesthetically in a wooden bowl. She put the lot on a tray and carried it carefully from the kitchen, pulling the door open with her foot and nudging it with her hip when it threatened to swing back on her.

In the hallway, she suddenly realised that she hadn't told Jack which room to go in. If he'd gone into the reception room she'd be acutely embarrassed. All her bedding was in there, including the big Snoopy T-shirt she was currently sleeping in. There was probably even yesterday's underwear strewn on the floor; the thought made her cheeks burn.

Then she heard a crackling sound coming from the second door along on her right. The first door was the downstairs toilet; the second led into the main sitting room with the cavernous fireplace. With a sigh of relief she walked over and pushed the door open with her foot. The instant she entered the room, a wall of heat hit her.

Jack was crouched on the hearth, his body outlined in flames that were leaping up the chimney. He was jabbing at the charring logs in the grate with an implement that looked more like a sword than a poker. He'd taken off the blue sweatshirt he'd arrived in to reveal a plain white T-shirt tucked carelessly into his jeans. The muscles in his arms were picked out in the pulsing, yellow liquid-light from the fire.

If Susan didn't know better, she might have believed that Jack had wanted her to find him like that, that he'd posed himself so that she'd see him when she walked in, powerful and in control, tending the magnificent fire he'd built. It made her realise that, despite her strong but still confusing feelings for him, she hardly knew him at all. He seemed honest, straightforward, incapable of deviousness, but was that really the case? Was that why she liked him so much – because she felt unthreatened by what she perceived as his simplicity? If so, she was doing him a disservice. So what if he *was* trying to impress her? If she found that a problem, then surely it was hers, not his.

She tried to push these thoughts to the back of her mind as she walked in, the heat bringing a response from her blood, making it pulse feverishly just beneath her skin. He turned to her, smiling, his face shiny, the fire dancing in his eyes.

'Is this all right for you?' he said, having to raise his voice above the crackling, popping, hissing flames.

She set the tray on the hearth, half-expecting the cheese to melt and the wine to boil in the bottle. 'I asked for a fire, not an inferno,' she said jovially. 'I'll just pop back and get a pig to roast, shall I?'

His smile widened into a grin, the fire turning his teeth to little pillars of white flame, and sat back. 'I think I might have overdone it,' he admitted, then swiped a hand across his glistening forehead. 'I'm sweating bricks.'

'I'll open a couple of windows,' she said. 'Why don't you put the guard over the fire? It might deflect some of the heat up the chimney.'

'Good idea.' He unfolded the big metal fireguard and dragged it into place. Immediately the mesh began to tink as it was struck by black splinters of wood that the fire had previously been spitting on to the hearth like teeth. Susan opened a few windows, but closed the curtains over them. She'd rather be too warm than have the room full of the furry grey creatures that scrabbled at the kitchen window at night and looked more like baby birds than moths.

She didn't feel tired any more. Jack's presence and the tension of the snake-hunt had filled her with energy. She crossed to the lamp in the corner that he must have switched on when he'd entered the room, and, feeling daring, said, 'Do you mind if I switch this off, Jack? I thought it'd be a bit more cosy just with the light from the fire.'

She dreaded his giving her a knowing look, and was therefore thankful when he simply shrugged as though it had never occurred to him that she might have an ulterior motive for creating a more intimate atmosphere. (*Is that what I'm doing?* she thought, surprising herself.) 'Whatever you like. Shall I pour some wine?' he said, reaching for the bottle.

In the firelight the wine glowed like a magic potion, as though tiny white tongues of flame had been sealed in lifeblood. She took the glass he proffered her and sipped from it. It was good wine, heavy and rich with fruit, but not acidic. It slid down her throat, smooth as honey. Her skin blazed anew. She gazed into the fire, relishing the moment.

'What are these black things in the bread?' Jack asked.

She looked at him. He was gazing suspiciously at the chunk of Ciabatta bread in his hand. 'They're olives,' she said.

'Perhaps we ought to give them back to her, then.'

She slapped him playfully. 'Peasant.'

He laughed and tore at the bread with his teeth. He chewed and swallowed, the bread leaving a dusting of flour on his top lip. As he ate with gusto, Susan picked and nibbled. She wasn't really hungry now; her stomach was too full of nervous anticipation, wondering where this might lead. Did she want it to lead anywhere? She wasn't sure. One thing she didn't want to do, however, was to force the situation on any further than she already had. From now on it was up to Jack to take the initiative, if he so desired. But how would she feel if he simply ate his fill and then went home? Both disappointed and relieved, she thought.

It was the situation, not Jack himself, that made her nervous. Indeed, she felt more relaxed with him than she'd felt with a man for a long time. In some ways he was even easier to be with than Gerry. She'd loved Gerry, but he hadn't been the most laid-back person in the world. As they sat on the rug in front of the fire and ate and drank, they chatted about this and that, about nothing in particular, and sometimes they lapsed into silence, and surprisingly that felt okay too. Usually, when speaking to someone she didn't know very well, Susan felt a need to fill in the silences, to plaster over awkward pauses with inane, sometimes desperate chatter. But she didn't feel that way with Jack. With him, even the silences seemed natural, comfortable. Again, she wondered whether it was the influence of the house, or of Longbarrow, or whether it purely came down to a question of her and Jack. Were there such things as naturally compatible people? Was it possible to meet someone with whom you immediately clicked?

The evidence is here, she thought, looking at him. He turned from the fire, caught her eye and grinned.

'What?' he said.

'What do you mean, "what"?'

'What were you thinking?'

'Nothing.'

'Yes you were. I could hear the cogs whirring.'

It was as if he was inviting her to take the plunge. For a second she pictured herself dithering on the side, and then all at once she leaped in. 'If you must know, I was thinking how well we get on, even though we hardly know each other. I feel totally relaxed with you.'

His expression didn't change. 'Yes, well, I'm a totally relaxing person.'

'I'm not,' she said.

'Yes you are. I'm happy enough.'

'But that's just the point – I'm not usually. I'm usually quite . . . uptight around men. Since my husband died, I haven't had what you'd call a proper relationship with anyone.'

His expression was suddenly more serious, his voice gentle rather than jocular. 'Is that what this is then – a proper relationship?'

She was surprised by the question. 'I don't know. Would you like it to be?'

Now he smiled. 'I asked you first.'

She was silent for a few moments, gazing into the fire, her thoughts a jumble. Finally she said, 'All I know is that I feel relaxed with you, and I like seeing you. But whether that's because everything's new and exciting or whether it's this place or whether it's you or whether it's me, I don't know.' She took a sip of her wine. 'How do you feel?'

'Happy,' he said.

'About me, I mean?'

'I like you a lot.'

She frowned. 'Yes, but you probably like a lot of people a lot, don't you? That doesn't mean . . .' She put a hand to her head. 'God, I don't believe we're actually having this conversation.'

'All right then,' he said, 'I like you more than a lot. I liked you from the first time I saw you. I'm just not very good with words, that's all.'

'I thought you were a great reader.'

'I am. But I'm not a great talker.'

They were silent for a moment, then she said, 'It's just. . . this isn't like me at all. I'm not usually so . . . spontaneous. And really, despite everything, I don't know the first thing about you. I'm terrified of making myself look stupid. I mean,

193

how do I know you haven't got a dozen girlfriends scattered around the village?'

'I haven't,' he said.

'But how do I *know* that?'

'You'll just have to trust me.'

She looked at him uncertainly. He said, 'I don't know what else to say. I haven't had a girlfriend for ages. Why, I don't know. Yes I do. It's because I never go anywhere to meet anyone. I work on my own or with other blokes; I go to the same pubs; I'm happy enough in my own company – I suppose I'm just a boring old bugger really. But it never bothered me until I saw you. And then – I don't know – something clicked. That sounds daft, I know, but that's what happened. Since you came here . . . well . . . I've been thinking of you a lot. But I never thought you'd feel the same way about me, never in a million years . . .'

He broke off, looking embarrassed. Susan reached across and touched his hand. He looked at it as though it was some precious jewel he didn't know what to do with.

'How do you feel now?' she asked.

'I don't know.'

'Still happy?'

'Yes.'

'Confused?'

'Yes.'

'Would you kiss me?'

'Yes.'

'Go on then.'

He shuffled towards her, put his right arm around her, touching her lightly in the small of her back as though she were made of the finest china. Firelight slid across his face as he tilted it towards her; her hair glowed like filaments of light.

Susan closed her eyes, but sensed his face coming closer, and then suddenly their lips were touching. Immediately her body began to tingle as though he was breathing electricity into her.

She moaned and reached for him, and as her hands slid across his back, so he responded. His touch sent sizzling waves of sensation through her skin. It was a long time since she had been touched like this, and she squirmed and gasped, her nerves jumping.

As their passion increased, so did her terror and exhilaration.

She felt she was on a roller coaster ride, out of control; she wanted to scream and thrash and writhe, but she didn't want it to stop, not ever. Her lips and hands became frantic, desperate. She clawed at him like a drowning woman voraciously clinging to life. She felt sensation building upon sensation inside her, layers of it, engulfing her thoughts, her rational mind. Her nerves were screaming now, the pleasure so intense it was almost unbearable, an exquisite torture.

'Make love to me,' she gasped, her voice raw, full of need. She began to tear at his clothes. 'Make love to me.'

She screamed when she came, as though he was murdering her. Later, when they were spent, their slippery, steaming bodies intertwined like battling snakes, she touched the question-mark scar on his chin.

'How did you get this?' she murmured.

'Fighting,' he said drowsily. 'Someone hit me with a beer glass. I was seventeen.'

She kissed the scar, crooning, 'My poor baby. My poor little bit of rough.'

He chuckled, the sound deep and resonant in his throat.

Later still, as the logs in the fire dwindled to white ash, enveloping their naked bodies with heat, they slept.

Chapter Twenty-Three

Before he even realised he was awake, David was standing on the landing below his room. Although the ponderous ticking of the clock in the hallway did not seem loud to his ears, he felt it pulsing through his body, shivering up through his feet, vibrating minutely in his teeth like an ebbing but persistent itch. He walked, his feet bare, to the head of the staircase and began to descend. Darkness flowed around him like oil, or something thicker than oil – like a soft, warm jelly that slowed his movements and calmed his heartbeat and muffled his thoughts.

Walking down the stairs felt like sliding deeper into the gelid darkness. His plodding feet kept time with the plodding clock. He felt as though he were treading water; nothing around him seemed solid. Dark moved on dark in the hallway below, like barely glimpsed sea-creatures shifting sluggishly through the depths.

And then, drifting out through the dark like a phantom of itself, came the clock. At first David thought it *was* floating, and then he decided that *he* was floating towards *it*. The clock-face glowed like the moon, surrounded by a misty nimbus of light. Somehow David could not focus on the time; the hands seemed indistinct, or perhaps constantly moving.

The fat moon-face on the smaller dial was gone, as though consumed by the larger. In its place was a landscape blanketed in snow so virgin it looked like nothingness. David drifted closer to the clock, lifting his face to its cold light as if to kiss it. Somehow the snowy landscape gave the impression of extending far beyond the boundaries created for it. A few bare and charred-looking trees poked through the snow, resembling

196

black cracks across the orange screen of the sky. A sudden flurry of snow blew into his face, and David closed his eyes as they filled with flakes that stung like grit. He raised a hand, fingers splayed, to protect his tender skin. His feet suddenly felt heavy and huge, as though concrete was setting around them. Eyes still closed, face freezing, he tried to lift one of his feet, and was surprised at the resistance from whatever he was standing in – so much so, in fact, that he lost his balance, falling forward. He put out both hands to stop himself – and suddenly they were sinking into cold, soft, deep snow. On all fours now, he opened his eyes and looked around.

He was surrounded by an undulating blanket of snow which flowed to the burnt horizon on all sides. Here and there, trees that looked as though a child had sketched them in charcoal punctured the snow's white crust. Aside from the trees the landscape was featureless, and, because of this, oddly beautiful. David pushed backwards with his hands in an effort to raise himself to a standing position.

Suddenly he sensed a presence beside him, and then strong hands were curling around his upper arms, helping him to his feet. David had no idea where the newcomer could have appeared from; a moment ago he had looked all around and seen nothing but snow in every direction. Once David was standing, the newcomer released him and moved round to stand in front of him. A warm, earthy, somehow spicy smell that made David think of cinnamon buns and Bonfire Night drifted from the stranger's body, caressing David's face. He breathed it in, looking at the stranger, a tall man with a handsome, high-cheekboned face, flowing dark hair and a trim beard. The man was wearing a coarse brown robe, like a foreshortened monk's habit, and on his feet were boots that looked as though he had stitched them together himself from the hide of some dark, shaggy animal – a bear, or perhaps a moose.

'Thank you,' David said.

The man gave a brief nod of acknowledgement, and then, almost impatiently, as though eager to get down to business, he said, 'The Great Serpent has laid her eggs, each of which contains shadows and poison. Even here the shadows lengthen and the poison spreads. I know you, David. Do *you* know *me*?'

'Er . . .' David said.

'Watch.' The man reached into his robe like a magician searching for a rabbit, and then, to David's shock and alarm, produced a black snake as long and as thick as his own arm. He held the snake tightly behind its head so that it couldn't twist and bite, its skull jutting from his fist like a strange weapon. The snake's body hung down, dormant at first, but as soon as the cold air and the lightly falling snow touched it, it began to writhe and hiss. The man seemed unconcerned as the snake lifted its tail, first finding and then beginning to coil around his arm. Now it seemed that the man was wearing a fat black spiral bracelet. With his free hand – his right – he reached into his boot and produced a knife with a gleaming, serrated blade perhaps ten inches long. He pinched the snake hard behind its skull and gave a practised flick of his left arm, and suddenly the snake was cracking like a whip, and the next moment swinging from his hand again like a black pendulum.

'Is it dead?' David wanted to ask, but even as he licked his dry lips in readiness to form the question he saw that it was not. The snake began to writhe again, to lift its tail so that it resembled an inverted question mark. However, before it could regain its purchase on the stranger's arm, he rammed the knife into its body just below his left fist and cut down, slitting it open along its length. David gritted his teeth in revulsion and pity as the snake began to thrash in what seemed to him obvious pain. He expected to see blood or internal organs pouring from the snake's wound, but what he did see almost stopped the breath in his throat.

It began as a glimmer, a flicker, and then all at once crackles of blue-white lightning were pouring from the two-foot long gash in the snake's body. It was like barbed wire made of raw electricity. It spiralled and spun around the snake, frantic stitches of energy and light.

The stranger opened his mouth and suddenly the energy was pouring into *him*. David saw it jumping around his teeth in white sparks, bleaching his gullet with light. As though the stranger was an empty vessel and the energy a liquid that was filling him up, David saw crackles of light first brimming and then spilling from the stranger's eyes. Like twitching, radiant tears, the energy obliterated the stranger's pupils, danced across his cheeks, and then began to move both upwards into his hair and downwards into his beard. When the stranger spoke, his voice crackled and sizzled with the energy that now seemed to be saturating his body.

'You know me,' he said.

David was not sure whether the stranger's words were intended as a statement or a question, but all at once he realised that, yes, he *did* know this man.

'Who am I?' the stranger said again, his voice sounding how an electricity pylon might if it started to talk.

David's own voice sounded small and feeble by comparison.

'You are Decumen,' he said.

Part Four
The Barrow (2)

Chapter Twenty-Four

What day is it? Kerr thought. Wednesday? Thursday? Friday? And what time is it? He tried to focus on his watch, but the little hands and numbers might have been smears of dirt for all the sense they made.

His head throbbed, his mind a stew of confusion, filled with fragments, half-remembered bits of days. What was happening to him? Why couldn't he think straight? Had he been asleep? It seemed so, but for how long? Why couldn't he remember?

It occurred to him, in a vague, cloudy way, that his disorientation ought to be frightening him, that if his shattered thoughts didn't start fitting themselves together soon he ought to feel the first bright spasms of panic. He'd always been terrified of the notion of going mad, losing his faculties and dignity and control. He'd found the idea of that far worse than the idea of death, which was after all merely obliteration, a non-experience, no worse than the time before his birth, when the world had functioned adequately without him in it.

But, like his memories, his emotions seemed distant, distant enough certainly to be ungraspable. They were like tiny figures trudging up the slope of a far-off mountain. There was anger, there fear, there happiness, there sorrow. They were recognisable, but there was no contact to be had with them. It was nice in a way – in a vague, unthinking kind of way. Bye bye world, bye bye life, cut my string and off I drift.

Have I taken an overdose? The voice, only mildly interested, spoke silently inside his head, giving Kerr the odd (but in his state of mind perfectly logical) idea that he was onion-man, composed of many layers, many skins, each of which contained its own personality.

The idea was . . . interesting. An overdose. Hmm. Of what? Not that it mattered if the entire ride was going to be like this. He didn't want it to start hurting, though; that would spoil things.

What was he looking at? White. A screen? But not bright white. Dim. Almost grey. Shadows. A ceiling.

Yes, that inner voice said again dreamily. *I'm looking at a ceiling. That means I'm lying down. I'm in bed or on the floor.*

Now an even more peculiar idea came to him. He was Frankenstein's monster lying on a slab in a laboratory, full of dead or, at best, sluggish cells. And the voice was the electricity surging and resonating through him, stimulating and feeding those cells. He thought of the cells as tiny little light bulbs which were slowly but surely fizzing and sputtering back into life. And the light of each of those little bulbs was in fact a sliver of memory or awareness or information, which (in another sudden strange transformation of images) now made him think of jigsaw pieces, coming together to form a complete picture.

Not that the picture was complete yet, oh no. He still had a long way to go. He remembered some things, though. Remembered the wedding dress lying on the bed, how seeing it, and seeing Hilary too (*Had* he seen her? Yes, he had. In the mirror. But had he *really* seen her? Oh, please say he had) had sent him off the deep end for a while there.

Too close. Too painful. He had had to put some distance between himself and the . . . the *incident*. He'd had to fill the space with something to dull the pain so completely that it had become less an anaesthetic and more a broth of forgetfulness. He had drunk deeply of that broth, and, he was almost sure, he had lost quite a bit of time. What else? He couldn't remember. He didn't *want* to remember. He had been to a very dark place and that was all he needed to know.

The light bulbs were still coming on – *crackle, fizz, plink, sputter* – and now Kerr was no longer floating; now reality was gelling around him. He became uncomfortably aware of his body. It felt weighty and full of vague aches. Full of something else too, something less easily definable – the deep-set, exhaustive sickness of futility, perhaps.

He sat up slowly, and again thought of Frankenstein's monster rising from the slab. The dead given life, or a *sort* of life, he thought. He sighed and groaned. A sort of life that was no life at all. It was all he had now, for ever and ever, amen.

Sitting, he assessed himself. His head throbbed, his mouth was dry, his heart ached when it beat as though he'd bruised it. His fingers and toes felt numb as though his nerves couldn't quite stretch to his extremities. Emotionally, things were back to normal. Although the booze and the Valium provided him with an umbrella from the worst of the storm, it didn't stop him knowing that the storm was out there. And even with his umbrella he had to plod through it, head bowed, listen to its thunder and feel the cold, inescapable gnash of its teeth.

Something glimmered to his right. He turned and saw a figure floating, headless. No, not a figure. A dress. Hilary's wedding dress. And now – *fzzt* – another light bulb of memory ignited, perhaps a whole bank of them.

He had tried to fit the dress back into its box, but it wouldn't go. It was too big, too frothy; when he tried to fold it, the white silk bodice slithered beneath his hands and the layered lace skirt refused to co-operate, bulging out first one side and then the other. His hands had been trembling and he had been weeping uncontrollably. He had been terrified of creasing the dress or even tearing it. In the end he had reached into the wardrobe for a coat hanger, his hand clattering among them like a trapped bird, and had hung the dress up on the outside of the wardrobe door to prevent it getting squashed between his baggy suits.

With an effort he swung his legs from the bed, the dull throb in his head cranking up to actual pain now, pain so bad it almost made him gag. He imagined pieces of broken glass stuck in his brain, grinding together when he moved.

On his bedside table was a bottle of Bell's, only a quarter-full. Kerr reached out, grasped the neck, brought the bottle to his lips. The first sip made him want to throw up, but the second was better, and by the third he was suckling like a baby at its mother's teat. Slowly he began to rock back and forth; he found the movement comforting. He was all too aware that mad people did this, but there was no one here to see him, so what did it matter what he did?

He stopped rocking. No one here. No one to talk to. No one to love. No one to love him.

Oh, Hilary, why did you have to go away? Why don't you come back?

The despair that washed over him, shocking as being doused by cold water, coincided with the ringing of the telephone downstairs. Kerr couldn't think of anyone he wanted to talk to (except Hilary), but he automatically pushed himself to his feet and began to shuffle across the room.

By the time he reached the bottom of the stairs, clinging to the banister to prevent his clumsy, disobedient feet missing a stair and making him fall arse over tit to the bottom, the phone had rung twelve, fifteen, maybe as many as twenty times. It gave every indication of continuing to ring for all eternity if he didn't answer it. As Kerr made his unsteady way towards the lounge, he had the strangest idea that even if he were to go in there and pull out the plug, the phone would continue to utter its shrill and plaintive *breep-breep . . . breep-breep*.

He was perhaps four steps from the lounge – the lounge where he had discovered his wife, cold and dead, her uneaten lunch by her side – when the phone was picked up.

'Hello,' said a woman's voice.

Kerr froze. All at once his throat seemed to flood with the taste and smell of sour whisky. His head swam with the fumes. His left arm tingled like the onset of a heart attack.

'Hilary?' he croaked, and then he was lumbering towards the lounge door, slamming it open with the heel of his right hand. He burst into the room, breathing stertorously.

The room was empty, the telephone seemingly untouched.

And then the phone began to ring again, or perhaps it had never stopped. Kerr blundered towards it, fumbled it from its cradle.

'Yes?' he barked into the mouthpiece.

'Marcus?'

'Yes.'

'Hello, Marcus, it's Julian Hamilton. I was just ringing up to find out how you were.'

'How I am?' Kerr said stupidly. The man's enquiry seemed somehow beyond him.

'Yes, the flu.'

'Flu?'

Now the voice on the other end of the line was flecked with

206

exasperation. 'Yes, you rang in on Monday afternoon to say you wouldn't be coming back to the surgery because you thought you had a touch of flu. Don't you remember?'

'I . . . yes,' said Kerr. 'Of course.' He paused, wondering how wise it would be to ask the next question. He wished his brain was working properly. Instinctively he decided to take the plunge. 'What . . . what day is it now?'

There was a pause, and then the voice said carefully, 'What *day* is it?'

'Yes.'

'You don't know what *day* it is?'

'I . . . I've been asleep,' Kerr said desperately. 'I'm a bit . . . disorientated.'

This time he felt the man's disbelief flowing through the silence towards him. Then the man said curtly, 'It's Thursday.'

'Thursday? Yes, of course,' Kerr said, managing to hide his shock, thinking: *I've lost three days!* He blundered on. 'And what time is it? I don't seem to be wearing my . . . erm . . . ' He couldn't for the life of him think of the name of the thing that even now he was wearing on his wrist, but whose symbols were still a mystery to him.

'Twenty past ten,' the man said, then added with emphasis, 'in the morning.'

'Right . . . er . . . right, thanks,' Kerr said. He couldn't now remember who this was he was talking to or what the point of the conversation – if it had ever had one – had been.

'So when *can* we expect you back?' the man said.

'Back?'

'In the surgery.'

'Oh . . . yes. Tomorrow, without fail. Absolutely. No problem.'

There was a kind of smug concern in the man's voice. 'Are you sure you're up to it, Marcus?'

'Course I'm bloody up to it,' Kerr said, at the last moment rediscovering a little of his old brusqueness. 'I'll see you tomorrow. Goodbye.'

He put the phone down before the man could confuse him further.

Chapter Twenty-Five

'Jack o' Lanterns.'

Merely the phrase was evocative enough to send a little shiver of excitement up Chris Farrar's back as he whispered it to himself in the darkness. Tonight he was absolutely determined that he wouldn't fall asleep as he had done for the past five nights since seeing the Jack o' Lanterns bobbing through the graveyard for the third time last Sunday. Instead of going out that afternoon, he had stayed in and made himself lie on his bed with his eyes closed until he fell asleep. He had slept for over two hours, waking up just after half-five when Mum had called him down for tea. Now at ... he squinted at the glowing numerals of his watch ... ten to twelve, he was wide awake and ready for action. He was desperate to see the Jack o' Lanterns again – but not *just* to see them. He wanted to pursue and overtake them, to get to the church door before they did, so that he could see whether what Col had told him about them was true.

Chris couldn't help feeling that, despite his efforts, summer was petering out when there still seemed so much to cram in before the prison sentence that was school resumed in ten days' time. Since David's initiation on Tuesday evening, the three boys had barely seen each other. Col seemed to be taking what his grandmother had said to heart and making excuses to keep away, and David, although he'd been round a couple of times, was still spending a lot of time helping his mum get the house straight. 'When we're properly settled you can come round for tea,' he had said by way of apology for not coming out when Chris had rung him that morning, but when would that be? Once the nights started drawing in and the homework started piling up, there wouldn't be much time to do anything.

Chris was sitting in his accustomed place, on a chair facing the window, his elbows propped on the windowsill so that his cupped hands could support the weight of his head. He had ducked his head and shoulders under the curtains and was staring out at what he could see of the churchyard through the trees flanking the path that led from the door of their house to the garden gate. The silhouette of the church rose above the trees, resembling a giant fist with its forefinger extended, breaking through the crust of the hill and jabbing at the star-freckled sky. Though one or two of the gravestones were crested with arcs of pale, bluish light, the church itself was black and featureless, more like a hole waiting to be filled with a solid object than an object itself.

On the windowsill was a pair of binoculars which every so often he raised to his eyes. He was fully dressed, in jeans and trainers and a T-shirt. Though the night was warm, there was a jacket over the back of the chair in which he was sitting, with a torch in the right-hand pocket. His parents had come up to bed twenty minutes ago, and the house was now quiet.

Chris was a bit disappointed that nothing had resulted from David's initiation on Tuesday evening, though not altogether surprised. He hadn't really known what to expect, though he'd been half-hoping for something momentous and spectacular. There were so many portents around at the moment that the timing had seemed perfect. Not that he wanted anything bad to befall anyone; he just wanted something exciting to happen before the summer slipped away for good.

He looked at his watch again. Midnight. As if he had prompted it, the church clock began to strike. He raised the binoculars to his eyes, scanning the churchyard. He'd been sitting here for over an hour now and was feeling fidgety and nervous, though he knew that the Jack o' Lanterns could appear at any time, that midnight held no special significance for them. The first time he had seen them it had been well into the early hours of the morning. He wasn't sure exactly what time, but he'd guess two or three o'clock. He'd woken up to go to the loo and on returning had noticed a green glow through a gap in his curtains. There had been four lights on that occasion, each as big as a man's head. He had watched them drift through the churchyard about four feet above the ground like puffballs of rot, his eyes wide with awe, heart racing with fear and excitement.

What had scared and thrilled him the most was that, although their course was slow and meandering, the lights had nevertheless seemed to move with a sense of purpose and deliberation, as if they had a controlling intelligence. Before Colin had passed on what his grandmother had told him they were, Chris had come to the conclusion that they were either ghosts or aliens. He had particularly favoured the aliens theory, surmising that the reason they had come to Earth was to find food in the form of dead bodies. He pictured each of them perched on a grave, extending some form of proboscis into the ground, which they would use to gnaw through the wood of the coffin below before sucking up the rotting meat inside. Chris had wondered whether they knew he was watching them, and if so how they'd react. Perhaps they'd appear in his room in a blaze of light and abduct him like in *The X-Files*. The second time he had seen them he had lain awake in his bed for hours afterwards, rigid with terror, waiting for them to come and take him.

The fact that they weren't aliens didn't disappoint him, however. Jack o' Lanterns were just as good, even though he didn't know *exactly* what Jack o' Lanterns were beyond portents of doom. Were they ghosts or just . . . things? Could they think and see? Would they sense him moving amongst them? Would they attack him, and if so, how? Did they burn or bite or electrocute? Did they make you dissolve if they touched you, like some kind of alien death-ray?

Chris was scared, but he was excited too, ready to face whatever consequences might befall him. He wanted to do it partly to see the awed expressions on his friends' faces when he told them about it later, but mainly in order to (in the words of his big hero, Fox Mulder) 'open himself up to the realms of extreme possibility'. Fox Mulder was full of great sayings like this. Chris's favourite was: 'The truth is out there.'

He whispered this, and all at once it seemed that his words held the power of some weird prophecy, for the Jack o' Lanterns, whether they held the truth or not, suddenly *were* out there.

There were six of them this time, low down and off to the left, moving close to the Farrars' garden wall, though staying on the churchyard side. The grass and weeds grew long here, where there were not yet any graves.

Chris's mouth went dry and he fumbled for the binoculars, dread and excitement curdling in his belly. His hands were so clumsy that he clacked the eyepieces against his spectacles, the bar connecting his lenses jarring the bridge of his nose. As ever, the green lights moved slowly, methodically; partly obscured by trees and foliage, they flickered in and out of sight, like torches being switched on and off. Chris had never seen the Jack o' Lanterns this close to the house before. *Are they coming for me because they know what I'm planning to do?* he thought. He tried to stop his hands from trembling as he focused on them, but despite their relative proximity he saw just as few details as the last three times they had appeared. They were simply lights, nothing more, bright – almost white – in the middle, deepening to a sickly lime colour around the edges (if balls of light could be said to *have* edges).

This is it, he thought, *this is it*. It was the moment he'd been waiting for, but all at once he wished he *had* been disappointed, that the Jack o' Lanterns *hadn't* come back. He knew he didn't have to go outside, that he could simply stay here in the safety of his room, watching the lights through his binoculars if he wanted, and for a moment the idea of doing just that was very tempting.

Then he remembered boasting to his friends about how he was going to reach the church door before the Jack o' Lanterns next time they appeared and see whether there really were faces of the soon-to-be dead contained within the lights. If Col and David discovered he'd chickened out, he'd never live it down. Not to mention how disgusted he'd be with himself later if he didn't follow this through, how he'd regret not having done anything when he had the chance.

'Oh shit,' he muttered, and pushed the curtain aside as he ducked back into the room. He grabbed his jacket from the back of the chair and pulled it on, the heavy torch in the pocket bumping against his hip. The night was actually still warm enough for him to have managed comfortably without the jacket, but he felt less vulnerable somehow, having something bulky wrapped around him. He crossed the room, went out on to the landing and crept down the stairs, pursued by the gentle grind of his father's snoring.

He expected it to be cooler outside, but it wasn't. The honeysuckle climbing the trellis to the left of the front door made the air seem thick and sweet as syrup. Chris looked left and right, but the Jack o' Lanterns were nowhere to be seen. He couldn't shake off the suspicion, however, that they had drifted in through the garden gate when he'd been coming down through the house and concealed themselves behind several of the trees flanking the path, perhaps prior to swinging out and confronting him like a cluster of glowing, disembodied heads.

For a few moments he hovered by the front door, trying to decide whether it would be wiser to proceed with caution or just to put his head down and run full-pelt at the garden gate. At least once he was in the churchyard there wouldn't be so many places where the Jack o' Lanterns could hide, not until he got closer to the church itself. His heart felt like a hamster on a wheel, racing along without getting anywhere; his body twitched and trembled, his nerves jumping. *Right, here I come*, he thought, and began to jog up the tree-lined path towards the gate.

When he caught a glimpse of a green glow through the trees to his right, he was so alarmed that he staggered and almost fell. His head jerking towards the glow, Chris fully expected the Jack o' Lanterns to loom from behind the trees in a slow and terrifying ambush. But at first he saw nothing except the trees themselves, too many of whose trunks looked like dark, motionless figures until his jerking eyes focused on them fully. Then, like a match flaring green, he saw another flicker of light, and then another. It took him a moment, however, to realise that the Jack o' Lanterns were not in the trees at all, but still in the churchyard, though now off to the right, moving away from him.

Relief flooded through him. If the Jack o' Lanterns continued their meandering, zig-zagging route, then all he had to do to avoid encountering them between here and the church door was to walk straight up the slope. While he'd been descending the stairs in the house, they must have drifted right past the gate. He wondered why they followed such a circuitous route. Maybe they were aimless, after all, or maybe their journey was a kind of ritual. Or maybe, he thought, fighting a nervous urge to giggle hysterically, they just like reading the inscriptions on the gravestones.

He reached the gate and peered through it cautiously to ensure none of the Jack o' Lanterns had stayed behind to surprise him. No, all six of them were seventy or eighty yards away, still moving off to the right, away from him and at this moment away from the church too. He set foot in the churchyard and began to jog up the slope towards the dark fist of the church. The Jack o' Lanterns were either unaware of his presence or considered it insignificant; they changed neither course nor speed.

It was not a strenuous climb to the church, but the nervous quivering in his belly enervated him. Neither did the jacket help; it seemed to soak up the moisture in the muggy air, and within minutes was heavy as chain-mail. By the time he reached the first of the gravestones, Chris was gasping for breath, sweat prickling in his hair. The going became not more treacherous, but certainly more complicated here. He would have to use the torch to negotiate the short flights of steps and yew trees and sprawling, spiny bushes that were stuffed between the gravestones like the work of a landscape gardener employed by the Addams family. This, of course, meant losing sight of the Jack o' Lanterns for a while. He glanced to his right, and for an instant felt certain they were rushing towards him. They weren't; it was an optical illusion exacerbated by his tiredness. However, they *had* changed course, though only because they had now reached the stone-walled boundary of the churchyard.

As Chris watched, they began to drift up the hill, paralleling his own route, approaching the first of the gravestones tucked beneath the shelter of the perimeter wall far away to his right. As they reached the stones and then passed between them, they doused each one in light the colour of putrefaction. Then the first of the trees over on that side of the churchyard seemed to lean forward and reach out with spiny limbs, like a mother welcoming her children home, and next moment the Jack o' Lanterns had drifted into that dark and hungry embrace and could no longer be seen.

Chris blew out a long breath and reached for the torch in his pocket. He wondered how quickly the Jack o' Lanterns could move. He'd only ever seen them floating along, slow as balloons, but that didn't neccessarily mean they *couldn't* move quickly, did it? He switched on his torch and immediately the

213

gravestones seemed to bulge, mushroom-white. It was a lot more fun *thinking* about doing this than actually doing it, Chris thought, but began nonetheless to follow the path between the headstones, the grass ahead of him springing to attention in white spikes as if his torchlight had awakened it.

For the next couple of minutes he plodded up sets of crumbling stone steps, crouched beneath the protective umbrellas of yew trees to peer round corners and slipped between tombstones like a ghost. He switched his torch on and off depending on how exposed he felt, and only once did he see a flicker of green to his right, or thought he did – in the instant it took him to turn properly to check, it was gone.

At last he was standing on the stone-flagged path that circled the church, the path that David had lapped seven times three days ago as his initiation into the Barrow Boys. The ground sloped away from him now, the trees and bushes and gravestones a jumble of black, hunched shapes beneath the night sky. He couldn't see the Jack o' Lanterns at all, had no idea where they might be. From now on, the risk he was taking was not even a calculated one; he simply had to trust to luck.

Switching off the torch, he began to creep around the church, keeping close to the wall. This would make a great story to tell the lads tomorrow, but he wished it was over now.

He reached the church door without incident, entered the vestibule and sank down with his back to the smooth, worn wood. He was exhausted, felt like closing his eyes, sleeping till morning. It certainly felt warm enough, especially with his jacket to drag around him like a duvet. Though familiar, the route from the house up to the church had seemed like dark and alien territory, and so it reassured him now to see the orange glimmer of a street lamp beyond the lych-gate, the tip of the war memorial above the trees.

Maybe the Jack o' Lanterns wouldn't come to the church door, maybe Col's grandmother had been wrong about them. Chris supposed that if they didn't come, he would feel a bit disappointed in the morning, but not much; after all, he'd done his bit, he couldn't be blamed for chickening out now. One thing he had learned from this was that ghost-hunting on your own wasn't much fun. He had stopped feeling excited the instant he had stepped out of the safety of the house. Next time, if he wasn't with his friends, he wouldn't bother.

'You'll need this,' Mr Toot was saying, holding out a big, old-fashioned key.

'What is it?' Chris asked.

'It will open the door that you need to open the most,' the grocer said, smiling.

Chris took the key, but suddenly it wasn't a key any more, it was something alive. It squirmed in his hand as though desperate to get away. Chris tried to cup one hand over the other, to make an egg of his hands, but the living creature that had previously been a key wriggled out through a gap in his fingers. The creature slithered down his chest and across his legs. It was a small black snake. Chris cried out and awoke, his eyes snapping open.

The Jack o' Lanterns were coming.

He saw them, a slow procession of green candles whose bearers couldn't be seen, drifting among the trees and tombstones to his right. Presumably they had followed the line of the perimeter wall as though marking the distance. Chris felt sure that once they reached the lych-gate they would begin floating up the path towards him.

It wasn't too late to get away, he thought. He could run home. They wouldn't come after him. But something held him there – a terrified, desperate curiosity, a sense of duty.

Unhurried, the first of the Jack o' Lanterns reached the lych-gate, and, as Chris had known it would, began to float up the path towards him. Now he couldn't have moved even if he had wanted to. His limbs seemed atrophied, no energy left in them whatsoever.

The Jack o' Lantern came closer and closer, a bobbing green head of light. Chris's terror mesmerised him, locked him inside himself. He couldn't move, couldn't speak, couldn't scream.

Something squirmed within the ball of light. Now it resembled a glowing womb in which a foetus struggled feebly. Chris saw shadows, shapes, something swarming and bulging, trying to rise from beneath the surface of the light.

It was a face. Oh God, it was a face. Col's grandmother had been right. Chris could see the dark pits of the mouth and eyes, the swelling of the nose. Now the Jack o' Lantern seemed composed not of light but of some viscous, glowing substance – clay that moulded itself.

215

The Jack o' Lantern was no more than twenty feet away now, and still the face it was becoming ran like tallow, the features refining themselves. It was as though an invisible sculptor was shaving off a little flesh here, adding a touch more definition there.

Ten feet, and suddenly Chris's eyes widened, his mouth whooping in air. Now he recognised the face. Though it was a death-mask its features were unmistakeable.

He was looking at himself.

All at once he rediscovered the ability to scream. He did so, loud and long, and his scream seemed in turn to unlock his limbs. He scrambled to his feet, still yelling but beginning to cry now too.

'*Gerraway from me!*' he bawled, flailing his arms, and turning blindly began to run back along the flagstoned path that would take him round the back of the church and down the slope to home. He was driven by the desperate, instinctive notion that if he could reach the warm security of his bed without incident, then everything would be all right.

I'm not going to die, I'm not going to die, his mind chanted as he ran, his breath tearing at his throat like jags of metal, his feet slapping the flagstones that were not really flagstones but tombstones, laid over the bones of the long-dead. He ran round the corner of the church, whereupon the street lamp outside the lych-gate seemed to wink out, though its bonfire glow had only been blocked by the church wall.

Chris didn't even break his stride; he kept running, nettles thrashing at his legs. *I'm not going to die, I'm not going to die, I'm not going to die.*

Here, almost hidden among tangles of foliage, was the first flight of stone steps. He lunged for it like a sprinter going for the tape, and as his left foot hit the top step he threw himself forwards, kicking his right leg out in a huge balletic leap.

He almost made it. An inch further and he would have been okay. But as he came down, his heel hit the very edge of the bottom of five steps, and it was like being shoved from behind before he could regain his balance.

His body shot forward down the slope, his natural momentum carrying him far quicker than his legs could. He began to fall forward as his legs crumbled, his hands going out to stop his face hitting the ground first. Eight feet in front of him, directly in his path, was a tombstone. Chris could do nothing to arrest or even change his course. It might have been better if he had allowed himself to go down and to have rolled into it, but instead he made the mistake of trying to stay on his feet.

He hit the tombstone with immense force, his left thigh and pelvis taking most of the impact. He heard a sound that made him think briefly of crunching a plastic cup in his fist, and then he was drowning in pain. The pain was of such unbelievable intensity that for a few seconds he couldn't see, couldn't scream, couldn't think. And then it had yanked him down into unconsciousness.

When he surfaced again, so suddenly that it was more like being switched on than waking up, he was in a world of agony. He was crying in little shrill gasps; it seemed such a pitiful and inappropriate reaction to such an immense hurt. The pain engulfed him, it *was* him; there was nothing else in the world, never had been and never would be. In his mind's eye, Chris saw the death-mask of his own face hovering before him, and he begged, desperately and silently as he lay broken, *Please make it soon.*

Chapter Twenty-Six

Jason Sheridan left it until Saturday morning before going back to the woods to retrieve his magazines. He had been planning to leave it a whole week, but by Saturday he was all but climbing the walls, desperate to see what the children who lived within the glossy pages were eager to show him. Besides, he felt fairly sure that he had managed to outwit Des Brewer by this time. Jason hadn't seen the policeman since he had tried to trick him into going home on Monday. When Jason *had* finally gone home, many hours after Brewer had told him to, he had been relieved to find that Dad wasn't there. Then Mum had told him that Dad had been arrested for fighting in the pub, and Jason had wondered whether that was just part of the trick, whether Dad and Brewer were in it together, trying to trap him.

If so, they hadn't succeeded. Jason had given nothing away. He had been pleased with his performance, had kept his head even when Dad had reappeared on Tuesday, claiming to have spent a night in the cells. On Tuesday night Jason had heard Dad hitting Mum, her crying out, begging him to stop. The next day she could hardly walk, or at least she *pretended* she couldn't. Jason had looked at her face and arms and legs closely, but had not been able to see a single mark on them. This had made him wonder whether in fact they were all in it together. Maybe they thought that he thought Dad would stop hitting Mum if he confessed. They must think he was stupid if they thought he was going to be taken in by that, which made *them* twice as stupid. Jason kept expecting one of them to crack, to try to make him tell them where the magazines were, but if they did that he'd just deny everything. The magazines were so well hidden that no one would ever find them.

Just to ensure he wouldn't be followed, he got up extra early on Saturday morning, setting his alarm for four a.m. It was still dark when he crept downstairs, though he knew it wouldn't be very much longer before pale blue worms started wriggling across the sky. He gobbled down a bowl of Cornflakes, holding his breath because the milk didn't smell too good, and when he left the house at 4:15 he took his fishing rod, keep net and creel with him, just so that if he *was* spotted he'd have a ready-made excuse for being out so early.

This was the only time of day when it felt anything like cool. It wouldn't last long, though. Soon the sun would come up, splashing the sky with light the colour of tinned salmon. Not long after that it would start to get warm and then hot, and it would stay hot until the sun went down again at about ten p.m.

Jason was often out early (though not usually *this* early). He liked to walk the streets before most people got up, and once they *did* start getting up, he'd usually head off to the woods or the river, somewhere he could be alone.

He didn't like people much. They asked him questions he couldn't answer and gave him funny looks and made him feel awkward and stupid. Some of them, like Kim Ellis, called him names; others, like Dad, just wanted to hurt him.

If Jason had his way, he'd get rid of them all – well, all except for Cassie Herron. Not for the first time he wished Cassie was with him now. He imagined the two of them walking towards the woods together, hand in hand, finding a quiet place to play their games. Maybe it wouldn't be very much longer before he could make the fantasy a reality. He was sure he'd be able to persuade her to come to the woods with him soon, and it wouldn't be a trick, not really; he'd just tell her he had something he wanted to show her, which was true enough, wasn't it?

Thinking of Cassie, of the things they might soon be doing together, made him feel light-headed, made his cock grow hard in his jeans again.

He wondered what Cassie was doing now. Sleeping probably.

I bet she looks just like an angel when she's asleep, he thought.

He didn't see a soul during his walk, though he kept

glancing behind him just to make sure he wasn't being followed. He was heading for the top woods up by the river, beyond the big house which he knew was there behind the wall that ran all the way round it, but which he had never seen up close. From down in the village you could see the roof of the big house poking above a load of trees on top of the hill if you were standing in the right place. Jason had heard vague rumours that the old woman who had lived there had died and some new people had moved in, but he didn't know who they were. All he *did* know was that they must be two things: rich and unfriendly. Rich because no poor person could ever live in a house like that, and unfriendly because with those big gates and high walls they couldn't want visitors.

One day, he thought, *I'm going to live in a house like that, and then I'll never have to see anybody. Except for Cassie. She could live there with me. We could play games all day long and no one would be able to stop us.*

Where the house was, it was quite open, cornfields replacing the woodland on both sides of the road, but once you came to the corner of the wall that faced on to the road, the land dropped away again, the woodland crowding in, becoming denser as you headed down to the river.

This was the way Jason went now, following a trail that led around the edge of the woods. Everything was green, and glowing like mad despite the recent drought; birds were starting up their dawn chorus and the air was full of good, fresh smells.

Jason felt happy and excited. The closer he got to where he had hidden the magazines, the faster he walked, almost breaking into a trot at times, the creel bouncing on his hip. His stomach flick-flacked with anticipation; blood made both his head and his cock feel engorged.

At last the river came into sight through the trees, blue and sparkling like a diamond. The banks were high because the water level was so low. Rocks were sticking up through the surface like the backs of stranded whales.

The woods came almost up to the river's edge on this side and then stopped. On the opposite side, fields stretched away into the distance, but here trees threw shadows on to the water, making it seem grey and murky up close.

Jason dumped his fishing stuff and began to walk along the

river bank into the woods, looking for a particular tree he had marked with a cross. He knew it was about five minutes' walk from his starting point, but that didn't stop him checking every tree to make sure.

He was just beginning to get worried when he saw it. It was a smaller tree than he remembered, little more than a sapling. In fact, now he thought about it, he recalled how the sap had run like blood when he'd cut into the trunk, how his knife had kept getting stuck in the gluey, fibrous bark.

He had thought it was a neat little cross he'd made, only noticeable to someone actually looking for it, but now he winced at the sight of the great wound in the vague form of a cross hacked into the trunk of the tree. He examined the ground round about, but the grass was lush and springy; it didn't look as though anyone had been here, at least not today.

Jason looked behind him once again, and then, using the tree as a marker, began to walk in a straight line, away from the water, deeper into the woods. He counted the paces he was taking as he did so, whispering the numbers under his breath. When he got to forty-five he stopped.

And there was the tree he was looking for, a massive horse chestnut whose smooth green buds would soon become conkers in their spiny coats. Jason stood at the foot of the tree and squinted up into the branches, his eyes trying to make sense of the collage of overlapping scraps of shadows that were leaves.

When he'd hidden the magazines in the hole in the trunk that was about twenty feet off the ground, it had been mid-afternoon, the sun so high and bright that every leaf, every tree trunk, every blade of grass had seemed to glow. The hole in the trunk then had been the only place where the shadows had seemed black; it had made the tree look as though it was yawning.

That was not to say that the hole had been immediately noticeable. If a squirrel hadn't shot across his path and scampered up the tree in a blur of grey fur, Jason would probably not have seen it. As soon as he did, though, he knew there was only one place he could hide his magazines. He had scrambled up the tree almost as quickly as the squirrel, his lithe limbs reaching unerringly for hand- and footholds. He had always been good at climbing; it was the only thing he *was* good at. He had climbed a lot at school – the geodome, the chain-link fence at the edge of the playground, the bars in the gym – until some of the kids started calling him 'monkey man', after which he had only climbed when he was alone.

Some people wouldn't know where to start on a tree like this, where the lowest branches were eight or ten feet from the ground, but to Jason the bulges and depressions in the trunk were like steps. He reached up and found a handhold, and was just raising his leg to find a foothold that would boost him up towards the branch he wanted (he had already plotted the route he would take in his head), when he heard the sound of giggling behind him.

His heart jumped, and he used the tree trunk to roll himself round so that he was facing back the way he had come. His pale face was a mask of shock, his fingers splayed, gripping the tree behind him. To anyone watching, he must have resembled a huge, etiolated lizard making ready to bask in the morning sun.

But there *was* no one watching. Jason had half-expected to see Mum, Dad and Des Brewer all standing in a row, laughing at him, but as far as he could tell he was as alone as he ever had been.

Except that he *couldn't* be. He *had* heard giggling, he was sure of it, though now he came to think of it, it was more the kind of sound a child would make than an adult. Realising this, the hard block of fear in his stomach began to soften around the edges, and then to dissolve, and as it dissolved it tingled, a sensation that Jason recognised as hope and growing excitement. Maybe, if there *were* children in the woods, he could persuade them to play some games with him. Maybe he could even show them his magazines, make them promise not to tell.

He pushed himself away from the tree and walked towards where he thought the giggling had come from, which was back towards the river, but veering into the trees on the right rather than following the straight line he had walked. It occurred to him to wonder what children would be doing out here at five o'clock in the morning, but he quickly dismissed the thought. After all, *he* was here. Why shouldn't somebody else be?

The trees seemed to step back as he approached, or rather to peel apart like a gate made of many layers, allowing him through. The sky was a pearly blue now, shreds of darker cloud hanging in it like rags, but the woods were still thick with shadow, and the impression of the trees moving as he did was making Jason's eyes go funny.

He considered calling out, but even though he wanted to find the children, he was still reluctant to draw attention to himself. He wondered whether the children had seen him, whether it was him they'd been laughing at. He hoped not; he hated being laughed at. The photograph of the girl he'd been told was Kim Ellis in the hospital flashed into his mind, together with a ghostly echo of the psychiatrist's voice: 'Were you trying to kill her, Jason?'

'No,' he thought, then realised he'd spoken aloud.

As though reacting to his voice, he heard the giggling again; it was high-pitched, girlish. It seemed to come from the trees just ahead of him.

Jason broke into a trot, hands reaching out for trees which he pulled himself round like an ape. He saw a small figure crouched at the base of a tree ten feet away, except that when he ran up to it he realised it wasn't a figure at all, but a bush. He wished the sun would come out and make the shadows disappear. In this semi-light there were still too many silhouettes, too many dark shapes that weren't what they seemed.

He jumped as something flapped above his head, and looked up to see a ragged black shape that could only be a crow moving swiftly across a dark mesh of branches. He grimaced and lowered his eyes – just in time to see another bush sitting in a clot of shadow fifteen feet away unfurl into the shape of a small figure and slip silently away through the trees.

This time Jason was so surprised that he did cry out. 'Hey!' he called, loping forward. 'Hey, wait!'

He reached the place where the figure had been crouching and put out his hand to swing himself round the tree it had disappeared behind.

Then he recoiled, snatching his hand back. The tree appeared to be covered in ridges of flesh so soft that his hand had sunk right into it. Sickened, holding the tainted hand out from his body, he peered at the section of bark he had touched. The sight of the partly liquefied yellow fungus that clung to the tree made him curl his lips in disgust.

He stooped briefly to wipe his hand on the ground, then

223

gave chase. He couldn't see the figure now, though the woods were getting so dense that he might run right past it without realising. After fifteen or twenty seconds, he stopped and looked around him. He saw trees and bushes stitched together by shadow, all sprouting from a thick, undulating carpet of bluebells and long grass and wild garlic. Above him, through a spiky lattice of branches, the hazy, insipid blue of the sky was warmed by the faintest suggestion of rose-pink light.

This was hopeless. If the children didn't want to be caught they wouldn't be. If he wanted to play with them he had to make them come to him.

'Hello,' he called softly. 'Hello, are you there? Can you hear me?'

Was that another giggle, faint as a breath of wind, or just his imagination?

'My name's Jason,' he said. 'I want to play with you. Are you there?'

No response. Reluctantly Jason decided to head back the way he had come. At least he had his magazines to look forward to.

He was actually turning away when he glimpsed movement ahead. He turned back to see the second of two small figures step out from behind a tree some thirty feet away. The two figures stood side by side, and though their faces were in shadow, Jason felt sure that they were observing him keenly. Despite himself he felt a quiver of unease. They were so motionless, so silent, like statues, and now that his eyes were adjusting he got the odd impression that it wasn't shadows that were obscuring their faces, but curtains of long dark hair.

'Hello,' he said tentatively. 'My name's Jason. What are yours?'

In eerie unison the two children (*girls*, Jason thought) turned to face each other, their dark hair swishing. Jason got the weird feeling that they were talking to each other without saying anything. Suddenly he wondered whether following these girls so deep into the woods had been such a good idea, after all. And then hot on the heels of that thought came another: Had he been lured here?

Suddenly he felt scared. He decided that he didn't want to play with these children, after all. He just wanted to get his magazines and leave.

'It's all right,' he mumbled, 'I'm going.' He turned and began to hurry back through the woods. With each step the unfocused fear inside him increased, climbing to panic. Soon he was not just hurrying, but tearing through the trees, hands held out in front of him, his breath like a rusty saw cutting back and forth through his chest. He told himself he was being stupid, that there was nothing to be scared of, that they were only children. But when he thought of how silent and still they had been, how their heads had turned like mirror-images towards each other, and most especially how they had appeared to have not faces but simply hair (*shadows, that's all*, his mind implored him to believe), the panic soared inside him to such an extent that by the time he reached the tree where he had hidden his magazines and collapsed in a heap at its base, he was sobbing with terror.

He lay there for a few seconds, trembling uncontrollably. It was only the thought that the . . . the children might be coming after him that encouraged him to climb shakily to his feet. His legs felt like rubber. Maybe he'd leave the magazines for today, come back for them another time (*or maybe never*). Yes, that was what he'd do. He took a staggering step forward.

And one of the children stepped out from behind the tree, blocking his path.

Jason gaped at the figure, barely aware that he was making small, inarticulate sounds at the back of his throat. It couldn't have got here before him, it just *couldn't*. Due to the figure's proximity he could see it clearly now. It was small as a child, but somehow he knew that it wasn't a child, even though its features were obscured by lank, dark hair that hung down over its face. It was wearing trousers made of some grey sacking-like material, over the top of which was a smock that came almost to its knees.

Jason backed away, taking small, almost dainty steps. 'Go away,' he whimpered, 'leave me alone.'

The figure reached up with tiny hands which were more like paws and parted the curtain of hair, revealing its face. It was not a human face. It was covered with soft grey fur and its eyes were black and bulging; it looked more like a seal than a man.

'No,' Jason said, his voice small, almost inaudible. His legs gave way and he plumped unceremoniously on to his backside.

He began to scrabble at the ground like a wounded crab, his heels and elbows digging into the earth.

The creature opened its mouth and hissed like a snake, revealing dozens of small but razor-sharp teeth.

Chapter Twenty-Seven

On Saturday morning Susan was grinning even before she had opened her eyes. The first thing she was aware of was the delicious anticipation which started in the pit of her stomach and radiated outwards, tingling like heat in her fingers and toes. The three days since she and Jack had made love in front of the fire had been strange ones, full of paradoxical thoughts and emotions. She had relished the days and yet at the same time had longed for them to pass quickly, and even now, although she was aching to see Jack again, she couldn't deny that there was also a part of her that was dreading it.

The thing was, she wanted everything to be perfect. She didn't want what they had shared to be spoiled by awkwardness or embarrassment. She had good reason to hope it wouldn't be; they had spoken on the phone and everything had been fine. But face to face was often very different to voice to voice. The distance of the telephone could make you bold, whereas the intimacy of eye contact could encourage all those inhibitions you thought you'd buried to come stammering and blushing their way to the surface.

Susan had never been as passionate, as hungry, as abandoned as she had been with Jack on Tuesday night. Not even with Gerry, not even in the early days; thinking about it later, realising what she was capable of, had been almost frightening. She didn't like surprising herself, and she had always hated losing control, and yet making love with Jack had been such an incredible experience that she knew she wouldn't hesitate in doing it again.

But would it be so incredible the next time? Did she *want* it to be? Could she cope with that kind of intensity every time she and Jack had sex?

For a while, she thought, and a bubble of laughter escaped her, echoing in what she still thought of as the nursery, in where she had slept for the first time last night. The room was carpetless and smelled so strongly of paint that it made her throat sore, but it was hers, and that was just one of the many things in her life that felt good at the moment.

Oh, Beth, she thought, *you'd be so proud of me*, and she laughed again, and rolled over in bed to look at the clock. She'd bought this bed, a big single, not long after Gerry had died. She had bought it because she'd been unable to bear sleeping in their double bed alone. And yet it was only last night, as she and David had carried the bed from one of the empty rooms where it had been stored into the nursery, that it had occurred to Susan how closed she had been these last seven years, how firmly – and yet in many ways unconsciously – she had vetoed the possibility of further relationships after Gerry's death. Last night it had hit her with the force of a revelation. For the first time she had looked at her single bed and had seen it as a symbol of the forest of thorns she had thrown up around herself. Now Jack had turned up on his trusty steed and had hacked his way through the forest to reach her. But how, when so many others had failed?

'He must have a magic sword,' she murmured, and this time *shrieked* with laughter.

It was 8:05. Jack was picking her and David up at 10:30. Susan smiled, thinking of the note he'd left her, which – like a schoolgirl – she'd read and re-read numerous times these last few days.

She hadn't noticed the note at first. Indeed, for a few moments after waking up naked on Wednesday morning, wrapped in a duvet and lying on a rug in front of a huge fire whose logs had burned down to embers, she'd felt nothing but a sense of disorientation. She'd stared at the fire she'd been facing when her eyes had opened and wondered where the hell she was. Then, as though contained in the warmth of the fire, memory had crept over her and she had whispered, 'Oh my God.'

It had been like remembering a scary but wonderful dream. She had felt the blood rise to the surface of her skin, making

228

her cheeks burn, her breasts tingle. She whooped in a breath that seemed to inflate her lungs until they were tight as balloons on the point of bursting, and for a few moments was unable to release it again. A sense almost of awe filled her. *Did I do that?* she thought. *Was that really me? Oh my God!*

For the first time since Gerry's suicide she had made love, and it had felt so good, so right and natural, and yet at the same time so . . . so *dangerous*. She would never have believed love could be so powerful, so terrifying.

Is he behind me now? she thought. *Is he sleeping naked beside me?*

Again, the prospect was intensely exciting and yet scary enough to make her stomach feel as though it was folding in on itself. For a few minutes she simply lay there, trying to pluck up the courage to move. Finally, unable to stand the suspense any longer, she rolled slowly on to her back. *Oh, please let both of us say and do the right things*, she pleaded silently. *Please let us not spoil what we had.*

But he wasn't there, even though she'd been sure he would be. She had even envisaged him in her mind's eye – lying on his back, muscly arms up over his head, mouth slightly open, closed eyelids looking oddly delicate, like lilac butterfly wings. This, she realised, staring at the trailing edge of duvet under which he should have been lying, was how David used to sleep as a baby. Again, upon discovering his desertion, opposing emotions battled inside her: keen disappointment on the one hand, relief on the other.

She sat up, the duvet slipping to her waist. Automatically she reached for it, intending to cover her exposed breasts, but then she realised that no, that would be the wrong thing to do. After last night any bashfulness on her part could only be a backward step.

But where was he? In the toilet? Making coffee? Or had he woken up sober, realised with horror what he had done, and sneaked away like a thief?

She wouldn't have been able to bear it if this had turned out to be the case, though at the time it seemed the most likely possibility. She pushed the duvet away from her and stood up and stretched, almost wishing that Jack would walk in at that moment and see her naked. She found her pants among the crumpled strew of clothes on the floor – her own clothes, she noted with a sinking heart, none of Jack's – and pulled them on. Then she found and pulled on the T-shirt she had been wearing the previous night – at which point she noticed the note.

It had been folded into three and propped up like a tiny tent on the settee, a sheet of lined notepaper from her telephone pad. Her name was written on the side facing her in big, blocky capitals that seemed so typically Jack.

With a fluttering heart she picked up the note and opened it out. She read it so eagerly the first time that she had to make herself calm down and read it again. He had written:

Dear Susan

Sorry I'm not there to kiss you good morning, but I've got an early start and had to be off. I didn't want to wake you because you looked so peaceful, although you nearly woke up when I put the duvet over you. You rolled over and said something, but I couldn't tell what it was.

Last night was very special to me. I hope it was special to you too.

The next few days are really chock-a-block with work for me, but I wanted to ask if you and David would like to come to the village show with me on Saturday? It's an agricultural show with cake stalls and things. We have one every year. If it's not your sort of thing then that's okay, but it would be great if you could come. It's usually quite good fun and you'd be able to meet a few people.

I didn't want to rush you. I thought you might need a bit of time to think about things after last night.

Anyway, ring me when you've decided, though if you want to catch me in you'll have to ring after 9 at night because I'm working with a builder friend of mine over in Harrogate these next few days and won't get back until then.

I'll look forward to your call. I hope you decide to come on Saturday.

All my love,
Jack   X

She had grinned then, so hugely that it had felt like a crescent moon in her mouth, and hugged the note, then kissed it tenderly as if it was Jack himself. She read the note twice more, each time lingering over the words, 'Last night was very special to me'. She even ran the tip of one finger gently over the sentence as if it held some emotional residue, some aura of Jack that she could extract from the page.

I'll ring him now, she thought, *and leave a message on his answerphone.* She padded across the room, still dressed only in pants and T-shirt, composing in her head what she would say: 'Hi, Jack, this is Susan. I've just read your note, and I know you're out, but I just wanted to say yes, Davey and I would love to go to the village show with you on Saturday.' Then what should she say? 'Last night was very special to me too'? Or should she even mention last night? Should she ask him if he wanted to come round after returning from Harrogate or did that make her sound too eager, too desperate? Maybe *he* wanted a little bit of breathing space, time to think things through. This thought dismayed her a little, even though she told herself that it shouldn't. No, she thought, best leave things as they stand. Not seeing Jack until Saturday would give both of them time to get last night into perspective. It would be better in the long run.

She went out into the hallway, the tiles cold on her bare feet, and then faltered, her heart jolting her happy mood out of her, alarm flooding into the gap it had left. David was lying on the floor by the grandfather clock in his pyjamas. He looked as though he'd fallen downstairs.

She rushed across to him, calling his name. To her relief she saw him stir, but when he tried to raise his head she fell to her knees beside him, crying, 'Don't try to move. Just lie still.'

As she was examining him, he said groggily, 'Mum, I fell asleep.'

She looked at him sharply. 'What do you mean, you fell asleep? You didn't fall down the stairs?'

'No,' he said, 'I fell asleep after meeting Decumen.' He gestured vaguely at the clock. 'He was in the snow. He showed me . . . showed me some things.'

'And you're sure you're all right?' she said, assuming he was getting his dreams muddled up with reality. 'You're not hurt?'

'No, I'm fine. I fell asleep, that's all. He must have brought

231

me back.' He blinked at her curiously. 'But what about you? Are *you* all right? You've hardly got any clothes on.'

She felt herself blushing, reached out and hugged him fiercely so that he wouldn't see her flushed face. 'Oh yes,' she said. 'I'm *very* all right. In fact, I feel wonderful.'

Chapter Twenty-Eight

Ten-month-old Zack Brewer was screaming at the top of his lungs. His mother, Alison, was in the bathroom, stooped over a sink, her hair a meringue of shampoo suds. Five minutes ago Zack had been in the bathroom with Alison, but after he'd dropped a flannel into the toilet and stuffed toilet paper into his mouth for the fifth time, Alison had scooped him up, carried him to his room and dumped him in his playpen.

His playpen was full of toys. *You'd think the little sod would be glad to be in there,* Alison thought with a viciousness she wouldn't have believed herself capable of before Zack's birth last October. But no, the instant she had walked out of the room he had begun screaming. She'd been told that as a mother she wouldn't mind her own child's cries as much as she did other people's, that she would feel sympathy rather than irritation, but when Zack cried for any length of time it ground in her teeth like a dentist's drill, and she felt as if a steel band was tightening around her brain.

'I'm obviously just a shit mother, aren't I, then?' she muttered savagely under her breath.

She really believed that. She *was* a shit mother. She couldn't cope. She resented Zack so much that it made her sick with guilt and shame. Did she love him? She honestly didn't know. Her emotions were a maelstrom that wouldn't stop churning long enough for her to evaluate them.

All she *did* know was that she woke up in the morning bowed down by the weight of her depression, spent the day brimming with rage, and went to bed at night exhausted and wondering whether her waking nightmare would ever end, sometimes even wishing she could fall asleep and never wake up.

It had to change soon. If it didn't she'd go stark staring mad. She didn't even feel as though she could go to anyone for help. She'd tried, but nobody had been able to reach her. Nobody understood what she was going through. Nobody at all.

'*Will you bloody shut up!*' she suddenly screeched, her head whipping round so that clots of shampoo flew across the small room, turning the blue walls into a clumsily rendered starscape. Zack paused, as though shocked into silence by the vehemence in his mother's voice – and then began screaming even more frantically than before.

'Right,' Alison muttered, the angry buzzing in her head almost drowning out her baby's wails, 'right, that's *it*.' She clawed at her scalp, then threw water over her sudsy hair, not caring that it was splashing over the carpet. She yanked a towel from the rack so hard that it fell off the radiator it had been hooked to, and stomped out of the room, rubbing at her hair as though it had offended her.

Zack was sitting in his playpen, clinging to the bars, his face red, cheeks wet with tears, snot dribbling from his nose. When he saw Alison he sucked in a breath, then let loose another protesting wail.

Alison felt the band tighten another notch around her brain. She scrunched up the towel she'd been using to dry her hair and threw it at her son.

It missed Zack, but struck the bars of his playpen with a wet slap and slithered to the floor. Zack glanced at the towel, but continued to scream.

Alison lurched forward. '*Shut up! Just shut up, you ungrateful little sod! We've bought you all these things, so why don't you play with them and STOP FUCKING CRYING!*'

This time her raised voice didn't shock Zack into silence. This time, evidently terrified, he redoubled his efforts. Before she knew what she was doing, Alison had taken two strides forward and delivered a stinging slap across the baby's cheek. She felt a savage, soaring glee as he fell sideways, his little arms coming up, his head crashing into the bars of his playpen. Then the glee was gone, overwhelmed by horror, pity and self-disgust as she realised what she had done.

'Oh God,' she whimpered. 'Oh Zack, I'm sorry, I'm sorry.'

Zack was lying amongst his toys, looking stunned. His

cheek where she had hit him was so red it looked like a hand-shaped birthmark. His lips were opening and closing, and he was making an awful mewling, gasping sound that frightened Alison badly. She was almost relieved when he finally drew a shuddering breath into his lungs and let loose an ear-splitting screech of bewilderment, fear and pain.

She dropped to her knees and shuffled over to the playpen. She felt wretched, felt like the worst kind of bully. When she reached out to pick him up, she was sobbing. Seeing her hands coming towards him, Zack wailed in obvious fear and tried to wriggle away, which made her feel as though her heart was splitting in two.

'Come on,' she sobbed, 'come to Mummy.' She picked him up and began to rock him. As tears poured down her face, she murmured, 'I'm sorry, I'm sorry, I'm sorry.'

Zack stopped crying a long time before she did.

Chapter Twenty-Nine

Old Jonas, who at fifty-one was not really old, had never killed anyone. He had never molested children, never eaten human flesh, never been in a mental institution and never received electric shock treatment. An only child, he had lived with both parents in the centre of Longbarrow until the age of twenty-seven. That was how old he had been on the day his father went out for a packet of cigarettes and never came back. Eight years later, when Jonas was thirty-five, his mother died from cirrhosis of the liver. People said that Jonas was to blame for the fate of both his parents. His father, they claimed, had left because he couldn't cope with his crazy loon of a son any longer. And his mother, rather than walking away like his father or placing Jonas in the institution most villagers agreed he should have been placed in at birth, had graduated from a dedicated drinker to a truly spectacular one.

On the day his mother died, Jonas had gone to see Mr Toot, who was the only person who had ever understood him, the only one whose words had ever been able to penetrate the complex obfuscation of Jonas's thoughts. In his intricate, roundabout way, Jonas had told Mr Toot what he planned to do, and Mr Toot, understanding and supportive as ever, had wished Jonas well and assured him that he would deal with the mundane practicalities that Jonas had neither the inclination nor the aptitude for. The arranging of the funeral, the selling of the house, the paperwork, the dealings with solicitors, regis- trars, bank managers, even the informing of relatives – all of this could be left to him. In effect, Mr Toot cut the balloon string that allowed Jonas to float away from the routines that dragged him down, the pills that tethered thoughts that longed to soar, the litter of discursive voices and minds that he had been forced for so long to wade through.

Finally Jonas was the wind, he was part of the Great Wheel. He was free.

Ever since he could remember, Jonas had seen the shape of creation. He saw beyond what most people saw – above and around and behind it. People to him were like apes – they had no insight, no vision, no sense of the Circle, the Great Wheel. They were blind and they were deaf, though they attempted to conceal their disabilities in the obsessive minutiae of their paltry lives. They shunned him because the truth he tried to speak to them, as simple as he made it, filled them with a terror they refused to recognise. Even the Leviathan did not know his true nature, though he must in time, because if he insisted on remaining blind, then the darkness would not be his alone. In all the energies around him, Jonas sensed the coming of a great and destructive change. Already the sickness was creeping invisibly through the earth. Soon it would blacken the roots of the Great Tree at the edge of the world and the fruit would wither and darkness and famine would split the ground.

This, at least, was how Jonas would attempt to simplify it for whoever cared to listen. For how could you explain a feeling that was so intrinsic it possessed neither form nor substance? It was like trying to explain the texture of an emotion, the colour of a personality, the shape of a human soul. Death, famine, plague, decay, suffering – these at least were words that conjured up recognisable images, concepts that hopefully even the blind and the deaf could understand.

Jonas watched and he waited. He had tried to warn the Leviathan too, to explain his knowledge in the best way he could, but he had been too eager and the Leviathan had made itself blind and deaf behind its fear and anger. Now, as Mr Toot had reminded him, Jonas must hope that the serpent sang softly whilst the Leviathan slept. If not, then the ensuing tumult would drown its song, and he must add his voice to that tumult if all was not to be lost.

As ever, Jonas was only peripherally aware of the physical plane. His body was a vehicle that he fed with fuel and sometimes warmth in order to keep it working, and that was all. If asked where he lived, he would be able to lead the asker there, but would not be able to translate his homing instinct into speech, would not be able to explain the location of the dwelling he had constructed deep in the woods from tarpaulin and timber, or even describe it.

The woods. The river. The sky. It was all one to Jonas. All part of the same body, all part of the Wheel. He found it hard to distinguish one element from another except in abstract symbols. There was the Great Tree, the Great Wheel, the Great Serpent, but there were no snakes or trees, for that was all one. To differentiate between them was so irrelevant that to him it became meaningless.

Nevertheless, he recognised Death, for that was a power that stood alone and apart. And he recognised it today. Death in the . . . in the . . .

'Water,' he croaked, dredging the word up from some storehouse of trivia deep inside him.

Death in the water. Yes. A body. Without hesitation, Jonas stepped into the sluggish, low-lying river and waded across to where the body floated on its front, arms akimbo, clothes ballooning with air.

He took hold of the body with his long, strong hands. It bobbed in the water like a marker buoy. He turned the body over and gazed with dispassion at the red meat where its face had been.

'Death wears many faces,' Jonas murmured and began dragging the body towards the river bank. He gazed at the bright summer sky, though saw only the descending darkness.

'Sing, serpent, sing,' he implored softly.

Chapter Thirty

By 9:15 Susan was in the shower, relishing the hot water battering on her head and shoulders. Now that the hour when she would see Jack again was almost upon her, she found that the excitement that had enlivened her earlier was turning to nervousness, making her jittery.

Her mind was growing increasingly crowded with anxious questions: How would Jack act towards her today? Would he expect too much or be offhand? And how should she react to him? If he put his arm around her, should she let him? And if she *did* let him, what would David think? She hadn't plucked up the courage to broach the subject with him yet. What if he was angry, or shocked, or upset? What if he didn't want to share his mum with anyone? And in the long run, could this relationship (if it *was* a relationship) really work, or was the novelty of it blinding her to the reality of the situation, which was that she and Jack were far too different to be compatible?

Though the drumming of the water drowned the questions out for a little while, by the time she had dried herself and pulled on a pink T-shirt and white shorts, they were back and louder than ever.

She looked at her watch – 9:35. She really ought to talk to David before Jack appeared, otherwise she would spend the whole day on tenterhooks, even if Jack's handling of the situation turned out to be as impeccable as she would wish it to be.

She made her son his usual breakfast of Frosties with milk, toast with strawberry jam and tea with two sugars, and carried it up to him on the same tray she'd used to carry the plate of sandwiches up to Jack a few days earlier. When she knocked on his door he shouted, '*Entrez beaucoup*' (the way he pronounced it he made it sound like 'On-tray boo-coop'), a private joke which made her smile.

When she entered, he was sitting up in bed reading a book – Alfred Hitchcock and the Three Investigators in *The Mystery of the Talking Skull*. He'd been reading a run of these lately. It was his usual pattern – find an author or a series of books he liked, devour the lot, then move on to something else.

'Room service,' she said, forcing herself to widen her smile even though her nervousness was now making her lips feel as though they were being twitched by thread.

David smiled back at her and carefully marked his page with a leather tasselled bookmark, gold-embossed with sites of Edinburgh. Putting the book aside, he said, 'What's this for? I'm not ill.'

'I thought you needed rousing,' said Susan. 'Jack's coming to pick us up at half-ten to go to the village show, or had you forgotten?'

She had the impression that saying his name might somehow have betrayed her feelings for Jack, but if so, David hadn't noticed.

'Course I hadn't forgotten,' he said. 'I was going to read until ten and then get ready, but now that you've made my breakfast I suppose I might as well eat it.'

'Such gratitude,' Susan said dryly and laid the tray across his knees.

As David began to eat, she gravitated almost unconsciously to the velux window out of which she and Jack had gazed a few days ago. She found herself searching among the distant jumble of matchboxes for his house before turning away guiltily, certain that David would become suspicious and ask her what she was doing.

'Do you like your room then?' she asked, looking around at the posters and pennants and bookshelves; the trainers toe to toe on the floor; the football perched on the chair like a brown egg in a nest; the stacks of board games on top of the wardrobe; the Mac on its desk which they had had to take apart to carry up the winding attic staircase; the skateboard propped against the wall like a giant plectrum with wheels.

He nodded, his cheeks hamster-fat with Frosties, lips glossy with milk. Finally he swallowed. 'It's brilliant. The best room I've ever had.'

'You've only had two.'

He frowned at the irrelevancy. 'Yeah, well, this is the best.'

She licked her lips which still felt as though they were being manipulated by some unseen puppeteer, and looked around the room once more as though searching for some means of diverting the conversation back towards Jack without making it too obvious.

'Are you all right, Mum?' David asked.

Her head jerked to look at him. 'Yes, why?'

'You just looked a bit . . . I dunno. I wondered whether maybe you were missing London.'

She blinked at him. 'No, of course I'm not. I love it here. Are *you* missing London?'

'No.' He shook his head vigorously. 'I love it here too. But.' He waggled his head and wrinkled his nose as if uncertain whether to continue.

'But what?' she said.

'But . . . well, I've made some friends, haven't I? You haven't. I was just worried that you were a bit . . . lonely.' He gritted his teeth in apology as though fearful of offending her.

Susan, however, was so astonished that she couldn't prevent herself from releasing a disbelieving laugh. 'Who says I haven't made any friends?' she said.

Now it was his turn to look surprised. 'Have you?'

'I might have.'

'Who?'

She couldn't meet his eye, but hoped her glance at the blank computer screen was suitably casual. 'Well, there's Jack,' she said.

David's look of expectation became a dismissive raising of the eyebrows. 'Oh, Jack.'

'What do you mean, "Oh, Jack"?'

'Well, he's just the handyman, isn't he? We *both* know him. I mean, he's nice and everything, but he's not really a proper friend, is he? Not like Beth.'

He's certainly *not* like Beth, Susan thought, but when she said, 'No, he's not like Beth', she did so guardedly. She paused a moment before adding, 'But . . . well . . . I really like him. Don't you?'

'Well . . . yeah,' said David. Suddenly his eyes narrowed shrewdly. 'Mum, have you and him got a thing going?'

Now Susan felt as though her cheeks were soaking up the heat of the thick gold columns of sunlight slanting into the room. She'd wanted to break this to David gently, but as usual he'd been far more perceptive than she gave him credit for. Now, defences down, she could only bluster, 'I don't know what you mean!'

David seemed unruffled. 'Mum, you don't have to pretend,' he said. 'I'm not a little kid.'

'Who says I'm pretending?' said Susan, backtracking wildly.

'You've gone bright red.'

'I haven't.'

'Yes, you have.'

She touched her face. Her cheek felt sizzling hot. She took a deep breath and smiled nervously. After a moment she said, 'All right. How would you feel if Jack and I did . . . have a thing going?'

David didn't even consider it. He simply shrugged and said, 'Okay.'

Susan was flabbergasted. Could it really be this easy? 'You honestly mean that?' she said.

He nodded. 'Yes. I like Jack a lot. He's really nice.'

'And you don't mind about . . . about your dad?'

He gave her a guileless, wide-eyed look. 'Dad's dead. You're not.'

Susan felt a surge of love for her son so strong it almost brought tears to her eyes. She crossed to him in three strides, reached down and hugged him tightly, making the tray shift on his knees, the crockery clink together.

'You never cease to amaze me,' she said. 'I don't half love you, you know.'

When she released him, he grinned at her, then took a bite of the toast he was still holding in his hand. 'So you and Jack *do* have a thing going?' he said.

Now her smile was coy. 'We might have. I'm not quite sure yet. We'll see how things go.'

'You look happy,' he told her.

She touched her face again, as though surprised by the expression he saw there, perhaps wanting to feel it for herself. 'I am happy,' she said. 'Happier than I've been for a long, long time.'

'Happier than you were with Dad?'

She paused before replying, then said, 'I honestly don't know, Davey. I can't remember that far back any more.'

'Are you happy even though weird things keep happening?'

She thought of the moving box of books and the phantom snake in the cellar, neither of which she had told David about, and of the things he *had* told her: the bloodstain in the church, the tramp who had accosted him in the village, and most recently of his dream about Decumen and the snake.

She nodded. 'Yes. I mean, nothing's happened that's been really threatening or frightening, has it? Well, apart from the tramp perhaps, but that was just a tramp, it wasn't anything . . . unusual.'

'What he said was pretty weird, though,' said David, 'and then what Decumen told me sounded like a warning.'

'But that was just a dream, wasn't it? You told me so yourself.'

He wrinkled his nose. 'Yes,' he said doubtfully, 'but it felt like more than a dream. It felt like I was in . . . another place.'

She sat on the bed beside him. 'Do these things frighten you?' she asked.

'No, they're just . . . weird. But Colin's grandmother keeps saying something bad is going to happen.'

'Not to us it isn't,' said Susan firmly. 'We're indestructible.'

David, however, now looked uncertain. Susan couldn't help wondering whether his uncertainty was actually to do with her and Jack, despite what he had said. However mature and perceptive he seemed, he was still only twelve years old, and he was being asked to accept a great deal of change in a very short time. Was there any wonder that his anxieties took the form of vivid dreams and this recent predilection for seeing dark omens everywhere?

But you were the one who heard the snake in the cellar, a voice whispered an instant before she could quell it. Sternly, as though to convince herself as much as him, she said, 'You know these things aren't really real, don't you, Davey? You know they can't hurt us?'

'Ye-es. But—' He shrugged.

'But what?'

'Well . . . have you noticed the clock these past couple of days?'

She thought for a moment. She'd seen the clock, certainly,

but had she really *looked* at it? She'd had too much of Jack on her mind to really notice anything at all.

'I don't know,' she said. 'Why?'

'Well, if you look you'll see that the moon face is moving over and the next picture is starting to appear.'

'Is it?' said Susan, knowing what he was going to say even before he said it.

He nodded. 'Yes. And if you go right up to the clock and bend your head a bit to look through the gap, you can see what the next picture is. It's the snowy place from my dream.'

Chapter Thirty-One

At first Reverend Farrar thought the dark bundle beside the tombstone was a discarded bin bag and a flicker of annoyance ran through him. A dozen steps closer, however, and he was able to see what the long grass had initially concealed: a denim-clad leg jutting from the motionless heap, a white, blood-soaked Reebok on its foot. His shock made him forget how to walk for a moment and he clumped to a halt. A wondering, almost idle thought trickled into his mind: *Our Chris has got a pair like that*. Then, forgetting his oft-repeated admonishment to his son not to take the Lord's name in vain, he muttered, 'Sweet Jesus', and began to run up the slope as fast as the heat and his dread-heavy legs would allow him.

Chris was lying on his back, his waxen face turned up to the sky. His eyes were closed and his lips were the colour of blueberries. His arms were outflung as though he'd been pleading for salvation when he'd . . .

(*passed out!* Farrar's inner voice shrieked at him frantically).

When Farrar saw the way his son's leg was twisted into an impossible angle below his left thigh, a jagged spar of bone sticking out through torn, blood-soaked denim, small black insects working busily at the bone marrow, he had to clamp a hand to his mouth to stop himself retching into the grass.

The nausea subsided quickly, but left Farrar trembling and dripping with sweat. He felt almost drunk with shock, shrouded in a fug of dizziness and unreality. He fell to his knees beside his son, barely even aware that he was whispering, 'Oh Jesus, oh Jesus', over and over again. At least Chris's eyes and mouth were closed; wasn't that a good sign?

He reached out a shaking hand which looked distorted, as though he were viewing it through the wrong end of a telescope, and placed it heavily on his son's forehead. Chris's flesh was clammy despite the sun's heat. Farrar croaked his name, but there was no response. When he bent forward to listen to Chris's chest, his head felt heavy as a boulder and he feared he might never be able to lift it again. However, the erratic beat of his son's heart fluttering against his ear filled him with such fierce joy that he sprang upwards on his knees as though he had been yanked from behind.

Chris was alive! He was *alive*! In Steven Farrar's world, that simple fact, which he had woken up this and every other morning taking for granted, was all that mattered. Suddenly he was filled with urgency, a feeling that he was racing against the clock. What should he do? Pick Chris up and carry him home? But ought he to be moved with his leg in that state? Might it result in even greater damage?

He hated leaving his son, but there was no alternative. He pushed himself to his feet and began to gallop down the slope as fast as his legs would carry him. He crashed through bushes and leaped down steps with scant care for himself, little knowing that it was similar recklessness by his son that had caused his horrific injuries. And as he ran his thoughts ran with him, a beseeching, endlessly repeated phrase: *Lord be merciful, Lord be merciful, Lord be merciful*.

Chapter Thirty-Two

When Susan answered the knock on the door at 10:32, her stomach cartwheeling, it was to be confronted by a man whose head was a bunch of flowers.

'Delivery for Susan Wisher,' the flowers said.

Susan smiled. 'Hang on a moment. I'll see if she's in.'

The flowers were lowered and Jack was grinning his goofy grin that Susan suddenly realised she adored. There was something different about him today. It took Susan a moment to pinpoint what it was: for the first time since she had met him, he had combed his hair.

'Hello,' he said, 'how are you?'

'I'm fine,' she said brightly, though her guts were still doing the samba. 'How are you?'

'Bit nervous to be honest,' he admitted. 'I haven't been out on a date for . . . oh, ages.'

'Me neither,' said Susan, 'and if it's any consolation I'm nervous too.'

'That's good,' said Jack.

'*Good*?' Her tone was mock-indignant.

'Yes, cos if you're nervous it means this is important to both of us.' Then he looked doubtful. 'Doesn't it?'

'I suppose it does,' she agreed, laughing, and stood back. 'Come in, Jack, and take the weight off your dahlias.'

He stepped into the house, holding the flowers out to her. 'These are for you by the way, if you hadn't already guessed.'

'Thank you, Jack, they're lovely. No one's bought me flowers since . . .' she thought back, but couldn't remember Gerry *ever* buying her flowers, '. . . for a long time,' she finished lamely.

'Well, I was just pulling up in front of your house and I saw them in the flowerbed, and I thought they looked so nice I just had to pick them.' He had delivered this solemnly, but now he grinned to show he was joking.

'I'll put them in water,' she said, smiling. 'We're nearly ready to go.'

As she turned away he leaned forward and said quietly, 'Susan.'

She turned back. 'Yes?'

He flipped a thumb at the ceiling. 'Have you told David about us?'

Us. It was the first time he had referred to them as a couple, and it sent a warm shiver of pleasure through her.

'Yes,' she said, 'he's all for it. He thinks you're a really nice person.'

He looked surprised and touched. 'Really? He said that?'

'Why don't you ask him yourself? If I'm not very much mistaken, that great clomping noise is the sound of him coming downstairs.'

She went into the kitchen to put the flowers in water. As she filled a bucket at the tap, unable to locate a vase, she thought to herself: *This is going to be great.* Another warm shudder of pleasure went through her, and she hugged herself, relishing the moment. Leaving the flowers to drink their fill, she went back into the hallway to find David and Jack standing in front of the clock. David was pointing up at the smaller dial where the snowscape he claimed to have dreamt about was now clearly visible, and Jack was nodding and looking serious.

'He slit the snake right up the middle and all this sort of lightning poured out of it,' Susan heard David say as she walked across. 'Then all this lightning went into his mouth and his eyes and all over him, but it didn't hurt him or anything. He asked me if I knew who he was, and suddenly – I don't know how – I *did* know. It was as if the lightning had made me see. And do you know who he was?'

'Who?' asked Jack.

'Decumen, the wizard who had the battle with the Seven Sleepers.'

'The mage,' said Jack.

'That's right – mage. That was the word I was trying to remember.'

'Hello, you two,' said Susan.

They both turned. 'Hi, Mum. I was just telling Jack about my dream.'

'So I heard. What do you think, Jack?'

He pursed his lips. 'I don't know. Sounds to me as if David's got friends in high places. But if you want to know what it's really all about, the best person to ask'll be Mr Toot.'

'Will he be there today?' David asked.

'I should think so. Everyone'll be there. It's a big annual event, this show. Last Saturday in August every year.'

'What's it for? To celebrate the harvest?' asked Susan.

'I think it used to be. Now it's more just a chance for every-one to get together.'

They drove down to the village in Susan's car, which she was pleased about because it meant that Jack would have to come back later to collect his van. David, who usually sat next to her in the passenger seat, today got into the back without being asked (not that Susan *would* have asked him). Having Jack sitting next to her as she drove was – like all aspects of their burgeoning relationship – new and strange and exciting. Once, she brushed his leg as she was changing gear and he turned and smiled at her. She glanced into her rear-view mirror to see how David was taking all this, but he was lost in his book again, his brow furrowed in concentration.

The show was situated not in the centre of the village, but on its outskirts in a huge field, half of which had been roped off to create a makeshift car park. The queue to get in was a dozen vehicles long and slow-moving. 'My treat,' Jack said when they finally got to the front of the queue where a plump girl in her late teens with a sunburned face asked for five pounds admission. After he had leaned across Susan to hand over the money, they jolted across the rutted field in pursuit of the line of cars in front of them, and were ushered into a space by one of a group of bored-looking teenagers wearing yellow bibs emblazoned with the words TRAFFIC CONTROL. There were plenty of horse-boxes in evidence, and indeed horses, being groomed by girls wearing camel-coloured jodhpurs and knee-high, shiny black riding boots that always made Susan think of Nazis.

They got out of the car and began strolling towards the dozen or so marquees situated around the main show ring. A brass band was playing in the ring, its rumbustious music filling the air. As well as horses and horseboxes, there were plenty of people wearing Barbour jackets and green wellingtons, even in the heat, as though it were a uniform. There were men in tweed caps carrying shooting sticks and women in blazers and Alice bands, their hair braided like French bread. There were farmers and farm labourers, red-faced and thickset, most of whom were congregated around the beer tent, supping frothing pints and having belly-laughing competitions. Aside from the marquees there were vintage cars and hot dog stands, a potter, a glass blower and a hurdle maker, and chickens and rabbits and goats in pens for the children to coo over.

In the marquees the really important business was taking place. Judging had already begun to find the lightest sponge cake, the tastiest scone, the sweetest honey, the biggest marrow, the juiciest plum. Everything that could be baked or grown was under scrutiny from judges who nibbled and scribbled and nodded solemnly as they conferred. As they passed the fairy cakes, where a fat, bespectacled man was grimly sampling each entrant's efforts and jotting his observations down on a clipboard, Susan couldn't help but giggle.

'What's up?' asked Jack, smiling.

She raised a hand to her mouth and leaned towards him. 'I don't mean to be rude, Jack, but don't you find this all a bit . . . silly? I mean, it's so quintessentially English, but it's like something out of the 1950s. I didn't realise this sort of thing went on any more.'

He grinned. 'I know what you mean, but I'd miss it if it stopped. I've been coming here for years and . . . I don't know . . . it sort of reminds me of when I was a kid, when things seemed so much more . . . simple and innocent. Do you know what I mean?'

She nodded. 'Yes. I suppose it's sort of comforting, isn't it? Like baked beans on toast in front of *Doctor Who* on a Saturday tea-time.'

He smiled in acknowledgement, then said, 'All this food is making me hungry. Does anyone fancy any fudge?'

'Yeah!' cried David, his eyes lighting up. 'Rum and raisin?'

'Whatever you like.'

David scampered ahead as though afraid all the fudge might be gone if they didn't hurry. As Susan and Jack stepped into the brilliant sunshine, Susan felt Jack's warm hand coupling with her own.

They bought three types of fudge – rum and raisin, cherry and vanilla, and chocolate and hazelnut – and ate it whilst sitting on the grass at the perimeter of the show ring, basking under the noonday sun and watching a number of lovingly maintained steam engines chug in a circle like a very slow merry-go-round. Susan was about to tell David he'd be sick if he ate any more when Jack said, 'There's someone over there you could meet.'

He was nodding towards a marquee they hadn't been in yet. Susan followed his gaze. 'Who?'

'She's just gone into that tent. Miss Morrow. She's the headmistress of the local secondary school. I thought if David was going there, it might be an idea to say hello.'

'Might as well,' said Susan, getting to her feet. 'Come on, before we lose her.'

'Aw, Mum, do we have to?' said David. 'I'll meet her when I go to school.'

'There's no harm in saying hello now,' said Susan. 'The more people we meet the better.'

David dragged himself unwillingly to his feet. Looking apologetic, Jack said, 'She's really nice, Davey, honestly. She likes a good laugh, or at least she did before her friend died. They used to come in the Druid's Arms a lot.'

'Her friend?' said Susan.

'Yes. She used to live with this older woman – Audrey, her name was.'

'So when you say friend, do you mean friend or *friend*?'

Jack glanced at David, as if unsure what to say. 'Well, they . . . they lived together like . . . like a married couple, I suppose you'd say.'

'They were gay, you mean?' said David casually. He nodded. 'That's cool.'

Jack looked surprised. 'Yes, well, that's what I reckon. Each to their own, I say.'

'Me too,' said Susan. 'So come on.' She led the way into the marquee.

Dairy products were doing battle here. Judges were debating over cream, butter, yoghurt, and most especially cheese, every conceivable kind of which appeared to be on display.

'There she is,' said Jack, indicating a tall, willowy woman in her late fifties who possessed such a natural grace and elegance

251

she looked as though she might once have been a ballet dancer.

Susan, who was still in the lead, waited for Jack to catch up and overtake her, then followed him across, David bringing up the rear. Joyce Morrow was nibbling a sliver of dark, rubbery-looking cheese, an intent expression on her face. The three of them waited for her to make a note on the clipboard she carried, then Jack said, 'Excuse me, Miss Morrow.'

She turned, blinking her large doe-eyes with their long lashes. Susan wasn't sure whether it was simply because Jack had told her about the death of Miss Morrow's partner, but she sensed an innate sadness about this woman.

'Hello, Jack,' Joyce Morrow said, her voice quiet and cultured, 'how are you?'

'Oh, I'm fine,' Jack said, and turned to indicate Susan. 'Miss Morrow, can I introduce you to a couple of friends of mine? This is Susan Wisher and her son, David. David'll be starting at your school next week. They've just moved in to the big house.'

'Oh, you lucky things,' said Joyce, taking Susan's proffered hand. 'So you're relatives of Mollie Boscombe's.'

'Only through my husband.' Susan glanced at Jack and added awkwardly, 'He died a few years ago. Mrs Boscombe was his aunt.'

'Ah,' said Joyce, 'and how are you settling in?'

'Very well,' said Susan. 'We love the village and the house, and we've met some really nice people, haven't we, Davey?'

David nodded. Joyce Morrow said, 'Well, it'll be nice to see you at school next week, David, though I don't suppose you're looking forward to it, are you?'

'Er . . .' David didn't know what to say.

Joyce Morrow smiled and, as though reading his mind, said, 'It's all right, I won't be offended if you say no. Coming back to school after the summer holidays is always pretty ghastly. And starting a new school where you don't know anyone can be even worse.'

David smiled back. He had no idea head teachers could be so understanding. The headmaster at his last school, Mr Egerton, had been a fearsome, rather elusive individual, whose widow's peak had earned him the nickname 'Dracula'.

'I've got some friends who go to your school,' he said, 'and they've told me all about it. It doesn't sound so bad.'

'Well, I'm pleased to hear that they didn't fill your head with horror stories. What are their names?'

'Colin Dyer and Chris Farrar.'

Immediately Joyce Morrow's smile stiffened. 'Ah,' she said.

'Is something wrong?' Susan asked.

'I just hope I'm not the bearer of bad tidings, that's all. Are you aware, David, that Christopher had an accident last night?'

'No,' said David. 'What happened?'

'I'm not entirely sure. I received a phone call from the organisers of the show this morning, asking if I would take over Reverend Farrar's judging duties. I was told simply that Christopher had had rather a serious accident.'

David immediately thought of Colin repeating his gran's warning of impending disaster, of Chris gleefully ranting on about portents. 'I hope he's all right.'

'As do we all, I'm sure,' said Joyce Morrow. 'Christopher's a very likeable young man, if a little . . . lively at times.'

The conversation drifted on to other things, but David hardly heard it. He was wondering how he could find out about Chris. If Chris was badly injured he didn't want to go round disturbing his mum and dad in case they were worried and upset. Maybe Col would know. Perhaps he ought to wander round for a bit by himself and try to find him. He was about to suggest this to his mum when a voice murmured in his ear, 'You dream a great deal, don't you, David?'

David spun round, startled. Mr Toot was standing behind him, the sun shining on his bald head. He was beaming as usual.

'What do you mean?' David asked.

'What I say,' Mr Toot replied, then raised a hand as though in apology. 'I see it in your eyes. Your dreams swim there like fish. You look troubled, David.'

'I'm worried about my friend, Chris Farrar. I've just heard he's had some sort of accident.'

'Ah,' said Mr Toot sadly.

'I don't suppose *you* know what's happened to him?'

'I don't suppose I do,' Mr Toot said. 'Sometimes your dreams seem so real, don't they? So real that you don't know what's true and what isn't?'

Taken aback by the abrupt switch between subjects, David

said, 'Yes.' And then, after a pause, 'How do you know so much?'

Mr Toot pointed to his eyes and then his ears. 'I keep these open all the time. Most people only pretend to. Tell me about your dream, David.'

David paused, and then said, 'It was about Decumen – you know, the mage in the legend of the Seven Sleepers?' For the second time that day he found himself recounting the details of his dream. When he had done he said, 'Do you believe in the legend, Mr Toot?'

'I believe in everything,' Mr Toot said candidly.

David was not sure how to take that. Did that make Mr Toot intelligent and open-minded or stupid and gullible? Certainly David did not always follow a great deal of what the little grocer said – much of his conversation was like a slippery eel, hard to hold on to.

'So do you think the Seven Sleepers will ever wake up?' David asked.

Mr Toot answered his question with one of his own: 'When do *you* wake up, David?'

Puzzled, David said, 'When I've been asleep. In the morning usually.'

'But not all creatures wake in the morning, do they?'

Feeling as though he was somehow being tested, David wrinkled his nose. 'No,' he said cautiously. 'Some wake at night. Like owls and bats.'

'Creatures that hunt in the darkness,' Mr Toot said, his voice suddenly quiet. He was staring at David so intently that David felt hypnotised. 'Look to the shadows, David. Look to the shadows.'

Chapter Thirty-Three

Five minutes after saying goodbye to Jack Bradley, his new friend (who Joyce suspected was already rather more than just a friend) and her son, David, Joyce Morrow was interrupted again. Not that she minded to be perfectly frank. She was getting to the stage where one piece of cheese was becoming indistinguishable from the next, and had decided even before Jack showed up that she was going to break off soon for a cup of tea.

The voice that addressed her was low-key, hesitant. She turned from her contemplation of a crumbly, rather bitter cheese to see two of her ex-pupils, Jake Sissons and Lucy Benson, standing beside her with the kind of taut, nervous expressions usually worn by recalcitrant pupils who had been summoned to her office.

'Hello, you two,' she said. 'I haven't seen you all summer. How are you both?'

At once Lucy's bottom lip began to tremble, and next moment she was trying to conceal the fact that she was crying.

Jake looked at his girlfriend with an anguished expression and placed an arm around her heaving shoulders. 'Hey, Luce, shh, don't cry,' he said miserably. He glanced around and then, a note of desperation creeping into his voice, 'Come on, Luce. People are looking at us.'

Joyce positioned herself so that Lucy was less noticeable to the passing crowds, and said gently, 'What's wrong, dear?'

'Sorry about this, Miss,' Jake said. 'She's had a lot on her mind just lately. We both have.'

Joyce waved away his apology. 'Perhaps we ought to find somewhere a little quieter. This way.' She led the couple between two trestle tables groaning with plates of cheese to a flap at the back of the marquee that had been opened to allow in some air. She stooped through and the two teenagers followed. Now they were at the back of the marquee, away from the crowds.

Lucy had recovered a little by now. She was wiping at her eyes and sniffing. 'Sorry, Miss,' she said. 'I didn't mean to blub. Things just got a bit too much for me all at once.'

'So I see,' said Joyce. 'But I won't ask why if you don't want to tell me. Just so long as you're all right now.'

'No, but we *do* want to tell you, Miss,' Jake said, glancing at Lucy who was nodding. 'That's why we came over. We decided that you were the best person to ask for advice.'

'Advice?' Joyce said. 'About what?'

There was a pause, as though Jake and Lucy were both waiting for the other to speak. Then Lucy reached out for Jake's hand and took a deep breath.

'I'm pregnant,' she said.

She looked defiant now, almost proud. Jake squeezed her hand.

'In that case,' said Joyce with a calmness that belied the sinking feeling in her stomach, 'we'd better sit down.'

They did so, on a flat, dry patch of grass. Though Joyce appeared composed, her mind was whirring. She knew from experience that Jake and Lucy would be looking for practical advice, encouragement and assurance, not gloom and commiseration and dire warnings about how hard it was going to be – despite the fact that these latter responses were her instinctive ones. The irony that she was the one they had chosen to come to for advice was not lost on her either.

'How many weeks pregnant are you?' she asked when they were settled.

'Eight and a half.'

'And have you both told your parents?'

Jake and Lucy glanced at each other. 'No,' Jake said.

'Why not?'

He looked uncomfortable. Hunching forward, he began to tear blades of grass from the ground, his blond hair gleaming like gold. 'It's just . . . hard,' he said, 'finding the right time. Our Gary's been giving Mam and Dad a lot of hassle this week.'

256

This time Lucy squeezed *his* hand, though Joyce noted that her smile of sympathy was somewhat forced. She looked up and said, 'My parents would kill me if they found out. They don't even like me *seeing* Jake. You know what they're like, Miss.'

Joyce did indeed know what they were like. John and Julia Benson had been among Anne Darracott's staunchest supporters during the campaign to get her ousted seven years ago. Not that she was petty enough to hold that against their daughter, who, despite her upbringing, seemed a sensible and open-minded girl (*though not sensible enough to take precautions against getting pregnant*, Joyce thought with a certain amount of resignation).

'I know it's going to be difficult,' she said, 'but nevertheless you *must* tell them, and preferably sooner rather than later. After all, you can't keep it a secret for ever, can you?'

'Well, we were wondering whether you could help us get something done on the quiet, like,' said Jake awkwardly.

'An abortion, you mean?' Joyce looked at Lucy. 'Is that what you both want?'

Lucy grimaced and placed a hand on her stomach. She glanced at Jake and then said hesitantly, 'I don't know. I . . . I think I want to keep it.'

Jake looked as though he'd sat on a porcupine. 'You never said that before.'

'I never said I wanted to kill our baby either.' Lucy looked confused. 'I'm still not sure *what* I want, to be honest.'

'What do you think, Miss?' asked Jake, and at that moment he looked like a lost little boy.

Gently Joyce said, 'I can't make that decision for you, Jake, but I do know that if you *do* both decide to keep the baby then you're going to need the help and support of both sets of parents.' She saw Lucy's look of despair and said quickly, 'They may surprise you, Lucy. They may not be happy with the idea at first, but they love you and they're hardly going to throw you and their grandchild out on the streets, are they?'

'You don't know them like I do,' said Lucy.

'I know they're decent people,' said Joyce, mentally biting her lip. 'I know they've given you and your sisters all that they could and have brought you up the best way they know how.'

Lucy still looked dubious. Joyce said, 'How about your parents, Jake? How do you think they'll react?'

'I think they'll give me a good hiding,' Jake said. Then he shrugged. 'But once that's over with, I reckon they'll be all right.'

'Why don't you tell them first then?' said Joyce. 'Both of you. They may not be so angry if Lucy's with you.'

Both of them looked reluctant. In a coaxing voice, Joyce said, 'I know it's not something to look forward to, but you both know it's something that has to be done, don't you?' She paused, and after a moment the two of them nodded grudgingly. 'Good,' she said. 'I'm sure you'll find that once all this is out in the open, everything will seem much brighter.'

They looked unconvinced, disappointed, as if they had been relying on their former headmistress to reel off the solutions to all their problems. Knowing she'd let them down, Joyce felt a sense of her own futility creeping over her, which was a feeling she had experienced often since Audrey's death. Sometimes she wondered why God bothered to keep her alive at all. She was, to coin a phrase dear Audrey had used often (though never about her), 'neither use nor ornament'. Attempting to swallow her self-pity, she said a little more harshly than she intended, 'I'm sorry there aren't any easy solutions, but there just *aren't*. Whether you decide to keep the baby or not, you're going to have to tell your parents and it's not going to be easy.'

'I know that, Miss,' said Jake, trying to smile, and then he added hopefully, 'but if we *do* decide not to keep it, *will* you help us out?'

Joyce looked at him incredulously for a moment and then shook her head. 'No, Jake, I won't fix up a termination for you. Imagine the headlines if the newspapers got hold of it: HEADMISTRESS IN SECRET ABORTION PACT WITH TEENAGE PUPILS.' (Gay headmistress, she amended silently to herself. Even better.)

'Course we wouldn't expect you to do that,' said Lucy, frowning at Jake, 'but. . .' She broke off, looking sheepish.

'But?' said Joyce with a sigh.

'Well, I was wondering . . . When we tell my parents, would you come with us?'

Joyce imagined the scene. John Benson would be bound to use her sexuality as a weapon against her. He already thought her perverse. Knowing him, he'd probably say that she encouraged her pupils to have sex, and that now she was encouraging them to go against their parents' wishes. She shuddered inwardly. She couldn't face that. The way she was feeling at the moment, she'd crumble.

However, when she saw the hope on Lucy's face she found herself saying, 'We'll see.' Then, thinking of Audrey and trying to make it sound convincing, she added, 'But in the meantime try not to worry. These things usually have a way of working out in the end.'

Chapter Thirty-Four

It was quiet in the surgery on Saturday. Most people were at the show. Too bloody busy enjoying themselves to think about getting ill, Kerr thought. Funny how most people only got ill when they had nothing better to do.

He had kept his word and returned to work yesterday, had made a point of breezing in, in fact, calling out hearty good mornings to everyone. He had rapped on Hamilton's door before morning surgery, and entered without being invited.

'Ah, Julian,' he had barked, 'sorry if I sounded a bit off it when you rang yesterday. Your call woke me from a very deep sleep.'

It was only when he reached the privacy of his own room and had shut the door that his legs had begun to give way. He had just about managed to make it to his chair, and had sat down, sweating and trembling. How he had got through the day he would never know, though the Valium he kept delving into his briefcase for had had a lot to do with it. A hundred years ago, when Hilary died, Kerr had started with a nice acceptable thirty milligrams a day, just enough to tide him over; now he was nudging two hundred.

Something had happened during his absence, because yesterday Kerr had found he could no longer cruise along in low gear as he had done previously, his favourite drugs buzzing pleasantly through his system. Yesterday he had had to concentrate *so hard* to prevent the words his patients were speaking to him from dissolving into gobbledygook. Even when he did understand, chances were he had completely forgotten what was wrong with them five minutes later. At times he had had to grip his desk as though it was the rim of a big black hole he would fall endlessly into if he let go. Today was only marginally better because he had had fewer patients to see. In fact, he had only had three so far – it should have been five, but two had failed to turn up.

At least the surgery closed at lunchtime today, which couldn't be far away now. That gave him the rest of today and all of tomorrow to recover before Monday. He had had a tough week, but he was sure that all he needed to set him back on course was a couple of good nights' sleep. All right, so he had been overdoing it with the pills and the booze, but it would be easy enough to cut down. He just needed to get home where he could have a rest and think things through without interruption.

Absently, Kerr reached into his jacket pocket for one of the little white pills he had deposited there and popped it into his mouth. If he had been asked how many of the pills he had taken today, he might have made an honest guess at three or four, though in fact this was his seventh. He swallowed the pill without water, closed his eyes for a moment like someone relishing a particularly fine chocolate, then stood up and walked over to the window. His room overlooked the small, hedge-enclosed car park at the rear of the new (it had been built in 1978) white-stoned medical centre.

His wife, Hilary, was walking across the car park towards the medical centre, wearing a navy-blue dress that Kerr recognised as the one she had been wearing when he had seen her reflection in the mirror at home a few days ago. She looked up at him, smiled and waved, then continued walking. Kerr was so stunned that he merely raised a hand in an instinctive response, and didn't react fully until she had got so close to the building that she had passed out of sight.

Then he made an odd, strangled sound and began scrabbling at the glass as though he believed his stubby fingers could tear through it like polythene. When he recovered enough of what remained of his wits to grope at the catch, sweat was pumping out of every pore in his body. He tore a fingernail so badly that it filled with blood in his increasingly frantic attempts to get the window open, but he didn't even notice. When he did finally manage to shove the window up and lean out so far he almost toppled thirty feet to the concrete below, Hilary was nowhere to be seen.

She must be in the building. She'd be in the waiting room now, perhaps strolling to the reception desk to ask for him. Still sweating profusely, Kerr turned from the window and blundered across the room. His hip collided with the edge of the treatment table, causing pain to flare brightly in the bone and fan out through his pelvis. 'Fuck. Ow,' he growled, limped to the door and threw it open.

He almost expected her to be sitting on one of the chairs out here, flicking through a magazine. But there was only a young mother and her toddler daughter, who were evidently waiting their turn to see Dr Hamilton or Dr Fanukin, and who regarded him with wide, alarmed eyes as if they were afraid he might insist on seeing them. Kerr swayed in the doorway for a moment as he considered asking them if they had seen Hilary, then he launched himself with a shove towards the heavy glass-panelled one that led to the staircase.

He ripped the door open, stumbled through, and began to descend the staircase, his squealing, sweaty grip on the banister stopping him from falling headlong. The only thing that mattered to him was to reach Hilary before she drifted away again, before she floated out of his life for good. She was trying her hardest to get back to him, but so far he had been too slow and too stupid to take advantage of her efforts.

If only he could touch her, speak to her, everything would be all right, he was sure of it. He reached the bottom of the stairs and let go of the banister, lunged forward and crashed through the door into the reception area.

Everyone jumped, heads snapping up, eyes widening to show their whites, mouths opening to utter cries of shock. The reception area was spacious, airy, full of light. To Kerr's right was the reception desk, to his left the alcove that was the main waiting room with its linked chairs lining the walls, its low table covered in magazines, a few children's toys scattered on the floor.

There were eight patients waiting to be called upstairs, none of which was Hilary. Behind the reception desk, Naomi, who was in her early twenties and had greasy hair and a spotty forehead, craned forward to look at him, while grey-haired Morag, who had worked at the new surgery ever since it opened and at the old one for twenty years before that, pursed her lips disapprovingly.

For an instant Kerr saw himself as these people saw him – sweaty, dishevelled, wild-eyed, gasping for breath, swaying like a drunkard – but felt no shame, merely impatience and contempt. What did they know, with their petty complaints? What did they know about real suffering?

He stumped to the reception desk and all but sprawled over it, inadvertently elbowing a telephone, which jangled briefly in protest. The roaring pump of his body seemed to fill the room, which was otherwise silent. Naomi stepped back as he advanced, watching him with a kind of nervous fascination as if he was an interesting but potentially dangerous animal, but Morag stood her ground, her face like stone.

'Did someone just come in here?' Kerr demanded.

Naomi glanced at Morag, who narrowed her eyes behind her pale-framed spectacles. 'People come in and out of here all the time, Dr Kerr.'

Kerr's anger was like pain, sharp and white, sliding into the underside of his brain. 'Don't be bloody obtuse, woman, you know what I mean. A woman. Did a woman just come in here?'

He heard a shifting behind him and turned round. A plump woman with mottled cheeks and a tight perm which merely emphasised the roundness of her face, was cautiously raising a hand.

'Er . . . I just came in,' she said. 'Well, a . . . a couple of minutes ago. I'm due to see Doc—'

'Not *you!* ' Kerr barked, making the woman flinch. 'Why the bloody hell would I want to see *you*?'

'Dr Kerr!' Morag's voice was low, but forceful enough to make Kerr turn. She hadn't moved, but her eyes were blazing. In the same low voice that nevertheless carried throughout the room, she said, 'You're making a scene, Dr Kerr. And you're being rude to the patients.'

Kerr goggled at her, for a moment too incredulous to speak. When he finally managed to do so, his voice was an octave higher than before, and more breathless than ever.

'Don't you tell me what I'm doing and what I'm being,' he said. 'I'm a doctor. You're just a bloody receptionist. I can bloody well fire you if I want to.'

'No you can't,' she muttered, barely moving lips which were

stretched so tightly over her teeth they had gone white, 'not any more.'

Rage filled Kerr's head, seemed to brim in his eyes like black liquid so that he could barely see. He was shaking like a volcano about to erupt, but Morag looked undaunted. If he hadn't had other things to think about, he might have put his hands around her wrinkled throat, shaken her until her teeth fell out, then kicked her out of the door and told her never to come back. But he didn't have time; he couldn't let this harridan detain him. He turned to Naomi.

'You tell me,' he said. 'You tell me where the woman in the blue dress went.'

Naomi looked as though she was about to burst into tears. 'I . . . I haven't seen a woman in a blue dress,' she whispered.

'She just came in here!' Kerr roared. 'What's the matter with you? Are you fucking blind or something? Or just stupid, is that it?'

'Dr Kerr!' Morag interceded, stepping forward as Naomi cowered back. Kerr swung on her, would have hit her if the world hadn't jolted on its axis just then, making him stumble and clutch at the edge of the desk for support.

Blood roared in his ears, but he could still hear Morag's voice, her clipped words slapping tinnily against the shutters that were slamming down in his head. 'For goodness sake, calm down,' she was saying. 'Perhaps if you tried to explain to us who this woman was we'd all understand a bit better.'

'She's my wife, you stupid fucking woman!' Kerr screamed. His voice seemed very far away, as did Morag's face, though he saw it flower into astonishment very clearly.

'Your wife?' he saw her lips say, though he didn't hear a thing.

'Yes!' He wanted to sob; perhaps he was sobbing. 'Now tell me where she is. I need to know. I need to see her.'

For the first time Morag looked uncertain, and something else too – pitying perhaps. 'I'm afraid your wife's dead, Dr Kerr,' he barely heard her say.

'Do you think I don't know that? My God, I'm not stupid, woman. That's why I need to speak to her *now*, before she goes away again. Can't you see?'

Morag obviously couldn't; she stood there, perplexed. Kerr swung round to address the room, once again grabbing hold of the edge of the desk to stop himself from falling.

'Aren't any of you going to help me?' he pleaded, and saw immediately that they were not. Most people averted their eyes; those who didn't wore expressions of contempt or hostility.

Kerr pushed himself away from the desk and towards the double doors that led outside. 'All right, don't bother,' he snarled. 'I don't need you. I know where she'll be.' He dragged the right-hand door open, though it seemed intolerably heavy. 'I hope you all die of cancer,' he shouted, and drew at least a scrap of satisfaction from the gasps of shock that he trapped inside as the heavy door banged shut behind him.

The brightness of the day seemed to be trying to bear him to the ground as he crossed the car park to his car. His clothes, drenched in sweat, were like lead. Even the blood pounding round his body seemed as dense as mercury. By the time he reached his car and slid into the driver's seat he was breathing as if he'd run a marathon.

He could barely see, his vision full of black clots that reduced the view through his windscreen to an unrelated collection of lumpy shapes. However, this would not deter him from driving home. He had to get there as quickly as possible if Hilary was not to elude him again. He started the engine and jerked out of the car park, then drove home in a blur, his hands and feet moving instinctively, as though guided from afar.

When his car jolted into his drive, he blinked as if he had just woken up. He fumbled for long seconds at the seat belt across his chest before realising he wasn't wearing one, then opened the car door and all but rolled out on to the Tarmac. His sweat-slippery hands climbed the car as he hauled himself to his feet, then he staggered towards the front door of his house, which was ajar.

Had he left it like that? Surely not. Then he realised that Hilary must have left it half-open, perhaps out of eagerness, perhaps as an invitation. She would be waiting just inside for him, willing him to hurry. He imagined touching his wife again, speaking to her, imagined shrugging off this hell that his life had become, and he felt so giddy that he almost passed out.

He went into the house and there she was, floating down the stairs in her wedding dress, a vision of white, like a light at the end of a long, dark tunnel. She must be wearing it to let him know that she wanted to start her life with him all over again.

He couldn't see her face, the dress was so dazzling. As she reached the bottom of the stairs and floated along the hallway towards him, he reached out to her, spoke her name.

She didn't reply, and still he couldn't see her face, nor her hands; surely he hadn't been too late, after all? But no, apparently not, at least not entirely, for as the dress got closer he saw it slowly lift its empty sleeves towards him.

Chapter Thirty-Five

For Joan Dyer, fear was a constant companion. It filled her so utterly that she was no more than a hollow vessel for it. She couldn't eat, couldn't sleep, couldn't even find the still, silent place inside herself any more. Indeed, the shadow of the evil that was coming to Longbarrow was so black and stifling now that sometimes Joan could barely breathe. She had tried pleading with Brian until she was blue in the face to take the family away, but he had remained adamant that they would stay and face whatever was going to happen together. She could see in his eyes that he actually thought nothing *was* going to happen, that he was merely humouring her. Could see too that the more frantic she became, the more he became convinced that she was slipping into a paranoia that could only become a dementia.

That was it then. She had lost. All she could do now was wait for the inevitable. She found herself wishing that death would come and take her before she was forced to witness her family being consumed by whatever form the oncoming evil might take. Even madness, which her constant state of terror ought to be pushing her towards, would be preferable to seeing them suffer.

The irony was, her family thought she *was* going mad, mainly because of the way she sat and gazed into space with increasing regularity. The truth, however, was that her body was still and her face blank not because there were too few thoughts in her mind, but too many. Today Sheila had been so worried by what she perceived as her mother-in-law's deterioration that she had been prepared to stay home from the show with her, to forsake her long-standing position as one of

Longbarrow's leading cake and scone makers. Joan, however, had roused herself a little, had patted her daughter-in-law's hand and urged her to go, assuring her that she would be all right. In the end, after much persuading, the family had left the house, promising that they wouldn't be long.

Joan found her fear a little easier to face alone. When her family were around her, despite the fact that she had never been a demonstratively affectionate woman, she found herself aching with love for them. Also, she was terrified of what she might see when any one of them walked in the room. Thankfully, there had been no recurrence of Monday's terrible vision when she had seen her grandson's skull gleaming through the jellyfish-transparency of his flesh, and the death-birds, as she had come to think of them, hatching from his body. Perhaps this meant that he had heeded her warning to stay away from the new boy in the big house, after all. Could she take solace from this? Could she dare hope that her family might survive whatever was to come? It was a question that she found impossible to answer. Her dread was so all-consuming that there seemed no room for hope.

She wished she could sleep some of her fear away, or at least black it out for a while, but since Monday she had done nothing but doze fitfully. It was as though the approaching evil had an energy all its own, a strange, dark electricity that buzzed constantly in her mind, keeping it active, refusing to let it rest.

She closed her eyes now, knowing she would get no peace, knowing that even if she did manage to slip below wakefulness, she would wake up exhausted and distressed, her mind full of jagged, messy images too incomprehensible to be termed dreams or even nightmares. Nevertheless, she had to try to sleep, if only because she longed to do so. She pushed herself down inside herself, so desperate for some respite from the constant, grinding ache of her fear, that she was prepared to search over and over again, through the same dark and terrible places, for the oblivion she craved.

Almost immediately she began to dream, which was odd because she had not dreamed in a long time. However, this dream had a strange texture. It was like a waking dream, like reality viewed through a filter. Joan Dyer had never been drunk or taken drugs, but she had always imagined that this was what it would be like. Although she was in her accustomed place in the dream, sitting in the green armchair by the unlit fire, looking out across the small sitting room that had become her world, the light was diffuse, treacly; sounds were muffled, her thoughts and movements slow and dragging.

When she looked down at her gnarled hands curled around the chair's arms like strange roots, her head seemed to take an age to tilt. It occurred to her to wonder – the thought drifting to the surface of her mind like a globule of coloured oil in a lava lamp – whether her eyes were open or closed. In slow motion she raised her hands to her face, her withered fingers uncurling. When she discovered that her eyes were open, a dreamy, intense terror that she couldn't explain seeped through her. As her hands floated back down to the arms of the chair, weightless as feathers, she heard footsteps.

They were coming along the hallway towards the sitting room, slow and measured, reverberating dully, the hollow sound of hard soles on polished wood. Joan raised her hands slowly to her ears to block them out, only to discover that the sounds were in her head as well as outside it.

The footsteps halted outside the closed sitting-room door. Slowly, slowly, the door swung open. There was no one there. No one at least that she could see. But Joan felt something enter the room, felt the fingertip caress of absolute, awful evil.

She wanted to die then, wanted her heart to stop. This, she knew, was what had cast its shadow before it into Longbarrow; this was what she had been waiting for. She squeezed her eyes tight shut, but felt compelled to open them again when she heard the frenetic whisper of beating wings.

The evil had found a shape.

A man with a thatch of red hair and skin the colour of bread was standing motionless in the corner of the room, wearing a suit made of white, fluttering shapes.

Joan tried to look at the man's face but she could not. It was as though her eyes refused to linger on his features, as though her vision slid away before it could focus. With a tremendous effort she forced herself to speak.

'What are you? Why have you come here?'

She felt a fluttering whisper in her head: *I am Redcap. I sleep no more.*

Then the white shapes exploded from his body and descended on her, filling her with the beating of their wings.

Chapter Thirty-Six

'Want to try again?' Mary Sheridan said, nuzzling up to Mike French's shoulder.

Mike smiled sleepily. Only his fear of the two of them being discovered in a post-coital stupor by Mary's husband, Ted, had prevented him from dozing.

'You're insatiable,' he murmured and swivelled round to kiss her.

'And don't you just love it?' she replied before her mouth met his and her hand slid down to enclose his already-stiffening cock.

As usual that morning he had glanced up at the bedroom window, seen the open curtain and entered the house. He had been, if anything, a little more nervous than normal, because this was Saturday, after all, and Ted was unlikely to be at work.

Mary had met him in the hallway. She had done her hair the way he liked it, and had been wearing the same towelling dressing gown she had been wearing the first time he had met her. As soon as he had closed the front door, she had pulled the dressing gown open to reveal a red basque and stockings. She was beautiful, apart from the bruises on her back and ribs and arms that were the result of the beating Ted had given her after being released from police custody on Tuesday. When he had first seen the bruises, Mike had vowed angrily to avenge her, but she had just smiled and murmured, 'My brave soldier.'

'Listen,' she had said this morning, smiling teasingly and pulling the dressing gown closed again, 'why don't you come back after your round and we'll spend the day together? We won't be disturbed. Ted's at the show, getting pissed with his mates.'

'What if he comes back?' Mike had asked.

'He won't. Once Ted starts drinking, he doesn't stop until chucking out time. I won't see him before midnight.'

'What about Jason?'

'Don't worry about him. He'll be out all day doing whatever weird things it is he does. Besides, he hasn't got a key to the house. We can lock the door.'

Despite his reservations, Mike had finally agreed to go back. When it came right down to it, he always ended up doing what Mary asked of him. He couldn't help it.

Now she broke their kiss and shuffled her body lower in the bed. She nuzzled his nipples, then moved lower still, raining light kisses on his stomach. When she dipped her head to take him in her mouth, he let out a gasp and reached up to grip the headboard. She was swivelling her body round so that he could do to her what she was doing to him when the doorbell rang.

'Fuck!' he said and jerked upright, almost choking her. She reared back, glaring at him angrily.

'For fuck's sake, just relax, can't you?'

'Somebody's at the door!'

'So what? It's probably just Jehovah's witnesses, come to save us both.'

'What if it's Ted?' Mike whimpered.

'It won't be fucking Ted. Ted wouldn't ring the doorbell. He'd use his key, or else bray on the door and shout a lot.'

'What if it's Jason then?'

'If it's Jason we won't let him in,' she said, speaking as though to a child. 'He'll get bored soon enough and piss off again.'

'I think you'd better see who it is,' he said.

'Oh, for fuck's sake.' But she swung her legs from the bed, picking her dressing gown up off the floor as she strode naked to the window.

When she had put the dressing gown on and tied it at the waist, she pulled the edge of the curtain back with her forefinger and peeked out. 'Oh shit,' she said.

'Who is it?' Mike asked, his voice brimming with panic.

'Des Brewer.'

'The police?' He leaped from the bed and began picking up items of his clothing that were strewn on the floor, frantically dressing himself. 'You don't think he's here about us, do you?'

271

She looked at him almost contemptuously. 'Don't be soft. Why should he give a shit about us?'

'Well . . . isn't adultery a crime?'

She sighed deeply and shook her head. 'Just calm down, will you, Mike. You're not thinking straight.'

Mike dragged his boots on and began fumbling with the laces. 'All the same I think I'd better go.'

'Why, for God's sake?'

'Well, what if . . . what if he wants to come in and speak to you? What if he's here a long time?'

She sighed again, then reached for her cigarettes on the bed-side table. Tightly she said, 'All right, you bloody go if you want to. Just let him in on your way out, would you?'

He looked at her in horror. 'I'm not going out the front. I don't want him to see me.'

Her face glowed orange from the flare of the match as she lit her cigarette. Smoke like ribbons of grey silk coiled through the air. 'I know,' she said tersely, 'I was joking.'

The doorbell rang again.

She crossed to the window and yanked the curtains open, filling the room with sunny light. Mike cowered like a vampire as she yanked up the catch and shoved the window open.

'What?' she shouted.

Des Brewer looked up at her. He didn't look happy. 'Ah, Mrs Sheridan . . . Mary,' he said. 'Could I speak to you for a moment?'

'Can't you say what you've got to say there? I'm not dressed,' she said.

He glanced up and down the street, as though looking for eavesdroppers. 'I really think it'd be best if I come in.' Then his face adopted a look of anguished sympathy. 'I'm afraid I've got some rather bad news.'

Chapter Thirty-Seven

'Fancy a pint?' said Jack.

Susan, who was leaning back on the grass on her elbows, tilting her face to the sun, squinted at him. 'Do you?'

'Yeah, I wouldn't mind. I'm a bit thirsty after those fish and chips.'

'All right then.'

They got up, Jack helping Susan to her feet. A man in red hunting gear was riding around the ring now, directing a pack of hounds which all the children, standing watching with their parents, were cooing over and pointing at. At a given signal from the huntsman, the hounds stopped running in circles and collected together in a group, their tongues lolling from their mouths, their tails wagging. The children were then allowed to run into the ring to pat and stroke the hounds.

'Indoctrination,' said Susan.

'What?'

'It's making out that hunting's okay, isn't it? They don't tell those children what those hounds are really used for. Getting dressed up to go out and kill things.' She pulled a sour face. 'It's sick and it's stupid.'

Jack shrugged. Susan said, 'Don't tell me you agree with it?'

'I'm not bothered either way,' he said. 'It's not my idea of fun, but that doesn't mean I wouldn't shoot a fox if I were a farmer and it was worrying my chickens. They can be vicious buggers, foxes. Sometimes they bite the heads off chickens just for fun. They don't always kill for food.'

'Yes, well, they don't know any better, do they? It's instinctive with them. With us it's just . . . sadistic. I mean who in their right mind could possibly get any satisfaction from watching a living creature being ripped to pieces?'

'Don't ask me,' said Jack. 'I'm a football man myself.'

They strolled around the perimeter of the ring, making for the beer tent. David had gone off to look for his friend, Colin Dyer, giving Jack and Susan some time on their own. Jack loved being in Susan's company. He might still have a lot to learn about her, and they might not always see eye-to-eye on certain things, but he didn't think he had ever felt quite so relaxed with anyone before. Even when he had been a youngster, even when he had gone off the rails a bit and got himself into bad company, he had always preferred being alone to being with his friends. It was not that he didn't like people, it was just that life seemed so uncomplicated, so much more settled, when he didn't have anyone else to worry about. He didn't know whether that made him selfish or weird or what, and he wasn't really bothered; as long as he was content, then who cared what other people thought?

But Susan was different. She had awakened something in him that he hadn't even been aware was asleep. He couldn't explain why, but almost from the start they had just sort of clicked. If it didn't sound so daft, he would have said that it was almost as if he had been waiting for her to show up in his life, that there was even a part of him that had always known she would. It seemed crazy to be having such thoughts when he had only just met her, when in fact they had only spent a total of perhaps two days together (not forgetting, of course, that one incredible night), and yet at the same time it seemed like the most natural thing in the world.

Predictably, the beer tent was packed and hot as a sauna. A lot of people were sitting or standing around on the grass outside with their drinks. Susan eyed the crush inside the tent with reluctance. 'I don't fancy squeezing my way through that lot,' she said.

'Why don't you wait here, then, and I'll get them in. What do you fancy?'

'Do you think they might do white wine?'

'They might.'

'Okay, I'll have a glass of white wine if it's cold. If not, I'll have a half of whatever you're having.'

He nodded. 'This may take some time.'

274

'If you're not back in an hour, I'll come after you with a shoehorn.'

He grinned and waved and pushed his way into the crush of people. ''Scuse me, 'scuse me,' he repeated like a stuck record, trying to avoid jogging elbows that were part of arms attached to hands holding drinks. Within seconds he was drenched in sweat, and wondering whether this had been such a good idea, after all. Did he really need a beer this badly? The answer was no, but the bar was in sight now. It would seem pretty tame if he went back empty-handed.

Then, above the general hubbub that filled the tent, someone suddenly roared, 'Fuckin' say that again!' Immediately the buzz of conversation wound down as if a plug had been pulled on a power tool, then ceased altogether. Heads began to turn. Jack stood on tiptoes, craning his neck, but he couldn't see what was going on. The voice sounded as if it had come from six or eight feet in front of him, close to the bar. It had been booming and slurred and oafish. It had also sounded familiar, though for the moment Jack couldn't quite place it.

Then another voice, younger and defiant, though laced with a hint of fear, said, 'Say what?'

'What you just said to this fuckin' cunt here,' the voice bellowed, and all at once Jack knew who it belonged to. Ted Sheridan, one of his old partners in crime. They had been mates once . . . well, kind of. Even now, on the rare occasions that their paths crossed, they still exchanged nods. Jack had heard all about the trouble Ted had caused in the Druid's Arms when he had popped in for last orders on Wednesday night after getting back from Harrogate. Trevor Paine's face had been a right mess. Ted had spent a night in the cells for it, and had an assault charge pending. Jack couldn't believe Ted was causing trouble again now – or maybe he could. The man was an animal, after all, incapable of intelligent thought.

Now that everyone was standing still, trying to see what was going on, it was easier for Jack to push through the crowd. ''Scuse me,' he murmured, wriggling his way towards the disturbance. He had an idea that he might be able to calm things down, nip the situation in the bud before it could escalate. It was probably a vain hope, but worth a try. He had never been the sort of person who could walk away from an incident where someone was likely to get hurt, or even stand around and watch it happening.

He squeezed through a space between two farm labourers he occasionally played pool with in the Druid's Arms, and suddenly found himself in a small clearing that had been created by wary onlookers pressing themselves as far back into the crowd as they could. On one side of this mini-arena was Ted Sheridan and two of his leering, bloodthirsty cronies, on the other side two teenagers whom Jack recognised as Gary Sissons and Ben Darracott. It was ironic, really; Anne Darracott saw herself as the self-appointed guardian of Longbarrow's morals, as a crusader against subversion, little knowing that her fourteen-year-old son and his friends were responsible for much of the petty crime that she was often heard declaring was the result of inadequate parenting.

It was Ben Darracott who had spoken to Ted. He was trying hard not to look scared so that he wouldn't lose face with his friend. Gary Sissons, of course, looked as arrogant as always. He was crazy enough to be constantly spoiling for a fight, whoever the opponent, and thus was not unlike a younger, smaller version of Ted Sheridan himself.

Gary was responding to Ted's latest outburst as Jack emerged from the crowd. Stepping forward, adopting an openly aggressive stance, the teenager snarled, 'Who are you calling a cunt, you fat bastard?'

'Hey, lads, calm down,' Jack said placatingly, and raised a hand towards Ted, half in greeting, half in a holding-back gesture. 'All right, Ted, how you doing?' he said, as if he thought this might detract Ted from wading forward and twisting Gary Sissons' head off with his bare hands.

Ted's bead-like eyes flickered towards him, but he made no reply, his face dangerously deadpan. Like a shark abandoning one potential meal for a closer one, Gary Sissons now swung towards Jack.

'Who the fucking hell are you?' he said.

'A friend, just wanting a quiet drink like everyone else.'

'Yeah, well, this has got nothing to fucking do with you, so fuck off.'

Jack raised his hands, refusing to lose his temper. 'Look, there's no need for all this. Everyone's just trying to have a good time here.'

'That little shit was saying stuff about my wife,' Ted rumbled, jabbing a thick, dirt-ingrained finger at Ben Darracott.

Ben did his best not to quail. 'I was only telling Gary something I heard my mum talking about,' he said.

'Yeah,' said Gary, turning back to Ted. 'We were having a private conversation, so just fuck off out of it, you fat bastard.'

Sheridan began to lumber forward, his lips writhing in his thick beard. Gary raised his fists, eyes shining with anticipation. Jack leaped forward and grabbed Ted's massive arms, trying to hold him back. Jack was not a small man, but it was like trying to halt a runaway bulldozer. 'Ted,' he shouted, 'Ted, think about this. You're in enough bother already. He's only a kid, he's not worth it.'

'What's a matter, fat boy? Can't you get it up?' Gary was screaming behind Jack. 'Is that why your slag of a wife has to shag the postman every morning?'

Sheridan roared like a bear and swept out his arm in an arc, flinging Jack away from him. Jack reeled backwards, losing his balance, and was only prevented from falling by helping hands that reached out from the crowd and steadied him. Ted and Gary clashed in the middle of the arena, like animals ill-matched in size but equal in viciousness. As they began to exchange punches, Gary's hands quick and frenzied, Ted's arms swinging round to connect with sledgehammer blows, Ben Darracott pressed himself back against the edge of the bar and looked as if he bitterly regretted having the village gossip as a mother.

Jack was looking around for anyone who might be willing to help him break up the fight, when a dark-suited figure burst from the crowd and began grappling with the combatants. Jack was so surprised that it took him a moment to recognise Des Brewer in his police uniform. 'Pack it in! Bloody pack it in!' Des was shouting angrily.

Whether by accident or design, Des's helmet was knocked off. The big policeman swore, but it didn't deter him from grabbing Gary Sissons in a headlock and twisting him away from Sheridan so that Des's broad blue back was between Sheridan and the teenager. Sheridan tried to punch Gary over Des Brewer's shoulder. The teenager's face was pouring with blood, but he was still screeching, 'Come on, you fat cunt, come on!'

Jack ran forward again, grabbed hold of Sheridan's punching arm and clung on for dear life. He added his own voice to the cacophony, yelling directly into Sheridan's bearded face, 'Ted, calm down! Calm down!'

More people came forward from the crowd now to help subdue the violence. With three people clinging to him, Ted Sheridan finally admitted defeat. He stopped trying to punch Sissons through the crowd and simply stood there, his face as deadpan as before as he watched half a dozen people bear the still-struggling teenager to the floor. Panting, Des Brewer knelt on Sissons' back and put handcuffs on him. Sissons was spitting blood, but that didn't stop him continuing to issue curses and threats.

Des Brewer wiped an arm across his brow and looked up at Sheridan. 'Don't you ever stop?' he said.

Sheridan simply stared silently back at him. It was one of his cronies who piped up, 'Ted never started anything. It was these kids here, telling lies about his missis.'

'I'm not interested,' Brewer said harshly, and the man fell silent, retreating sheepishly into his beer. Brewer looked at Ted and his voice carrying throughout the now-silent tent, said, 'If you can refrain from hitting anyone for five minutes, Ted, I'd like you to come outside with me. I've got something important to tell you.'

Chapter Thirty-Eight

By the time he got home, Mike French was hot and flustered. He'd known Mary could be a bit fiery, but he had never known her be downright nasty before. However, as he had leaned forward to kiss her goodbye before sneaking out the back door, she had deliberately raised her cigarette to her lips and muttered, 'Fuck off.'

'Please, Mary,' he had said, 'don't be like this.'

'Don't you fucking tell me how to behave,' she had snapped.

'I wasn't. I just didn't want us to part on bad terms, that's all.'

'You shouldn't be so bloody spineless then, should you?'

He had frowned, miserable and frustrated. 'I'm not being spineless, I'm just being careful.' When she had simply looked away in disgust, he had said, 'See you on Monday?'

'I'll think about it,' she had said. 'You'd better go if you're going.' The instant he was out the door, she had slammed it behind him.

He walked through the downstairs rooms of the silent house to the kitchen and poured himself a glass of water. He was glad his parents and younger sister were at the show; it hadn't escaped his mother's attention how preoccupied he had been these past few weeks. He had told her it was the prospect of going to university, but she hadn't seemed convinced. As he tilted the glass to pour the last of the water down his throat, the telephone rang.

He considered letting it ring; he didn't feel like talking to anyone just now. But when it showed no sign of stopping he reluctantly made his way into the lounge and snatched it up from the nest of its own looped lead on the windowsill.

'Hello,' he said into a flood of static that sounded both raw and fierce.

The woman's voice that replied seemed to form from the static. 'Ted knows about us,' it said.

Instantly Mike's sweat turned as cold as the water in his belly. 'Is that you, Mary?'

The static-filled voice ignored the question. 'Listen, we need to talk.'

'When?' Mike said in a small voice, his head spinning.

'Now. Meet me in the woods in half an hour. Take the path down to the river beyond the big house.'

'I don't know if I—'

'Don't let me down, Mike,' the voice said. The crackle of static was replaced by the empty hum of the dialling tone.

Mike stood with the receiver in his trembling hand for a few seconds, staring at it in anguish and disbelief. Then he lowered it, clattering, back into its cradle, and wrapped his arms around his stomach.

Suddenly he felt horribly sick. Clamping a hand to his mouth as he gagged, he rushed into the kitchen and vomited all the water he had drunk into the sink. He continued to retch even when his stomach was empty, the contractions so violent that tears were squeezed from his eyes.

It was ironic that the potential consequences of this affair that had made him feel so adult were now making him feel like a child again. He felt an urge to do what he had done when he was six or seven years old and had woken from a nightmare, which was to crawl under his bed where he believed the monsters couldn't get him. The prospect of venturing out of the house terrified him, but then so did the thought of remaining here, waiting for Sheridan to turn up. What if Sheridan should appear, ranting and raving, when Mum and Dad and Donna were home? Mike didn't think he'd be able to bear it if his family ever found out what he'd been up to.

At last his stomach began to settle. He rinsed out his mouth, then splashed water on his face and dried it with a tea towel. His legs felt hollow as he walked back into the lounge and peered cautiously through the net curtains. As far as he could see, the garden and drive and the street beyond that were clear. Of course, Sheridan could be crouched behind a wall or a tree, but Mike doubted he would be that subtle. He felt dreadfully vulnerable as he crept out of the house and hurried along the street, head down. His heart leaped every time someone came into view, because for a split-second his imagination made *everyone* look like Ted Sheridan. Even eighty-five-year-old Mrs Standing, who walked with a stoop, was momentarily Sheridan crouched forward like an ape; even a ginger-haired girl of about ten, erupting from her driveway on a pink bicycle, was Sheridan bursting from ambush astride a Harley Davidson.

Before meeting Mary, Mike would never have considered himself timid or paranoid, but now he couldn't help thinking that every situation had been contrived to place him in danger. Every engine he heard as he left the streets of the village behind and began toiling up the sun-dappled road that wound through the first of several clumps of woodland made him glance nervously around and edge closer to the railings that dropped down into the woods, which would provide him with his only possible escape route if Sheridan *should* appear.

Even arriving without incident at the path that led down to the river didn't make Mike feel much better. As he set off along it, he couldn't help wondering whether Mary had made her phone call to him under duress, whether in fact he was walking into a trap.

His surroundings *seemed* peaceful enough, but the trees and bushes provided plenty of places to hide, and certainly Mike thought that if *he* wanted to lure someone to a place where he knew he wouldn't be disturbed, then this was the obvious location. For this reason, by the time the river came into view he was wound up so tight that the first sign of trouble would have reduced him to a blur leaving a trail of fire in its wake. His head flicked back and forth like a bird's, his accentuated senses registering every nod of leaf and wind-stirred blade of grass, as he made his way through the trees that marched down to the river's edge. There was no sign of Mary, which of course didn't neccessarily mean that anything was wrong. She might simply have been hiding for fear of Ted showing up, or waiting for him further along the river, or maybe she was not even here yet.

Nevertheless he came to a halt, moving closer to a tree whose protective capabilities were merely psychological. 'Mary,' he called softly, 'Mary, are you there?'

The only reply was the constant idiot drone of insects fat with summer's bounty. Mike sighed and moved down to the river, half-thinking that if Sheridan should appear, he could always jump into the water and swim for it. It was shallow and slow-moving at the moment and Mike was a strong swimmer, which was something he couldn't imagine Sheridan being. So yeah, if he couldn't run for it, he would swim for it. There was always a way out.

What if he's got a gun? The thought came to him as if someone had whispered it in his ear. Mike clenched his fists as he felt something turn over inside him. Shit, why hadn't he thought of that before? Sheridan might be in the trees, pointing a gun at him at this moment.

Oh, why had he ever allowed himself to get into this mess? 'Mary,' he said, his voice cracked and snappish with tension now, 'Mary, if you don't show yourself in five seconds, I'm going home.'

He glanced quickly along the river bank, right and left, but there was no sign of her in either direction. He returned his attention to the trees he had just emerged from, alert for a glint of metal or an inexplicable shadow. He saw neither, and was just about to call out his lover's name once more when a woman's voice that seemed to come from nowhere said, 'Don't be afraid, Mike.'

Mike was so surprised that he almost stepped back into the water that was no more than a couple of paces behind him. 'Mary?' he said, but he knew even as he said it that it hadn't been Mary's voice he had heard.

It had been a strange voice – old and yet not old, and somehow ethereal.

'No,' the voice said, confirming his doubts. 'And yes,' it added, puzzling him.

Then there was a rush of static like a bad radio signal, and through it Mike heard the voice say, 'Listen, we need to talk.'

He went cold inside. This was part of his telephone conversation with Mary. How had whoever this was managed to tape it and why? Perhaps she was working with Sheridan.

His body felt jittery with fear, but he braced himself to run. 'Who are you?' he demanded.

'No,' the young-old voice said, 'who are *you?*' It seemed to find this amusing. 'Who are *you*, Mike?'

Mike's head snapped this way and that, but he could see no sign of anyone. 'What do you mean, who am I? You know who I am.'

'Yes,' the voice said, 'I do. But you don't, do you, Mike?'

'I don't know what you're talking about,' Mike said, his nerves and lack of understanding making him angry. 'What do you want?'

'I want *you*, Mike,' said the young-old voice that seemed to come from nowhere and everywhere.

'Well, you can't have me,' Mike said. 'Is Mary here?'

'No.' There was a sound that might have been a chuckle. 'She never was. It was me all along.'

'*You*? You mean, the phone call and everything?'

'Yes.'

'But why?'

'I need you, Mike. I need your body.'

Mike was clenching his fists, trying not to show how much he was quaking inside. 'Fuck that,' he said, and suddenly started running along the river bank to his left.

He ran awkwardly, his limbs stiff with fear, his head hunched down into his shoulders. If whoever had lured him here *did* have a gun or any other type of weapon, now might be the time when they would use it.

However, it was not a weapon that stopped him in his tracks, but something altogether more extraordinary. Suddenly, in his path, appeared a wall of fire, rising up as if from nowhere.

Mike staggered to a halt, his mouth dropping open. The fire raged with green and yellow and purple flames, like a burning rainbow, but it was no hallucination. He could feel its tremendous heat stinging his skin, causing the ends of his hair to curl and crisp. He staggered backwards. What the fucking *hell* was going on here? He turned to run in the other direction, but the fire was too quick for him.

Like a living thing, it sped across the ground in an impossibly thin band, making him think of a wall that appeared through the trickery of animation to build itself. The fire overtook him easily, and then curved round in front of him, blocking his way. He stumbled to a halt, now completely trapped in an impossible yet no less real semicircle of iridescent flame.

His body seemed to turn to mush, and his legs gave way beneath him. He fell on to his knees on the grass with the river behind him, his eyes staring, his mouth hanging slackly open. He panted like a dog as his heart pummelled his chest. This couldn't be happening, it *couldn't* be. He was seeing things, he was going mad.

He couldn't even swim for it. He was in no fit state to do anything but remain here and accept whatever terrible fate awaited him.

All at once, through the ten-foot high wall of flame, he saw something, a shadow, a blur, that grew steadily larger and darker until he recognised it as an approaching figure. The figure stood on the other side of the flame-wall, its features, even its sex, indeterminate. Then, before Mike's disbelieving gaze, it began to rise from the ground, to levitate from a standing position, until its head was level with the top of the flame-wall, then cresting it. Mike looked up, but sunlight flooded his eyes, reducing the figure to a black silhouette haloed in white light. He squinted and blinked, but not until the figure's feet had touched down on the ground on his side of the barrier was he able to focus upon it.

Standing in front of him was a frail old woman. Although he recognised her, it took him a moment to put a name to her.

'Mrs Dyer,' he finally whispered wonderingly.

Joan Dyer smiled, revealing almost a full set of grey-yellow teeth. 'Hello, Mike.'

Her voice was all wrong. Mike could only think that it sounded like someone young using the old woman's vocal cords.

'Mrs Dyer, what's happening?' Mike whimpered.

Again, Joan Dyer did something very odd, very uncharacteristic. She sat down cross-legged on the ground in front of Mike, her bony knees sticking out.

'I'll tell you,' she said, 'but only if you call me by my proper name.'

Mike felt like an invalid, so enfeebled by illness that he couldn't grasp the jist of his companion's conversation. 'Your . . . proper name?' he said.

'Yes,' said the old woman. 'Joan Dyer is merely a skin, a means of communication. I'm borrowing her for a while. I'm using her memories, her experiences, her knowledge, to

284

acclimatise myself to my new surroundings. My real name is Redcap.' She paused as though expecting some kind of reaction from him. When she next spoke she sounded a little petulant. 'You haven't heard of me?'

The name did in fact ring a distant bell in Mike's mind, but in his present state of confusion he couldn't recall it. 'I'm not sure,' he admitted.

'Oh dear,' said the old woman. 'Joan Dyer knew me, but then she was steeped in folklore. Perhaps you've heard of the Seven Sleepers?'

'Y-yes,' Mike said. 'Everyone in Longbarrow's heard that legend.'

'It's no legend,' said the old woman. She leaned forward, another smile stretching her wrinkled lips. 'The Sleepers are real, Mike. *We're* real. And we sleep no more.'

Mike looked into the glittering eyes of Joan Dyer and in that moment he realised she was mad. However calm and reasonable and friendly she sounded, she was quite definitely several spices short of a chicken tandoori, as his best mate, Will Trent, was wont to say. He had no idea how she had created the fire-wall, or how she had apparently levitated over it – perhaps her madness was catching and he was imagining all this. All he knew was that she was insane, crazy, nuts, bananas, mental. Her eyes crawled with it.

'Oh,' he said, 'right. I see.'

'No, Mike,' she said mildly, 'you don't see. You don't see at all. But soon enough you will.'

She settled herself into a more comfortable position on the grass. Mike thought he heard her bones creak. 'This may be hard for you to believe, Mike, but you and I are related. Yes, we are. The first time my colleagues and I came to Longbarrow, we made certain provisions in case our plans should go awry. We impregnated some of the local women with our enchanted seed, thus creating a lineage that survives to this day. I can see by your thoughts, Mike, that you don't believe a word of what I'm telling you, but whatever you believe or disbelieve is irrelevant to me. You, Mike, are nothing more than a vessel, a host. You were created by us, to serve us. We need you to house us, Mike, to carry us during these early days of our re-birth, until we defeat Decumen and take his power for our own, whereupon we will shed our mortal skins.'

The old woman smiled, stood up, stretched out her arms. 'It is *so good* to be alive again, Mike. *So good*, even in this decrepit body. The omens have been gathering for our re-birth for some time now. It was inevitable. Decumen's influence is weak, whereas ours is strong, and growing stronger by the hour. Soon we shall be whole again.' She raised her face to the sky and suddenly screeched in such a raw, crazed voice that Mike cowered, raising his arms, 'And then, Decumen, you shall choke on our revenge!'

She composed herself in an instant and turned to him, smiling sweetly, holding out her hand. 'And now, Mike, it is time for you to meet another of your fathers. His name is Gerennius, the fire-maker. You and he will become closer than you can ever imagine.'

Mike scrambled back as she came for him, right up to the water's edge. 'No,' he jabbered, 'keep away from me.' He glanced behind him, intending to plunge into the water, after all. But before he could move, the old woman sprang forward with astonishing speed and closed her bony hand around his wrist. Mike tried to shake her off, but she simply tightened her grip; her strength was phenomenal.

'Let go,' he shouted, then cried out as he felt his bones grinding together. 'Oww . . . you're hurting me.'

'Be still and watch the fire,' she ordered.

Mike had no choice but to do as she asked, his teeth clenched in pain.

Throughout the exchange, the fire-wall had maintained its position, almost as if the flames were enclosed in glass, but now Mike saw a section of it begin to bulge outwards. He bit his lip, drawing blood, as the bulge began to take on the vague shape of a human form, then started shaking his head in denial as the figure tore itself from the wall, trailing flame, like a man leaping through a sheet of thin fabric. For a moment there was a gap in the fire-wall from which the figure had emerged; through it, Mike could see a patch of woodland, bathed in sunshine. Then, like an instantly healing wound, blue and green and violet flame surged into the gap, closing it up.

Mike began to sob as the fire-form, crackling and hissing, lumbered towards him. It left charred footprints in the grass behind it. Its head was a tapering ball of blue flame, its thick arms ending in paws of fire. Mike struggled frantically, but the old woman's grip was immovable. The fire-form raised its hands as though to touch his face. Mike felt heat searing his cheeks, and at last he found the voice to scream. The blackness of unconsciousness began to press in on all sides, but he didn't pass out until a maw full of crimson fire opened in the centre of the thing's burning head and it began to speak.

Chapter Thirty-Nine

It was the longest day Steven and Helen Farrar had ever known. The instant the ambulance had screeched to a halt, lights flashing, in front of the Accident and Emergency department of Ripon General Infirmary, the doors had been thrown open and Chris had been rushed through to theatre for emergency surgery.

As well as smashing his femur, he had also severed his femoral artery and lost a massive amount of blood. He had already had one cardiac arrest in the ambulance on the way to the hospital and had been pulled back from the brink thanks only to the quick work of the attendant paramedics. Since then his heart had been fibrillating wildly, resisting all attempts to stabilise it. The Farrars had been informed that due to the excessive blood loss, their son's chances of survival could be placed at no more than fifty per cent.

All that had happened over three hours ago. Since then there had been no news. If purgatory was a real place, as the Catholics believed, Farrar thought, then it must look and smell and feel like this.

He and Helen were sitting on dun-coloured plastic chairs with no armrests in the hospital's reception area. As waiting rooms went it was pretty grim, clinical at best: ivory-coloured walls, fluorescent lighting, ringing telephones, footsteps echoing on tiled floors, the smell of sanitised fear.

And people, of course. People who for the most part looked as pensive and bewildered and afraid as Farrar felt. People who, like himself and Helen, were waiting for news of loved ones whom today Fate had decided to pick out for special treatment.

Farrar had not been blind to the hopeful, almost longing looks that some of these people had given him. It was an attitude he was used to. Wear a dog collar in a hospital and you were immediately expected to offer comfort and advice, perhaps even to dole out a few miracles.

Well, not today, he thought, unable to help feeling both resentful and ashamed. Today, if any miracles should happen to come his way, he'd be saving them for his only son. Perhaps his attitude would be seen by some as selfish, unChristian even, but Farrar didn't care. He was only human, after all, with a human being's foibles and failings. He was no saint, and had never made claims to be one. He knew that the world was rife with atrocity and depravity, that even as he was sitting here countries were being torn apart by war, that across the globe men, women and children were being raped and tortured and murdered. He knew this, and yet today he prayed for only one thing. Today all that was important was the life of his son. Nothing else mattered.

He looked at his wife. Helen had become hysterical in the ambulance when Chris had had his heart attack, but since arriving at the hospital had seemed to withdraw into herself. Her hands were clenched tightly in her lap and she was gazing down at them, lips pursed, as if she had never seen them before and couldn't work out what they were.

Farrar leaned towards her and touched her elbow gently. When she glanced up at him, he asked, 'Are you all right?'

She gave a small, tight nod, though Farrar wasn't sure she had even heard the question.

'Can I get you anything? Tea? Coffee?'

She shook her head and looked down at her hands once again. Farrar shifted his weight, preparing to stand up.

'I think I'll just—' he began, then lapsed into silence as a young female doctor with short blonde hair and a carefully neutral expression appeared through the swing doors that led from the operating theatres and marched towards them as though determined not to falter.

Farrar rose anyway, but more slowly than he had been about to, to meet her. Helen remained seated, her eyes wide and wary, like a child anticipating punishment from a parent.

'Mr and Mrs Farrar?' the doctor said in a voice as measured as her expression.

'Yes,' said Farrar, suddenly afraid to ask the questions that were crowding his mind.

'Do you think I might have a private word with you both? There's a consultation room just round the corner we can use.'

Steven and Helen exchanged glances, then he nodded. 'Er . . . yes, of course.'

'If you'll follow me.' She strode off. Farrar helped his wife to her feet, and then they followed the doctor, albeit less briskly, their limbs hampered by tension.

The doctor, whose name badge Farrar noticed read Dr A. Vine, offered them a quick smile as she held open a door out of sight of the reception area. The two of them entered, Farrar so preoccupied with what she might be about to say that his eyes slid over the details of the room without registering them.

Dr Vine entered, closing the door behind her, and turned to face them.

'I won't beat about the bush,' she said carefully. 'We did all we possibly could, but I'm afraid we weren't able to save your son. I'm very sorry.'

Farrar stared at her. He had heard the words, but he knew they couldn't possibly be true. 'No,' he said, 'I don't believe you.'

Dr Vine's face was sympathetic, her voice soft. 'I'm afraid he had lost far too much blood. He died on the operating table. His heart simply gave up. I assure you he didn't suffer.'

Helen put her face in her hands and began to weep.

'No,' Farrar said again. 'No. No.'

Denial after denial dripped from his numb lips, each as small and pointless as his life seemed suddenly to have become.

Part Five
The Red Church

Chapter Forty

Jack could not have wished for a more perfect day. Sitting in the car while Susan drove them back to Longbarrow House after the show, he felt as happy and complete as he could ever remember. Even the incident with Ted Sheridan had been nothing more than a minor blip. He glanced at Susan, who was trying to blink away the sunlight that was flashing through the trees into her eyes, and thought: *I love you.*

Perhaps he would tell her soon, when the moment was right, though the prospect of doing so alarmed him as much as it excited him. He had never before had cause to tell anyone that he loved them. He'd had girlfriends, certainly, but he had felt no more than a fondness for any of them, and sometimes not even that; sometimes the attraction had been nothing more than physical.

He glanced at David in the back seat. The boy was staring out of the window, though he appeared to be taking nothing in.

'You all right, David?' he asked, earning himself a little smile of appreciation from Susan.

David looked up, blinking. 'I was just thinking about Chris. Do you think I should ring up his house when we get home, Mum, to find out what's happened to him?'

Susan shrugged. 'You can if it's worrying you.'

'It is. Col didn't even know he'd had an accident.'

As soon as they pulled up beside Jack's van, David was out of the car and running up to the front door of the house. He jiggled impatiently from foot to foot until Susan let him in, then dashed inside as though there was a race for the telephone. He whispered the Farrars' number as he punched it in, as though only by hearing himself saying it aloud could he remember it.

'I'll put the kettle on, shall I?' Jack said.

'No, it's okay, I'll make the tea. You go and sit down.'

He leaned forward, lowering his voice. 'I'd rather be with you.'

She laughed. 'Come on then, Mr Leech.'

They went into the kitchen and busied themselves making tea. As Susan reached up to the cupboard for teabags, Jack came up behind her and embraced her, his arms encircling her stomach. She wriggled round to face him, so that they were almost nose to nose.

'See what I mean?' she said.

'What?'

'About leeches. They cling to people, don't they?'

They kissed, long and tenderly. Jack felt the scintillating echo of it rippling right through his body, tingling in his scalp and his toes. He had never known anything like it. Her touch was like delicious electricity.

'Wow, baby, you do things to me,' he said in a gravelly American accent.

'Oh God, you're not going all Barry White on me, are you?' she murmured, but she was dewy-eyed, somnolent, like a contented cat.

They broke apart, not guiltily, but slowly, smiling, as they heard the telephone receiver ching back into its cradle and footsteps approach the kitchen. David appeared, looking flustered. 'There's no answer,' he said.

Susan completed the task she had been performing when Jack had made his move and took the teabags down from the cupboard. 'Try not to worry, Davey,' she said. 'I'm sure everything'll be all right.'

'Yeah,' said Jack, 'he's probably just fallen off his bike and banged his head, something like that.'

'But if there's no answer, maybe his mum and dad have gone with him to the hospital, which means they've been there all day, which means it must be serious.'

Susan put three teabags into a pot shaped like a pumpkin with a handle and spout. 'I'd still try not to worry. He might have broken a bone, which means he'll have to have it examined and x-rayed and put in plaster and everything. These things take time, David. You know yourself how busy hospitals can get.'

David nodded reluctantly. 'I suppose so. But can I try again later?'

Susan put her arm around him and kissed the top of his head. 'Of course you can.'

Jack stayed for a dinner of salmon baked in mustard, served with potatoes and mangetouts. They washed it down with a bottle of elderberry wine and afterwards ate a tub of homemade lemon ice-cream which Susan had bought at the show.

She made some coffee while David tried the Farrars' house again, with no success. They retired to the main sitting room to drink and chat. By 9:30, David was falling asleep. Susan leaned forward and shook his knee gently to rouse him. When he frowned and murmured and opened his eyes just enough to peep at her, she said, 'Come on, sleepy head, time to hit the sack.'

He went without protest, dragging his feet up the stairs as if there were weights attached to them. Jack and Susan listened to him ascend, then Susan smiled at Jack and snuggled up to him.

'Mmm,' she said, 'you're just like a big cuddly bear.'

'Fat and hairy, you mean?'

She yawned hugely. 'Warm and snuggly. Wake me up in the morning.'

She put her head on his chest and closed her eyes. Jack held her for a while, luxuriating in the soft warmth of her body, the dizzyingly clean fragrance of her dark hair and velvet-smooth skin. Only when his right arm, which was taking most of her weight, began to go numb did he kiss her forehead and say, 'Susan, are you asleep?'

She made a contented sound. 'Nearly,' she said.

'Perhaps I'd better make a move, let you get to bed,' he murmured.

The way she peeped at him through hooded eyelids was exactly how David had looked at her a little earlier. 'You can stay if you like.'

He smiled and kissed her again. 'You're dead on your feet.'

'We don't have to do anything. We could just snuggle up together, go to sleep.'

He had to admit it was a tempting offer, but he said, 'Don't you think it might be a bit soon for David if I came down to breakfast in the morning? I mean, it was only today that you told him about us.'

She forced her eyes to open a little wider. 'Don't you want to stay?' she said, her voice still so sleepy that he couldn't tell whether she was teasing or hurt.

'Of course I do. I just don't want to upset David. I want everything to be perfect between us – between all three of us.'

'For ever and ever,' she murmured.

'That's right,' he said, smiling, 'for ever and ever.'

She raised her head and kissed him on the lips. 'You're a lovely person, Jack Bradley.'

'Thanks,' he said, 'so are you.' He wanted to tell her he loved her then, but, despite everything, was afraid of destroying the moment, scaring her off. Instead he said, 'Do you want to do something tomorrow? We could go for a drive out in the country, take a picnic. Then maybe you and David could come back to my house and I could cook you some dinner.'

'That sounds wonderful,' she said. 'What time?'

'Pick you up about eleven?'

'Fine.'

They disentangled themselves and stood up, Susan stretching and yawning. 'I'm sorry I can't keep my eyes open,' she said.

He kissed her again. 'That's all right. We've got all the time in the world.'

They walked to the front door hand in hand. Jack opened it and they strolled out together to his van. It was another balmy night. Even wearing only her T-shirt and shorts, Susan was not cold. They lingered for a while by the van, kissing and canoodling.

'I feel like I'm fifteen again,' she said.

'I never felt this good when I was fifteen,' said Jack. 'In fact, I've never felt as good as this in my life before.'

They said their goodnights and see you tomorrows and then Jack got into his van and drove away, waving, until the house with Susan's slim figure standing in front of it was swallowed by the trees. Using his key, he unlocked the big gates at the end of the drive, drove through them, then locked them up again. Not caring that he might look soppy, he blew an extravagant kiss at the gates and called out, 'Goodnight, gorgeous', before getting back into his van. Not until he caught a glimpse of himself in his rear-view mirror, as the trees petered out and were superseded by street lamps, did he realise he was grinning.

He was too full of happy energy to go home to bed. He glanced at his watch: 10:40. Time for a quick couple in the Druid's before last orders.

The pub was packed when he walked in, and thick with smoke that felt damp and warm as sauna steam. It was always like this after the show. In fact, this was the first time for years that Jack hadn't been in the pub from seven o'clock onwards, getting plastered with the rest of them. Not surprisingly, the volume level was high. Men whose faces were so red that the colour had seeped into the whites of their eyes greeted Jack like a long-lost brother, though ordinarily they might acknowledge him with nothing more than a curt nod if they passed him in the street. Middle-aged women with smudged make-up and gaudy jewellery were being clumsily flirty; one of his customers, Vivian Morgan, sidled up to him, placed a hand on his backside, and said in a Pernod-scented whisper, 'And who was that very pretty girl I saw you with this afternoon, Jack?'

'Pint of bitter please, Janice,' Jack said when he had finally made it through to the bar.

Janice, big and sexy with a personality to match her proportions, waggled her eyebrows lasciviously. 'And where have you been all evening? With this new mystery woman of yours that everyone's talking about?'

'Everyone? What do you mean, everyone?' said Jack, thinking of Vivian Morgan, whose clutches he had had to negotiate himself out of carefully.

'Well, I've heard one or two people mention that they saw you at the show with her, looking like the cat that's got the cream. If it's true, you'll be breaking a few hearts in here tonight, Jack – mine included, I might add.'

'Give over,' Jack said. 'She's just a good friend, that's all.'

'Oh yeah?'

'Yeah.'

'What's her name then?'

'Susan.'

'Is it true she's the woman who's moved into the big house?'

'Yes. Her husband – her *dead* husband – was Mrs Boscombe's nephew.'

'So you'll be marrying into money, then, will you?'

'Who said anything about marriage?' Jack said, knowing he was blushing now, but hoping it might be construed as nothing more than a heat flush. He nodded towards the landlord, Trevor Paine, who was serving someone further down the bar. 'How's Trevor's face now, by the way?'

'Healing nicely,' said Janice. 'One eye's still giving him gyp, though – and us. He never stops moaning about it. But never mind changing the subject. Tell us about this lass of yours.'

'Maybe I'll bring her in one day next week, then you can meet her for yourself,' Jack said, taking his pint and handing over his money.

'I'd scratch her eyes out,' Janice said, grinning. She handed him his change. 'Nah, good luck, Jack. You deserve it.'

Jack smiled his thanks and moved away from the bar. Amid the revelry he noticed Des Brewer, sitting alone, gazing glumly into his pint. As Des was the only person who looked as sober as Jack felt, Jack made his way across. Des didn't notice Jack until he was standing right over him, then he looked up.

'Oh, hello, Jack,' he said, 'how's it going?'

'Not bad. Mind if I join you?'

Des wafted a hand at the only stool in the vicinity which wasn't occupied. 'Feel free.'

Jack sat down. 'It's lucky you showed up when you did this afternoon.'

'Eh?'

'The beer tent at the show. If you hadn't turned up when you did, Ted would have turned that Sissons lad into mincemeat.'

'Oh aye,' said Des. 'It were just coincidence, that. I'd come to see Ted about something else, as it happens.'

'Had you?'

'Aye. You've not heard what's been going on then?'

Jack shook his head. 'No, what?'

'All bloody hell's broken loose. I've never known a day like it. We've had one murder, another death which we're currently regarding as suspicious, and two disappearances.'

'A murder?' said Jack, gaping at the policeman. 'Who?'

'Ted Sheridan's son, Jason. Old Jonas found him floating in

the river this morning.' He crooked a finger and leaned forward, a confidential look on his face. When Jack mirrored his movement, Des murmured, 'He were such a mess we still can't work out exactly what he died of. He *looked* as though animals had had a go at him after he were dead, but if that were the case, what was he doing in the river?'

'Bloody hell,' said Jack. 'Do you think Ted might have done it?'

'No reason to suspect him so far – except for the fact that he's a right nutter, of course.'

'How did he take the news?' asked Jack.

'Well, you can't tell with Ted, can you? He never gives a right lot away. He's not the sort to break down, and to be honest I don't think he and Jason ever thought that much of each other. When I told him he just swore and then went quiet. I got the impression he were more angry than anything. Almost as if his son was property that belonged to him that no one else had a right to touch. I think he'd have reacted the same if someone had nicked his car and torched it.'

Jack sat back, shaking his head. He took a swig of his pint, then asked, 'So who else has died?'

'Young Chris Farrar, the vicar's son. If anything, his death's even more of a mystery than Jason's.' He explained the circumstances and the state in which Steven Farrar had found his son that morning.

Jack listened, the memory of David's anxiety about his friend making him feel sick to his stomach. It was awful to think that David was asleep now, unaware of what had happened, that he had the shock of his friend's death to face in the morning. Jack resolved to ring Susan first thing and tell her, so that she could be the one to break the news to David if she wished. It would not be a pleasant task, but it was better than him finding out via other, less delicate means.

'Then on top of that, a couple of people seem to have disappeared into thin air. One's Joan Dyer, Brian Dyer's mam – you must know her, Jack?' Jack nodded. 'Aye, well, the family went off to the show this morning, leaving the old woman at home, and when they got back later she were nowhere to be found. Brian says his mam's been going a bit doolally lately, and they're worried she might have wandered off by herself, but I'm damned if we can find her. We're resuming the search first thing in the morning – six a.m. If you've got nothing better to do, Jack—'

'I'll be there,' Jack said.

Des nodded. 'Mike French is the other one who's disappeared. He's Sam French's son – you know, the union man. He's eighteen. Temporary postman. No one's seen him since he finished his round this morning. Normally I wouldn't be that worried about him at this stage, but in light of what's happened to Jason Sheridan . . . Jason was a similar sort of age, you see.'

'You think all these things are connected then, do you?'

'I don't know. Probably not. Not all of them anyway.'

Jack asked more questions, which Des answered willingly. He found it macabre to be sitting here talking about all the terrible things that had befallen the village over the past twenty-four hours, whilst all around them people were enjoying themselves as if nothing had happened.

Though, to be fair, the majority of the people here were probably still unaware of what *had* been happening. If this had been any day but the day of the show, the news would have spread through the village like wildfire, no doubt courtesy of the all-seeing, all-knowing Mrs Darracott and her jungle telegraph. Tomorrow, Jack supposed, would be the day when all that Des Brewer had told him would become public knowledge. People wouldn't be able to *escape* the news tomorrow, if only because Longbarrow would, in Des's words, 'be crawling with coppers'.

When last orders were called, Jack made his way to the bar and bought himself and Des another pint. Twenty minutes later, with the pub emptying rapidly, he offered Des a lift home, but the policeman said he'd rather have a walk to clear his head. 'See you at six then,' Jack said, standing up and clapping Des on the shoulder.

It had been so hot in the pub that it actually seemed chilly when he stepped outside. Immediately the fresh air rushed into his head, dizzying him, making him realise he wasn't quite as sober as he'd thought. He supposed, looking back on it, he had drunk a fair bit – a couple of pints at the show, half a bottle of wine at Susan's, another couple of pints just now. Maybe it would be a good idea to leave the van here overnight and come back for it in the morning. It was only a fifteen-minute walk, and if there were more coppers around than usual because of all that had happened today . . .

His feet, it appeared, had decided for him before his brain could. He was strolling away from his van, across the pub forecourt towards the exit.

What a day, he thought, his mind buzzing with thoughts and alcohol. He didn't know whether to feel deliriously happy at the way his life was turning out, or shocked and saddened by everything else that had happened. A murderer, here in Longbarrow? It seemed inconceivable. Would it be an outsider or someone local? *Could* Ted Sheridan have killed his own son? And what about Chris Farrar? How had Des phrased it: 'It was as though the boy had thrown himself, or been thrown, full-force, at the gravestone, smashing his leg'? That's what he'd said, or something like it. Jack thought of Susan and David, up at the big house on their own, separated from the rest of the village by over a mile of woodland. He felt a twinge of anxiety. Maybe he ought to go back up there, make sure they didn't come to any harm. But he was in no fit state to drive, and besides, Susan would most probably be fast asleep now; he didn't want to scare her half-witless by braying on the door loud enough to wake her up.

He comforted himself with the thought of the high wall topped with broken glass running all the way round the property, of the spiked metal gates which, although not impossible to scale, would surely not be worth the hassle for any potential intruder.

No, he thought, they'll be okay. I'll give them a ring in the morning, when I get back from helping the search party. He was over halfway home now and the streets were quiet, no sign of any police anywhere. He came to what was generally regarded as the centre of the village, where the road branched around both sides of the war memorial, like water around an obstruction. He walked along the right-hand pavement beside the church wall, the church tower rising blackly into the night above the trees, the graveyard quiet and still. When Jack had been a boy, he remembered standing on the path in front of the church tower and squinting up at it framed against the bright blue sky. He remembered staggering backwards because the tower had seemed as though it was toppling, like a vast felled tree, towards him, and his mam laughing and saying,

'Oh, I shouldn't worry, our Jack. I think this old church will still be standing long after I'm gone.'

Last night a boy died in there, or as good as, Jack thought, looking over the wall. What terrible pain he must have been in. He wondered, if he had been walking home at this time yesterday, whether he could have saved Chris Farrar, whether he would have heard him moaning or screaming or crying for help.

The street lamps ahead of him cast little puddles of tangerine light at regular but widely spaced intervals along the pavement; between them trees laden with summer plumage craned over the wall. The puddles of light merely accentuated the areas of blackness between them, transforming the trees into the silhouettes of huge, misshapen figures dressed in rags. Jack's footsteps in the silence approaching midnight echoed grittily. Ahead of him, in the blackness between the next street lamp and the one beyond it, a dark shape flowed like oil over the wall and across the pavement.

Jack stopped and peered ahead. Had he really seen that or was his mind simply creating shapes out of shadows, the way it did when you looked up at the clouds? There certainly seemed to be nothing there now. He started walking again, albeit a little more cautiously.

Over by the war memorial something moved. Jack turned, his eyes aching as he tried to penetrate the darkness that had gathered there like fog. Could he see a shape, something squat and muscular, bull-like? He was breathing quickly, but he got the odd impression that an echo of the sound he made was bouncing back at him from the direction of the monument. He gulped in air and held it in his lungs. No, it was not *his* breathing he could hear, it was something else's.

And it was not breathing, but panting.

There *was* something there. Something big and black. Some animal.

He heard Des Brewer's voice in his head: *'He looked as though animals had had a go at him after he were dead, but if that were the case, what was he doing in the river?'*

Jack felt the hairs quilling at the nape of his neck. What should he do now? Go back slowly the way he had come, retrieve his car and drive home, after all? He certainly didn't feel the slightest bit drunk any more. He wondered whether the thing by the war memorial had seen him, wondered too what it was. A big cat, like a puma maybe? He'd heard the stories like everyone else, but had never believed them. Yet all at once it seemed to make sense. A puma could have killed Jason Sheridan, and been responsible for Chris Farrar's death too. Maybe it had terrified the boy so much that he hadn't been looking where he was going, and he had fallen and—

Then the thing by the war memorial moved out of the shadows and Jack saw that it wasn't a puma.

It was a dog.

It was huge and black and rippling with muscles, like an extra-large mastiff on steroids. Despite this, Jack might almost have believed it was just a normal dog if it wasn't for the fact that each time it panted a strange oily vapour curled from its jaws and its eyes glowed a brilliant red.

Jack went cold all over and had to clench his fists to stop himself from shaking. The dog curled its jowls back, revealing teeth like a great white shark's. It appeared to be grinning at him.

Jack began to move backwards slowly, keeping his eyes fixed on the dog, careful not to make any sudden moves. The dog watched him, its eyes like laser-points; Jack almost expected to see two thin red beams suddenly come shooting out of them. As he edged backwards, the dog plodded forwards. Though compact, there was not an ounce of fat on it; its muscles moved beneath its black coat like those of a prize racehorse. The creature radiated a kind of dark power, and not just because of its size and appearance. Jack was not a man who scared easily, and yet at this moment he was terrified.

He continued to move slowly backwards while the dog watched him and kept pace. Something had to happen soon. Jack couldn't keep this up all the way to the pub car park. He couldn't shake off the feeling that the dog was somehow marking him, that it had *allowed* him to see it, and that that was not a good omen.

All at once his left foot came down on something that had been discarded on the pavement – a drinks can from the sound and feel of it – which skidded out from under his foot, causing him to stumble backwards a few paces.

It was this that broke the spell. The dog charged.

Not at him, though. With astonishing speed, a blur of black

fur and muscle, it streaked across the road and leaped over the church wall, back into the graveyard from where it had come. Jack expected to hear it land with a meaty thump, but in fact he heard nothing. It was as though the dog, on re-joining the darkness had blended back into it.

Jack turned and ran. Fear filled his throat, and his legs felt as though they were full of spaghetti rather than muscle, but he ran as he had never run before. He kept looking over his shoulder, but nothing appeared to be following him. However, it was not until he was inside his van with the doors locked and the engine running that he even began to feel anything like safe.

Chapter Forty-One

'Do you want to see my scar?' asked Chris.

David nodded. He couldn't recall why Chris was here in his room, or when he had arrived, but it was good to see him; he'd been worried.

Not that he'd tell Chris that. He didn't want his friend thinking he was a wuss.

'I'll have to take my trousers down,' Chris said, and looked at David warningly, 'but that doesn't mean we're going out or anything.'

He unzipped his jeans and pulled them down to his knees. Chris's scar resembled a large Y that he'd drawn on his leg with a maroon felt-tip pen. The tail of the scar was just above his knee. It branched off around his thigh, one stem curling round the back of his leg, the other disappearing under the hem of his boxer shorts.

'Wow!' David said, impressed. 'Frankenstein City.'

'Pretty good, huh?' said Chris, grinning. 'Bloody hurt, though. Come on.'

He pulled up his jeans and made for the door.

'Where are we going?' asked David.

'Outside.'

'What for?'

'You'll see.'

The two boys went out on to the landing, David barefoot, wearing his pyjamas. The house was dark and as still as it can only get in the dead hours before dawn.

'Hurry up, we have to meet someone,' Chris said, loud enough to make David wince.

'Shh, you'll wake my mum.'

'No, I won't, she can't hear us.'

'Why not?'

'She just can't, that's all.'

David thought about this for a moment, then said, 'Who do we have to meet?'

'You'll find out if you stop asking questions, won't you? Come *on*.'

Chris led the way downstairs. A little moonlight, tinted green and blue and red by the stained-glass panel above the front door, gave the hallway some definition. David noticed that there were two grandfather clocks, tall and dark, edged with green light, standing side by side. Then one of the grandfather clocks stepped forward and David realised it was a man. He came to a halt halfway down the stairs.

'Who's that?' he whispered.

'It's who we have to meet,' Chris said, making no attempt to lower his voice. 'It's all right, don't be afraid. He's a friend.'

'I wasn't afraid,' David said. 'I was just wondering, that's all.' Yet he proceeded cautiously, until he got close enough to smell the spicy cinnamon smell coming from the man's body. Then he said, 'It's you.'

Decumen inclined his head. Now David saw the faint green light outlining his bearded face, flashing in his eyes like emeralds.

'How did you get out of the clock?' David asked.

'He doesn't *live* in the clock, you dork,' said Chris, rolling his eyes. 'He can go where he likes – well, more or less anyway.'

'How come *you* know so much about it?'

Chris shrugged. 'I've learned a lot of things since my accident.'

David leaned closer to his friend and murmured in his ear, 'So why is he here?'

'He needs to show you something. Look.'

Decumen reached beneath his robe and produced not a black snake this time, but a white one. David gritted his teeth in a grimace.

'You're not going to cut it open again, are you?'

Decumen smiled as if he found the question amusing. 'For every poison there must be an antidote,' he said. He tossed the snake away from him.

It landed on the wooden floor of the hallway with a soft

thump, like a coil of rope. With sinuous grace it unfurled, its head questing forward, and then it began to move in a rippling S-shape across the hallway.

'Where's it going?' David asked, a little alarmed. He didn't think his mum would take too kindly to having a five-foot long snake roaming the house.

'It goes where it goes,' Decumen said. 'Follow it and see where it leads you.'

'Come on,' Chris said, 'before it gets away.'

Already the snake had slithered across the hallway and was disappearing down the corridor beside the staircase that led to the kitchen.

The boys hurried after it, David wondering whether the creature was poisonous. He felt he ought to trust Decumen, but he couldn't help having his doubts.

It appeared that the snake was indeed heading towards the kitchen. It bypassed all the other doors along the corridor, but it was only when it reached the kitchen door that David realised it was closed.

We've got it cornered, he thought. Now it'll turn on us. But in fact the snake simply passed through the door as if it wasn't there.

David gaped, then grabbed Chris's arm. 'Did you see that?' he said. 'It just went straight through the wood like a ghost.'

Chris shrugged. 'So what? You can do that sort of stuff in dreams. You can fly and everything if you want to.'

David could hear his bare feet slapping on the floor, could feel the hardness of the wood beneath his soles. 'What do you mean?' he said. 'This isn't a dream, is it?'

'You should know,' said Chris. 'It's *your* house.'

Before David could think about the apparent illogicality of that statement, Chris had shoved open the door that the snake had just passed through and entered the kitchen. The snake was a white moving scar on the dark floor. 'There,' Chris said, pointing at it.

The snake reached the far door that led into Aunt Mollie's little garden and passed through that too. 'Come on,' said Chris, picking up speed, 'it'll be harder to spot outside.' He turned the key in the lock of the back door, pulled it open and went outside.

David hesitated a moment, thinking of his bare feet, then he followed.

The snake was winding its way up the path, travelling at jogging speed, though its movements were lazy, relaxed. The boys followed it through the flower garden and out into the paddock beyond, where the moonlight made the long grass seem frost-rimed. The snake was easy to spot, the grass twitching as it passed through, springing back into place in its wake. Then suddenly the snake seemed to disappear; the grass became still.

'We've lost it,' said Chris, disappointed.

'Looks like it', David was about to say, and then it suddenly came to him. 'No, we haven't. I know where it is.'

He hurried to the place where the snake had disappeared, the grass prickly beneath his feet, and dropped on to his knees. He began clearing away grass and weeds with his hands and within seconds had uncovered the round black hole of the well.

'That's where it went,' he said.

Chris dropped on to all fours and peered dubiously into the stone-lined shaft. 'Well, we can't follow it down there, can we?'

'No,' David said, and was about to stand up when he felt something beneath him: a rhythmic tingling like a faint but rapidly increasing heartbeat deep in the earth.

'Can you feel that?' he said, and then his eyes widened. 'Chris, look!'

All around them the earth began to glow, as lines of energy – ley-lines – became visible, converging on the well from all directions. The well filled with an incandescence that was more than light, more than energy; it was beauty and goodness in its purest form. David watched it, goosebumps rippling over his skin. It was such an incredible, enchanting sight that it made him want to weep. He reached towards the well instinctively yet hesitantly, then drew his hands back, uncertain.

'If you feel you must drink, then drink,' a voice beside him said.

He glanced at where Chris had been just a moment before. Now Decumen stood in his place. This sort of thing happens in dreams all the time, David thought vaguely.

'It is . . . safe, isn't it?' he asked.

'Only those who take risks can ever truly taste life,' said Decumen.

David plunged his cupped hands into the well, and when he drew them out again they were full of the clearest water he had ever seen. He remembered Decumen's words: *For every poison there must be an antidote.* He wasn't entirely sure what the words referred to, but they were comforting somehow.

He drank.

Chapter Forty-Two

Since Des Brewer had given them the news of their son's death, a kind of limbo had descended over the Sheridan household. Ted had spent all of his time sitting on the settee, drinking can after can of beer and saying barely a word, scowling at the TV which had been on constantly. Mary had spent her time tiptoeing around, trying not to draw attention to herself, afraid that if she disturbed her husband's simmering mood it would spill over into something worse.

She still hadn't decided exactly how she felt about Jason's death. Her mind and body were a stew of emotions. She had cried at first, but only because of the shock, and because it had seemed the right thing to do. In all honesty, however, she could hardly have described herself as grief-stricken. She and Jason had been growing apart ever since his first day at school. In the intervening years, the gap that had begun to open between them around that time had widened into a chasm. Though they lived in the same house, the two of them had only spoken to each other when it was absolutely neccessary. Mary didn't actually *know* her son at all, didn't know how he spent his time, what went on in his head, who his friends were. If asked what sort of boy he was, she would have said 'weird'. His company unsettled her, and part of her, she had to admit, felt a measure of relief that he was gone.

All this, of course, only served to make her feel terribly guilty. What sort of mother was she to feel relief at her own son's death? She felt embittered by her own emotions, and by the life that had led her to this point. Looking back, all she saw was a wasteland, the years poisoned and laid bare by pain and unhappiness and missed opportunities. She didn't want much –

love, a little security, a little happiness . . . that was about the sum of it. But even these small ambitions seemed beyond her. She had about as much chance of being happy as she had of winning the lottery.

Sitting on her bed, smoking a cigarette, she wondered how it would all end. Her life felt as though it was already over, just more of the same from now on, for ever and ever, a-bloody-men. But she was only thirty-six, for God's sake! She and Ted had been married for . . . what? Seventeen, eighteen years? They might have another forty or fifty ahead of them yet.

'No fucking way,' she murmured to herself. She'd rather get cancer and die young than have to face that. She'd leave tomorrow if she had somewhere to go, or a little money to take with her. But she had nothing. Nothing at all.

Ted was coming upstairs. She heard his heavy tread and hated it, his laboured breathing and hated that too.

I wish *you'd* fucking die, she thought savagely. I wish you'd drop down dead right now of a fucking heart attack. I'd watch while your face turned blue and your eyes bulged. I'd watch until you stopped breathing, and I'd enjoy every second of it.

Ted went into the bathroom. She heard him grunt, then start to piss. He always pissed like a fucking horse. There'd be a fat yellow rope of it, splashing endlessly.

Finally he finished and she heard him zip himself up. As usual he didn't bother flushing the toilet. He came into the bedroom.

'Who the fuck is he?' he said.

She looked up. His eyes were blurry with alcohol. 'What?'

'You heard, you fucking slag. Who have you been shagging?'

Mary was scared, but she was also angry. 'I haven't been shagging anyone.'

He lumbered towards the bed, fists clenched and swinging. 'Don't fucking lie, just tell me his name.'

'How can I tell you his name when there isn't anyone?' she said.

He reached out, grabbed hold of her feet and yanked her towards him.

'Let go of me, you fucking bastard!' she screeched.

He swung his free fist in a lazy arc and connected with the side of her skull, snapping her head sideways. There was a crunch. She thought her eardrum had exploded. She screamed with the pain.

He hit her again, smashing her nose. Again: her lip. Again: her eye.

She was screaming and crying and pleading.

'Tell me his name and I'll stop,' he said, and as he said this he took hold of the little finger of her right hand and began bending it back.

'All right, all right, I'll tell you,' she babbled. 'Just please stop, please stop.'

She told him what he wanted to know. Ted yanked her finger back, breaking it with a crack.

Leaving her screaming and writhing on the bed, trying to curl herself around the pain and smother it, he walked out of the room.

Chapter Forty-Three

It wasn't you it wasn't you Hilary because when I took you in
my arms you just folded up just a dress empty nothing up your
sleeves nothing inside just nothing just emptiness and so I
cried and I called your name in the garden just crying and
calling your name and I've tried so hard Hilary I've tried but
nothing is worth anything without you and so I decided and I
went upstairs and I looked in the mirror and you weren't there
either and you weren't anywhere and so I decided I didn't want
to try and I didn't want to hurt any more I wanted it to end
this is no life no life better off dead better where you are on the
other side of the mirror truly together and so what I did was
drinking and drinking pickling my liver cirrhosis yes please
except that would be too slow and too painful and I don't
want pain I've had enough pain without you is all pain and so
this is what I did I lined them all up all my pills everything I'd
collected everything I could lay my hands on and I remembered when I was a boy lining up my soldiers all ready for
battle and I thought that was only yesterday I was only a boy
yesterday and now it's all over and this is it my last battle my
little soldiers all lined up and I started killing my soldiers one
after the other ending it all one bit at a time killing my soldiers
and killing myself swallowing and swallowing until they were
all gone and I didn't feel any different except free like a great
burden had been taken away the battle lost and so finally won
and I went up to our bed where you never got pregnant
because you couldn't but it didn't matter because we loved
each other we had each other for ever and ever amen except
that was a lie wasn't it nothing is for ever it all ends and there's
always pain and misery and death at the end of every life and

so we invent God to make it all better but we know deep down that really it's all rot and decay isn't it it's all just unhappy endings and we die and the world goes on and our children die and the world goes on and our grandchildren die and the world goes on and soon we never existed we never mattered we're not even a memory any more our lives full of joy and love and laughter and things that mattered and things that were important never really mattered after all because they never existed they become less than memories and everything rolls on and things end in pain and death and sadness and it's all so pointless and I don't want to have to think about it any more I don't want to pretend and so I lay down and I closed my eyes and I welcomed the darkness my old friend I've come to talk to you again and then my eyes were open and I don't remember how and I saw you in the mirror and I thought you were going to take me back there back to where you were so we could be together but you didn't you came out of the mirror and you said no it's not over yet not yet this isn't how it ends and I said please Hilary just let me go and you said no and you took me lifted me up like a feather I was floating and we were in the bathroom and you made me sick you made my head in the toilet being sick wanting to close my eyes and come through the darkness to the other side of the mirror but you made me sick and sick and I saw all my little soldiers one two buckle my shoe twenty lots and lots a hundred and thirty-ten a trillion million all up out of me in the toilet gone and the bad end not over yet and I just wanted to close my eyes and know no more and I said why Hilary why are you doing this I just want us to be together on the other side of the mirror and you said my name's not Hilary it's Pyewackett and I said that's a funny name.

Chapter Forty-Four

Steven Farrar stood at his pulpit and looked out over his congregation. For the first time the rows of faces staring up at him seemed unreal, a collection of masks on to which expressions had been moulded: pity, sympathy, grief, expectancy, confusion, fear. For the first time too he felt that he had nothing to offer these people.

What did they expect of him? Comfort? Explanations? Did they expect him to be serene despite his loss, untouched by grief, bolstered by his faith? If so, they were going to be disappointed. He was shattered, devastated, felt as though such a gaping hole had been torn in his life that it could never be repaired. His faith was still strong, but that didn't prevent his being human, didn't stop his feeling the sting of death as keenly as the next man.

He had planned nothing, had only come here today because there hadn't been time to make alternative arrangements, and because it had seemed to him that in light of the evil, or misfortune, or whatever one wished to call it, that had befallen the village, it was more imperative than ever that today's period of worship should be observed, that the church should be open for those who wished to use it.

Not that that made it any better for him, any easier. He was not full of righteous anger, or defiance, or even determination. It was too soon for that, too soon for anything except a grinding pain that he couldn't imagine ever going away.

He realised he had been still and silent too long when a troubled murmur began to rise in the congregation, when feet began to shuffle nervously, when heads began to turn uncertainly towards their neighbours. He leaned forward, his

315

hands gripping the wooden rail in front of him as though he might fall without its support – as well he might. At this shifting of his weight, the collective murmur quietened, heads turned back towards him. The Reverend cleared his throat.

'As many of you are no doubt aware,' he said, letting the words tumble out, not knowing what he was going to say until he said it, 'my dear – my *beloved* – son, Christopher, died yesterday.' His voice faltered a little; he cleared his throat again. The congregation was silent now, their eyes fixed on him. 'At this stage police are uncertain whether his death was an accident or whether it was the indirect result of some kind of . . . of physical assault.

'However, as no doubt most of you are also aware, Chris's death is not the only . . . ah . . . tragic incident that has blighted our village this weekend. A teenage boy, Jason Sheridan, whom many of you knew, has been brutally murdered, his body found dumped in the river up in the top woods. Furthermore, two people – young Michael French and Joan Dyer, who has been a valued member of this community for many years – have gone missing, and so far a police search, which I understand many of you participated in this morning, has revealed no trace of either of them.

'The police have asked me to ask you that if any of you out there have any information that could lead them to the whereabouts of either of these missing people, or if you have any information relating to the deaths of either Chris or Jason, then please don't hesitate to call them. Even what seems to you the smallest, most seemingly unimportant detail may be vital to the inquiry, so please, please don't hesitate.'

He closed his eyes briefly and took a deep breath. Standing here, talking like this, was such a strain, not only mentally but physically. He opened his eyes again; his congregation hadn't stirred.

'Obviously this is a bad time for all of us. Not only for myself and my wife and the other families involved in these dreadful events, but, I suspect, for many of you too.' He raised a hand and waved it out over the congregation as though scattering seed. A number of people nodded.

'When incidents like this happen, they affect the whole community, especially when that community is as close and as warm and as loving as that which we have here in Longbarrow.

'That's why in what may prove to be difficult days and weeks and months ahead we must strive to retain that community spirit; we should provide support and friendship for one another, be Good Samaritans, if you like, for our friends and neighbours. We should be watchful without becoming paranoid, and careful without becoming afraid to venture out of our homes. We should help the police in whatever way we can. They are going to be coming round to all our homes, asking lots of questions, over the next few days. But please try not to look upon their presence as intrusive or unwanted. Their aim, as well as ours, is to restore all of our lives to normality again as soon as possible.'

Was he rambling? Laying it on too thick? Was his own perception of events clouded by his closeness to them? Certainly his congregation still seemed riveted by his words, but were they only maintaining their silence out of respect or sympathy?

'Do any of you have any questions to ask or comments to make at this point?' he said, his own train of thought having become temporarily derailed.

There was silence for a moment – people looked at one another or at the floor, as if fearing they might get selected to offer some opinion like children in a classroom.

Then, tentatively, someone near the back raised a hand. Farrar couldn't see who it was until they stood up, and then he recognised Joan Dyer's son, Brian.

'Brian,' he said, 'you wanted to say something?'

Brian Dyer looked around as though gauging his fellow villagers' mood before nodding. 'Aye,' he said, 'it's just . . . well, this may sound a bit daft, but my mam always had what I suppose you'd call the second sight. She knew things were going to happen before they did.'

The murmur started up again, swelling to the high vaulted ceiling. Brian looked around uncertainly, then saw that many of the villagers were nodding their heads in grave affirmation. This seemed to give him the impetus to go on.

'Aye, well, just recently she's been saying that summat bad's coming to Longbarrow. She didn't know what, but she kept trying to get us all to leave. She said that if we stayed we'd be doomed with everybody else.

'I have to say, I thought she were going a bit doolally. I

317

mean, I know she's seen stuff in the past, but she's always been sensible about it. Sometimes it bothered her, but it never scared her.

'These last few weeks, though, she's been terrified. I kept trying to calm her down, kept telling her that if summat was going to happen we'd face it together, but I never really thought there were owt in it. I thought, you know, she were getting old, and that her mind weren't as strong as it used to be.

'And now she's gone, and no one knows where. I thought at first that she'd wandered off, but in light of everything else that's happened – your lad, vicar, and the Sheridan lad and all that – I'm beginning to think that she might not have gone off by herself, she might have been taken.'

The murmur rose to a hubbub, and though individual words were indiscernible, Farrar sensed a mood of both speculation and fear. He raised his hands for quiet, and was at least partly successful in achieving it.

'But *who* do you think might have taken her, Brian?' he asked quietly.

Brian shrugged, looking uncomfortable. 'Well ... I don't know. Whoever did for Sheridan's lad, I suppose.'

'But *why*, Brian? Why would Jason Sheridan's killer kidnap your mother?'

'Mebbe because she knew too much. Mebbe he did it to keep her quiet.'

Again the murmur rose, accompanied by vigorous nods of assent.

Farrar raised his hands again. 'But how would the killer know?' he said. 'Your mother hardly leaves the house these days, does she, Brian? It's not as if she was broadcasting her doom-laden prophecies far and wide and drawing attention to herself, is it?'

Brian looked sullen. He shrugged.

'I think this is what we have to guard against,' said Farrar. 'We shouldn't speculate, we shouldn't read things that aren't there into the situations presented to us. If we do that we'll panic, we'll begin to see shadows in every corner, make this whole thing out to be far bigger than it really is. What we have here are a number of incidents that the police have no reason to believe at this stage are even connected.'

318

Someone stood up near the back and put up a hand. For one ludicrous moment, Farrar thought that Brian Dyer was shrinking, getting younger, and then he realised it was not Brian, but his son, Colin, who had stood up.

'Yes, Colin,' he said.

Colin looked around, evidently intimidated by the amount of people surrounding him, waiting to hear what he had to say, but determined to say what was on his mind nonetheless.

'What about the portents?' he said.

'Portents? I don't quite follow.'

'Before he . . . well . . . died, Chris kept going on about portents. Like my gran, he said he knew that something was going to happen. He saw green lights in the churchyard – Jack o' Lanterns, my gran said they were. She said that if you could get to the church door before they did, you'd see the face of someone who was going to die in the light. Maybe that's why Chris was in the graveyard on Friday night. Maybe he was out looking for the Jack o' Lanterns.'

Speculation and fear. It rose again, a great swell of it, washing over Farrar like a wave. He gripped the edge of the pulpit, his knuckles white. He wasn't up to this, this debate, this discussion.

He said, 'We mustn't do this. We mustn't let ourselves fall prey to rumour and superstition. We mustn't.'

Colin said something to his father. Brian stood up again and said, 'My son says there's something under that rug in the aisle that we all should see.'

Farrar slumped, sunk his head into his hands. When he looked up again, Brian Dyer had edged his way along to the end of the pew and was making his way down the aisle towards the rug covering the bloodstain.

It won't look that impressive, Farrar thought. It'll look like nothing more than a spillage of ink. As Brian stooped to lift the rug, people crowding to the ends of the pews or even standing on them, craning their necks to watch, Farrar closed his eyes and began to pray silently to himself.

The cries of horror and disgust and fear were bird-like, echoing, spiralling to the high ceiling and bouncing back off the stone walls. Farrar opened his eyes and gasped. The bloodstain was no longer black and dry; it was red and glistening and fresh. And what was more it was spreading, oozing up

319

through the tiles of the church floor. It was as though the lifting of the rug had acted like the removal of a tourniquet, causing blood that had been staunched to now gush forth as if from a terrible wound.

Chapter Forty-Five

'Give us a blow job, Sheila.'

'Fuck off.'

'Ah, go on. I've never had a blow job at eighty miles an hour before.'

'Well, that's tough shit, isn't it? You won't be getting one from me.'

'You've never had a blow job in your *life* before,' Ben Darracott said, twisting round in the passenger seat.

'Piss off, Darracott, who asked you? This is between me and her,' replied Al Lebsen, his bullet head with its dyed blond number-two cut thrusting forward aggressively.

'Don't be a greedy cunt, Lebbo,' Gary Sissons, who was driving, said. 'It's between all of us. Just cos you're in the back with her don't mean you can keep her all to yourself.'

'Hey, I'm not some fucking piece of meat, you know,' protested Sheila Holmes. 'I do have a fucking say in this.'

'Fuck off, you fat tart, or you'll be walking home. If I decide I want to put my cock in your mouth, then I'll do it, all right?'

'Yeah, and if you fucking try it, you'll get it fucking bitten off.'

Gary laughed. Ben and Lebbo dutifully joined in while Sheila sat, scowling. Life with Gary was unpredictable, sometimes scary, sometimes dangerous, but it was never boring, Ben thought.

They had nicked the car, a top of the range Mondeo, from the car park behind the Pricecutter supermarket ten minutes earlier. Or rather, Gary had nicked it. He'd broken the window, got inside and hot-wired the thing in about ten seconds flat while the others kept watch. It had been a risk, what with all the coppers around, but then virtually everything Gary did was a risk. They had screeched out of the car park and through the streets of the village with Gary at the wheel, Ben trying to put his seat belt on, Sheila shrieking with laughter, and Lebbo jabbing V's at the disapproving faces that turned to regard them. They had narrowly missed an old biddy with a shopping trolley on the zebra crossing by the bank. The car had whipped past close enough to cause the hem of the coat she wore despite the heat to flap. 'Fucking old bitch,' Gary had snarled. 'I'll get her next time.' Gary hated old people. They were slow and miserable and boring, and they went on about the fucking war all the time, and they wore coats in the summer, for fuck's sake!

Gary had driven the car out of the village and up the road towards the woods. Now they were tearing through the country lanes at a steady eighty, slowing only marginally on the bends, the back wheels slewing and shrieking, trees whipping past, the engine roaring as Gary over-revved it.

Gary wanted to go and find the place where Shez had died. Shez had been a mate – sort of – and Ben had been shocked when he had heard (via his mum, of course) that Shez had been found dead in the river, apparently with his face torn off. When Ben had told Gary, though, Gary had been neither shocked nor upset. Instead, he had grinned, and a bright, feverish excitement had come into his eyes. 'Really?' he had said. 'Wow! Fucking cool!'

Gary loved serial killers as much as he hated old people, and ever since he had heard about Shez and that Farrar kid he had been harbouring hopes that one of them was stalking Longbarrow. He wanted to go to the woods, Ben suspected, to see if there was an atmosphere about the place, to see if he could pick up any residue of evil from what had happened there. Ben had told him that the place would be crawling with coppers, but Gary had waved away his protests.

'So fucking what? They're not going to fucking arrest us, are they? The worst they can do is tell us to fuck off.'

Ben had reluctantly agreed, but that had been before they nicked the Mondeo. Now the coppers would have every reason to arrest them, if only because of the way Gary drove.

The car crested a rise towards an impossibly blue sky and for a breathtaking moment it felt as though Gary had

Chapter Forty-Seven

They sat around the big fireplace in the main sitting room. David, looking distressed, was hunched forward, his hands clenched together between his knees. Susan seemed dumbstruck by what she had just been told, but not for long. 'I don't believe it,' she said, shaking her head slowly.

'Afraid it's true,' said Des Brewer. He had hardly said a word while Jack related the events of the past two days. He had been content just to let Jack get on with it and to observe the reactions of Susan Wisher and her son. He had heard on the grapevine that a young mother and son – relatives of Mollie Boscombe – had moved into the big house, but this was the first time he had seen them. They seemed nice enough – and Jack was sweet on the mother; Des would have been able to tell that even if Jack hadn't already told him.

'But how can so many terrible things happen in so short a time in a place like this?' Susan said.

'A whole year's worth of tragedy in a single weekend,' confirmed Des Brewer, shaking his head. 'Five unnatural deaths – all young people – and two, possibly three, disappearances, if our theory that the driver of the crashed vehicle crawled away or was dragged away from the wreckage is correct.'

'Have you any idea who the driver of the car might have been?' Susan asked.

'We're not certain at this point, but we've got one or two ideas. Once I've done here, I'm off up to the Sissons' farm to see if their youngest lad, Gary, is around. You wouldn't happen to know him by any chance, would you?'

Susan shook her head.

'David?'

David frowned as though the policeman had disrupted his train of thought. 'No. Chris and Colin told me about him, though. They said to stay out of his way.'

'Good advice,' said Des. 'I mean, don't get me wrong, I hope the lad's fine, but there's no denying he's a troublemaker.'

'It was him who started that trouble yesterday, in the beer tent,' said Jack.

Susan nodded distractedly. 'I still don't understand why you're here, though, officer. I appreciate that you've had an unprecedented run of tragedies to cope with, but I don't see what it's got to do with us.'

Des glanced at Jack. 'I'm just making general enquiries, Mrs Wisher. But now that you mention it, there are one or two things that I'd like to ask David.'

'David?' exclaimed Susan. 'Why David?'

She looked at her son. He was still in the same position, hands between his knees, shoulders hunched as though he was cold. He looked resigned but guilty, as though he fully expected the policeman to accuse him of all the things he felt he was responsible for – waking up the Sleepers, making things come true by dreaming about them, indirectly causing his friend's death.

'If you'll just bear with me, Mrs Wisher. This shouldn't take more than a few minutes. David, you don't mind if I ask you a few questions, do you?'

David looked trapped, but he gave an abrupt shake of the head. Des smiled, hoping to reassure the boy.

'Yesterday, David, I was talking to your friend, Colin Dyer,' he said, 'in connection with his grandmother's disappearance. He told me that his grandmother seemed very insistent that Colin keep away from you, that she seemed to think you were a bad influence of some sort. Have you any idea why she might think this?'

David glanced at his mother as if for guidance. She raised her eyebrows as though encouraging him simply to tell the truth.

'No,' he said, 'not really. I mean, I'd only just met Colin and I've never met his gran. But Col told me about her. He said she was psychic. I think she must have had one of her funny turns and . . . and seen something.'

'And what sort of "something" might she have seen, do you think?'

David hesitated, looked at his mother again, took a deep breath. Finally he said, 'Maybe she saw that I'd be the one who'd wake up the Seven Sleepers.'

Des blinked. 'Sorry?'

Quickly Susan said, 'Chris Farrar dared David to run seven times round the church because he said it would wake up the Sleepers . . . you know, the ones in the story?'

'Yes, I know the legend. Go on.'

'Well, that's it, really. David now seems to think that because of what he did everything that's happened is his fault.'

'I have dreams too,' David said defiantly. 'I dream about things before I know they've happened. Like I dreamed about Chris last night, and he showed me the scars on his leg and everything, but I didn't know properly what had happened to him until Jack just said.'

'I see,' said Des. He offered David another smile and held up a hand. 'Look, David, this stuff about dreams and legends is all very interesting, but my job, you see, is to deal with facts. I'm not saying you're lying, but do you think we could forget all this Seven Sleepers stuff for a minute and concentrate on what we know rather than what we think?'

David frowned, but nodded.

'Right then, so you say you've never met Colin Dyer's grandmother? You've never seen her, never even spoken to her on the telephone?'

'Yes,' David said. 'I mean no, no I haven't.'

'And apart from what you've told me, you've got no idea why she should warn her grandson away from seeing you?'

'No.'

'I mean, have you ever got Colin into trouble?'

'No, I only met him last week.'

'And you yourself have never been in any trouble – with the police, for instance, where you used to live?'

David was about to shake his head when Susan interjected angrily, 'What are you suggesting? My son's not a troublemaker.'

Des held up a placatory hand. 'I'm sorry, Mrs Wisher, I'm just trying to get to the facts of the matter. I'm not accusing David of anything. To be honest with you, I'm clutching at straws a bit here, trying to work out how all this lot fits together – if it does, that is. It's just that with your son being a friend of Chris Farrar's and Colin Dyer's he sort of links two of the events.' He puffed out his cheeks. 'Look, like I said, I was clutching at straws. I'll not take up any more of your time.' He stood up.

'So that's it then, is it?' said Susan.

'Aye, for the time being.'

'You mean you'll be coming back?'

Des shrugged. 'Only if I feel I have to.' He looked a little awkward, then said, 'This may sound daft, Mrs Wisher, but it's nice to meet you. I'm sorry it had to be in such ... um ... formal circumstances. I hope you'll be very happy here in the village. I'm sure you will. It's usually a good place to live – quiet, peaceful. It's not always like this.'

Susan's icy demeanour thawed a little. 'Thanks ... er ... what do I call you? Officer Brewer?'

'Just Des'll do.'

'Des,' said Susan, nodding. She stood up and shook his hand. 'I hope you manage to sort everything out.'

'I'm sure we will. Thanks again for your time. Goodbye.'

'Goodbye,' said Susan.

'Bye, Jack.'

'Yeah, see you later, Des,' Jack said.

Susan saw Des out and he walked down the steps, got into his car and drove away. As the trees engulfed the house behind him, he wound down his window, partly to get rid of the smell of baking leather which filled the hot car and made him feel sick, and partly in the hope that the fresh air would stimulate his brain cells.

What the bloody hell was happening in Longbarrow? Were the deaths and disappearances all linked in some way that he couldn't yet fathom; were they partly connected; or was he dealing with a cluster of unconnected events whose timing was merely coincidental? Personally, he favoured the middle ground. He couldn't see how old Mrs Dyer's disappearance could be linked to the car accident that morning which had claimed the lives of three Longbarrow teenagers, for instance, but surely it was not unreasonable to speculate that whoever had killed Jason Sheridan could also have abducted Mike French (unless, of course, French had killed Sheridan and was currently hiding out

336

somewhere). But if Mrs Dyer had simply wandered away, where the hell was she? She was too frail to wander far unless she had been picked up (perhaps by the killer?).

DI Stamper, head of the team who had been drafted in to deal with the investigation, was currently operating with the theory that the killer was local – someone who knew the area well and had a house or an outbuilding where his victims, be they dead or alive, could be kept with little fear of immediate detection. Des knew it was a reasonable assumption – an extensive search of the local fields and woodland had unearthed nothing – but at the same time he found it hard to believe. He knew Longbarrow and its inhabitants well, had lived here all his life, and though he wasn't too naive to realise that evil often wore a mask of respectability, he still couldn't conceive that a person capable of the savagery he had seen inflicted on Jason Sheridan could live in the village for any length of time without arousing at least some suspicion somewhere along the way. Oh, Longbarrow had its share of troublemakers, child abusers, wife beaters and weirdos, but Des liked to think he had tabs on all of them. Besides, over the past twenty-four hours, most had been questioned and eliminated from the inquiry. Today, police frogmen would be dragging local rivers and ponds whilst the house-to-house operation got underway in earnest. Hopefully that would turn something up. If not, they would have to become more intrusive, would have to start examining garages, garden sheds, cellars, barns and stableblocks, which would be bound to lead to bad feeling.

Des drove through the big metal gates that Jack had left open and turned left towards the village. The sun's radiance turned the ears of corn in the field to his right into shining yellow filaments. The boundaries of both the field and the high wall that surrounded Longbarrow House ended abruptly, giving way to immediately dense woodland. Driving between trees which arched over the descending slope of the road was like entering a chute full of green shadow. Shattered fragments of sunlight bounced off the car's windscreen and bonnet.

Suddenly something that Des could only think of as a fireball exploded out of the trees on the right-hand side of the road thirty feet ahead of him and came to rest in a shower of sparks directly in the path of his car. Instinctively he stamped on the brake, his seat belt locking across his body, preventing him from being thrown forward. His immediate thought was that someone had set a barrel alight and rolled it down on to the road. The car screeched to a halt, Des grunting as he was jolted back against his seat. His heart was racing and his head seemed to be pulsing in rhythm with it. He took a couple of deep breaths, then fumbled to release himself from the seat belt that had probably saved his life. That done, he shoved open the car door and got out, trying to stamp some strength into his shaky legs.

The fireball was still burning so fiercely that Des couldn't make out what was at the centre of it. Indeed, he had to screw up his eyes against the creamy glare of the flames, and even here, a dozen feet away, the heat was causing his skin to break out in blisters of sweat.

He looked in the direction from which the fireball had come, but saw nothing except trees. He had a fire extinguisher in his car, tucked under his front seat. He was about to turn away to get it when the fireball changed shape. It seemed to elongate, to grow taller and thinner, and oddly made Des think of a man who had been squatting now standing up. At the same time the fire began to die back, revealing a dark shape at the centre of it. Des squinted, trying to make the shape out, and then his eyes opened wide in astonishment.

The shape in the centre of the fireball was indeed a man. As Des watched, he saw the flames disappearing into the man's body, as though sucked in through the clothes and skin, leaving the man himself completely unharmed. Even the blue postman's uniform he wore showed not the slightest sign of charring. The man opened his mouth and the last of the flames rushed down his throat and disappeared.

Now Des saw that he wasn't actually a man at all, but a boy, a teenager. And what was more, he was the missing teenager, the one everyone had been looking for: Mike French.

For a few moments Des didn't know what to do or say. His mind was racing, trying to come to terms with what he had witnessed. It must have been a trick of some kind, an illusion. There was no other explanation for it. 'Mike,' he said, his voice weak, gravelly.

He cleared his throat, was about to say more, when he sensed movement in the trees to his right and his left. He glanced to either side of him. People were emerging from the undergrowth. From the right came Joan Dyer who had been reported missing eighteen hours earlier and for whom an extensive search had been carried out that morning. She was moving with a litheness that was somehow unsettling in one who was so old and appeared so frail. From the left came Gary Sissons, blood trickling down his face from a gash on his forehead, and old Dr Kerr, who Des knew had been badly hit by the death of his wife a year or two ago.

None of the quartet said anything, and they had strange, eager looks on their faces. Des felt his stomach grow cold with fear. These were people he had known for years, and yet in a sense they weren't. They were different somehow. They had changed.

He tried hard, however, not to show the dread that was mounting inside him. Gruffly he said, 'What the bloody hell's going on here?'

Joan Dyer's lips curled upwards in a slow grin. It was ghastly, cadaverous. Unhurriedly, silently, the four very different figures began to walk towards him.

'Just stay where you are,' Des said, and this time was unable to quell the waver of panic in his voice. The quartet ignored him. They continued to advance.

Des began to back away. There was something dreadfully wrong here. He turned, intending to run to his car, lock himself in, radio for help.

However, when he saw what was standing on the roof of his car his legs almost gave way. He cried out, a shrill, inarticulate sound of fear.

A huge black dog, as big as a puma and twice as broad, peered down at him with eyes that glowed like hot coals. Energy draining out of him despite his desire to get away, Des fell to his knees.

The dog jumped to the ground, its body landing with a soft thump. Des heard the shuffle of unhurried footsteps behind him. The dog seemed to be looking not at him but into him, its eyes boring deep into his soul. Des could find no strength to defend himself, could only whimper, as the dispossessed of Longbarrow surrounded him, their faces alive with a savage hunger.

Chapter Forty-Eight

'Sorry about that,' said Jack.

'What are you sorry for?' asked Susan.

Jack shrugged. 'I thought Des just wanted to tell you to be careful and to let him know if you saw or heard anything. I didn't know he was going to upset you.'

'He didn't upset us,' said Susan. 'Did he, Davey?'

David shook his head.

'Are you sure?' said Jack.

'Absolutely. Obviously what's happened is upsetting, but that isn't Des's doing, is it?'

Jack looked uncertain. 'I suppose not.' Glancing at David he added quietly, 'Sorry about your friend, David. He was a nice kid, Chris Farrar.'

David looked down at his hands. 'Yeah, well.'

'Look, if you don't want to go out, that's okay.'

Susan shook her head. 'No, let's go out. It'll help take our mind off things. What do you reckon, Davey? Do you still want to go?'

David looked as though he couldn't care one way or the other, but he nodded. 'Yeah, we might as well.'

'Right, well, I'd better just pop home and get the picnic then,' said Jack. 'I was going to call and pick it up on my way here, but what with needing to open the gate for Des, and him being in such a hurry, I didn't get the chance.'

'We could have lunch in a pub if you'd rather,' said Susan.

'You're joking, aren't you? I was up half the night making sandwiches and salad and stuff.'

'Oh, Jack,' said Susan, touched, 'you shouldn't have gone to so much trouble.'

Jack looked embarrassed. 'It's all right, it didn't really take me that long. Look, I'll pop back and get it. It'll only take me ten minutes. There's a bottle of wine in the fridge as well. I hope it'll be all right for you. I don't know much about wine, but the woman in the offy said it was a good one.'

'I'm sure it'll be perfect,' said Susan. As Jack stood up, she stood up too and kissed him lightly on the cheek.

'See you in a bit,' Jack said, blushing, and left the room.

'Are you all right, Davey?' asked Susan, sitting beside her son and putting an arm around him.

He nodded, though his 'Yes' sounded like a sigh.

'Oh, damn,' said Susan suddenly. 'I forgot to show Jack the well.'

'You can show him when he gets back,' said David. 'He'll only be a few minutes.'

Chapter Forty-Nine

It took a long time before the pain of her broken finger and smashed face subsided enough to enable Mary to move. By then it seemed she'd spent hours drifting in and out of a state of semi-conscious nausea, occasionally retching, but producing nothing except gasps of agony. She'd been in too much pain even to clean up the blood that had poured from her shattered nose, pooling on the sheets around her face, drying to a black crust on her skin and in her hair. The only emotion she had been aware of during this time was hatred directed towards her husband, the only thought a fierce resolve that once she was able she'd either leave Ted or kill him, and stuff the consequences.

In the end it was the intense urge to pee that encouraged her to rouse herself. Judging by the ache in her bladder it had been there for a while, albeit stifled by the more immediate concerns of her hand and face. Gingerly holding her throbbing right hand away from her body, she used her left arm to lever herself upright. For a moment the bloody sheet came too, sticking to her face, and then it peeled redly away. She closed her eyes, breathing deeply to fend off a fresh wave of dizzy nausea, and then she inched herself round on the bed until she could touch the floor with her feet. Every little movement sent a jolt of agony into her broken bones; a number of times the urge to sink back on to the bed, close her eyes and simply let her bladder go was almost overwhelming, but she forced herself to resist it. She would not allow Ted to take away any more of her dignity than he already had.

When she finally rose to her feet, it seemed for a moment as though her head would continue to float upwards until her thoughts touched the black airlessness of space. Closing her eyes and counting to ten felt like the only way she could anchor her mind. She made her way to the bathroom, shuffling like an old woman, gritting her teeth against the shudders of pain that accompanied even the lightest of footsteps. She wondered whether Ted was still in the house. The TV was still droning downstairs, but that was no indication one way or the other.

His piss was still in the toilet bowl, oily and yellow. She flushed it away, the rushing of water making her bladder ache all the more. Awkwardly, using only her left hand, she pulled down her knickers, sat on the cold seat and let go. She sighed with relief and imagined that Ted was beneath her, drunk and snoring, and that she was pissing into his open mouth, drowning the bastard. Sitting there, she examined her right hand for the first time. The sight of it brought on a fresh wave of nausea. Her little finger was bent back at an alarming angle, the area around it and the finger itself horribly swollen, the flesh black with bruising. When she had finished on the toilet, Mary hobbled over to the sink, turned on the cold tap and thrust her right hand beneath it. The force of the water on her tender flesh almost made her pass out.

Crying with the pain, she sank to her knees, though she tried to keep her chin above the rim of the sink in case she needed to be sick. Despite this she forced herself to hold her hand beneath the tap until the cold water began to make it numb. Only then did she remove it, turning off the tap with her left hand, then crawling across to the toilet and yanking off lengths of toilet paper which she used to dab her hand dry, whimpering all the while. When that was done, she allowed herself to rest for a few minutes, just until the throbbing, which seemed to be reverberating through her entire body, had lost its edge, then she shuffled on her knees back to the sink, used it to haul herself to her feet and looked in the mirror.

Her face was a mess. She looked as though she'd been in a car crash. Of course, the dried blood which coated her chin and the left side of her face like a giant scab didn't help, but even without that her nose would still resemble a blob of plasticine that had been smeared across her face, and her eye a purple golf ball lodged in the socket, her pupil glittering blackly from a slit in its centre.

Mary put the plug in the sink and filled the bowl. She used a flannel carefully to remove most of the dried blood. Soon the water was a murky pink, flakes of black blood floating on its surface. She needed to change her top and her bra, both of which were blood-stained and sticking to her skin, and then the bedding – could she do all that with one hand?

Then again, why *should* she do it? This was all Ted's fault, and therefore his mess. Why should she be the one to clear it up? Because she knew that if she didn't he'd be liable to break the rest of her fingers, the mood he was in.

God help Mike if Ted managed to find him. And yet part of her hoped that Ted *would* find him – at least then he'd take the rest of his anger out on Mike and not her. Who knows, Ted might even get arrested and chucked into a cell again. If that happened, she'd make good use of the time by gathering her things together and getting out. There were places where women like her could go, refuges for battered wives, abused women. She'd swallow her pride and ask Des Brewer how she could find such a place; he'd know what to do. The more she thought about it, the more determined she became to ensure that Ted never hurt her ever again.

She was cleaning the rime of blood off the sink with toilet paper when the doorbell rang. Her immediate thought was: *I can't let anyone see me like this!* Then hard on the heels of that came another thought: *No, why should I be ashamed? If I'm going to get away, then I can't hide the truth any more.*

Defiantly yet gingerly she exited the bathroom, moved across the landing and started down the stairs. The doorbell rang again.

'Answer the fucking door, you lazy bitch!' Ted yelled from the living room.

She jumped and almost missed a stair, the sudden movement causing a sharp, dark jag of pain to jump into her right hand. She stifled a cry, though couldn't stop tears springing to her eyes. Her reaction had been one not so much of fear but startlement; she'd got it into her head that Ted had left the house, that he was roaming the streets looking for Mike.

Now the pain seemed to act as fuel for her anger. She wanted to scream at him, fly at him, tear him apart, but she forced herself with an effort to remain calm. She was in no state to fight him; even fully fit she was no match for his lumbering, brutal strength. No, the best way to hurt him was to do as he said. She'd answer the door in her blood-drenched top, her face beaten to a pulp, and if it was Des Brewer on the doorstep, which she half-expected it would be, then so much the better.

She reached the bottom of the stairs and pulled open the front door. Mike French, still in his postman's uniform, was standing on the doorstep, beaming at her.

'Hello, Mary,' he said, showing no reaction whatsoever to the state of her, 'I thought I'd just drop by to say hello. Mind if I come in?'

She stared at him, mute with shock.

'What's the matter?' he said. 'Cat got your tongue?'

'You . . . you . . .' she stammered.

He arched an eyebrow enquiringly. 'I . . . I . . .?'

She glanced behind her, half-expecting to see Ted framed in the living-room doorway, swaying from side to side like the king of the apes. She positioned her body in front of Mike and raised her left hand. 'Ted's here,' she hissed, 'and he knows about us.'

She expected Mike to crumble, expected to see his face blanch with horror, but instead he actually rubbed his hands together and grinned. 'Excellent,' he said cheerfully. 'That'll save me the bother of looking for him then.' He took a step forward.

Mary stood her ground, refusing to let him through. 'Are you mad? Look what he's done to me, Mike. This is nothing compared to what he'll do to you.'

Mike looked at her almost pityingly. 'Compared to what he would have done to Mike, you mean?'

'What?'

He grinned again. She had never seen him look so self-assured. He said, 'You may find this hard to believe, Mary, but I'm not Mike any more.'

She was totally confused now, and her confusion was making her angry. 'What the fuck are you on about?' she said.

'My name is Gerennius. I'm simply using Mike – his body, his thought processes, his speech patterns. I have access to all his memories, of course. I know all about you. You were very important to him. Which is why I thought I'd come and say hello.'

'Oh fuck,' Mary moaned, again glancing at the living-room door. 'What the bloody hell are you on, Mike?'

'On?'

'Drugs. You must have been taking something to behave like this. Look, never mind, I don't want to know. Just go home and sleep it off, okay?'

'But I want to see Ted.'

'No you don't, believe me. Look, Mike, I'm doing you a fucking favour. Now go!'

She gave him a little shove in the chest with the fingertips of her left hand. Instantly, she snatched her hand back, so surprised that she was unable to stifle a cry of pain.

His chest was hot! Not just hot but *hot*. Hot as the glass door of an oven that was turned to the highest temperature. Hot enough, she realised, looking at her hand with astonishment, to raise angry-looking heat blisters on her fingertips.

'Mike, what—' she began.

And then from behind her Ted snarled, 'Who the fucking hell is this?'

Mike smiled and stepped forward again. Mary moved back out of his way, wincing at the pain that her rapid footsteps caused to jolt through her right hand.

'I am Gerennius,' Mike said. 'Hello, Ted.' He held out his hand.

Ted stared stupidly at the hand for a moment and then his piggy eyes shifted to Mike's face. Like a slow child on whom the solution to a mathematical problem has finally dawned, he said, 'No, you aren't. You're that fucking Mike French. You're the cunt what's been shagging my wife.'

Mike sighed good-naturedly, then winked at Mary as if they were sharing a joke. 'All right,' he said, 'let's say for the sake of argument that I *am* Mike French. Why don't we just shake hands and forget about this whole thing?'

'I'm gonna tear your fucking head off and shit down the hole!' Ted bellowed.

Mary scampered out of the way, awakening yet more pain in her hand, as her husband powered forward like a tank.

'*No, Ted, don't*!' she screamed as he drew back the fist he had used to transform her face into a Halloween mask earlier that afternoon. Mike simply stood, smiling, as Ted pistoned the fist

346

forward. Mary winced, expecting to hear the crunch of bone, to see teeth and blood flying in all directions, Mike collapsing pole-axed to the carpet, but in actual fact an astonishing thing happened. Almost casually Mike raised his hand and caught Ted's fist in mid-air. And not only did he catch it, but he stopped it dead and then simply held it, his body relaxed, his arm immovable as rock.

Mary looked at the expression on her husband's face and almost shrieked with hysterical laughter. Ted's mouth, a red flap in his bushy dark beard, was gaping with bewilderment, and his eyes were all but popping out of their sockets.

'What the fuck—' he said, and then his eyes became even more bulbous, and an incredible expression, an expression that it took Mary a few moments to realise was fear, appeared on his face, making him look oddly vulnerable and child-like despite his bulk.

Smoke was rising from between the fingers of Mike's hand that was curled around Ted's fist, and with the smoke came a smell, the pungent, fatty smell of charring meat.

Ted howled and writhed, but he couldn't free himself from Mike's grip. He took a swing at Mike with his other hand, but Mike caught and held that too. Now it seemed that the two were locked together in an odd dance, Ted taking increasingly frantic kicks at Mike's legs, Mike stepping nimbly out of the way. Smoke was rising from both of Mike's fists now, turning thicker and blacker and more pungent. Finally, as though this was a game he was getting bored of, Mike raised his arms, forcing Ted to his knees.

Mary watched all this with a kind of detached horror. She couldn't quite believe what she was seeing, couldn't understand how Mike – who must have been half the size Ted was – was getting the better of her husband. And where was the smoke coming from? Mike seemed almost to be burning Ted just by touching him. Was that possible? She couldn't deny that she had blistered her fingers simply by touching Mike through his clothes. But where had this . . . this power come from? Had he known about it when he had been with her? Could he just turn it on and off at will? She felt confused, light-headed, as though she was on the verge of dreaming or about to faint.

Now Mike was bending down towards her husband, as if he

was about to kiss him. When Mike briefly opened his mouth, Mary was certain she saw a flicker of flame in there.

Then Ted's beard was all flame. It rushed upwards to engulf his head as though he'd been doused in petrol. Within seconds his head was a ball of crackling yellow light. He jerked madly in Mike's grip, but made no sound. Mary, however, screamed so loudly that something seemed to tear in her throat. Her legs gave way and she fell down, instinctively putting out her hands to break her fall. Pain exploded up from her broken finger, shooting through her arm and into her head. The pain was big and black and swamped her thoughts. She passed out.

She must have been unconscious for no longer than a minute, perhaps less, for when she opened her eyes Mike and Ted were still in the same position. Ted's head was little more than a blackened skull now, oddly shrunken, around which flame flickered. Mike opened his hands and Ted's lifeless body hit the floor with a dull thump. Suddenly Mary's mind jumped back two decades to when she'd been sixteen and in love not so much with Ted, but with his exciting, dangerous image – fearless leader, hard man, psycho biker. Showing off, Ted had shot a cow in a field with his father's shotgun, blown half of its head away, and the cow had collapsed just like that – no preamble, just straight down, thump, the end.

Mike looked at her and smiled. Fire was dancing between his teeth.

Mary began to whimper and plead. 'Don't hurt me, Mike, please. Please don't hurt me.'

'I'm not going to hurt you,' Mike said. 'I'm not going to hurt you.' He stepped over Ted's body and came towards her. He had no eyes now, only fire. His smile widened. She felt the heat of his breath.

'Just one kiss before I go,' he said.

Chapter Fifty

In many ways, not knowing where Gran was was worse than knowing she was dead. At least when someone died you knew their suffering was over. But Colin had no idea whether his gran was suffering or not. For all he knew someone could be sticking needles up her fingernails at this very moment. Or burning her with cigarette ends, or pouring boiling water over her head, or twisting her arms until her bones broke. These mental images made him feel sick but they kept coming and coming. On a couple of occasions Colin had thumped the sides of his head until his brain hurt in a vain attempt to dislodge the thoughts.

The house was silent, as it had been almost all the time since Gran had disappeared. The Dyers were not ones for weeping and wailing. They kept their emotions bottled up, and although sometimes that made Colin's stomach churn, made him feel that a terrible pressure was building up inside, it was still better than losing control.

Losing control was like going mad, giving in to the demons; it was like things unravelling until they got to the point where you couldn't make them right again. It was like what seemed to be happening in Longbarrow, things unravelling, coming apart, just as Gran had said they would. They should have got out when she'd told them to, but it was all very well thinking that now. Now they couldn't get out and leave Gran to the mercy of . . . whatever. Now they had to see things through to the end.

So Gran had been right all along. Even Chris had been right – him and his portents. But in the end it hadn't done either of them any good, had it? Colin thought of what had happened

349

earlier that morning – his dad lifting the rug in the church, the blood oozing up through the floor. It had caused a stampede. A few people had been hurt. Chris's dad had collapsed, and those that hadn't fled towards the back of the church, among them Miss Morrow, Colin's headmistress, had rushed forward to help Mr Farrar.

Dad hadn't said a word since the incident. They'd driven home in stony silence. Colin wasn't sure whether Dad was angry with him for getting him to lift up the rug. He'd wanted to say, 'I didn't know that was going to happen, Dad. I didn't know it was all going to come up through the floor like that', but one look at his dad's face had convinced him that perhaps it might be best simply to keep quiet.

Colin was in his room now, lying on his bed, staring into space. He didn't know where his parents were, though he'd guess that his dad was in the garage, tinkering with the motorbike he was building from scratch, and his mum in the kitchen, making the Sunday dinner. Not that any of them would feel hungry, but no doubt they'd all still sit down and stolidly plough their way through roast beef, Yorkshire pud, potatoes and veg. They'd do it simply because that was what they did on a Sunday, and not to do it would be like admitting that nothing meant anything any more.

Colin decided to go and see if his mum wanted any help with the dinner, though what he really wanted was to ask her if Dad was mad with him. He got up off his bed and went downstairs. Sure enough, the smell of roasting meat was beginning to fill the house. It made him feel even more sick than he was feeling already, and also a little ashamed to think that they would all be sitting down to Sunday dinner as normal whilst Gran was God knows where.

To get to the kitchen, Colin had to cross the lounge, and as he pushed open the door he braced himself to look at Gran's empty chair, which was sitting in its usual place by the fire.

He entered the room and, unable to help himself, glanced across at the chair.

A feeling of shock and delight shuddered through him. His mouth dropped open, his legs turned to straw.

Gran was sitting in her chair, smiling at him.

'Hello, Colin,' she said.

Colin's mouth moved, but no sound came out.

'What's the matter? Cat got your tongue?' Gran said, and then cackled as though she found this incredibly funny.

'No, I . . . hi, Gran,' Colin said. His mind was bursting with questions, but for the moment his astonishment blanketed them.

Was it him or did Gran seem different somehow? It was hard to put his finger on, but the expression on her face, the position of her body, even the way she had spoken, seemed . . . not quite her.

Her eyes were glittering, watchful. Colin had been longing to see his gran alive and well again, but all at once he felt unnerved by her presence.

Half-turning towards the kitchen, he called out, 'Mum.'

He heard the clatter of crockery, then his mum's voice. 'What is it?'

'Gran's here.'

There was a moment of absolute silence, then the door from the kitchen opened behind him.

'What do you—' his mum said, then she stopped dead, staring at the old woman in the chair. 'Oh my God,' she said slowly.

'Hello, Sheila,' said Gran. 'Surprised to see me?'

Mum nodded dumbly, then she managed to stammer, 'Where . . . where've you been?'

Gran smiled, and again Colin felt uneasy. It wasn't like her normal smile, it was . . . wolfish. Yes, that was the word for it. He thought of the story of Little Red Riding Hood (*My, what big teeth you have, Grandma*).

'I've been on a strange and wonderful journey,' Gran said. 'Fetch Brian and I'll tell you all about it.'

Mum looked at Gran for a moment, almost as if she was going to defy or challenge her; if she did, it would be a first. Then she turned to him and said, 'Go and fetch your dad, Colin.'

'Where is he?'

'In the garage.'

Colin nodded, but hesitated a moment. He had an urge to ask his mum whether she would be okay, but that was daft, wasn't it? Of *course* she'd be okay.

'Well, go on then,' said Mum.

'All right.' Colin offered his gran a hesitant smile and her wolfish grin widened for a moment in response, then he sidled from the room. He went along the hallway and out the front door into brilliant sunshine. The garage door was open and Dad was in there, stripped to the waist, the bike upside down, the concrete floor round about scattered with oily components. Dad was trying to do something with the front wheel of the bike, messing with the spokes, his fingers black with oil, his face set. It looked a fiddly job. Sunlight was gleaming on the sweat on his dad's broad back.

Colin stood in the garage doorway, his shadow stretched out across the floor in front of him, nudging his dad's heel. Dad was either ignoring him or was so absorbed in his work he didn't know Colin was there.

'Dad,' Colin said.

His dad's fingers stopped what they were doing for a second, then resumed. 'What is it?' he grunted. 'Dinner ready?'

'No.' Colin swallowed. 'Gran's home.'

Now his dad stopped what he was doing altogether and looked up. 'What do you mean, home?'

'She . . . she's just home. She's come back.'

'Did she say where she'd been?'

'No. She said to get you and she'd tell us.'

His dad looked at him for a moment, then said, 'Right.' He wiped his hands on a towel advertising Tetley Bitter and pulled his T-shirt over his sweaty torso. 'Let's get this sorted out then, shall we?' he said. He stumped towards the house, Colin following. He opened the front door and made his way down the hallway without wiping his feet on the mat. Colin trailed his dad into the lounge. Gran was still sitting in her armchair, but there was no sign of Mum and no sounds of activity from the kitchen.

'Hello, Mam,' Dad said, as if Gran's return was nothing special, as if she had just been to the shops or something. 'You've come back then?'

Gran smiled – a little slyly, Colin thought. 'Yes, I have.'

'Where's Mum?' Colin asked.

Gran looked at him, still with that sly look on her face. 'She had to pop out for a minute.'

'Why?' said Colin.

'I don't know. She didn't say.'

'Well, where did she go?'

'I don't know that either.'

'So where've you been, Mam?' Dad said. 'You've had half the bloody village out looking for you. Our Sheila's been worried sick.'

'All in good time, Brian. Give us a chance to get settled.' She raised her thin arms towards him. 'Aren't you going to give your old mother a welcome home kiss first?'

A look of alarm crossed Dad's face. 'A kiss?' he said.

Colin could understand his dad's surprise and reticence. His gran was not the sort of person to kiss people or even hug them. And neither had Colin heard her refer to herself as 'mother' before; she always said 'mam' or 'gran'.

'Aye, just one,' Gran said, still with her arms held out, 'seeing as what I've been through.'

Dad looked bemused, but took a step forward.

'Don't, Dad,' Colin warned.

His dad turned to look at him. 'Eh?'

'Don't kiss her.' And then before he even knew what he was going to say, Colin blurted, 'She's not Gran.'

Now his dad blinked as though someone had slapped him across the face. 'Not your gran?' he said. 'Don't be daft, lad. Who the bloody hell do you think it is then? Bloody Queen Mother?'

'I don't know,' Colin said unhappily, 'but it isn't Gran.'

Gran simply sat there, looking amused. 'What's up with your lad, Brian?' she said mildly. 'Has he gone barmy while I've been away?'

Dad shrugged. 'The whole bloody place has gone barmy, Mam. There's all sorts going on.'

'Aye, well, I'm back now to sort it all out. Give us a hand up, Brian, love.'

She reached long bony fingers towards him. Unhesitatingly, Dad took her hand in his own.

With astonishing speed, Gran swung up from her seat, clamping her other arm around her son's back. Dad looked startled. He and his mother were pressed together like smoochers to a slow song at a party, their faces an inch apart. Gran grinned her wolfish grin, showing old yellow teeth, grey gums.

'Give us a kiss, Brian,' she said.

'Give over, Mam.'

'A nice big kiss. Get your tongue right in there.' Her hand moved up to the back of his head and she pressed their faces together. As she ground her mouth on his, Dad tried to struggle free, but her grip was immovable. All Colin could see of his dad's face was one of his eyes, wide and glaring with revulsion.

At last Gran removed her hand from the back of Dad's head, allowing him to pull himself free. He staggered backwards, swiping at his mouth with his forearm. Colin saw that there was blood around his gran's lips.

A greyish tongue like a slug slithered from her mouth and licked the blood away. She giggled. 'Ooh, you bit me, you naughty boy.'

Dad stopped rubbing at his mouth just long enough to shout, 'What the bloody hell's the matter with you?'

Gran tilted her head coquettishly. 'Just because I'm not feeling quite myself doesn't mean you have to shout at me, Brian.'

'You need a bloody doctor, you do.'

'Not as much as Sheila does,' Gran said.

'What do you mean?'

'Where *is* Mum?' Colin demanded.

Gran spread her hands and shrugged. 'I'm afraid she's gone the way of all flesh.'

Dad scowled. 'What are you bloody on about? What have you done to her, Mam?'

'It's easier for me to show you than it is to explain,' Gran said. 'Watch.'

She opened her mouth in a wide O. Her cheeks seemed to bulge and Colin saw something white pushing against the back of her teeth. At first it made him think of a magician producing ping pong balls from his mouth, but when the white thing began to wriggle and jerk as it squeezed its way out between his gran's lips, he was reminded instead of the time he had seen puppies born on his Uncle Terry's farm.

'What the bloody hell . . .' Dad said as the white thing finally slid free and rather than falling to the floor seemed to open vestigial wings and flutter to the ceiling. Colin tried to focus on the creature, but it made his eyes go funny. It was moth-like, bird-like, and yet it was neither of these things. It moved so fast it seemed almost transparent, and appeared to be changing form constantly.

'What's that?' Dad said weakly.

Gran didn't answer. More of the things were hatching from her mouth – and not just from her mouth now, but from all over her body. They were coming out of her ears and her nostrils, out of her eyes like swollen white tears, even out of her hair and the ends of her fingers. They made no sound, and yet Colin fancied he could hear the rapid, moth-like fluttering of their wings. The dozen of them that were in the room quickly multiplied to twenty, then forty. Now Gran was alive with them. They were moving under her clothes, enveloping her head in a white cloud.

Colin made for the door. 'Get out, Dad, get out,' he shouted.

His dad, however, appeared not to hear him. He was staring up at the white writhing mass on the lounge ceiling with an almost idiotic look on his face. Colin yanked open the door that led into the hallway. 'Dad, come *on*.'

Finally, slowly, his dad turned his head to look at him. He looked hypnotised, as though he didn't know quite where he was. Then understanding dawned on his face and he took a step towards his son.

It was too late. With a shrill bleating that Colin seemed to hear only inside his own head, but which seemed no less real because of that, the creatures coalesced into a solid-looking mass above his dad's head and simply fell on to him. It was like watching him being covered with a white blanket. He screamed briefly and then made a sort of choking sound and fell silent. When, a few moments later, the creatures rose into the air like disturbed birds, Colin saw that his dad was gone.

Half-sobbing, unable to catch his breath, he stumbled into the hallway. His legs refused to work properly; he felt weak and uncoordinated. He had an idea that if he could make it outside he would be safe, because evil things always died in the sunlight. He was less than six steps from the door when he heard the beating of a thousand wings in his head. He was actually reaching out for the door handle, unaware that he was screaming, when the white darkness closed over his face.

Chapter Fifty-One

'How are you feeling now, Reverend?'

Steven Farrar was sitting on the threadbare settee in his study, a tartan blanket around his shoulders. He was clutching the cup of tea that Joyce had made for him and urged him to sip. However, despite the blanket, the tea and the heat of the day, Joyce saw that he was trembling like an addict denied a fix. His skin was as grey as his hair and there were dark circles around his eyes.

'Fine,' he murmured, nodding vaguely, 'thank you.'

'You don't feel sick or dizzy? You haven't got any pains in your chest?'

He blinked slowly, like a turtle. 'No, no, nothing like that.' Then he looked up at her, frowning. 'Where's Chris?'

Joyce sat beside him, placing a hand on his forearm. 'Chris died,' she said gently. 'Don't you remember?'

A shadow of anguish flitted across his face, then he became composed again. 'Oh,' he said, 'yes, of course. I'm sorry to put you to so much trouble. I don't normally do this sort of thing. I didn't get much sleep last night, you see, and . . .' His low, rambling voice tailed off mid-sentence.

'Good Lord, you don't have to apologise,' said Joyce. 'As long as you're all right, that's the important thing.'

'Oh yes,' he said unconvincingly, 'yes, I'm fine. I have the Lord to sustain me.' He gazed into space for a moment and then he murmured, 'I was forty when he was born, you know. Helen was thirty-six. We both thought we'd missed our chance of having children. He was always such a happy boy, so full of life.'

Suddenly his face seemed to fold in on itself and he slumped forward, weeping. Joyce took the mug from his hand for fear that he'd drop it. She placed the mug out of the way, then put her arms around him and held him.

At last he stopped crying. 'Thank you. I'll be all right now,' he whispered.

'Would you like me to stay with you for a while? I don't mind. I've nothing else to do.'

'No, no, you've done more than enough. You've been very kind. Thank you, Miss Morrow.'

'Oh, you don't have to thank me. And call me Joyce.'

He nodded, gave a vague smile and said nothing.

A silence fell between them. Joyce looked around the study. It was full of books and chunky dark furniture that had seen better days. Dust teemed like pond life in the syrupy sunlight that fell through the window. In more favourable circumstances the room would have seemed cosy. Today it seemed merely dismal.

At last Joyce stirred and said, 'Look, Reverend, I know it was just stress and exhaustion that caused you to collapse in church like that, but all the same I'm not entirely happy about leaving you alone. Is ... er ... your wife in the house, or somewhere nearby where I can contact her?'

'When I came out this morning I left her in bed,' Farrar said. 'She's probably still there. She was quite heavily sedated. Chris's death has hit her very hard.'

'Would you like me to go up and speak to her, explain what's happened?'

'No, no, leave her. I'm perfectly fine, really, just very tired. Perhaps I'll lie down here for a little while, try to get some sleep.'

'Yes, perhaps that might be best,' Joyce conceded. 'Is there anything else I can get you before I go? Another blanket? More tea?'

The Reverend assured her that there wasn't. Joyce urged him to ring her if there was anything at all she could do, then she said goodbye and left.

As she trudged up the tree-lined path to the gate that led into the churchyard, she reflected on the awful tragedy of Chris's death. She wondered how a person could keep faith in a God that allowed such things to happen. She knew how bitter she had felt when Audrey had died, but at least Audrey had lived a relatively full life. She could only admire Steven Farrar for turning up in church that morning – it had been a brave and selfless act, though perhaps in the circumstances ill-advised.

She moved slowly up the slope towards the first of the gravestones, wading not only through the long grass but through the heat as well. She had her head down and was thinking of the things she had seen and the things she knew to have been happening in Longbarrow, trying to make sense of it all, when a flash of red in the corner of her left eye made her look up. What she saw was so incredible, so shocking, that reality actually seemed to shift out of phase for a moment – she felt as though she had become weightless, as though she had stepped into a dream without realising it.

The church was full of blood. She could see it at the windows, the sunlight making it look unreal as shiny red plastic. Perhaps she might have believed that was all it was if it hadn't been for the fact that it was oozing through the stonework like liquid through a porous pot. Even as Joyce watched, more blood appeared, speckles of red that swelled to the size of boils, then burst and trickled down the walls where they merged with other trickles to form rivulets. Slowly but surely, before her eyes, the church was turning red. The Eye of God, the witchcraft eye, carved into the church tower, appeared to be weeping tears of blood.

Joyce's legs felt weak, spindly. Her heart seemed to swell and crash against the thin crust of her chest. What she was witnessing was abominable, but it was also compelling; she couldn't tear her eyes from the sight. She ought to tell someone, but who? The Reverend? No, he was too fragile; something like this might break him. Des Brewer? Yes, she'd tell Des, if someone hadn't already.

She forced her legs to move, to carry her totteringly forward. She felt loath to approach the bleeding church, but she had no alternative unless she was prepared to make a wide detour and climb over a four-foot high wall. She moved between the gravestones and the foliage and the craning yew trees, so light-headed that she felt rather like a ghost, or would have if her body hadn't felt so clumsy, so uncooperative. She had never suffered from asthma, but climbing the little flights of stone steps between the different levels of the churchyard made her breath wheeze in her chest.

In areas the trees became so dense that the church, and even the tower, would disappear from view for ten or fifteen seconds. When the trees fell away and the ground rose and the tower poked into view again, it always seemed redder than before. In fact, the blood had now covered over half the stone. It must be soaking into the ground already, but how long would it be before the ground became so saturated that it began to seep outwards into the churchyard and beyond? Was it possible that the blood would never stop flowing, that it would flood first Longbarrow and then the surrounding countryside and then the towns beyond that? No, of course not. Such a thing was ludicrous. She was letting her imagination run away with her.

She was on the same level as the church now. She moved towards it, keeping to the shadows cast by the yew trees flanking the path, as though afraid that somehow, because the church could bleed, it meant it had acquired a kind of pseudo-life and was watching her approach.

As she got closer, she could smell the blood. It smelt rank and coppery in the heat. Up to now, the ground had been hard and dry, the grass yellow and stiff as straw, but all of a sudden the earth gave a boggy squelch when she set her weight on it. She looked down.

Blood was seeping out of the ground around her foot. And ahead of her the earth looked . . . flushed. It reminded Joyce of sunburned skin.

Sickened, she pulled her foot from the marshy ground. It came free with a slurping noise. The blood had soaked into the ground far quicker than she'd thought it would. If she wanted to reach the gate, she would have to cross that. The alternative was to get off the path, cut through the trees and climb over the perimeter wall on to the pavement. The wall was just over waist height here, which would be an awkward climb, but she thought she could manage it.

She stepped off the path, towards the trees. Just as she did so a figure appeared from behind one of the trees a little way ahead of her, where the ground was boggy. Joyce turned her head to look, wondering if it was someone she knew. The figure hovered in the dark shadows of the trees, and Joyce got the impression that it was an old man – bald and wizened, thin almost to the point of emaciation. Perhaps a pensioner come to visit his wife's grave, bewildered by what was happening, trying to find solid ground where the yew trees grew. Whatever, Joyce was glad of the prospect of human company and raised a hand.

'Hel—' she began, but her voice shrivelled in her throat as the figure stepped into the sunlight.

It wasn't an old man at all, not a living one at any rate. The figure was naked, and looked emaciated because its brown, leathery skin clung tightly to the bones beneath. Its face was little more than a skull. It had no eyes and its lips had peeled back from its teeth which looked protuberant, monkey-like. A few wisps of colourless hair clung to its dusty scalp.

Impossible as it seemed, Joyce was looking at a walking corpse.

For a moment Joyce and the corpse stood facing each other, each as still as the other, and then the thing began to lurch towards her. Joyce felt terror sluice through her. She wanted to scream, but her throat was frozen. Clumsily she turned and stumbled away. She felt sick, her lungs ached, her legs felt as though they were clamped in wooden splints, but she dare not stop. If that thing so much as touched her, she felt sure she'd drop down dead with the horror of it, and then what would it do to her body? She felt that she was teetering on the edge of madness and couldn't help wondering whether in fact she *was* mad. All this couldn't possibly be real, it just *couldn't*, and yet to her it seemed as real as anything she'd ever known.

She had no idea how fast the thing could move, how close behind her it was. She had no idea either where she was running *to*, though just getting away was good enough for now. As grass thrashed her ankles and steps appeared with an abruptness that seemed to suggest they were determined to make her fall and injure herself, Joyce found it hard to shift from her head the image of the wizened, leathery figure scampering like a monkey to intercept her. Perhaps it was waiting just ahead, behind a bush or a gravestone, its eyeless face turned in her direction, its lips shrivelled back over bared teeth.

No, she mustn't think that. If she did, she'd slow down whenever a potential hiding place came into view, and then she would surely be caught. She had to keep going, had to hope that the thing could move no faster than she could.

She brushed against a yew tree as she rounded it, knowing that just ahead there was another short flight of three or four stone steps as the land dipped away again. She had always liked the fact that the churchyard was a higgledy-piggledy mass of intimate nooks and crannies in which a person could wander, shielded from prying eyes, but now the place seemed claustrophobic and she isolated, vulnerable. Even with the sun blazing down, the place seemed full of dead ends, shadowy corners.

Here were the steps, four of them, cutting through a bulk of foliage. She clattered down them, terrified of slipping. The steps opened on to a sort of plateau containing a dozen graves, flanked by thorny bushes. Instantly Joyce registered movement to her right. Her head darted in that direction.

Another corpse, this one fresher than the ravaged thing that was pursuing her, was hauling itself from its grave.

Joyce stopped, the strength going out of her. She stumbled sideways and clutched at a headstone to stop herself from falling. This time when her mouth opened, a shrill wheezing sound came out that at least had the ambition to become a scream. Beyond the emerging corpse, the church tower, running with blood, split the summer sky.

Dirt fell from the thing's hair and shoulders, pattering to the ground. Though this corpse was more recently dead than the first, it was impossible to tell whether it was male or female. Its clothes were filthy and stained with rot, its head puffy and slimy and grey, the colour and texture of old mushrooms. Furry blotches of turquoise mould obscured its features. At the sight of it and the sickening, overpowering smell of it, Joyce bent double and vomited, violently and copiously.

The thing turned its hideous, rotting puffball of a head in her direction. It made no sound, but its struggles to free itself became more urgent. Its hands were furry, shapeless lumps of grey-green decay which it was using to try and dig itself free. Whimpering, her breath ragged, her strength sapped by terror, Joyce staggered away.

She couldn't believe her heart hadn't burst already. She would have welcomed oblivion if only to erase what she had seen, but not here, not amongst these terrible things. Her only thought now was to retrace her steps back to the sanctuary of the Reverend's house. At least there she could lock doors, barricade windows, use the telephone to summon help.

There was a scrabbling to her left. Joyce saw skeletal fingers, like strange shoots, pushing themselves up through the turf covering a grave. She stumbled on, and a little further ahead encountered the corpse of what was undoubtedly a little girl, wearing a dress which might once have been worn to birthday parties, but which was now the colour of sludge. The girl was dragging herself along the ground. She had no legs, and like the first corpse Joyce had encountered, was in an advanced state of decay. Joyce passed so close to the girl without seeing her that another step forward and the corpse would have been able to grab her ankle.

She ran on, sobbing, her heart on fire. She was almost at the periphery of the graves now, at the place where the land became a meadow of long grass and buttercups that sloped gently down to the wall surrounding the Reverend's house. Only when she was safely past the last of the graves did she glance back.

The church tower was a column of blood; not an inch of stonework was visible. And in the red swamp that was spreading ever more rapidly from the red church at its centre, Longbarrow was giving up its dead.

Joyce could see a dozen corpses now, maybe more. Those that still had faces gazed at her without expression. Those that were still mobile enough lurched on stiffened limbs. Others – those that had been under the ground a long time, or whose injuries or level of decay prevented upright movement – shuffled or even crawled along the ground. All were moving in her direction. It was as though they sensed that her heart was still beating and that blood ran in her veins, and they resented it. The nearest was still some distance away, and it seemed that even the most mobile was unable actually to run, but Joyce found it difficult to glean much comfort from this. Turning, she stumbled towards the gate in the wall. She reached it in perhaps twenty seconds, burst through, and ran up the path between the trees to the door of the house.

She reached for the door handle, suddenly certain that it would be locked and that the Farrars would be inside, sound asleep, unable to hear her pleading to be let in. However, the door wasn't locked. It opened easily. As she stepped into the house, she looked behind her once more. The walking dead were now descending the slope beyond the graves, the nearest some fifty yards or so from the gate. Nevertheless it would only take them a minute or two to reach the house. That was how long she had to ensure that all the doors and windows were locked.

She slammed the front door behind her, slid home the two heavy bolts, top and bottom, and twisted the key in the lock. She looked wildly around for a moment, not knowing where to start, not even knowing how many points of access there were in the house, and then she decided to wake the Reverend. The twenty or thirty seconds it would take to impress upon him the urgency of the situation would be worth it if it meant they could lock up the house securely, methodically, thoroughly.

She ran down the hall to the study door, hoping he was still lying on the threadbare sofa where she had left him. She almost slipped on the tiled floor, had to slap a hand against the wall to prevent herself from doing so. Her shoe came off. She left it, staggering lopsidedly to the study door, and went into the study. He was still there, curled up, his back to her, obviously asleep.

'Reverend!' Joyce shouted, her voice shrill, splintery with panic, 'Reverend!'

She ran over to him, grabbed his shoulder, shook him vigorously.

He rolled over towards her. His face was purple, his eyes open and staring.

Heart attack, she thought bitterly. She should never have left him, should have insisted he see a doctor.

Then she noticed the marks on his neck.

The door slammed behind her. Joyce whirled round. Despite the state of the body, she recognised the figure standing there straight away.

She fell to her knees. 'Audrey,' she whispered. 'Audrey, no please.'

Her dead lover moved towards her, arms outstretched.

Chapter Fifty-Two

She'd hit him again. She hadn't been able to help herself. This time she hadn't just slapped him, she'd punched him full in the face. And for what? Covering the kitchen floor in a snowfall of soap flakes from the box of Persil that she'd carelessly left by the washing machine. He'd been chuckling as he did it, thinking it was a game, and she'd got so mad, *so mad*, that she hadn't even realised what she was doing until he was lying on his back on the lino, blood pouring from his little nose.

She'd felt awful, of course, but by then it had been too late. She'd crawled to him on her hands and knees, sobbing, 'Oh Zack, oh Zack, I'm so sorry, I'm so sorry.' She'd picked him up. He hadn't even been crying – just whimpering, his eyelids flickering, his face a mask of blood. She had carried him through into the lounge and laid him on the settee. Now she was in the bathroom, dunking a flannel in a basin of warm water. She was sobbing and trembling. She needed help and she would get it now, she really would. This couldn't go on. She had hurt Zack for the last time.

She was stepping out of the bathroom with the warm, damp flannel in her hand when she heard the front door open downstairs. A bright flash of panic went through her. Oh God, this was either Des home early, or his interfering cow of a mother come to check up on her. And Zack was lying on the settee, semi-conscious, covered in blood!

She tore downstairs, hoping that she could somehow deflect whoever it was away from the damning evidence of the violence she had inflicted on her baby son. However, the hope was a forlorn one, and when she entered the lounge it was to find Des reaching down to gather Zack up in his arms.

Alison wanted the ground to open and swallow her up. She felt so ashamed, so utterly wretched. She dropped to her knees, her sobs intensifying.

'Oh, Des, I'm sorry, I'm so sorry, I didn't mean to, I couldn't help it . . .'

He turned to her. She'd expected to see anger on his face, fury even, but the expression he wore was even more unsettling. His eyes were glittering and there was a strange half-smile on his lips.

His voice, too, was strange – soft and hypnotic. 'You've hurt him, haven't you?' he said. 'You've hurt my little familiar.'

Alison, still kneeling on the floor, sniffed and wiped her face, and looked at her husband, wide-eyed. She'd expected to be shouted at, she *deserved* to be shouted at. Des was normally a blunt man, straightforward. She'd never seen this weird side of him before. It was creepy. It made her stomach crawl.

'I . . . I . . . yes,' she stammered, now unable to raise her voice above a murmur. 'I did . . . I hurt him. I need help, Des. I can't cope. Please help me . . . please . . .'

But now, astonishingly, Des appeared to have lost interest in her. He was rocking his son in his arms, crooning words that either Alison wasn't hearing properly or that were unknown to her.

It must be the shock, she thought. That was it. That's why he was behaving so strangely. She held the flannel out to him.

'Des, would you—' she began, and then stopped.

Her eyes were playing tricks on her. She blinked, feeling dizzy, and looked again, but the illusion persisted. Something appeared to be happening to Zack. It was crazy, but he appeared to be changing form in her husband's arms.

'Des . . . what's happening?' she whispered.

He made no reply.

I'm going mad, that's what, she thought. *I'm finally going round the twist.* It seemed to her that Zack was shrinking, that his skull was changing shape, that he was *growing fur*!

She closed her eyes tightly and shook her head. She opened them again – and screamed.

Des had dropped Zack on to the settee. Except it was no longer Zack. In his place was a large brown hare.

The hare twitched its nose at her, its ears laid flat along its back.

'Go, my familiar,' said Des.

Alison screamed again as the hare coiled up like a spring and then leaped from the settee, bounding across the room and out through the door.

She watched it go, then turned back to Des. 'What's going on? Where's Zack?' she demanded shrilly, her voice as ragged as her thoughts.

Des put a finger to his lips, offered her a serene smile. 'Hush, my lady,' he said.

'What do you mean, hush? Where's Zack? Des, what's going on?'

He leaned down to her and lightly trailed his fingers across her nose and mouth. Alison wanted to ask him what the hell he was doing, why he was behaving so oddly, but when she tried to open her mouth nothing happened.

Her first reaction was one of surprise rather than fear, but then she realised that not only could she no longer open her mouth, but for some reason she could not seem to draw air in through her nose either. Which meant she couldn't breathe! She felt an immediate pressure in her throat and chest, coupled with the first sparks of real panic in her brain. Had he put something over her face? Some kind of tape perhaps? She put her hand up to explore and a sick, heavy terror settled inside her.

She had no mouth, and no nostrils! All she could feel was smooth, unbroken skin. Panic-stricken now, she clawed at her face, but it made no odds. She was desperate to draw in breath, but she couldn't. Already her throat and chest and head seemed to be swelling with airlessness. Her lungs were hurting, but the worst thing was the absolute, uncontrollable terror of being unable to breathe.

She fell to the floor, thrashing and convulsing desperately. Her eyes were bulging out of her head, her brain seemed to be on the point of bursting. A horrible buzzing blackness closed in as the pressure and pain in her lungs became indescribable. The last thing she saw as she looked up was her husband's dispassionate face as he watched her die.

Chapter Fifty-Three

Speaking to Miss Morrow had finally convinced Jake and Lucy that they could no longer put off the inevitable. They had to tell their parents about the baby. They had decided to start with Jake's mum.

Jake met Lucy at the farm gate and together the two of them walked down to the house hand-in-hand. Jake's dad was out doing a few chores around the farm, as Jake had known he would be. His mum was inside, preparing the Sunday dinner. The smell of roast pork that greeted them as they entered the kitchen made Lucy want to throw up, but she forced herself to smile as Bridget Sissons turned from the sink where she had been peeling potatoes.

'Hello, Lucy,' she said, 'this is a nice surprise. Are you stopping for dinner?'

It was impossible to envisage her own mother greeting Jake like that. The thought of telling her what they were about to tell Jake's mum made her feel even sicker than the smell of the pork did.

Lucy shook her head and tried hard to keep her voice from wavering. 'No, I don't think so, Mrs Sissons. I'll have to get back.'

'Oh, that's a shame. Well, there's plenty to go round if you change your mind.'

Jake glanced at Lucy, his face pensive, then said, 'Mam, can we talk to you about something?'

She went back to peeling the potatoes. She was a plump, pretty woman in her late forties whose hair was as blonde as her eldest son's. Lucy had always thought of her as the sort of woman who took things in her stride. She hoped she wasn't about to be proved wrong.

'I'm all ears,' Bridget said, her back to them. 'It's nice to have a bit of company when I'm cooking.'

Jake and Lucy exchanged another glance. Jake looked anguished. Lucy gave him an encouraging nod.

Jake walked forward and pulled a chair from beneath the big kitchen table. 'Could you sit down a minute, Mam? It's important.'

She turned from the sink, a peeler in one hand, a dripping potato in the other. 'More important than your dad's belly? You know how famished he gets. He's like a bear with a sore head if he has to wait too long for his food.'

'It is quite important, Mrs Sissons,' said Lucy. 'I think it'd be best if you *did* sit down.'

Bridget Sissons narrowed her eyes shrewdly as she looked from her son to Lucy, then back to Jake again. She placed the peeler and the potato down on the draining board and wiped her hands on her apron. 'Are you going to tell me what I think you're going to tell me?' she said as she moved across to the table and sat in the chair that Jake was holding out for her.

Jake looked startled. 'I don't know. What do you think we're going to tell you?'

Lucy sighed and sank into the chair opposite Bridget. 'I think we are,' she said. 'You've guessed, haven't you, Mrs Sissons?'

Bridget Sissons looked at her for a moment and then at Jake – she appeared to be appraising them, sizing them up. Then in a serious but not unkind voice she said, 'Aye, love, I reckon I have. So when's it due?'

'End of March,' said Lucy.

Jake, still standing, looked indignant, almost as if his mother had stolen his thunder. 'How did you guess?' he said.

'What else could it have been?' said Bridget. She frowned. 'Stop hovering, Jake, and sit down. You're making me nervous.'

Jake sat, puffing out his cheeks. 'Aren't you mad?'

Bridget considered the question. 'Aye,' she said, 'part of me is. Mad that you weren't more careful. But there's no point shouting and bawling, is there? It won't change anything now.'

Lucy shook her head. 'Thanks, Mrs Sissons. We've been dreading telling you. Well, not just you. Everyone.'

'Your mam and dad, you mean?' said Bridget.

'Yeah, and Dad,' replied Jake. He hesitated a moment, then asked, 'What do you think *he'll* say?'

Bridget sat back, blowing out her cheeks. 'I dread to think. He'll not be best pleased, I can tell you that.'

'I know,' said Jake, grimacing. 'When do you think we should tell him? I thought he might take the news a bit better if Lucy was here.'

'You thought you'd be able to hide behind her, you mean?' said Bridget.

Jake blushed. 'No, I just meant he might not blow his top in front of her.'

'You're probably right. Your dad's not one for showing himself up in front of folk.' She pursed her lips. 'Would you like me to tell him?'

Jake's eyes lit up at the prospect, but before he could speak, Lucy said firmly, 'No. I think it's up to us, isn't it, Jake?'

He looked at her disbelievingly for a moment, then he sighed and nodded. 'Yeah,' he said, 'I suppose so.'

'I don't reckon I'd tell him until he's come in for his dinner and he's got a beer in his hand, then,' said Bridget. 'In the meantime, we'll have a cup of tea and you can tell me what you think you're going to do.' She stood up. 'Jake, you make the tea. I'd better get on with the dinner.'

She was moving back across to the sink when the back door was thrown open with such force that it slammed against the wall, making them all jump.

Jake whirled round, certain that his dad had somehow overheard their conversation. He expected to see him standing framed in the doorway like a bull that had discovered the ability to walk upright, fury on his face.

It wasn't his dad who stood there, however, but Gary. His eyes were wide and spacey below a cut on his forehead and he had a strange, manic grin on his face. Jake's emotions switched almost instantaneously from fear to relief to dismay. This was all he needed. Gary looked as though he'd been down the pub with his mates, getting fighting drunk.

Bridget recovered her composure quickly. In a cool voice she said, 'Decided to join us, have you?'

Gary turned his head to look at her. It was an odd, unsettling movement, slow and smooth and somehow robotic.

Jake glanced at Lucy and saw that she was looking at Gary with unease. Mind you, that wasn't unusual. In his brother's presence Lucy was always uneasy – and with good cause.

'Where is he?' Gary said.

Bridget looked at her youngest son coldly. 'Where's who?'

'Dad. Where's Dad? I want to talk to him.'

'Aye, and I expect he'll want to talk to you when he sees the state you're in. Been bloody fighting again, haven't you?'

Gary entered the room, moving like a panther, prowling. 'That's not important. Fetch him for me,' he said.

'Oi, don't talk to Mum like that,' said Jake. 'If you want to speak to Dad, *you* go and find him.'

Gary stopped prowling and stared at his brother. 'Who are you?' he said, and then before anyone could get over their surprise enough to answer him, he said, 'Oh yeah – Jake. Big brother, big nobody. And you're Lucy. Posh bird, nice tits.'

Jake jumped up from his chair, clenching his fists. 'You shut your bloody mouth or I'll shut it for you!' he shouted.

Lucy raised her hands as though to reach right across the room and pull Jake back into his seat. 'Forget about him, Jake, he's not worth it. He only said it to get a reaction.'

'But he can't talk to you like that,' said Jake. 'I won't have it.'

'Forget it, Jake,' Lucy repeated firmly. 'I'm not bothered by anything your brother says. As far as I'm concerned, *he's* the big nobody. Sorry, Mrs Sissons, no offence meant.'

'None taken, love,' Bridget said. She scowled at Gary. 'And you, young man, can apologise to Lucy and your brother.'

Gary, however, merely glanced contemptuously at his mother and then stomped out of the kitchen into the yard. 'Good riddance,' muttered Jake, but a moment later they all heard Gary shouting, 'Dad! Dad! Come here, I want to talk to you!'

Bridget sighed. 'That won't put your dad in the best of moods. I'd better go and see if I can calm the lad down.'

'I'll come with you, Mam,' said Jake.

'Me too,' said Lucy, standing up.

'You don't have to. You can stay here if you like,' Jake told her.

'Don't be daft,' said Lucy. 'If I stayed here, who'd keep you under control?'

They trooped out into the yard. Gary was standing in the middle of it, still shouting for his dad. He was crazy at the best of times, but today he seemed to have an extra edge of craziness, an added intensity. Not that the chickens, strutting around his feet, pecking up seed that Jake had scattered for them earlier, seemed to notice.

'Gary—' Bridget said sharply, but just then her husband appeared round the corner of a barn, scowling, a hammer in his hand.

'What the bloody hell's all this shouting about?' he demanded.

Gary turned to face his father, grinning fiercely. 'Ah, there you are. What kept you? I've been shouting for hours.'

The irritation on Bill Sissons' face deepened to red-faced anger. 'Don't you talk to me like that, you cheeky bugger.'

'I'll talk to you how I like,' Gary said. 'I'm in charge here now.'

'Oh aye? We'll see about that.' Bill Sissons threw the hammer aside and began to unbuckle the belt of his trousers.

'Bill,' Bridget warned, 'I'll not have you hitting him with that.'

The burly farmer yanked the belt free as he strode across the yard and let it dangle from his hand. 'You keep out of it, woman. I should have given him a thrashing years ago. It might've knocked some respect into him.'

Gary looked around, seemingly unconcerned by the fact that his eighteen-stone, belt-wielding father was now closing on him fast.

'I don't like these chickens,' he said thoughtfully. 'I think I'll get rid of them.'

The words were barely out of his mouth when in an eruption of guts and blood and feathers one of the chickens exploded.

Lucy jumped back as blood speckled her legs, letting out a little scream. Jake and his parents froze, staring in stupefied shock at the gory mess that two seconds earlier had been a perfectly healthy chicken.

The feathers were still settling when a second chicken exploded, then a third and a fourth. Lucy covered her face with her hands and screamed, 'Stop it! Stop it!'

Bill Sissons' head jerked as he looked from one exploding

371

chicken to another. His face was swelling with rage, turning purple, his eyes bulging.

Finally he lurched into motion again, advancing on his youngest son with huge, heavy strides, drawing back the arm that had held the belt.

'You bloody vandal! You've gone too bloody far this time!'

Even now chickens were bursting as though they had swallowed firecrackers. Gary stood in a mist of gore and fluffy brown feathers, smiling with a kind of crazed serenity.

Jake rediscovered the ability to speak just as his dad reached Gary. 'Dad, don't,' he shouted, but it was too late. Already the belt was flailing through the air towards the boy, the buckle flashing in the sunlight.

And then there was a brighter flash, and suddenly the belt leaped from his dad's hand. It sailed through the air and landed ten feet away in a cloud of dust, the buckle clanking. Bill Sissons yelped with pain and snatched his hand back. Another two chickens exploded. Gary didn't bat an eyelid.

Someone's shooting at us, Jake thought suddenly. *One of Gary's crazy mates is killing the chickens one by one. He must have shot the belt out of Dad's hand too.*

He looked around wildly, but could see no one. Whoever was shooting must be using a silencer, must be a hell of a shot too, Olympic standard.

'Come on, Gary, stop this!' he shouted, holding up his hands. 'Tell your friend to stop shooting.'

Everything seemed to go quiet then, though in fact the chickens had made virtually no sound as they had exploded. Jake glanced quickly at the others: Lucy looked repulsed by the carnage around her, Mam was almost expressionless with shock, and Dad was still purple-faced with anger, but bewildered now too, and shaking the hand that had been holding the belt as if the pain in his fingers could be flicked away like water.

Gary looked amused. 'You've got such a boring mind, Jake, so *practical*. Don't you recognise magic when you see it?'

'I'll bloody magic you,' Bill Sissons said, recovering a little, and reached out to grab Gary's arm.

And then he stopped, became motionless, as though playing at statues. An expression of utter confusion crossed his face.

'Bill, what's wrong?' Bridget cried.

He answered her only with a great deal of effort, his face turning an even deeper shade of purple. 'Can't . . . move . . .' He screwed up his face and clenched his teeth like a weight-lifter going for a world record. Clots of foamy spit collected at the corners of his mouth.

'What do you mean, Dad?' Jake asked.

'He means what he says,' said Gary. He grinned at his father. 'Do you want to see another trick, Dad? Look at that cow over there, the one by the tree. I'll let you move your head so you can see it.'

They all looked at the cow Gary had indicated. It was in the field by the big barn, nibbling grass beneath the shade of a tree. It was standing a little apart from the rest of the herd.

'Now watch,' Gary said, raising his fist in the air and clench-ing it.

At once the cow began to buck and thrash as though attacked by a swarm of wasps. Then it started to scream, a high-pitched, distressingly human sound. And then, before their astonished and horrified eyes, great chunks of flesh began to tear themselves from the cow's body, trailing blood which sprayed in all directions. Now it was as though the cow was being attacked not by a swarm of wasps but by a pack of invisible wolves.

Seconds later the cow's legs gave way and it crashed to the ground. The force that had torn it apart continued to work on its body for a moment, furiously hurling hide and flesh and shredded internal organs into the air. Then it stilled and died, leaving the cow's body a shapeless mass on the blood-soaked ground, half-concealed beneath the shadows of the tree.

Jake turned to his brother, sickened, cold inside. In a hoarse, horrified voice he said, 'What did you do?'

'I killed it,' Gary said simply, and smiled. 'I hold the power of life and death over all of you.'

Lucy let out a little sob. At some stage during the cow's frenzied death, she had clapped her hands over her ears and squeezed her eyes tight shut.

'Gary, love, look—' Bridget Sissons began.

Gary rounded on her. 'I'm not Gary. Haven't you realised that yet? My name is Uther. But I feel Gary's hatred inside me. He hates you so much. *So much.* But he hates him the most.'

He swivelled, pointing a finger at Bill, still immobile. 'Do you want to know *how* much he hates you?' he said softly.

'Gary, don't,' said Jake.

'This much.' Gary squeezed the thumb and forefinger of his left hand together as though squashing a bug.

Bill Sissons made a choking sound, like a man with something stuck in his throat. His bulging eyes widened in disbelief, which quickly became panic, as though he could feel something happening inside him. Then he gagged and suddenly blood was coming out of his mouth.

'*Gary*!' Jake yelled.

His brother ignored him.

Jake considered rushing his brother, grappling with him, but remembered what had happened when his dad had tried to hit him with the belt. If Gary had that kind of power, fists alone would not be enough to subdue him. Jake looked around desperately, spotted the hammer that his dad had discarded earlier and ran towards it. With each step he expected his brother to use his new powers to stop him, but Gary's attention was focused wholly on his father.

Blood was now leaking from Bill Sissons' ears and nose and even his eyes, and he was rapidly losing consciousness, his legs buckling beneath him. Only the lock that Gary had somehow put on his body held him upright. Then Gary threw up his arms, letting go, and his dad crumpled to the ground, his face hitting the dusty cobbles with a wet smack, chicken feathers adhering to the blood on his cheeks and chin. Bridget Sissons was cramming her fists against her teeth as though to stifle a scream.

'It was quite quick,' Gary said, disappointed.

'He's not dead?' Bridget said in disbelief, her voice muffled by her fists.

'Yes he is,' Gary said brightly. 'But don't worry, you'll be joining him soon. Now, in fact.'

He turned towards her, once again pressing his thumb and forefinger together. Instantly Bridget's eyes rolled up into her head so only the whites could be seen, and blood spilled from her mouth.

At the same instant, Jake drew back his arm and hit his brother as hard as he could on the back of the head with the hammer. There was a wet clunk and Gary dropped to his knees as though praying. Jake hit him again.

374

Gary fell forward like his father had done a few moments before, his eyes fluttering, mouth open, gurgling sounds coming from his throat. Blood was spreading over the back of his skull. Blood and hair matted the head of the hammer. Jake hit his brother a third time, then threw the hammer aside.

He was sweating and shaking, distress on his face. Lucy still had her hands pressed against her ears, but she had now opened her eyes. She stared at Gary and then at Jake, and then in a splintery, hysterical voice she said, 'You've killed him! Jake, you've killed your brother!'

Jake glanced down at Gary's prone body. Unconvincingly he said, 'No, I haven't, he'll be all right.' Then his face screwed up with anguish. 'You saw what he was doing. It was either him or us.'

Lucy was about to reply when Bridget Sissons' knees buckled and she folded almost gracefully to the ground, her mouth, nose and one ear leaking blood.

The two of them looked at her stupidly for a moment, then Jake dropped to his knees beside her. 'We've got to get help,' he babbled. 'You go into the kitchen, get the keys for the Range Rover. They're hanging by the sink. I'll carry Mum over to it and open the gate.'

'What about your dad?' asked Lucy.

'Dad's dead. Now hurry.'

Lucy did as Jake had asked her, stumbling across the yard, trying to avoid the strewn chicken guts and pools of blood. Her legs felt like string, her breath coming so quickly and shallowly that it was making her feel dizzy. She found the keys and stumbled back across to Jake who was waiting by the Range Rover, straining beneath the weight of his mother's plump body, which he was trying to hold upright.

'Open the doors,' he said, but Lucy was already attempting to do so. Her hands were shaking so much that it took several attempts before she managed to get the key into the lock of the passenger door. Once that was open, Jake reached in and unlocked the back door, then together the two of them hauled Bridget's body on to the back seat.

Jake took the keys from Lucy and got behind the wheel. She climbed into the passenger seat next to him. Lucy had Jake's mum's blood on her clothes, but Jake had more of it on his, and he was also speckled with blood that had squirted out of his brother's head when Jake had hit him with the hammer.

Lucy glanced back at the yard, saw the motionless bodies of Mr Sissons and Gary lying there amid the blood and guts of a dozen chickens, and felt suddenly sick and woozy. She put a hand to her pounding forehead as black sparks danced in front of her eyes.

'You all right?' Jake asked, his voice seeming to come from far away.

She blinked, tried to make herself breathe calmly and deeply, and after a moment the blackness passed.

'I will be in a minute,' she said. She swallowed, trying to get rid of the lumpy saliva in her dry mouth. 'Are you just going to leave Gary there?'

Jake didn't even look back at his brother. He started the engine, his face set. 'I'll tell them about him when we get Mum to the doctor's. We're not taking him with us. If we do and he wakes up he'll kill us.'

They drove away from the farm, jolting over the rutted ground baked dry by the sun. Lucy sank back in her seat, hugging herself. It was hot in the Range Rover and smelled of leather and something raw that she tried to tell herself was not blood. She felt sick to her stomach, but now that they were leaving the carnage behind, she became aware of a creeping numbness that was spreading throughout her entire body. It was ridiculous, but she wanted to go to sleep; her mind felt so tired. Defence mechanism, she thought vaguely, and closed her eyes.

The next thing she was aware of was a voice saying, 'What's going on?'

She came awake with a jolt, instantly terrified, her mind swelling with nightmarish images.

'*What*?' she shouted, her breath coming in great panting gasps.

She couldn't work out where she was, what she was doing, but she had the feeling that something awful had happened, or was about to. She felt a hand on her arm and looked into Jake's face and it all came flooding back. Remembering gave her no comfort at all.

'It's okay, Luce,' Jake lied, 'it's okay.'

She blinked, looked around. 'Where are we?'

'Just outside the village. Look.' He nodded ahead.

Lucy looked. They were approaching the clump of woodland that wound down to the valley in which Longbarrow nestled. Beyond the trees dark smoke was rising into the air.

'What is it?' Lucy asked.

'That's what I'd like to know.'

'It looks like something's on fire.'

'Something big,' said Jake.

The first of the trees flanking the road folded their branches over the vehicle, blotting out the smoke. The two of them fell silent again as Jake guided the Range Rover through a tunnel of wavering green shadows. Apart from the occasional gear crunch, he was handling the vehicle well. He had only driven the car around the farm before. He was too young to take lessons or even to hold a provisional licence.

The woodland petered out and they entered the outskirts of the village. Now they could see that the thick black pall of smoke in the air above Longbarrow was rising not from a single source, but from several different locations.

Lucy looked at Jake uneasily. 'I don't like this, Jake. What's happening?'

Jake looked equally uneasy. 'I don't know. I've still got to get help for my mum, though, haven't I?'

Lucy nodded and glanced over her shoulder at Jake's mum. She saw that Bridget was now awake, silently watching her.

'How are you, Mrs Sissons?' she opened her mouth to ask, but then realised that Jake's mum was not looking at her at all.

She was not looking at anything. Her eyes were open, but glassy. The blood on her face was darkening as it dried. Bridget Sissons was motionless, and Lucy knew that if she touched her skin she would feel it cooling.

'Oh no,' she said quietly.

'What?' Jake scanned the road ahead as though he had missed something. 'What?'

Lucy swallowed. 'I think your mum's died.'

Jake's eyes widened and then he scowled. Angrily he said, 'Don't be stupid, she can't have done.'

Lucy turned and looked at Bridget Sissons again, as if she half-believed that the vehemence of Jake's denial would be enough to revive her.

However, Jake's mum's glassy-eyed stare had not changed.

Lucy looked away. 'Sorry, Jake, but I think she has,' she said softly.

Jake slammed on the brakes and the Range Rover screeched to a halt. Twisting in his seat, hampered by his seat belt, he said furiously, 'She's not bloody dead. She *can't* be. Not her *and* my dad. We were only talking to her half an hour ago. We'd only just told her about the baby. She was cooking the Sunday dinner. She *can't* be dead.'

He started to cry and shake. Still tangled in his seat belt, he reached across the back seat and shook his mum by the shoulder. Her head lolled horribly; her neck seemed boneless.

'Come on, Mum,' Jake sobbed, 'wake up, wake up.'

Lucy put her hands on him, trying to calm him, though she felt anything but calm herself. Softly she said, 'There's nothing you can do for her, Jake.'

He continued to shake her, but then his sobs overtook him. He turned and slumped back in his seat. Lucy reached for him and for several minutes they clung to each other, Jake sobbing, she numbed, disbelieving.

Finally, as if by some silent mutual agreement, they broke apart. Jake sniffed and wiped his eyes. 'What shall we do now?' Lucy said.

Jake looked momentarily at a loss, then he said, 'We'll go to Des Brewer's, tell him what happened.'

'Are you sure you're okay to drive?'

He nodded fiercely. 'I'll be fine.'

He restarted the engine and they moved forward. Round the next bend were Longbarrow's busiest streets, where most of the village's shops and offices were concentrated. Here there would be people about, even on a Sunday. They drove round the bend – and straight into a nightmare.

Heaped up in the middle of the street outside the Nat West Bank was a pile of human bodies, ten feet high. Lucy screamed. Jake's feet jerked from the pedals as his whole body lurched in shock. The Range Rover stalled violently, throwing them both forward, cutting off Lucy's scream. Their seat belts locked and they jerked back into their seats. They both stared out of the windscreen at the impossible sight in front of them, unable to take it in.

Men, women and children were stacked up like timber on a human bonfire. Lucy quickly covered her face with her hands,

378

but Jake looked long enough to realise that these people had not all died in the same way. Some had been burned, others savaged as though by wild animals, and some seemed to have died of some kind of disease, their faces and arms and hands swollen with huge black boils. And as well as these, there were plenty of others whose cause of death was not immediately apparent.

'Make it go away,' Lucy moaned. 'Make it go away.'

'Who could have done this?' Jake whispered. 'Who could have killed all these people?'

Lucy looked at him through her fingers. Distress made her angry as she shouted, 'Just drive away from here, Jake. Now. *Now*!'

'All right, all right,' Jake said. He started the engine, but for a few moments his hand hovered over the gearstick as if he had forgotten how to use it.

'What are you *doing*? Why aren't we *moving*?' Lucy yelled at him.

He scowled at her. 'Don't shout at me. This isn't my fault. I'm just trying to work out whether I can get between . . . them and that lamp post.'

Lucy refused to look up to see how tight the gap was. 'Just reverse,' she said, 'turn round, go a different way.'

'It'd take ages to get to Des Brewer's that way. I'd have to go all the way round the . . . what's the matter?'

A look of horrified realisation had suddenly appeared on Lucy's face. 'Oh my God,' she said, 'what about Mum and Dad? What about Emma and Stacy? Oh God, if anything's happened to them . . .'

'It won't have,' Jake said. 'They'll be all right.'

'How do you know?' She looked stricken. 'How do you bloody know that?'

Jake thought of his own parents – his dad lying dead in the yard at home, his mum lifeless on the seat behind them – and his brother, whose head he had been forced to bash in with a hammer to make him stop. He felt a bitter, uncontrollable fury twisting inside him. He wanted to scream at her, 'What about *my* mum and dad? Yours can't be any worse off than mine!' but he forced himself to keep the words inside.

Instead he muttered, 'I'm just trying to be positive, that's all. There's no point thinking the worst, is there?'

She merely stared at him, her breath coming in short, panicky gasps.

'I'm going forward,' Jake said. 'Watch that side for me. It's going to be tight.'

He put the Range Rover into first and inched forward towards the pile of bodies. As he got closer he tried not to look at the gaping mouths and staring eyes, tried to view the heap as nothing more than an obstacle, something to be negotiated.

'I want to get as close as I can to the lamp post without actually crashing into it,' he said to Lucy. 'It doesn't matter if I scrape a bit of paint off, and don't worry about the wing mirror, okay?'

Lucy nodded curtly. Jake took a deep breath and attempted to squeeze the vehicle between the pile of bodies on his right and the lamp post on his left. He heard the left wing mirror go with a tortured, tearing sound, felt the jolt of it in his hands through the steering wheel.

Dead bodies filled the driver's side window. Jake glanced to his right and saw the black, bloated face of a toddler staring in at him with its one remaining eye. He shuddered and faced forward again. A hand covered in black boils flopped against the windscreen. As the Range Rover moved forward, it slid up and over the roof, leaving behind a smear of yellow pus. The Range Rover jolted as something crunched and then seemed to burst under its tyres.

Then they were through.

In the next street a car had smashed into a baker's shop, its front end and the display window of the shop a fusion of broken glass and twisted metal. Jake wondered what had made the driver lose control like that. He wondered too what had happened to the occupants of the car. Were they part of the pile of bodies in the street they had just left?

It was in this street, too, that they encountered the first of the fires. It was raging unchecked in a newsagent's shop, gutting the place. Jake drove past, the Range Rover's tyres crunching over broken glass from windows that had burst in the heat.

In the next street, which would eventually bring them round in a loop to the war memorial and the little row of shops opposite the church which included the Bensons' post office, was Des Brewer's house, with a blue POLICE sign outside. Three police cars were parked on the kerb – no doubt belonging to the extra men (wherever they were) who had come to investigate the murder that Lucy had told him about when she had arrived at the farm that morning. Jake had said then that he wouldn't have let her walk the two miles from the village if he had known there was a murderer on the loose. She had snorted contemptuously and told him about the techniques she had learned for dealing with attacks in self-defence classes at school. All that seemed such a long time ago now.

The door to Des Brewer's house was wide open. Jake brought the Range Rover to a halt just beyond the police cars, and after a moment's hesitation gave a short blast on the horn.

There was no response from inside the house. Jake looked at Lucy. 'I'm going to have a quick look, see if there's anyone about. You wait here and lock all the doors. If I'm not back in five minutes, drive round to the post office. You can drive, can't you?'

'A bit,' she said. Jake opened the door. Lucy grabbed his arm. 'But I'm not going to let you go off on your own. I'm coming with you.'

'No,' Jake said. 'You stay here. It might be dangerous. There's no point both of us . . . getting into trouble.'

'I don't want to be left on my own,' she said.

'It'll only be for a minute. I won't do anything daft, promise. I'll have a quick look and come straight back.'

She hesitated a moment and then let go of his arm. 'All right. But just go into the front of the house and shout. If Des's there he'll hear you.'

Jake nodded, looked around, then got out of the Range Rover. Lucy tensed as he set foot on the pavement, though she didn't quite know what she expected to happen. She watched him jog up the path to the open door of the house, hesitate a moment, then go inside. She didn't realise she was clenching her teeth, half-expecting him to call out in pain or shock or surprise, until her jaw started to ache.

She looked around at the deserted street, which the gritty, smoke-filled air seemed to make flat, colourless. What was happening in Longbarrow? It looked as though an invading army had passed through here, wiping out or abducting the entire population. But when she had left home to walk the two miles to the Sissons' farm less than two hours before it had seemed like a perfectly ordinary Sunday morning. Did it have anything to do with Gary and the terrifying powers he had displayed? She couldn't believe that the two things were unconnected, but Gary couldn't have done all this by himself, surely?

She wondered if anyone was still alive in Longbarrow, thought again of Mum and Dad and her sisters. She could only hope that some people were lying low in their homes, keeping quiet, waiting for the . . . whatever it was to pass.

'Come on, Jake, come on,' she muttered. As if she had willed it, Jake appeared in the open doorway of the Brewer house and jogged back up the path. When he got into the Range Rover, Lucy saw that he was ashen-faced.

'What did you see in there?' she asked.

'Something really weird. Des Brewer's wife. She was dead like everyone else, but . . . her face was . . .' He shuddered.

'What, Jake?' Lucy asked gently, not sure that she wanted to know.

'It was . . . she had . . .' his face creased for a moment as if he was in pain, ' . . . no nose and no mouth. There was just smooth skin. What could do something like that?'

Lucy was silent for a moment, shaking her head, then she said, 'There was no sign of Des Brewer?'

Jake shook his head. 'Just Mrs Brewer.'

'What about the baby?'

'There was just Mrs Brewer,' Jake repeated, frowning.

'Maybe Des took the baby and got out before . . .' She left the sentence unfinished.

Jake gave a final shudder as though attempting to shed the memory of what he had seen in the Brewer house. 'Let's go,' he said, starting the engine.

They drove away. Lucy braced herself as they rounded the loop that would bring them to the open area by the war memorial. Would it be the same as she had always known it – the little row of shops which included Mr Toot's, the estate agent's, and her mum and dad's post office? Would all the landmarks still be there, untouched by whatever mayhem had been unleashed in the village in the past two hours? The war memorial itself? The church tower, which was the first thing she saw when she looked out of her bedroom window every morning, the sight of which she had always found oddly comforting?

In fact . . . She turned her head, knowing that from here she should be able to see the church tower poking above the roofs of the houses. She let out a gasp.

'What's the matter?' asked Jake.

'Look at all that black smoke. It looks as though there's another fire near to where my house is. And . . . this is really weird . . . someone's painted the church tower red.'

Jake glanced to his left. 'Looks like blood,' he said.

She looked at him sharply. 'Don't be stupid. How can it be blood?'

'I didn't say it *was* blood, I just said it *looked* like blood.'

'It wasn't red two hours ago.' Lucy's voice cracked with despair and confusion. 'Oh, Jake, what's happening?'

He shook his head. 'If . . . if we can't find your mum and dad, we'll get away from here, drive to the next town and get some help.'

They rounded the corner, Jake taking a sharp left into Church Street. Now the war memorial was directly in front of them in the middle of the road.

'*Nooo!*' Lucy screamed.

It was the post office that was on fire. Already the building was nothing more than a black framework filled with savagely roaring white flame. Glass and charred debris littered the pavement outside.

'They must have got out,' Jake said. 'They wouldn't just stay inside.'

Lucy, however, was scrabbling frantically at the door handle. Next moment the door of the Range Rover swung wide with the vehicle still moving. Afraid that she was going to throw herself out into the road, Jake slammed on the brakes. The door, which had been springing closed again, now sprang back open.

'Lucy, hang on—' Jake began, but she had managed to unclip her seat belt and less than a second later had leaped down from the vehicle and was running towards the flames.

'Shit!' Jake said, frantically unclipping his own seat belt. What did she think she was going to do? Plunge into the burning building to look for survivors? If she did, she'd be dead within seconds.

He opened his own door, leaped down and ran after her. 'Lucy,' he yelled. 'Lucy, stop!'

He didn't know whether it was his voice that brought her to her senses or whether she was beaten back by the heat. Whatever, fifteen yards from the building he saw her stagger to a halt, throwing up a hand to shield her face.

He caught up with her, took hold of her. The heat was unbearable; already he was drenched in sweat. He coughed and screwed up his eyes as smoke billowed over them. Above the roar of the flames, they could hear the very structure of the place bursting, cracking, splitting apart. Lucy slumped against him as if on the verge of passing out, and made no protest as he dragged her clear.

She was wailing, almost screaming, her mouth open wide, her eyes screwed shut. Jake was frightened by the intensity, the rawness, of the emotion pouring out of her. He tried to calm her, to whisper words of comfort, but she seemed inconsolable. She reminded him of mad people he'd seen in films. Was that what had happened? Had her mind finally given way under the strain?

He put his arm behind her legs and scooped her up. He half-expected her to struggle, but in fact she snuggled into him, crying into his blood-speckled T-shirt. She was heavy, but he wouldn't have to carry her far. He turned back towards the Range Rover, which was still parked in the middle of the road, thirty yards away, its doors open.

Dead people were coming out of the graveyard and moving slowly across the road towards him.

Jake had always thought it a cliché, but a genuine chill of horror rippled down his back. There were perhaps two dozen of them on the pavement and road, but more were emerging all the time. They were in varying stages of decomposition, and as such lurched, shuffled or crawled depending on their level of mobility. The nearest, who had almost reached the Range Rover, had skin like soft, discoloured cheese and wore a suit stained with rot. Flies crawled over him, droning. He seemed unperturbed by the way they congregated in his eye sockets. Behind him was a woman who had small white eggs, like clusters of warts, glistening in the green, splitting flesh of her face. Behind her were others, equally fly-blown; others still who had gone beyond that, who were little more than collections of bones held together by dried-up strips of muscle.

There was no sound as they approached, save the idiot hum

of the insects that feasted on them. They seemed mindless, no longer capable of rage or hunger or envy, and yet Jake couldn't help thinking that they had displayed some level of guile by staying out of sight until he and Lucy had left the relative safety of the Range Rover behind and thus made themselves vulnerable. Perhaps the dead people had even started the fire, anticipating how Lucy would react? No, that was going too far. Somehow Jake couldn't imagine them formulating plans, and besides, how could they possibly have known that he and Lucy would be turning up here?

He wavered for a moment, not knowing what to do. What could they do now? They were cut off from the Range Rover and Lucy seemed in no fit state to run. Jake shouted her name, but she didn't respond, merely snuggled against him all the more and screwed her eyes up even tighter. 'Lucy,' he said urgently, 'there are . . . people coming across the road towards us. They want to hurt us. We need to get away.'

Still no response. Could he outrun the dead, carrying Lucy? For a little while, maybe, but if they didn't give up the chase before too long he'd be exhausted. Maybe they could find a car, though if they did he'd need the keys as well. He knew that car thieves made cars start by pulling out a couple of wires under the steering wheel and touching them together, but he didn't know whether he'd be able to do it. Maybe he'd get lucky; more likely he'd spend hours farting around, trying to make the right connection. He imagined himself frantically touching wires together even as the dead surrounded the car and reached in for him with their rotting hands. Where was Gary when you needed him? Maybe this was Jake's punishment for bashing his brother's skull in with a hammer. Oh come on, Jake, he thought, pull yourself together. He hefted Lucy in his arms and made ready to stumble away.

Before he could take even a step, however, a door opened behind him. Jake sensed a small figure standing by his right shoulder, and he twisted to look at it, the movement jerky, panicky. At first it seemed to him that the figure was featureless, its head a glowing orb, but then Jake realised that Mr Toot was standing there, smiling at him.

'Hello, Jake,' the little man said calmly. 'Come inside. I'll put the kettle on.'

Chapter Fifty-Four

Earlier – just as Lucy was arriving at the gates to Jake's parents' farm; just as Joyce Morrow was noticing that the church was oozing blood; just as Mike French was giving Mary Sheridan one final lingering kiss; just as Colin Dyer was running down the hallway in a vain attempt to reach the sunlight that he thought might save his life; and just as Des Brewer was reaching out almost tenderly to suffocate his unsuspecting wife – Jack arrived home.

He parked his van on the little driveway in front of the garage and got out. He lingered for a moment to peruse his small but lovingly tended front garden. His lilies and clematis were doing particularly well this year, and his sunflowers were now seven feet tall and still showing no signs of wilting. Soil looked a bit dry, mind, and the lawn could do with a trim. There were even one or two weeds daring to raise their straggly heads. Ordinarily he'd keep well on top of little jobs like these, but just recently . . . well, he'd had other things on his mind, hadn't he?

He smiled as he thought of the day ahead, though he couldn't help feeling a little guilty for being happy in light of all that had happened in Longbarrow this weekend. People dying, disappearing – he'd never known anything like it. There were one or two who'd helped in the search that morning who had been mumbling about ancient prophecies and dark magic and the coming of great evil. Jack knew all the stories, all the local superstitions; he had even had his own fair share of odd experiences up at the big house over the years, so he certainly wasn't about to dismiss such matters out of hand.

And yet, despite all of this, he was of the opinion that

everything that had happened this weekend could be put down more to bad luck than bad magic. In the light of another brilliantly sunny day, he had even managed to rationalise last night's encounter with what at the time had seemed far more than simply an ordinary dog. It had been dark and quiet, the streets deserted, he'd had a few pints, his head had been full of Des Brewer's stories – there was no wonder he'd allowed his imagination to run away with him. All right, so the dog had been huge and black and fearsome-looking, but that didn't make it a hell-hound, did it? It had been an extra-large Rottweiler, that was all, or a mastiff of some kind – more than likely one of these new foreign breeds that were coming on the market; you read about them in the papers all the time. And its eyes hadn't really glowed red – that had just been the blood vessels reflecting the street lights in the same way that people's eyes glowed red in photos taken with a flash. And the vapour that had seemed to curl from the animal's mouth – well, it had been slavering and panting, that was all, its breath emerging as steam; it must have been a cooler night than Jack remembered.

He had told Des about the dog that morning, and Des had said he would look into it, but hadn't seemed to find the incident of particular significance. Indeed, he had laughed and said, 'So what are you telling me, Jack? That you had a run-in with Black Shuck?' And Jack, embarrassed, had replied, 'Course not. I just thought you'd better know, that was all. Bloody big animal like that running about.'

Jack wandered up to his front door, unlocked it and went inside. People who visited him – there weren't many, but the odd one or two – were always surprised at how clean and tidy the place was. It was as if they expected inch-thick dust on every surface, dishes piled up in the sink, and the floor strewn with old socks and empty beer cans. In fact, many people – men and women alike – seemed to regard it as suspicious that the house *wasn't* in a state. The looks they gave him, as though they were convinced he had something to hide, made Jack feel awkward and guilty. But there was nothing sinister about his orderliness. It was merely that, living alone, he didn't make much mess, added to which he had plenty of time to clean up after himself.

But it was not *just* that the place was clean that seemed to get to people – it was that it was homely too. It was evidently not the done thing for a single man (especially one with his background) to spend his money on ornaments and rugs and pictures and tablecloths and lampshades and plants and furniture. He should be spending it on . . . what? Booze? Women? Flash cars? Power tools?

Needless to say, Jack didn't invite many people to his house. In fact, the prospect of Susan and David coming round for a meal that night after their picnic filled him with nervousness. Would Susan look at him as though he was weird? He'd be disappointed in her if she did, but at the same time he had to brace himself for the possibility.

The front door led into a small porch which contained a shoe rack, pegs for hanging coats on, a box of bulbs and seeds in packets, and a black umbrella propped in a corner. Jack unlocked the inner door, which opened into a three-foot-square hallway, a staircase directly in front of him, a door to his left.

This door, which he entered, led into the lounge. It was dark in the lounge, which was strange, because considering the brightness of the day it shouldn't have been. The fact that the curtains were closed accounted for a little of the darkness, but even so there should have been enough light coming through for the room to appear no more than dingy.

But this was weird. This was midnight blackness. Jack felt the hairs prickle on his arms and neck. He could make out nothing except a few vague, hunched shapes. He inched into the room, reaching out for the light switch on the wall to his left. Before his fingers could reach it, however, something growled softly in the darkness, no more than a few feet in front of him.

Jack froze, hoping that if he stayed still he would not be seen. He thought again of the dog he had encountered last night. Now, in this blackness, the incident was not so easy to rationalise. The dog had seemed to mark him with its red eyes. And there *had* been something about the creature, hadn't there, something he had refused to believe in the daylight, something he could only think of now as an overwhelming, palpable sense of evil? And hadn't it moved incredibly quickly, far quicker than any normal animal could have done? Hadn't it resembled a black blur of shadow?

He knew he ought to slide back along the wall and out of

the room (strange that the daylight from the hallway wasn't penetrating the darkness in here), but he was terrified that if he moved so much as an inch, something huge and black with red eyes would launch itself, snarling, from the darkness and open his throat with razor-teeth. So he stayed where he was, his back against the wall, his left arm stretched out along it. He tried to control his breathing, which sounded abominably loud to him, as though it was filling the entire room.

Then someone spoke. It was a voice he thought he recognised, but couldn't quite place. The words were soft, but their unexpectedness made him jump.

'Hello, Jack,' the voice said. 'We've been waiting for you.'

Jack didn't reply. He screwed up his eyes, peering in the direction from which the voice had come. It seemed that whoever had spoken was standing over by the fireplace, but Jack might as well have been wearing a blindfold.

'Aren't you going to come in and say hello?' the voice said a little mockingly.

'I ... I can't see,' Jack made himself reply. He tried to summon up a little indignation. 'What are you doing in my house?'

'As I said, waiting for you.' When the intruder spoke again, he sounded amused. 'Come on, Jack, we're not going to hurt you.'

Jack felt something brush by him, nudging his legs. It was the lightest of touches, though he nevertheless got the impression that he was in the presence of a large and powerful creature. There was something else too: even through his jeans, Jack experienced a brief but intense sensation of numbing cold in his thighs and knees.

He could hear the creature now, padding heavily across the room. It sounded more like a tiger than a dog. Suddenly Jack realised that not only could he hear the creature, but he could actually *see* it now too, an impression of it, at least. It was a compact, muscular shadow, black sliding across black. Jack looked around. The room was definitely a little lighter than when he'd entered it, though he got the impression that this was nothing to do with his eyes acclimatising themselves to the darkness. Rather it was as though the intruders in his house had *allowed* him to see a little more, as if they held thrall over

389

light and dark. This was a peculiar notion, he knew, yet he was convinced of its truth.

The room was still an alien landscape of hunched, dark shapes, but at least there was *some* definition now, separate gradations of darkness. Jack peered hard at where the voice had come from and saw a bulky figure in silhouette. A little bolder, he asked, 'Do I know you?'

The figure still sounded amused, mocking. Though Jack was scared, it was beginning to get on his nerves. 'Perhaps,' it said. 'Why don't you come closer and see?'

Jack stayed where he was. He wondered how fast the dog could really move, whether it would be able to catch him if he made a run for it. How long would it take him to reach his van – ten, fifteen seconds? If he managed to get into the hallway and slam the door behind him, that would gain him at least two or three seconds . . .

'What do you want me for?' he asked.

'We want to speak to you.'

'What about?'

The figure sighed. 'Why don't you sit down and relax, Jack? Why so tense?'

'Wouldn't you be tense if you got home to find the place darker than it should be, with a stranger and a . . . a bloody big animal in your house?'

The intruder chuckled. 'I take your point, but rest assured, Jack, we mean you no harm.'

'Why's it so dark then?'

'We like the dark. We find it restful.'

'Bollocks,' Jack said, and ran for the door.

He never saw the animal move, but suddenly it was there in front of him, blocking his retreat. Its eyes were twin red lamps, its jowls curled back, revealing pointed white teeth as long as Jack's fingers. It was snarling, a vicious, blood-curdling sound.

Jack raised his hands. 'Okay, okay, calm down, boy.' To the man he said, 'Call your dog off.'

'He's not my dog,' the man said. 'He's got a will of his own.' He chuckled. 'I think he wants you to sit down.'

'What for?'

The dog took a step forward, its snarls intensifying.

'All right, all right,' Jack said. 'Look, I'm sitting.' He

blundered across the room to the dark shape of the settee and sat down.

'That's better,' said the man. He stepped forward, from the dark into the semi-dark, and though his face was still in shadow, Jack now recognised him.

'Dr Kerr!' he said, surprised. 'What are you—'

'Shh,' Kerr hissed sharply, raising a hand.

Jack fell silent.

'My name is Pyewackett,' said Dr Kerr.

In spite of himself, Jack laughed. 'What do you mean? Pyewackett's the name of . . .' His voice trailed into silence as he remembered what Des Brewer had said to him that morning: *So what are you telling me, Jack? That you had a run-in with Black Shuck?*

Pyewackett. Black Shuck. They were supposedly names of two of the Seven Sleepers. This was crazy. Jack glanced nervously over his shoulder; the dog was prowling up and down behind the settee, its red eyes bobbing.

'What the bloody hell's going on here?' he said. He sensed, rather than saw, Kerr smile.

'You'll find out soon enough, Jack. For now we want you to lend us something.'

'Oh yeah? What?'

Kerr didn't reply. Instead he turned his head and said, 'Shuck.'

The dog padded round the settee, until it was standing directly in front of Jack. Now that Jack was sitting down, he and Black Shuck were eyeball to eyeball, their faces only inches apart. Jack didn't dare move. The dog's glowing red eyes filled his vision.

All at once he noticed a strange, sulphurous smell, and next moment felt something snag in his throat, something that burned. He tried to raise a hand to the pain, thinking he'd been cut, but found that he couldn't move. He tried to call out, but the instant he opened his mouth, what felt like a searing cloud of vapour rushed between his teeth, setting his tongue and throat on fire.

The pain was excruciating, but Jack could do nothing except endure it. Inwardly he felt himself quaking with agony, but outwardly he could not move a muscle.

He heard a sound accompanying the pain, a sort of soft

rushing like the wind through leaves, and all at once he realised what the dog was doing. It was filling his lungs with its own breath, or with the poison that passed for its breath. Jack thought of the black, oily vapour that he had seen curling from its panting mouth last night.

Then the pain swamped him and he blacked out.

He came to, trembling, sprawled on the settee, his throat scoured, his limbs drained of energy. The room was still full of shadows, still darker than it should have been. Jack made out the bulky figure of Dr Kerr still standing by the mantelpiece.

'Back with us, are you?' Kerr said lightly.

Jack opened his mouth to reply, wanting to know how long he had been unconscious, but somehow he couldn't get his voice to work. Despite his predicament, what worried him most at that moment was that he was going to be late for his date with Susan. With enormous effort, he dragged himself into a semi-sitting position and peered at the luminous hands of his watch. His thoughts were so muzzy that for a few seconds he couldn't work out why there only appeared to be one long hand in a vertical position, and then slowly it dawned on him. It was 12:30. He'd been unconscious for nearly an hour!

Urgency lent him strength and he scrambled upright. He felt as though he had flu – head spinning, limbs aching, throat sore. He made to push himself to his feet, but he interpreted a growl from the darkness as a warning to stay where he was. He looked up at Kerr, and again opened his mouth to ask a question and again couldn't get his voice to work. Frustrated, he raised a hand and gingerly massaged his burning throat.

'That won't do you any good, Jack,' Kerr said, 'but don't worry. Thanks to Shuck you no longer need to speak to communicate with us. We know what you're thinking before you even know it yourself.'

Jack scowled. What was the man talking about? As though he had asked the question out loud, Kerr said, 'Don't you remember me saying that we wanted you to lend us something, Jack?'

Jack nodded warily. The line of darkness that was Kerr's mouth curled into a smile.

'And have you still not guessed what that something was?'

Jack thought about it, but his mind seemed full of cotton wool. He shook his head.

'I'll give you a clue, shall I?' said Kerr. And then, imitating Jack so perfectly that Jack felt goosebumps bristle all over his body, he said, 'Susan, hi, this is Jack. I'm afraid I've got a bit of car trouble. The van's completely conked out on me. I'm going to see if I can work out what the problem is and have a go at fixing it. But if I can't do it I'll have to drop it in at the garage, which'll mean us having to use your car. Do you mind?'

Jack's eyes widened. *No*, he mouthed. It couldn't be true, could it? They couldn't possibly have stolen his voice?

Now speaking in his own voice again, Kerr said, 'I called Susan when you were asleep and told her what I've just repeated to you. She believed it, of course. She trusts you implicitly. Did you know that, Jack?'

Why, Jack started to say, but of course could make no sound. Furiously he thought: *Why are you doing this?*

'Old wounds, Jack. Ancient battles. Things left unfinished.'

What's that got to do with me?

'Everything, Jack. You're a vital pawn in a great and ancient game. You love Susan, don't you?'

Jack tried to make his mind a blank, but Kerr continued regardless.

'You feel you've been waiting for her all your life, don't you? As soon as you saw her, you knew that she was the one, that the two of you were somehow destined to be together. You'd never felt that way before, but the feeling was so intense, wasn't it, Jack, so *right*?'

Jack felt a sense of doom, of dread, of terrible destiny, burgeoning inside him.

'You are the trap, Jack,' Kerr said, 'and the trap will soon be sprung. Wheels have been set in motion. Forces are gathering. Soon we shall have a full complement, and then the final phone call will be made and *he* will come to us.'

Who? Jack thought frantically, fearing that he already knew and was denying it to himself. *Who will come?*

'I shall not name him,' said Kerr quietly.

Chapter Fifty-Five

Mr Toot stood by the window of his shop, looking out into the street. Jake and Lucy sat on plastic chairs by the counter, hands curled around mugs of tea. Jake's mug was almost empty, but Lucy's was still full. She stared down at it blankly as if she had no idea what it was or how it had got there.

Looking at the back of Mr Toot's gleaming bald head, Jake asked fearfully, 'Are those . . . things still out there?'

Mr Toot turned. 'Things?' He looked puzzled for a moment, and then his face cleared. 'Oh, you don't have to worry about those, Jake. Minor manifestations, that's all. Nasty but limited. I can deal with those.'

'Deal . . . how?' said Jake.

'How, when, what, where, why, who. I like people who ask questions, Jake. Questions are the product of a healthy mind. But time is of the essence. Already I've been waiting long enough for you to turn up.'

'Us? You mean . . . you knew we were coming?'

'You or whoever,' said Mr Toot airily, and crossed the room to peer down into their mugs. 'All finished? Good, good. In that case, we'd better go.'

'Go?' said Jake, alarmed. 'Go where?'

'To where this is going to end.'

'Where's that?'

'Longbarrow House. I'll need you to drive, Jake. I don't, I'm afraid.'

Jake shrank back into his seat. 'I'm not going back out there again.'

Unexpectedly, abruptly, Lucy mumbled, '*Can* you make all this end?'

Mr Toot smiled and spread his hands as she looked up at him. 'No,' he admitted, 'not alone. But with the right help, anything's possible.'

'*I'll* drive you then,' she said fiercely, pushing her hair back from her face.

Jake was startled and delighted by her sudden re-emergence. He had been beginning to fear that the trauma of the past couple of hours had caused Lucy's mind to collapse. Seeing her so evidently damaged by what she had been through, he had even been feeling guilty for not being in the same state as she was, for still being able to function, at least. He'd been wondering what that told him about himself. Was he so heartless that he really believed once all this was over everything could return to normal? Or was he just too stupid to accept that things would never be the same again?

Quietly, carefully, he said, 'Luce, are you okay?'

She looked at him as though he was mad. 'No. Are you?'

Jake was taken aback. He didn't know how to respond for a moment and then he shook his head. 'No, not really.'

Lucy turned back to Mr Toot and said almost shyly, 'I know you want to get on, Mr Toot, but could I ask you one question?'

'You want to know if your family is still alive,' Mr Toot said.

She swallowed. 'Yes . . . yes, I do.'

He looked into her eyes as though hypnotising her, and in a soft but compelling voice he said, 'And if I were to tell you that I never, ever lie, would you still want me to answer your question?'

Jake thought the pause as the two of them gazed at each other would go on for ever. He didn't realise he was holding his breath until Lucy shuddered and whispered, 'No.'

Gently Mr Toot said, 'We should go.'

Lucy nodded and shakily stood up. After a moment's hesitation, Jake stood up too. 'I'll drive,' he said.

Lucy looked at him almost resentfully. 'You don't have to. I can manage.'

'Maybe. But I'll drive. It's my car.'

That came out sounding more childish than he had meant it to. She glared at him. He thought she was going to start an argument and he dreaded it. When it came to arguing she could run rings round him, tie him into knots.

However she simply said, 'Let's go then.'

The two of them trailed Mr Toot to the door. As the little man reached out towards the handle, Jake said quickly, nervously, 'Hang on, I'm not sure about this. What if those things are still out there?'

As though he hadn't heard the question, Mr Toot pulled the door open and stepped outside. Lucy glanced at Jake and said, 'He said he could deal with them.'

'Yeah, but what if he can't?'

'He said he could, and he never lies.'

'How do you know?'

'He said so.'

Jake pulled a face. He'd heard stuff about Mr Toot, about some of the things he'd done, and you could tell just from being with him that the man was special. But these were exceptional circumstances, and Jake couldn't shake the feeling that Mr Toot was being far more confident than he had any right to be.

But it was too late to discuss it now. Mr Toot was outside, walking away from the shop. A moment later Lucy determinedly took a step outside the shop too. His stomach churning, Jake hurried to catch up with her. The instant he stepped into the daylight the sun sprang on him, blinding him. Jake screwed up his eyes, unable for a moment to see anything but indistinct shapes. For long seconds he felt horribly vulnerable. He brought up a hand to shield his face, fighting desperately to blink the light away as though it was dust.

Then, thankfully, his eyes began to adjust. The painful brightness sank back to a tolerable level. Jake looked around, and almost wished he had remained blind.

Dead people were milling around the Range Rover like the starving around a relief wagon.

There were around forty of them now, maybe more. They blundered into each other, stepped on each other. Droning flies hovered above them in a black cloud. They should have been pathetic, but they were terrifying. As Jake's eyes adjusted fully to the light he realised that the dead were not only *outside* the Range Rover but *inside* it too – crawling over the seats, pressing their rotting hands and slug-like faces against the windows.

396

The tea that he had drunk in Mr Toot's shop seemed to curdle in his belly.

'Mum,' he breathed.

Lucy, who had been walking six paces behind Mr Toot, her shoulders set determinedly, now faltered, then came to a stop. Jake thought at first that she too had seen the dead inside the car, but then he realised that in fact she was turning her head to look to her left. He, however, was more concerned with what the dead might be doing to his mother's body than with what had caught Lucy's attention.

When he came within earshot, she turned to him and in an eerily quiet voice said, 'Jake, what are *those*?'

'What?' Jake reluctantly tore his eyes from the melee around the Range Rover and turned to follow her gaze. His eyes widened.

A group of small children with their heads on backwards were walking towards them.

That was what Jake thought at first. But then he realised that the children simply had curtains of lank hair obscuring their faces. They moved with an eerie, unhurried grace, silent as cats. Something about them made Jake shudder, made him want to turn and run.

He looked to his right. More of the lank-haired children were moving towards them from that direction, their forms wavering in the heat-haze that pulsed from the still-burning post office.

'Mr Toot,' Lucy called nervously.

Mr Toot was close to the Range Rover now, ambling towards it as though out for an afternoon stroll. One or two of the dead seemed to have sensed his proximity, and had peeled themselves away from the main throng – quite literally – to face him. The little man turned and smiled at the teenagers.

'No need to worry,' he called cheerfully, 'everything's under control.'

The lank-haired children, perhaps a dozen of them on either side, were closing in swiftly. Lucy and Jake clutched at each other, not so much for protection as comfort. Jake saw one of the children reach up to part the curtain of hair over its face, and caught a glimpse of bulbous dark eyes and small but vicious-looking teeth.

Then Mr Toot opened his mouth wide and made the most astonishing, wonderful sound that Jake had ever heard.

It was a high, pure note – beautiful, shimmering, radiant. It was not a human sound; it was the kind of sound that Jake might have expected an angel to make. Despite the circumstances, it filled him with a sense of awe and incredible well-being. He looked at Lucy and saw that her mouth was hanging open in wonder, that already tears of joy were sparkling in her eyes, spilling down her cheeks.

The child-like creatures and the dead reacted to the sound in an altogether different way. The creatures began to writhe in obvious pain, clawing at their scalps. The dead simply shrank away, heading back towards the churchyard, and although they showed no particular urgency and made no sounds, Jake nevertheless couldn't help thinking that the sound distressed them.

It didn't distress him, though. Jake drank it in, allowing it to fill him until there was nothing else in the world. His surroundings and the notion of time bled away as his senses became completely overwhelmed. Now he wasn't simply hearing the sound, he *was* the sound. He felt as though he was floating in a limbo of infinite peace, felt like an infinitesimally small but vital part of something vast and timeless and wonderful.

This is it, he thought. *This is what we're born for. Nothing matters except this.*

Then he felt himself being tugged backwards and downwards as though by invisible threads. He felt no sense of regret, merely acceptance. The next thing he was aware of was opening his eyes and finding himself looking into Lucy's radiant, awe-struck face. He had never seen her look more beautiful, more full of life, than she did at that moment. He felt almost sick with love for her. He knew without having to ask that her experience had been the same as his.

For a few moments neither of them said anything, and then Lucy murmured, 'I'm not scared any more.'

'Me neither,' said Jake.

He looked around. The small creatures had gone, as had the dead. Mr Toot was busily wiping the seats and the interior windows of the Range Rover with a large white handkerchief. He was whistling as he did it, looking for all the world like a proud but over-fussy car owner. Although Jake knew that what he was really doing was removing as much evidence of decaying human matter from the inside of the vehicle as he could, he found that the thought didn't sicken him as much as it might have done a few seconds – minutes? – ago.

He and Lucy walked over. Mr Toot turned and beamed.

'All finished,' he said, and threw the soiled handkerchief into the air. Jake was not surprised to see it vanish.

'Is my mum—'

'Where you'd wish her to be,' said Mr Toot. Matter-of-factly, he added, 'They've taken her body, but you know that that's not important, don't you, Jake?'

Jake nodded. 'Yes. I know that they can't hurt her any more.'

'Mr Toot, that noise you made . . .' Lucy ventured.

But Mr Toot held up the keys to the Range Rover, which were looped around the end of his chubby right forefinger, and jangled them. 'Time to go,' he said.

They climbed into the vehicle, Jake and Lucy in the front, Mr Toot in the back. Jake twisted the key in the ignition and the engine roared into life. They drove away, leaving the gutted post office and the red church and Mr Toot's little shop behind them. Now that they were underway, Jake half-expected Lucy to ask Mr Toot again about the incredible sound he had made, but was not altogether surprised when she didn't. Lucy was usually persistent and determined, but both of them had learned in a very short time that there were some questions that Mr Toot simply didn't answer. It was not that he ever got angry; on the contrary, he was always perfectly genial. But there was something about him that dissuaded you from pushing him, something that went deeper than respect, deeper than shyness, deeper even than reverence. Mr Toot was an enigma. He gave the impression of knowing all the answers, and yet it was impossible to resent him for not sharing all that he knew with you, impossible to get angry with him or dislike him.

'Mr Toot, what's happening in Longbarrow?' Lucy asked, twisting round in her seat.

'There has been . . . an awakening,' the little man said.

'An awakening of what?'

'Evil.'

'Evil? But . . . how? Why?'

Mr Toot sighed and said regretfully, 'A child's game. Power

beyond understanding. Inadvertent but inevitable. Even the greatest of enchantments cannot last for ever.'

Lucy looked at Jake. He raised his eyebrows to show that he didn't understand either.

'I'm afraid you've lost us,' Lucy said tentatively. 'What does this . . . this evil want?'

'What do any of us want?' Mr Toot said. When Lucy looked at him, puzzled, he explained, 'To live. To grow. To bloom.'

'But evil isn't a . . . a person,' said Jake. 'It's a thing. It's what people do to each other. It hasn't got a brain.'

Mr Toot smiled and folded his hands in his lap. 'Evil is an energy,' he said, 'a force. It is bad magic. It lives in all of us. But sometimes it takes us over, it grows, and once it begins to grow it doesn't stop unless it *is* stopped.'

'But how does it grow?' asked Lucy, then she held up a hand. 'No, don't tell me. It feeds on people, doesn't it? Or not on people, but on . . . on misery and suffering and fear. It creates it and then it feeds on it, and the more it creates the more it grows.'

Mr Toot remained silent, but Lucy knew that she was right.

Jake said, 'But what about Gary, the things he could do? He's not part of this evil, he's just a kid. He's my brother.'

'He must have been . . . possessed,' said Lucy. 'Isn't that right, Mr Toot?'

'Evil needs a focal point,' Mr Toot said, 'which can often be achieved only through physical manifestation. In this instance, a series of hosts was required. Six hosts plus one watcher, making a total of seven.'

'Why seven?' asked Lucy.

'Numbers are important and powerful. They are magical principles which govern the entire universe. The seven deadly sins. The seven devils cast out by Christ. The seven-headed dragon.'

'So are you saying that this thing is like a . . . like a gestalt?' said Lucy.

'A what?' said Jake.

'A gestalt. A sort of . . . group creature. It's made up of separate parts, but when they come together they create a new and powerful entity.'

Jake raised his eyebrows, impressed. 'Blimey.' Then he

frowned and glanced at the little grocer in the rear-view mirror. 'How do you know all this stuff, Mr Toot?'

Mr Toot smiled. 'I know,' he said simply.

'But did you know before? Before all this happened, I mean? Did you know that this evil was coming?'

Mr Toot looked out of the window. They were leaving the silent, smoke-grimed streets of Longbarrow behind them now, climbing up into the sun-drenched woodland. It seemed so peaceful here, so normal.

'There were omens,' Mr Toot admitted. 'Certain manifestations.'

'So why couldn't you have done something about it then?' Lucy asked quietly. 'Why couldn't you have destroyed it, nipped it in the bud, before all this . . .' she wafted a hand in the air, ' . . . all this happened?'

Mr Toot regarded her steadily, serenely. 'Because it had to happen. Sooner or later, there had to be a final battle. Besides, how do you destroy something that is not yet truly born?'

Uneasily Lucy placed a hand on her stomach, thinking about her baby. 'Abort it?' she suggested.

Mr Toot smiled. 'You can't abort dreams and illusions. You can't destroy energy that comes and goes like a wish or a thought or a phantom.'

'But if you knew it was going to happen, surely you could have done *something*? I mean, so many people have died.'

Lucy was not angry, but she was insistent. Jake glanced at Mr Toot in the mirror again. He had never seen the little grocer look more serious.

'The magic was leaking out,' Mr Toot said. 'The enchantment was coming to an end. Trapping the Seven in sleep was only a temporary measure. Decumen was dying. He did just enough in the hope that when the final battle came, his line would be strong again.' The little man shrugged. 'He knew that the price would be high, but that events had to be allowed to unfold. If I had tried to stop it before it reached this point, I might have been destroyed, and the evil would still have worked its way free eventually. You do believe me, don't you?'

Lucy looked at him for a moment, her face troubled, then she nodded. 'Yes.'

Petals of sunlight flurried across the bonnet of the Range

Rover. Jake asked, 'Couldn't you just have found out who these hosts were going to be and killed them one by one?'

'Oh yeah,' said Lucy, 'you mean you'd have killed Gary in cold blood if you'd have found out what he was going to become?'

Jake looked uncomfortable. 'I might've. I did kill him in the end, didn't I?'

'Only because there was no alternative. You were driven to it. Anyway, you don't know for certain that he's dead.'

Jake pressed his lips together and said nothing. Despite what she had said to Jake, Lucy turned to Mr Toot and asked uncertainly, '*Would* killing the hosts have stopped all this, Mr Toot? I mean, six lives compared to . . .' she thought of the bodies heaped in the road, the silent streets, '. . . hundreds.'

'If you break the cup the poisoned water is still as deadly,' Mr Toot replied.

'You mean the evil would still have been there, biding its time, waiting for new hosts?'

Before Mr Toot could reply, they broke out of the trees into sunlight. The little man looked up, his spectacles flashing. 'Here we are,' he said.

They drove up to the gates of Longbarrow House, which were closed and padlocked. 'How are we going to get in?' asked Lucy.

Mr Toot, however, had already thrown open the door of the vehicle and was climbing down. He hurried up to the gates and reached out towards the big padlock with both hands.

There was a flash of light, like the reflection of sun on glass, though more intense. Both Jake and Lucy recoiled, Jake reflexively shouting, 'Whoa!', Lucy throwing up a hand to shield her eyes. For a few moments each of them blinked and rubbed at their eyes, trying to rid themselves of the burning red cataracts that obscured their vision. When the after-glare began to subside, they saw that Mr Toot had succeeded in opening the gates and was now scampering back towards the Range Rover, blinking like a large pink mole.

'What did you do?' Lucy asked when he had climbed in.

'I used my key,' he told her with a smile. 'On we go.'

Jake drove the Range Rover through the gates and up the long, twisting drive between the oak trees. Lucy looked around

402

with interest. She had lived in Longbarrow all her life and yet she had never been through these gates before, had never seen 'the big house', apart from a cluster of chimneys poking above the treetops on top of the hill.

The drive widened and the house came into view. It looked homelier than she'd thought it would, tall rather than expansive, not as ostentatious as she'd expected, but impressive all the same.

Jake parked and they got out. 'What do we do now?' he asked, but Mr Toot was already hurrying towards the steps that led to the front door. Jake looked at Lucy and murmured, 'I don't think there's anyone home. There's no car or anything.'

Mr Toot hopped up the steps and tried the handle, but the door was evidently locked. Lucy expected him to knock, but instead he murmured something she couldn't quite hear and turned the handle again, and this time the door opened.

Lucy looked at Jake, her eyebrows raised, but he was looking up at a carving on the wall above the front door. Lucy had thought at first glance that it was simply a spiral, but on closer inspection she realised that it was a coiled snake. 'You coming in?' she asked. Jake nodded and the two of them followed Mr Toot into the house.

They found him standing perfectly still in the middle of a large entrance hall, his head tilted up as though listening. Apart from the sedate ticking of a grandfather clock which was standing between two doors against the right-hand wall, the house was silent.

The instant she stepped over the threshold, Lucy felt a rush of warmth, a sense of well-being, nowhere near as intense as when Mr Toot had made that incredible sound back in the village, but enough all the same to cause a soporific smile to spread across her face. She looked at Jake and saw that he was smiling too, his eyes dewy; it was like the expression he had worn after the one and only time they had made love and she'd become pregnant.

'Feel it?' she whispered, knowing that she didn't really have to ask.

Jake nodded as though in slow motion. 'This is a good place, isn't it?'

'The best,' she said.

403

Mr Toot was still standing with his back to them, facing the stairs. Although she couldn't see his face, Lucy got the impression that he was concentrating hard, perhaps oblivious to their presence.

Now he raised his arms slowly, opened his podgy hands. He reached upwards, stretching his fingers, as though striving for something just beyond his reach.

'What's he doing?' whispered Jake.

'Shh,' said Lucy.

Mr Toot's body now resembled an X. His legs were rigid, feet spaced apart, arms reaching straight up into the air, head thrown back, a spot of light gleaming on his hairless scalp.

It looked an intensely uncomfortable position, and yet seconds seemed to stretch into minutes as Mr Toot stood there, motionless. Jake and Lucy stood motionless too, watching, not daring to interfere. Lucy was just beginning to wonder how much longer this was going to take when she caught a flicker of movement to her right. She turned her head in that direction and gasped. 'Jake, look.'

Jagged streamers of blue-white light were crackling and dancing over the face of the grandfather clock. It was, thought Lucy wildly, as though the bleak snowscape currently visible on the clock's inner rotating disc was in the raging throes of an electrical storm which was spitting jags of lightning out into the real world. This thought had no sooner formed in her head than more crackles of lightning, larger and fiercer than those sparking from the clock-face, began to form, this time curling from the walls, the ceiling, the floorboards beneath their feet.

Lucy felt her hair prickling, her fingers tingling, saw sparks dancing and twitching like sprites around her shoes. However, she was awe-struck rather than frightened by the phenomenon. It was as though the whole house had become 'live', its fabric suffused with raw electricity.

'It's him,' Jake breathed. 'He's drawing it into himself.'

It was true. Mr Toot was soaking up the energy, the juice of the house, like a human sponge. Crooked strings of lightning stretched from his fingers and his head as more lightning coiled around his body – so much of it, in fact, that the separate strands appeared to be coalescing, knitting themselves into a thick, blazing cocoon. He looked like a marionette made of light, the strings that held him up twitching and fizzing angrily.

And then, slowly, Mr Toot brought the sizzling clots of light that were his hands together. The instant his palms touched, there was an immense, powerful, *draining* sound, a sound that Lucy could only think of as incredible energy rushing in to a void. And indeed, for a moment Mr Toot blazed like a sun as all the lightning remaining in the house funnelled into his body. The final flare of light was far more intense and prolonged this time than it had been when Mr Toot had manipulated the padlock down by the gate. Both Lucy and Jake found that not only did they have to squeeze their eyes tight shut to counter it, but they also had to clap their hands over their faces. For a long time the darkness behind Lucy's eyes blazed orange, and then finally it subsided and she cautiously removed her hands and opened her eyes.

The first thing she saw was Mr Toot's serene, patient face. He seemed none the worse for his experience. She looked around. There was no evidence that anything unusual had happened in the house – nothing out of place, nothing burned or even singed.

'Wow,' Jake breathed, his hands falling slowly from his face. 'What happened?'

Mr Toot smiled, but his smile seemed distant, preoccupied. 'We have to go,' he said.

Chapter Fifty-Six

'This must be it,' said David.

Susan turned into the drive and parked behind Jack's blue van. She felt jumpy, nervous, but put it down to a touch of culture shock. Living in London all these years meant that she wasn't used to streets that were so eerily quiet. She knew it was Sunday, but even so she would have expected to see kids out riding their bikes, dads washing their cars or strolling to the pub for a pre-lunch pint. Maybe, she thought, everyone was watching the firefighters, or staying inside with their doors locked because of this murder.

She hadn't believed Jack at first when he had rung to say that a number of buildings in the village were on fire and that some of the roads were closed off.

'My God,' she had said. 'Longbarrow's worse than Brixton.'

He had laughed. 'It must be you. You're a jinx.'

'Bad news for you, then, isn't it?' she had said, and then had asked more seriously, 'Do they know what caused these fires?'

'Not yet, but I reckon it'll be kids, carried away with everything else that's gone on this weekend, trying to get in on the action.'

'So mindless,' Susan had said, shaking her head, and then had added regretfully, 'I suppose this means our picnic's off.'

'Course not,' Jack had replied. 'Go and get a pen and a bit of paper and I'll give you directions to my house avoiding all the main streets.'

That had been fifteen minutes ago, and now here they were, having followed Jack's directions to the letter. David had wanted to take a detour to see the fires, but Susan had told him they'd had enough hold-ups, and anyway Jack had said the roads were closed off.

They got out of the car, walked up to the front door and knocked.

'Looks a nice place,' said David.

'Yes,' said Susan distractedly.

She knocked again, wishing she could shake off her feeling of unease.

'Mum,' David said.

'Yes?'

'Do you think whoever killed that kid in the woods also killed Chris and those people who've disappeared?'

Susan frowned. 'I don't know. I doubt it. Chris's death was just an accident, wasn't it?'

'Jack said they *thought* it was an accident, but they weren't sure. He said that—'

'Oh, David, don't go on about it,' she snapped, and then almost immediately pulled an apologetic face. 'Sorry, it's just that today is turning into one of those days.' She scowled at the door. 'Come on, Jack, or have you been abducted by aliens like everyone else in this bloody place?'

'Maybe he's in the toilet or something. Why don't you try the door? He wouldn't mind.'

Susan shrugged and did so. The door opened and they stepped into a small porch. She tried the inner door; that opened too.

'Jack,' she called up the stairs that confronted her.

From behind the closed door to her left she heard a voice say, 'In here.'

She opened the door and stepped inside. 'Jack, are you all—' and then she realised how dark it was, '—right,' she finished uncertainly.

'I'm fine,' came Jack's voice from the depths of a darkness that seemed impossible, impenetrable.

'Why can't I see you?' Susan said. 'Why's it so dark? What's going on?'

Jack laughed. 'I've got a surprise for you. Come in.'

'But I can't see.'

'Just take five steps in front of you. You too, David. You won't bang into anything, I promise.'

'I don't like this, Jack,' Susan said.

'You will,' promised Jack. 'Come on, Susan, be a sport.'

Susan sighed and glanced at David, who shrugged. 'All right,' she said, 'but if this is some sort of practical joke, I won't be pleased.'

She reached out towards David and he took her hand. Together the two of them edged forward into the darkness. 'How did you manage to get it so dark?' Susan said, her voice wavering a little. 'There's not even any light coming through from the hallway.'

'Trade secret,' said Jack. 'Okay, you're fine there.'

The two of them came to a halt, still clutching one another's hands. Susan peered so intently into the darkness in front of her that the backs of her eyes began to ache, but she might as well have been blind.

'So what happens now?' she asked.

'This,' said Jack.

The door through which they had entered slammed shut behind them, making them both jump.

'Jack!' Susan shouted, annoyed. 'That was *not* funny!'

'Wasn't it?' said Jack.

'No. Now please could we have a light on in here?'

'Your wish is my command.'

There was a click and a lamp with a heavy red shade came on. The bulb beneath the shade appeared to be failing, which meant that the lamp cast only a small red pool of light around itself, barely penetrating the blackness at all. The lamp was set on a small side table, beside which was an armchair in which Jack reclined. The light made it look as though Jack was drenched in blood. He was smiling, his eyes closed.

'Jack,' Susan snapped, 'what are you playing at?'

Jack's smile widened, his lips parting, and he opened his eyes. Susan let out a little scream, taking an involuntary step backwards. A black, almost treacly mist was drifting from Jack's mouth and seemingly empty eye sockets.

In a ragged voice Susan said again, 'What's going on? Jack, what's happened to you?'

'I've seen the light,' Jack said and laughed, more of the black mist curling out between his teeth.

'What are you talking about? Stop it, Jack, please. I don't like this.'

Suddenly David's grip on her hand tightened. 'Mum,' he

said in a scared voice, twisting to peer into the darkness behind and to the sides of them, 'I can hear something.'

It was true. From all around them came the rustle of movement, as if unseen figures were shuffling forwards to surround them.

Susan was badly scared now. She and David clung to each other. 'Jack,' she pleaded, 'if this *is* a joke, please stop it now.'

Jack, however, merely waved his hand in an introductory flourish. 'Susan, David,' he said, 'I'd like you to meet my friends.'

The darkness began to disperse. It was like watching an accelerated film of dawn breaking in a pitch-black room. Figures loomed as the blackness peeled away from them. Susan saw an old woman, a stout man in his sixties, two teenage boys – one wearing a postman's uniform, the other with a shocking amount of mostly congealed blood caking his hair and running down his face – and a man in his thirties whom she recognised as Des Brewer, the policeman who had turned up at her house with Jack less than two hours ago.

Ordinarily, the sight of someone like Des Brewer would have reassured her, but not on this occasion. There was something about the manner of *all* these people that frightened her badly. They seemed . . . predatory, somehow. There was an expression in their eyes that seemed simultaneously crazed and blank.

What was happening? She couldn't believe this was a joke any more. She felt sure that she and David were in terrible danger. She squeezed David's hand, hoping he'd realise that she meant to rush the figures closing in on them. He squeezed back, and she braced herself, shifting her weight on to her right foot.

She had decided to go for the old woman, to shove her back on to the settee, thus creating a clear run to the door, when she heard a curious padding sound. She looked down and all but leaped backwards in shock. A huge black dog with red eyes emerged from behind the settee.

It bared its dripping teeth at them. Black mist curled out of its mouth like smoke.

'Black Shuck!' David yelped in panic, and clung to Susan as the dog prowled around them.

Susan's fear had sent her mind into such turmoil that for a

moment she didn't know what her son was talking about. Then she remembered the afternoon when they had first come to Longbarrow, sitting drinking tea in the back room of Mr Toot's shop while the little grocer and Jack filled them in on local folklore.

Don't be stupid, she wanted to say, *Black Shuck isn't real. This is just a dog, that's all.* But her throat was too dry and too paralysed with fear to work. Besides, her words would convince no one, least of all herself. Whatever this creature was, it certainly wasn't a dog. It gave off an aura of . . . of *evil* – that was the only word she could think of to describe it. Its very presence made her feel bad, sick to her soul. The creature was darkness and misery and terror in physical form.

Jack had leaned forward with interest at David's words. 'So you know us,' he murmured, 'but do you know yourself, I wonder?'

Susan hugged David to her and glared at the man whom, in such a short time, she had come to love and trust. Fear enraged her, enabled her to rediscover her voice, raw and shrill though it was. 'We don't know what you're talking about! Why don't you leave us alone?'

Jack, however, ignored her. Leaning forward even further, he addressed David. '*Do* you know yourself?' he asked.

'W-what?' David looked at Susan for guidance, but she was as confused as he was.

'You *should* know yourself,' Jack said. 'You were the one who imprisoned us and who, without knowing it, set us free.'

Black Shuck continued to prowl backwards and forwards in front of them. The others stood silently behind them in a rough semicircle. Susan felt David's body tense against hers. 'Oh no,' he said, his voice filled with such horror that she felt her stomach cramp.

'What?' she said. '*What*?'

'I know who they are,' said David quietly.

Susan's eyes darted from Jack to the prowling animal to the silent figures with the crazed eyes standing behind them. 'What do you mean, you know who they are?'

David slowly raised a hand and pointed a trembling finger at the figure in the armchair. 'That's not Jack,' he said.

Susan's fear and confusion boiled over into anger again.

410

'David, will you please tell me what you're talking about! If that's not Jack, who the bloody hell is it?'

He looked at her almost apologetically. 'It's one of the Sleepers,' he said. 'I'm not sure which one.'

'Vinegar Tom, at your service,' Jack said.

Susan felt as though reality was slipping away from her. 'This is crazy,' she said weakly. 'The Seven Sleepers is just a . . . a legend, a story. It's not real.'

Her voice trailed off. She couldn't deny the evidence of her own eyes.

'This is all my fault,' David said miserably. 'It was me who woke them up. I should never have run round the church.'

Susan looked at him sharply. 'I've told you before, Davey, you can't blame yourself for this. Over the years plenty of people will have run round the church.'

'True, but only one had the power to awaken us,' said Jack.

'Only . . . you mean *David*?'

'Not David,' said Jack. He pointed at the boy as if accusing him. 'He is the latest to carry the seed. The latest and the last.' He laughed. 'Even now he doesn't know himself.'

Susan licked her lips. 'Look, we don't know what you're talking about. Who do you think David is?'

Jack curled his lips in distaste. 'I shall not name him.'

'But I shall,' said a voice from behind them. Susan and David turned. It was the teenager with the blood-matted hair who had spoken. The lines of blood that had run down his face looked black in the gloom.

The teenager was baring his teeth in a mirthless grin. His eyes were full of hate and madness. 'He is Decumen and his reign is at an end,' he said.

He stepped forward, a knife suddenly appearing in his hand, and before Susan could react, he plunged it into David's stomach.

Chapter Fifty-Seven

Jake and Lucy had no idea where they were going until they got there. Mr Toot directed them through the silent streets of Longbarrow and finally said, 'Pull in here.'

Jake did so, and again no sooner had he cut the engine than Mr Toot had shoved open his door and leaped down on to the pavement. Jake and Lucy glanced at each other in brief puzzlement, wondering what was so important about this ordinary house in this ordinary street. They followed Mr Toot up a drive in which was parked a blue van and a red Citroën. He was standing with his hands pressed against the front door, a concentrated look on his face, as if feeling for vibrations.

'Mr Toot, what—' Lucy began.

He turned and pressed a finger to his lips.

She leaned towards him, whispering now. 'What's in there?'

He smiled, albeit distractedly. 'Dark magic.'

'Evil?' said Lucy.

He nodded. 'Perhaps you'd better wait in the car.'

'No way,' hissed Jake, trying to sound as if he meant it. 'You helped us, now we'll help you. We can't let you go in there on your own.'

'I have certain qualifications,' Mr Toot said.

'All the same, I think we'd feel safer with you,' said Lucy.

Mr Toot was about to reply when they heard a scream from inside the house. Instantly the little man whirled and entered first the porch and then the house proper, doors seeming to open before his without his touching them.

Taken by surprise, and unnerved by the scream, Jake and Lucy simply stood there for a few seconds, and then ran after him, Lucy in the lead. She saw Mr Toot enter a room to the left of the staircase and followed him in.

412

It was gloomy and full of people. It took her a few seconds to make sense of the scene that met her eyes. There was a young woman and a boy standing together, the woman with wide eyes and her fists pressed against her cheeks, the boy looking pale and faint. On the floor between them and a group of other people, someone writhed in pain, holding his stomach. Lucy couldn't quite accept that the slippery pink rope tumbling through the writhing person's fingers was loops of intestine. There was blood on the carpet, and a knife, and a massive black dog with glowing red eyes, like something out of a nightmare. But perhaps worse than all of these things was the atmosphere in the room. Thick as the smoke from the fires that were burning all over Longbarrow, was a palpable, all-pervading sense of what Lucy could only think of as evil.

The feeling made her skin crawl, her heart quicken, her stomach judder. For the first time since Mr Toot had made that incredible sound in the street outside his shop, she felt frightened. She was barely aware of Jake having entered the room behind her until he exclaimed, 'Gary!'

The word seemed to lift a screen from her eyes, and she realised that the person squirming on the floor, trying to push his escaping innards back into the gash in his stomach, was indeed Jake's wayward brother, Gary, whom they had left for dead at the farm.

The woman and the boy looked up, their eyes wide with shock. Mr Toot reached out and placed a hand on the shoulder of one of the quartet of people looking dispassionately down at Gary – a young man wearing a postman's uniform.

There was a flash that hurt Lucy's eyes, and a fizzle, as if Mr Toot and the young postman (whom she now recognised as Mike French, who had been in the sixth form at school and who Jake had told her was missing) were full of powerful but opposing charges of energy. Mike French jumped out of the way, clutching his shoulder, and Mr Toot stepped through the gap, hopped nonchalantly over the wriggling form on the carpet and went to stand beside the woman and the boy.

The black dog with the glowing red eyes snarled at Mr Toot, its slab of a head lowered between its massive shoulders as if ready to charge, but Mr Toot ignored it. 'Susan, David,' he

413

said warmly, as if they had met by chance in the street, 'how are you?'

The woman whom Mr Toot had called Susan looked as if the question was beyond her, but the boy, David, jabbered, 'He stuck the knife in me, Mr Toot. I felt it go in. But then he fell down and the knife was in him and I was okay, but I didn't do anything to him, honest.'

'No,' Mr Toot said gently, 'I know you didn't. It's all right.' He turned to the room at large, spread his hands and smiled, totally disregarding the squirming, blood-drenched figure at his feet. 'Well, here we all are again,' he said pleasantly.

Jake was still gaping down at Gary as if he didn't know what to do or say. Lucy took his arm and gently led him to the side of the room. She had no intention of running out on Mr Toot, but as soon as she had entered the room she had felt out of her depth here, had felt that she and Jake had no real part to play in whatever was going on, and that the best thing they could do was simply to stay close to the door and watch and keep silent.

One of the four people who had been looking down at Gary was an old woman whom Lucy vaguely recognised as some harridan who had used to come in the post office, but to whom she couldn't for the moment put a name.

'We wondered when you were going to show up, little man,' the old woman said. 'Been skulking in your shop, have you, afraid to show your face?'

'Redcap,' Mr Toot smiled, 'it's been a long time.'

Susan's eyes flickered from the old woman to the little grocer to the groaning figure on the floor. 'Mr Toot, will *you* tell me what's going on?' she said desperately. 'How do you know these . . . these people?'

It wasn't Mr Toot who answered Susan, however, but Jack. 'We go back a long way, Susan.' And then a trace of scorn crept into his voice. 'Ask the little man to tell you who he really is.'

There was a silence. Susan looked at Mr Toot. The little grocer sighed as if it was of no consequence and said, 'I'm a watcher, a guide. I was left here to help you.'

'You're *nothing*,' sneered the old woman to whom Mr Toot had referred as Redcap. 'You're a splinter, a shard.'

'A fleck of dirt from under Decumen's fingernails,' mocked Des Brewer.

The four people standing over Gary and the man in the armchair laughed.

Mr Toot smiled, apparently unperturbed. 'Why don't you destroy me then?' he said quietly. 'Why don't you destroy us all?' He looked down at Gary as if seeing him for the first time. 'Oh, I see you tried – and failed.'

The old woman smiled thinly. 'Sweet folly of youth,' she said. 'Uther has always been impetuous, more so when he has the thoughts of a reckless child to play with.'

'Nevertheless,' said Mr Toot, and for the first time Lucy heard his normally gentle, lilting voice harden, 'you thought that David could be despatched without Longbarrow House to protect him, which was why you drew him here. You miscalculated. You underestimated his power.'

'*His power*,' sneered Redcap. 'The boy has no power. Decumen's seed may be in him, but it is as dry and as dead as his bones.'

Mr Toot squatted beside Gary. 'What do *you* say?'

Gary's face was deathly white now, his hands and face soaked in blood. The wound in his stomach was gaping, intestines spilling across the salmon-coloured carpet of Jack's living room.

With an enormous effort, the boy raised his head and spat blood in Mr Toot's face.

Mr Toot produced yet another white handkerchief and unconcernedly wiped the blood away. He stood up and looked at Redcap. 'Uther is testament that Decumen's power lives on in David. Already you are diminished, Redcap. You can't hope to win.'

'No,' Redcap said, 'you are wrong, little man.'

As though at an unspoken command, the five sleepers came forward, crouched down and laid their hands on Gary. His show of defiance towards Mr Toot appeared to have drained the last of his energy. He was semi-conscious, breathing quickly and heavily, his intestines draped across his stomach and fanning out over the floor like a jumble of skinned snakes. However, as his companions touched him he began to moan and stir.

Light sparked and flickered from the fingertips of the five, to enclose Gary's body in what looked like a shroud of glowing brambles. Soon the jags of light had stitched themselves into such a tight weave that Gary's body could not be seen. Only his head was visible – eyes closed, mouth open.

Black Shuck padded forward, eyes like red lanterns, muscles rippling beneath its midnight-black coat. The dog's head swung down until it was nose to nose with Gary's. When Shuck opened its mouth, revealing teeth that a Tyrannosaurus Rex would have been proud of, Lucy had to stifle a scream. She felt certain that the dog was going to tear off Jake's brother's face, but instead the creature exhaled an oily black mist, which settled over Gary's face before rushing into his open mouth and up his nose.

The five stood as one, umbilical cords of light trailing from their fingers. Gary opened his eyes and sighed as though in contentment. Gradually the light began to soak into his body, like a layer of snow melting rapidly into the ground. When it faded they all saw that the wound had sealed itself with a minimum of scarring, his guts having somehow found their way back into his body.

Redcap gestured at Gary as he clambered unsteadily to his feet. 'You see, little man. He is whole again. We are not diminished. Unlike us, Decumen is dead. His power is no match for ours.'

'You still can't do anything to us, though, can you?' Susan blurted, her voice full of hysterical defiance. 'You can't hurt us and we can't hurt you. Stalemate.'

The creature inhabiting Jack's body, which had called itself Vinegar Tom, made the corners of Jack's mouth curl upwards in a ghastly grin. 'Ah, Susan, sweet Susan,' it crooned.

'Don't you Susan me,' she said angrily, though her voice was shaking. 'You're not Jack, you're just using him. You're a . . . a parasite.'

Vinegar Tom laughed.

'Why don't *you* tell Susan the truth, little man?' Redcap said.

'Truth?' Susan said, looking uncertainly at Mr Toot. 'What truth?'

Mr Toot looked as unruffled as ever. 'Don't worry, Susan. The truth as they see it is flawed.'

'You think so, do you?' said Redcap. The old woman turned to Susan, smiling mockingly. 'He can't accept it because it would be like admitting that his existence is worthless. But the

416

fact is, Susan, you are ... what is the phrase? Running on empty. Living on borrowed time.'

'You're lying,' Susan said.

Redcap shook his old woman's head. 'Oh no, I'm not. You see, it's the house that's protecting you at the moment. The *mage*' (she spoke the word as if it was an insult) 'built the house as a temple for his power, a repository for his magic. The bricks and the land are saturated with it. But that power is finite, Susan. It's draining away even as we speak. And as the power that is protecting you is being used, so it diminishes, and so our power grows.'

Susan turned to Mr Toot. 'Is this true?'

The little grocer shook his head. 'Decumen's power is finite, yes, but so is theirs. I couldn't stop them consuming the village, but I can stop them from extending their influence further. With Decumen's help I've constructed a barrier around Longbarrow. Once they reach that they will have nowhere else to go, and with nowhere to go their evil will turn inwards and consume itself.'

Redcap began to laugh. It was a hoarse, ugly sound. 'Barrier,' the old woman sneered. 'Here is how we deal with your barrier.'

In unison the six Sleepers threw back their heads and opened their hands, as if releasing something into the air. Susan, Lucy and David all cried out with shock as Mr Toot's benign, serene face twisted with sudden pain. He fell to his knees as if someone had coshed him across the back of the head. For a moment there was silence in the room, the Sleepers frozen in a position of triumph, Mr Toot slumped in apparent defeat.

'Mr Toot,' David said at last, his voice small, achingly boyish, 'are you all right?'

Slowly, as if it caused him great pain, Mr Toot raised his head. 'It seems,' he said quietly, 'I may have underestimated our opponents' strength.'

Susan's voice was breathless, alarmed. 'What does that mean?'

Mr Toot did not look at her. For a moment David wondered whether he had even heard the question.

Then in a flat, dull voice, totally unlike his normal mellifluous tones, he said, 'I'm afraid it means we have lost.'

Chapter Fifty-Eight

'Lost?' said Susan angrily. 'What do you mean – lost?'

Mr Toot shook his head. He looked an utterly broken man. 'I'm sorry. I did what little I could, but they're too strong for me. I'm afraid I've let you all down.'

'No you haven't,' Lucy wanted to shout from the far corner of the room, but she was too terrified to draw attention to herself. She couldn't bear the thought of the eyes of all those evil people turning to look at her. For the moment she and Jake appeared unnoticed; she supposed it was because they simply weren't important enough to bother about.

In a small, almost churlish voice, Susan said, 'But we *can't* have lost.'

'Why not? Someone has to,' Jack said, smiling smugly.

Susan looked at him. She appeared unable to decide whether to be angry or frightened. Finally she turned back to Mr Toot and said, 'So what happens now?'

'Why don't you tell her, little man,' Jack said.

Mr Toot sighed and pulled himself groggily to his feet. 'They'll destroy the house,' he said flatly, 'neutralise Decumen's power.'

Susan was horrified. 'They can do that?'

'Oh yes,' said Jack.

Susan pursed her lips. She leaned closer to Mr Toot. 'And what'll happen to us when they do that?'

The grocer didn't reply, but the expression on his face was answer enough.

'Shall we all go?' said Redcap. 'I'm rather bored with this tittle-tattle.'

The old woman made a gesture towards the door, looking at

Susan as if to say: After you. Susan, however, shook her head.

'We're not going with you,' she said. 'You can't make us, not yet.'

Mr Toot, who had already taken one weary step towards the door, turned back. 'There's no point resisting, Susan,' he said gently. 'We've lost.'

Susan glared at him, her face defiant. 'Maybe, but that's no reason to make it easy for them, is it? Why should we give them the satisfaction of making us watch while they destroy the house? Let them come looking for us when they've done it.'

Redcap smiled, as if full of admiration for Susan's fighting spirit. Then the old woman's head snapped round impossibly fast, like a viper's, and she glared at Lucy. 'Come here, child,' she murmured.

Lucy's eyes and mouth widened in shock and fear. 'W-why?' she stammered in a small voice before letting out a little scream as she took a lurching step forward. She took another step, then another and another, until she was standing in the middle of the room. It was clear from the look of bewildered horror on her face that her movements were entirely involuntary.

'Pick up the knife,' Redcap said.

Lucy shook her head, moaned, 'No, I don't want to', but moving like a marionette she bent and picked up the knife that was still lying on the carpet. She looked at the blood-stained blade with revulsion, the tendons standing out in her neck as she attempted to rear back from it.

'Now, Lucy,' Redcap said pleasantly, 'I want you to slice open your stomach, tear out the foetus inside and eat it.'

Revulsion turned to absolute terror before Lucy's face crumpled into tears. 'No,' she sobbed hysterically, 'please don't make me do this, please don't make me do it.'

The hand holding the knife turned the blade inwards towards her stomach. Lucy, eyes were stretched wide as she looked down at it.

'*No!*' she shrieked. '*No! No, please!*'

'*Stop this!*' yelled Susan. 'Stop it now! It's disgusting!'

Redcap looked up. The expression on the thin, lined face was rapt, eager, hungry. 'Is it?' the old woman murmured.

'You're sick,' Susan snarled. She looked around the room at the other Sleepers. 'You're all sick. Why can't you just . . .' Her voice choked off and she shook her head, unable to express the revulsion she felt.

'It's not sickness, Susan,' said Jack. 'It's power.'

Susan was still shaking her head from side to side, looking down at the floor. Bleakly she said, 'If we come with you, will you promise to let the girl and the boy go?'

'No,' Redcap said. 'We don't have to promise anything. But we'll consider it.'

The still-sobbing Lucy opened her hand and the knife fell to the floor.

Susan put her arm around David. 'Let's get it over with then.'

Chapter Fifty-Nine

The sixty-something man whom Susan didn't know drove her car. Next to him sat the teenager in the postman's uniform. Susan and David sat in the back, holding hands. They didn't talk; Susan was too busy staring out of the window, appalled by the sights that her earlier circuitous route around the village had prevented her from witnessing. She was also trying desperately to keep her imagination in check, fearing that if she started to wonder what the Seven would do to them once they had neutralised the house's power she might well lose it completely.

When they pulled up in front of the house and got out, the first thing Susan did was to raise her face to the sun and take half a dozen deep breaths of fresh air. Up here, she couldn't taste the smoke rising from the fires that were consuming Longbarrow. She remembered how she had felt that morning, strolling in her garden, finding the well full of water, revelling in her new life. Now all that was gone, destroyed in a few short hours. There had been some small, cynical part of her that had believed it was all too good to be true, but in her wildest imaginings she would never have conceived of it ending like this.

The other vehicles were already parked in the drive, people getting out of them. Black Shuck had spent the journey crouched on the roof of the Range Rover like the ultimate hood ornament, and now the creature sprang to the ground with a spurt of gravel and slunk to the front door, a dog-shaped piece of muscle-bound darkness invading the daytime.

Lucy's face was a plaster mask inset with dark-rimmed eyes haunted by what Redcap had almost made her do to herself.

Jake, who looked nearly as shell-shocked, was trying vainly to console her. Redcap ordered Mr Toot to lead the way, which he did, his shoulders slumped, sunlight bouncing off his bald head. At the top of the steps he put his hand on the door handle, murmured something and the door opened. Even now, despite everything, Susan felt a fierce spark of possessiveness as first Redcap and then the rest of the Sleepers barged uninvited into *her* house, pushing her, David, Lucy and Jake before them. As she stepped through the door she twisted her head to look at the sun, wondering if she was seeing the daylight for the last time.

Inside the house, Mr Toot seemed to know where Redcap wanted him to go. His heavy footsteps matched the tick of the grandfather clock as he led them down the corridor to the kitchen. As soon as he entered the room, Susan knew he would cross to the cellar, and indeed he did. Darkness rose from beyond the cellar door when he opened it like something soft and stealthy, like a secret that had swelled beyond recognition. Susan blinked, wondering where that thought had come from. As if slotted beneath Mr Toot's feet, grey steps led down.

Unlike in Jack's house, little was being said now. It was almost as though everyone knew what to do, as though they each had their designated role. Movements seemed automatic, ritualistic even. Susan felt a light prod in the back and she moved forward towards the cellar opening, still holding David's hand. She glanced at her son at exactly the same moment as he glanced at her. He looked pale, tight-lipped, his dark eyes wide as though he was drinking it all in, but he offered her a small, stiff smile, which she reciprocated.

She tried not to think how like being led to an execution this was. She had seen the films – everyone silent, moving with ordered precision, the air full of a weird kind of calm tension. When she stepped into the cellar opening, first having to relinquish her grip on David's hand, the darkness sucked her in. She saw Mr Toot's head bobbing below her, the hair of the old woman whose body Redcap had stolen like a drifting cobweb, an oil slick that was Black Shuck moving on the darkness. She put out a hand to the light switch on the wall, but a voice behind her, so soft and androgynous that she couldn't even begin to guess who had spoken, murmured, 'Leave it.'

She felt her way down in the darkness, her hand occasionally brushing the wall which was cold, rough. She heard David's breathing behind her, deep but measured. Though her stomach fluttered and she felt light-headed, she was not finding it difficult to keep panic at bay. Was that acceptance of the situation or was it merely that the positive vibes in the house, which she now knew to be the residue of Decumen's power, were calming her, dulling her fear?

By the time they had all descended the steps and were standing on the stone-flagged floor, the cellar was cramped. It was gloomy but not exactly dark; the door at the top of the steps had been left open, allowing a little daylight to struggle through. Redcap ordered her, David, Jake, Lucy and Mr Toot to stand with their backs against the far wall. They obeyed without question, Susan wondering what was going to happen as she put her hands out behind her to touch the rough stone. Her palms tingled as if she could feel the constant movement of the molecules inside it. The grey forms of the Sleepers took up what seemed to be prearranged positions, standing in two lines of three, facing each other as though about to begin a barn dance. Black Shuck prowled malevolently around them, appearing to trail wisps of darkness through the grey murk. There was a moment where no one moved or spoke, a moment almost of reflection, and then as one, the six human Sleepers raised their arms, fingers touching so that they formed an unbroken rectangle, and began to murmur words in a language that Susan didn't recognise.

Almost immediately, the section of stone floor within the human rectangle began to glow. The light lit up the faces of the Sleepers, which seemed bestial as they chanted – eyes rolling, nostrils flaring, lips curled back, saliva spraying and drooling from their mouths. The light within their cage of linked hands grew increasingly intense until it became so unbearable that Susan had not only to squeeze her eyes tight shut, but to turn her head away.

It seemed to take an age before the light began to fade. By then Susan was clenching her teeth, certain that her eyelids were going to shrivel away like cellophane. Finally, however, the pure burning whiteness acquired a hint of yellow, then darkened to orange, and gradually to red. Her neck felt stiff as she opened her eyes and turned her head. The Sleepers were still standing in position, fingers touching to form a rectangle. Now, however, the floor within the rectangle was no longer a floor but a black chasm.

They're going to throw us down there, she thought with a bright flash of panic that not even the influence of the house could protect her from. *They're going to throw us down there and we might never stop falling.*

Then she saw that the rectangular opening contained steps leading down. She could make out four steps before the darkness swallowed them like water. Black Shuck moved in a ripple of dark muscle to the top of the steps and disappeared down them. Redcap broke the rectangle by lowering Joan Dyer's thin arms, then turned and beckoned them forward. Susan glanced at Mr Toot, but he was looking down at the opening and she couldn't catch his eye. Wearily he pushed himself away from the wall and moved towards the opening. Susan followed.

When they were all standing on the edge of the opening, Redcap gestured at the steps. 'After you.'

'What's down there?' David asked, peering nervously into the darkness.

'You'll find out soon enough. Lead them down, little man.'

Unprotestingly Mr Toot began to descend the steps.

'I'm not going down there,' Lucy said suddenly, her voice shrill, chalky, echoing off the stone walls.

'We have to,' Jake said, putting his arm around her. 'They can make us.'

She struggled against him. 'I don't *want* to go down there. I don't *want* to.'

Glancing at Redcap, who was watching Lucy's distress with an eagerness that repulsed her, Susan reached out and caught hold of Lucy's flailing hand.

'Hey, come on,' she said. 'We'll be all right. I'll go first.'

Though her words were hollow, her tone of voice seemed to calm the girl. Lucy stopped struggling and looked at Susan. Her shoulders slumped and she nodded. 'All right,' she mumbled.

Susan led the way, half-twisted backwards so that she could keep hold of Lucy's hand. Behind Lucy came David and then Jake. Mr Toot was out of sight, and initially it was so dark that Susan could not even see the steps beneath her feet. After a dozen or so steps she kept expecting to alight on solid ground – though was constantly wary of stepping out into nothingness – but each time she probed ahead with her foot there was another step waiting for her, and another, and another.

Time passed, though exactly how much was difficult to tell. After a while her movements became so automatic that she felt as though she was on the verge of sleepwalking. With no visual reference point to latch on to, her mind began to drift, to entertain increasingly fanciful ideas. She found herself wondering whether this place, this realm, actually existed in the real world or whether it had been conjured by the Sleepers, like the hole in the floor.

Her legs started to ache, and her shoulders. She was still holding Lucy's hand, but had got so used to it by now that she could no longer actually feel the girl's flesh touching hers. It was as though Lucy's flesh was part of her, as if their linked hands had fused together into a knuckly, nodular growth.

How far beneath the earth were they? Half a mile? A mile? More? She wished she'd counted the steps from the beginning so that she would have some idea of how long they had been descending. She started now, but after six hundred she began to lose count and heart. She was just getting to the stage where she was thinking that descending through pitch darkness for all eternity with no hope of reaching a destination was the most appalling fate conceivable when she saw the light.

At first she thought she was dreaming or hallucinating. The light was no more than a golden glimmer far below her in the darkness. Susan screwed up her eyes, peered at it, tried to define it, but she didn't realise she was actually leaning forward like a woman on the edge of a cliff enticed by the sea churning on the rocks below until Lucy tugged her hand.

Feeling giddy, she swayed back, putting her free hand out to the wall to steady herself. She twisted her head in Lucy's direction, though of course could see nothing but blackness.

'Can you see it?' she hissed. 'Can you see that light down there?'

She sensed Lucy leaning forward too, albeit cautiously. 'Yes,' she whispered. 'What is it?'

'I don't know. Where we're headed, maybe.'

'What do you think's down there?'

'I don't know. Come on.'

They started moving again, Susan trying to concentrate on feeling ahead with her feet, trying not to be distracted by the golden glow which grew steadily brighter as they approached it. Within a few minutes, she was able to make out that the light was spilling from some unknown source over a patch of stone flooring that stretched away from the bottom of the steps which the climbing light turned into yellow rungs.

Almost excitedly she turned to Lucy again. 'I can see the bottom of the steps. There's some sort of corridor or passageway. That's where the light's coming from.'

'Oh,' said Lucy in a small voice.

Susan could just about make out Lucy's face now as a brownish mask whose eyes and nose were black triangles of shadow. She squeezed the younger girl's hand, but couldn't bring herself to tell her not to worry.

They continued down and a minute later were at the bottom of the steps.

After so long descending it felt almost unnatural to be standing on solid, flat ground. The muscles in Susan's legs quivered, and she couldn't stop herself lurching as she walked, as if one leg was longer than the other. Letting go of Lucy's hand was like peeling two toffees apart. She was flexing her fingers when David joined her, staggering a little.

'Are you all right?' she asked, hugging him.

He gave an unconvincing nod. 'Where are we, Mum?'

'I don't know.'

'Where's that light coming from?'

Susan turned and pointed. 'In there.'

They were standing in a narrow, low-ceilinged corridor, at the far end of which, some twenty feet away, was an arched opening that had been hewn from the rock. Golden light filled the arch and poured out into the corridor. Though the light gave the place an illusion of warmth, it was as cold as an icebox down here.

'I know that,' David said, 'but *what* in there?'

'Why don't you find out?' crackled Redcap in his old woman's voice.

Susan turned back to see Jake and Lucy cowering away from the old woman who had also now reached the bottom of the steps. Behind Redcap was Vinegar Tom. It still anguished

426

and infuriated Susan to see Jack's body used like this, to see his face contort with cruelty, scorn, arrogance – expressions it was never meant to wear. Susan longed to see his goofy grin again, longed to hear him laugh, longed to see the way his eyes sparkled when he teased her, the way his face and voice softened when he was concerned. She wondered where the *real* Jack was – dormant and waiting to emerge or gone for ever? She felt tears pricking her eyes and blinked them back furiously, turning them into anger.

'Why don't *you* take a running jump?' she snapped. It wasn't much of a riposte, but it was at least heart-felt.

'You won't be so defiant when we make you tear your son's liver out with your bare hands,' snarled the creature revelling in the twisted corridors of Gary Sissons' mind.

Susan went cold inside, but tried not to show it. She shrugged. 'However powerful you might be, however much you hurt us, it doesn't alter the fact that you're really nothing more than a bunch of petty-minded bullies. I feel sorry for you.'

Before any of them had a chance to reply, she turned and marched towards the golden archway, her head held high and her face set even though she was trembling inside and her heart was pumping madly in her chest.

She reached the archway and passed through it, treacly light coating her. However, when she saw what the room contained, she stopped dead, awe-struck.

'Wow,' breathed David behind her, stretching the word out, his voice soft and full of wonder.

The place they had walked in to was a tomb. The walls and floor were of rough-hewn rock, though so saturated with honey-coloured light that they shone like metal. In the centre of the floor, dominating the room, was a huge golden casket that glowed and pulsed with its own inner light. On the lid of the casket, carved in the metal itself, was the same design that appeared on the gateposts and above the door of Longbarrow House: a coiled serpent.

Mr Toot was standing against the wall, looking at the casket, his face unreadable. Black Shuck, as ever, was prowling, the golden light making no impression on the creature's night-black form.

Susan, still gazing at the casket, was not aware that the

Sleepers had entered the room, herding Jake and Lucy before them, until Redcap said, 'Stand against the wall.'

Susan blinked and looked at Redcap, irritated that her contemplation of such a beautiful object had been disturbed. However, to have retorted in a place like this would have seemed somehow crass, like starting an argument during a wedding ceremony. And so she merely shot the old woman a contemptuous look and, taking David's hand, walked over to stand beside Mr Toot.

The Sleepers fanned out either side of Redcap, adopting watchful, wary poses as if the casket was an escaped animal they intended to corner and overpower. Slowly they moved forward, surrounding the casket, and then, as one, they reached out and placed their hands on it.

Immediately the casket reacted. It seemed to convulse, its light flaring and dimming. Then, like sparks from a stone, Susan saw pixels of light rise from the lid of the casket, a whole stream of them, which before she could even blink coalesced and took the form of a seven-headed snake.

This creature, composed of pure, incandescent energy, lashed out at the Sleepers like a seven-tailed whip, each head instinctively seeking out a separate member of the group. For a moment each of the Sleepers was engulfed in crackling threads of energy as if they had been electrocuted. Susan saw Black Shuck snapping at the energy as if it were a troublesome fly buzzing around his head. She saw the energy tear into Jack's face, obliterating his features in a sizzling flurry of white light.

She squeezed her eyes tight shut and put her hands over her ears. She had no desire to see Jack consumed, could feel no sense of triumph in this scene, nor even relief. Even if her and David's lives were saved by what was happening here, she knew she would feel nothing but grief for Jack. The assault seemed to go on for a long time, but eventually the crackling began to die down. Susan removed her hands from her ears, and almost immediately heard Mr Toot, standing beside her, murmur, 'No.' Fearful of what she would see, she cautiously opened her eyes.

What she didn't expect to see was the Sleepers still standing. However, that was exactly what they *were* doing, and not only that but they were clearly winning their battle with the energy-creature. It was weakening, breaking up, coming apart, like a bad TV picture. It was still spitting gouts of energy, like venom, at the sleepers, but they were coping with it easily, the energy fizzling out as soon as it touched them, as if they were absorbing it.

Redcap laughed and looked at Mr Toot. 'Your defences are pitiful, little man,' she shouted.

The energy-creature was a collection of unconnected sparks now, buzzing around like blind fireflies. Then, in rapid succession, even these winked out.

For a moment the silence in the tomb was deafening. Redcap was grinning so widely it made the old woman's face look unnatural, corpse-like. As one the Sleepers moved forward again, and once more placed their hands on the casket. Susan cried out, raising her hands instinctively, as the energy they had consumed suddenly rushed out of them in a seven-pronged stream of incredible light and engulfed the casket. There was an almighty crack that reverberated around the tomb, and the lid of the casket split into four pieces and slid to the floor, each crash creating a cacophony of echoes that made it seem as if the roof was falling in on them. The Sleepers stepped back to avoid the falling slabs of metal. Without its lid, the casket reminded Susan of a vast insect whose carapace had been torn away.

She stood on tiptoe, craning her neck to see what the casket contained. Though two of the Sleepers partly obscured her view, she was able to make out a dust-grey skeleton, its flesh-less hands crossed over its chest, dressed in faded purple and golden robes.

'Decumen,' Redcap hissed. 'At long last.'

The Sleepers moved forward, like hunters closing in on their defenceless prey. Susan almost jumped out of her skin as Mr Toot, standing beside her, suddenly shouted at the top of his voice, '*No!*'

The cry was enough to make the Sleepers pause. In a smear of movement that was astonishing in one so portly, Mr Toot suddenly rushed past Susan and scooped up David as if he was a baby. Before Susan could react, Mr Toot had lifted her son above his head and was springing towards the casket in the middle of the room. The young man in the postman's uniform half-turned, raising his arms, but Mr Toot simply barged him out of the way. With a bone-chilling snarl, Black Shuck leaped forward, its mouth a blur of teeth and slaver, and closed its jaws around Mr Toot's right ankle with a crunch. Mr Toot screamed, pulled up short, but he didn't let go of David. Like a footballer taking a throw-in, he lifted David up behind his head and hurled him through the air.

Susan screamed, her hands flying to her mouth, as her son landed on top of the skeleton in the casket in a flurry of arms and legs. Clearly the skeleton was no more than a brittle shell, for it collapsed into dust beneath David's weight, robes and all. As if this was some kind of signal, the entire room seemed suddenly to come alive, runnels of energy appearing in the walls and across the floor and ceiling, like veins carrying blazing, thrumming life-blood to the vast heart that was the casket. Once again, the casket was consumed with intense, incandescent light, and this time David, struggling confusedly to his feet, was consumed too. He cried out, convulsing as the energy flowed into him. His hands flew out from his sides, his back arched, his head was thrown back; he looked as though he was being crucified.

Susan's body was tingling as though full of electricity, but her discomfort could not compare to the horror she felt watching her son. Black Shuck, its teeth still embedded in Mr Toot's ankle, was dragging the little grocer back across the floor, but Susan could feel little sympathy for him. She saw Mr Toot raise his head, his face contorted with pain. Looking at David, he shouted, 'Don't fight it, David. It's part of you, part of what you are.'

Whether David heard his words or whether he was simply learning for himself how to accommodate the energy Susan wasn't sure. Certainly David's body seemed, little by little, to be relaxing, his bowed back straightening, his taut, anguished face adopting an expression of acceptance, even serenity.

Aside from Black Shuck, the Sleepers seemed paralysed by what was happening. David's arms fell slowly to his sides, and, his eyes full of light, he looked around the room. His gaze seemed to fall on each of the Sleepers in turn, marking them. As if yawning, slowly and exaggeratedly, he opened his mouth wide.

Seven strands of energy, like crackling bolts of lightning, erupted from between his lips and sought out the Sleepers. This energy, channelled through David, was far fiercer than the energy the seven-headed snake had produced. It was, thought Susan fleetingly, like the difference between a forty-watt and a hundred-watt bulb. Thorny glowing tendrils wound themselves around the Sleepers' heads and bodies. Black Shuck began to buck and writhe as though the power was stinging him, releasing Mr Toot, who rolled clear.

In eerie unison the Sleepers began to scream. It was a high, warbling, continuous sound that made the hairs on the back of Susan's neck stand on end. Simultaneously, droplets of black oily fluid began to ooze out of the Sleepers' mouths and eyes and ears and nostrils, out of the pores of their skin, through their clothes. The black fluid flowed up along the coils of energy, into David's mouth. As the lassoes of energy tightened around them, so the fluid began to flow more freely, until soon it seemed as though the Sleepers were being sloughed of layer upon layer of tarry black skin.

This went on for a long time. Susan watched, transfixed with horror, though despite what was happening to her son and the man she loved she felt powerless to intervene. Finally, unable to bear the sight of Jack's rigid, screaming form any longer, or of David gulping down copious amounts of what looked like industrial waste, she tore her gaze away. Her eyes alighted on Black Shuck, who was reacting to the energy somewhat differently to the rest of the Sleepers.

Susan watched, appalled, as the huge black dog literally unravelled before her eyes. The creature was like a woolly jumper with a loose thread, the energy like a mischievous boy tugging remorselessly on that thread, slowly but surely undoing the creature even as it snapped and snarled and twisted and fought. There was no blood, no bone, no spill of innards. The dog was composed of darkness, nothing more, and yet for all that its demise was a ghastly spectacle. Susan watched until the dog was a head, and then a snout, and then a final flash of teeth, and then no more. When its work was complete, the tendril of energy retreated – or perhaps more accurately was sucked back – into David's gaping mouth.

The sixty-something man who had driven Susan's car was the first of the Sleepers to collapse. Drained of life-blood, of darkness, of evil, of power, he slid to the ground and lay motionless, the tendril of energy unwinding itself from his body and retreating back into David's mouth as the one that had consumed Black Shuck had done.

Next to fall was Gary Sissons, then Des Brewer, then Jack, then the boy in the postman's uniform. Despite the frailty of the host body, Redcap was the last left standing, though eventually even Redcap, whom Susan had come to regard – rightly or wrongly – as the leader of the Sleepers, succumbed. With a cracking of old joints, the body Redcap had inhabited dropped to its knees and swayed for a moment, looking oddly as though the old lady was pleading for mercy, and then fell forward on to its face.

The last of the tendrils of energy retreated, crackling, into David's mouth; the veins of energy striating the walls and floor and ceiling of the tomb faded to a dull glow.

Then all was silence.

Unable to believe that it was over, Susan simply stood for perhaps half a minute, hardly daring to move or breathe. The six bodies that the Sleepers had inhabited lay sprawled on the stone floor like the victims of a massacre. David still stood in the casket, his face blank, trance-like. Jake and Lucy were cowering against the wall, clutching each other. Mr Toot appeared to be removing something that had burrowed into his ankle. Susan saw him draw out what looked like a wriggling black worm. He dropped the worm on to one of the softly glowing veins on the floor, and immediately there was a flare of light, a crackle, and the worm was gone. Mr Toot climbed to his feet and smiled, apparently none the worse for his tussle with Black Shuck.

'What . . . what happened?' Susan asked weakly.

'We set a double trap for them,' Mr Toot said. 'We fooled them into believing that Decumen's power was weak, but it wasn't. David carried the seed of Decumen's power, and although that seed was dormant it was not dead. The casket was the source, the reservoir, David the conduit.'

'Wait a minute,' Susan said weakly, holding up a hand. 'What is all this about David carrying the *seed* of Decumen's power? Are you telling me he's actually descended from Decumen?'

Mr Toot nodded.

'So all this was manipulated? Bringing us here, to this

house? It was all just so that David could be ... could be plugged in?' Her voice became shrill with anger. 'You knew all this was going to happen, didn't you? All this death and destruction? You knew it and you didn't do anything to stop it.'

'It was inevitable,' Mr Toot said calmly. 'This was the best way. The only way.'

'Best for who?' said Susan bitterly. She looked away, shaking her head, and took a deep breath. Finally she raised her head again, to look not at Mr Toot, but at her son. 'Will he be all right?' she asked.

Mr Toot nodded. 'He'll be fine.'

'But all that ... all that stuff he swallowed. Isn't it inside him?'

Mr Toot walked up to the casket and said, 'David.' Slowly David turned his head. 'Open your mouth.'

David did so. Mr Toot opened his mouth too. Immediately black oily fluid flowed from David's mouth and into Mr Toot's. It flowed in a steady stream, horizontally, defying gravity. Watching it cross from the boy to the man was an unsettling sight.

It was several minutes before the fluid stopped flowing. In all that time no one moved or spoke. At last, however, the exchange was complete. In unison David and Mr Toot closed their mouths. David also closed his eyes, then swayed for a moment and sat down in the casket.

Susan stepped forward, alarmed. 'David?'

'He's fine,' Mr Toot said, turning. 'In a moment he'll wake up and remember nothing.'

Despite herself, Susan felt reassured by Mr Toot's words. She turned her attention to the six bodies on the floor. 'What about these people?' she asked, looking at Jack. 'Are they dead?'

'Dead? No,' Mr Toot said softly.

'So they'll be all right?'

'Why don't you go back up into the house where it's warm? Take David and Jake and Lucy with you?'

'I'm not going anywhere without Jack,' she said. 'Not if there's a chance that he ... not if he's still alive.'

'Don't worry about Jack,' the little grocer said soothingly. 'I'll see to him. And to these other unfortunates too.'

'How?' Susan asked, but before Mr Toot could reply, a bewildered voice behind her said, 'Mum?'

Susan turned. David was climbing unsteadily to his feet, looking around in confusion.

'Davey!' she exclaimed, and rushed to help him out of the casket.

'What happened? Why am I in this coffin? What happened to the Sleepers?' he mumbled, taking her hand.

'I'll explain later,' she said. 'Are you all right?'

'I . . . yes, I think so. A bit groggy.' Supported by Susan he climbed down to the floor.

'Go,' Mr Toot said again. 'It's a long climb. I'll take care of things here.'

Susan looked into the little man's round, earnest face, into his brilliant blue eyes. The sensation made her feel a little giddy. 'You promise to look after them?' she said softly.

'I promise,' Mr Toot replied.

Susan held Mr Toot's gaze for a moment longer, then turned away. 'Right then,' she said, 'let's go.'

The ascent to the cellar, though arduous, was nowhere near as bad as Susan had been expecting. Maybe it was because they were heading back towards the light, and therefore had cause for hope, whereas before their situation had seemed hopeless, or maybe it was simply that journeys that were unknown at the outset always seemed quicker on the way back. Or perhaps it was simply that the time flew because they were talking, their voices echoing in the darkness. Jake and Lucy falteringly told Susan who they were and how they had come to arrive at Jack's house with Mr Toot, and Susan told David what had happened after Mr Toot had hurled him into the casket, and what Mr Toot had subsequently told her.

Sooner than she could have hoped, Susan noticed a splotch of grey hovering in the darkness somewhere above her head. 'I think we're nearly there,' she called excitedly. 'I can see daylight.'

Sure enough, a few minutes later they climbed up out of the darkness and into the cellar, sweating and exhausted. Though gloomy and cold compared to the rest of the house, after what they had been through the cellar seemed like the warmest, homeliest place on earth.

Suddenly, as though she had been keeping it bottled up for

too long, Susan felt emotion surging through her. She began to shake, then simultaneously to laugh and cry. The inability to control her emotions frightened her a little, but it also felt good to be letting them all out.

Alarmed less by her abrupt tears than by the high, somewhat crazed laughter accompanying them, David put his arms around Susan and squeezed her.

'Hey, Mum,' he said soothingly, 'it's okay. It's over now. Everything's okay.'

She hugged him hard. He smelled of dust and dankness and sweat. When she was able, she whispered, 'I know, I know,' over and over as if trying to convince herself.

Eventually they went upstairs to the kitchen, squinting like moles emerging into the sunlight. Everything seemed so bizarrely normal up here. There were coffee mugs in the sink, crumbs on the kitchen counter, a pot plant dying of thirst on the windowsill, a pair of sunglasses on the table. After all she had been through, after experiencing events that in a few short hours had irrevocably changed her life, Susan found it hard to get her head round the fact that such mundane, unimportant things as these could remain unchanged. What had happened seemed to her so earth-shattering that surely *everything* should be affected by it? She looked outside and saw that the sun was still shining, that birds were still singing, that flowers were still nodding their heads in the gentlest of breezes. How could this be? How *could* it? The world had been turned upside down, so why did it still look the same?

They sat round the kitchen table, exhausted as athletes after a marathon. Lucy was slumped forward, arms forming a cushion for her head, eyes closed. Jake sat beside her, staring into space and absently stroking her back, as though practising for when she was in labour. No one spoke for a while; it was as if the daylight inhibited them. Finally David stirred and said, 'Does anyone want a cup of tea?'

Susan had to stifle a bark of laughter. Tea: the Great British Solution. 'Blimey, I've just seen half the world wiped out in an atomic war. Better put the kettle on.' However she nodded. 'I'll have a large whisky and six Valium in mine.'

'Me too,' said Jake. 'And two sugars.'

Lucy said nothing.

David got up and began to make the tea, moving like an

automaton. They all heard the sound simultaneously and looked up, Lucy included.

A slow smile spread across Jake's face. 'He's at it again,' he murmured. He shuddered with contentment and closed his eyes.

Susan felt her dark, jagged thoughts being smoothed out, purified, by the beauty of the sound she was hearing. She recognised it as the sound Mr Toot had made the first day she and David had come to Longbarrow, the incredible, piercing, unearthly note that for a while had seemed to untangle and repair the broken threads of the universe.

The note was faint and yet it seemed to fill the room. Susan knew that it was coming from beneath them, and yet it seemed to come from everywhere. Like Jake and now Lucy, she wanted to close her eyes, give herself up to it, allow it to wash through her and over her, carry her away. But she forced herself to concentrate, watching the open cellar door as the note rose in volume and intensity.

Just as the note reached a peak, just as she thought she would *have* to give herself up to it, she saw movement at the top of the cellar steps. Next moment the six people whose bodies had been possessed by the Sleepers filed out of the cellar, their eyes closed, their heads lolling, their arms hanging limply by their sides.

Bringing up the rear of the procession was Mr Toot, his mouth open. Susan, enraptured, felt herself beginning to slip away, and welcomed it. Then, abruptly, the sound stopped; Mr Toot closed his mouth. Susan blinked and reluctantly came back into herself.

The six people who had been hosts for the Sleepers crumpled to the floor and lay still. They looked pale, hollow-eyed, and their breathing was shallow. A little woozily, Susan looked at Mr Toot. 'Are they going to be all right?' she asked.

'Perhaps,' said Mr Toot. 'Goodbye.'

As he turned back towards the cellar door, Susan jumped up from the table. 'Hey!' she shouted, hopping over the prone body of Des Brewer. She caught up with Mr Toot at the cellar door. 'What do you mean, "goodbye"?'

'I have to go,' Mr Toot said calmly.

'Go? Go where?'

'Back down there.'

'But . . . but why did you say goodbye?' She laughed nervously. 'I mean, it's not as if you can stay down there for ever, is it?'

Mr Toot smiled. 'If you had a vial of some terrible virus, Susan, something that could wipe out millions of people if it was ever released, what would you do with it?'

Susan frowned, thrown by the question. 'I don't know . . . hide it, I suppose.'

'Would you perhaps put it in a safe and bury it deep in the ground where no one would ever find it, seal it up where it could never do any harm?'

'I suppose so,' said Susan guardedly, 'but I still don't see what—'

'I'm the safe, Susan.' His smile was almost apologetic. 'I have to go.'

'But you're a human being,' Susan protested. 'You're not an inanimate object. How will you—'

'Mum!' David's voice was urgent.

Susan half-turned. 'Just wait a minute, Da—'

'Mum, it's Jack and the others. I think they're dying.'

Susan whirled round, and immediately let out a cry of shock. The hosts did indeed look as though they were dying. Their faces were not merely pale any more, they were grey, and not only that but their cheeks and eyes looked sunken, as though their flesh was shrinking around the skull.

'Jack!' Susan cried and flung herself to her knees beside him. She lifted his head and put her face close to his. He barely seemed to be breathing and his skin was cold. Trying not to panic, she pressed her ear to his chest. His heart was beating, but so, so slowly. 'What do we do, Mr Toot?' she said, twisting round.

But Mr Toot had gone.

'*No!*' Susan yelled. She jumped to her feet, ran towards the cellar door, yanked it open, slapped her hand down on the light switch. 'Mr Toot, come back, we need you,' she shouted. When there was no response, she leaped recklessly down the steps.

Mr Toot was not in the cellar, and what was more, neither was the opening at the top of the steps that had led down to the burial chamber. The floor was whole again and seemed to be composed of solid concrete. There was not even a

437

single hairline crack to show where the opening might have been.

Susan felt like sobbing, screaming, tearing her hair out, but there was no time. She ran back up the steps and into the kitchen, to see David disappearing out of the back door carrying a red plastic bucket.

'Where are you going?' she shouted.

'I've got an idea. I won't be long,' he called back over his shoulder as he ran out of the house and up the garden path.

'Do you think we should give them heart massage or something?' Jake asked.

'I don't know. They haven't had heart attacks, have they? They're just sort of . . . fading away.' Susan pressed a hand to her head and muttered, 'Come on, think, think.' Suddenly her face cleared and she ran into the hallway. She snatched up the telephone and had dialled 999 before realising the line was dead.

'*Shit!*' she shouted, slamming the receiver into its cradle. She ran back into the kitchen. 'How are they?'

'Much the same,' said Jake. 'Maybe we *should* try heart massage. We can't just stand here and watch—'

His words were interrupted by the back door, which had swung shut behind David, banging open again. David entered, carrying a bucket full of water which slopped on to his shoes and over the floor.

'Well water,' he said before anyone could ask. 'I remember Jack once telling us that it could cure anything.'

Susan had forgotten all about finding the well full of water that morning, but she recalled now how the water had seemed to sparkle and glow, how incredibly clear it had been, how it had made her hands tingle when she scooped it up. She looked at David, eyes wide, then rushed to snatch a mug from the mug tree on the counter. David hardly had time to put the bucket down before she was plunging the mug into it, filling it. She drew the mug out, dripping, scrambled over to Jack, raised his head with one hand and tilted the mug to his lips with the other.

Some of the water trickled out over his face, but most of it went down his throat. Susan kept pouring until the mug was empty; she half-expected Jack to choke, but he didn't.

For a moment, nothing happened. Susan pulled Jack's head

on to her lap and, stroking his hair almost feverishly, mur-mured, 'Come on, come on.'

Then . . . was it her imagination or was there a slight bloom of colour in Jack's cheeks that hadn't been there before?

Suddenly his eyelids flickered. He moaned. The tip of his tongue appeared and licked his lips.

'Jack!' Susan cried. 'Jack! Can you hear me?'

His eyes opened. He looked up at her and smiled.

'Course I can hear you,' he said drowsily. 'There's no need to shout.'

Chapter Sixty

Hand in hand, Susan and Jack walked out into Mollie Boscombe's little back garden. Sunlight drenched them, but Susan felt unworthy of it. All things considered, she had got off lightly. She still had David, she still had Jack. There was no such relief for Jake and Lucy, and for poor Des Brewer who didn't yet know that his wife was dead, his baby son missing. For them (and possibly for some or all of the others too), survival meant nothing more than that their grieving could begin in earnest. And what of Gary, Jake's brother? Was he aware that his parents had died by his own hands? Would Jake be able to keep the truth from him?

There were horrors to unfold yet, black days to endure.

'Will it ever be over?' she said before realising she had spoken out loud.

Jack looked at her. 'What?'

'I mean . . . will things ever be the same again? Will Longbarrow ever recover?'

Although the village was not visible from here, they both glanced instinctively to the right. A basin of smoke dirtied the summer sky above where they knew Longbarrow to be.

'There must be survivors down there,' Jack said.

Susan paused before replying. She had given him a potted account of what had happened, but had been wary of laying any blame at his door. It was vital that those whom the Sleepers had used didn't feel responsible.

'You didn't see it, Jack,' she said. 'The place was deserted, except for the bodies piled up in the street. Buildings were burning . . .' She shook her head.

'Even so,' said Jack. He looked troubled for a moment, then

continued, 'People would hide, wouldn't they? In cellars and attics and the like. They'll be coming out soon. Things'll be getting back to normal.' He pulled a face. 'Well, not normal, but you know what I mean.'

They fell silent momentarily, lost in their own thoughts, as Susan opened the gate that led into the paddock. She wandered out, the long grass tickling her shins, rustling like wheat. It was only then that she realised she was leading Jack towards the well. She remembered how eager she had been to show it to him earlier. Could that only have been a few hours ago? It seemed like days, weeks.

She glanced at him. He seemed unaffected by what had happened to him. She kept expecting to see some shadow of his ordeal in his eyes, his face, some sign of inner trauma, some residue.

'Are you sure you're all right?' she asked.

He looked at her and smiled reassuringly. 'Never better.'

They reached the well.

'Oh,' said Susan.

There was no water in it. It was a stone throat stretching down into unseen depths. She knelt on the rim and put her hand down it, feeling the walls.

'They're bone-dry,' she said.

'Perhaps it's done its job,' said Jack, helping her to her feet. 'After all, you can't hold on to magic, can you?'

'Can't you?' Susan said. She slid her arms around his waist, raised her face towards his for a kiss. His lips were warm. She tingled with life, remembering the incredible sound that Mr Toot had made. 'This is all the magic I need,' she murmured.

He held her tightly. They stood there in the high grass for a minute or more, just trying to hold on to the moment, trying to make time stand still by doing so themselves.

Eventually, however, she stirred. 'So what happens now?' she asked.

'What do you mean?'

'Well . . . Longbarrow's a shell, isn't it? Maybe it would be best if we got out, started somewhere new.'

'Is that what you want to do?'

She sighed. 'I don't know *what* I want. Except you, that is. As long as I've got you and Davey, I'll be okay.'

441

'You've got me,' Jack said, 'whatever happens, and I'm happy to do whatever you want, only . . .'

'Only what?'

'Only if it was up to me I'd stay and help to rebuild the place if I could. This is my home – *our* home – and I don't think we should run away from it, abandon it, just because of what's happened.'

She looked at him. 'Maybe you're right. Maybe we've got a duty to put things right again.'

'Let's see what Davey reckons,' said Jack.

Susan nodded and held out a hand to him. He took it, gripped it tightly. Slowly, surrounded by the murmur of summer, they walked back towards the house. Away to their left, above Longbarrow, the smoke in the summer sky began to disperse.